welcome to picketwire

Tim Wintermute

Prismatist Press

ISBN 979-8-9894234-5-3

eISBN 979-8-9894234-4-6

TO KATHLEEN

contents

CHAPTER ONE

Howdy Hanks sat in the saddle of his motorcycle and looked across the prairie at his hometown of Picketwire. He tried to imagine the buffalo and the Indians who hunted them, and the conquistadors in search of cities of gold, and the mountain men on their way to Bent's Fort a few miles north on the Arkansas River where they would sell their pelts and get drunk and set off back to the mountains to start all over again, and the pack trains of traders on their way south to Taos and Santa Fe. Thirty years ago he'd read Thomas Wolfe's novel *You Can't Go Home Again* just after he'd left Picketwire on this same motorcycle. Wolfe's book was published posthumously and created quite an uproar in his hometown of Asheville.

Howdy's play was going to have its premiere in his hometown, and while he was expecting a similar uproar, he wouldn't be hiding from it six feet under. Of course, the cast had to be chosen, the rehearsals had to take place, and, probably most important, the play had to be finished. Then there was the girl he'd left behind, or did she leave him behind? Seeing her again was something he both wanted to return for and was scared to death of.

He pushed the kick starter on the old Indian. It coughed up some smoky phlegm from its exhaust then roared to life, which, considering its age, couldn't be taken for granted. He adjusted the throttle and the engine settled into the throb that was as familiar as his heartbeat. He donned his helmet, something he never would have worn in his hipster youth, but now that he'd somehow managed to make it past sixty, he didn't want to risk smearing what gray matter he had left on the blacktop like butter on toast. Besides, he preferred the anonymity it provided. In his youth he'd aspired to notoriety, but, despite his best efforts, he'd instead found fame as the so-called Sagebrush Shakespeare. Of course, in his youth his hair had been jet black while now it was more salt than pepper and Howdy liked to joke that some of the best lines he'd written were on his face.

Howdy didn't ride straight into Picketwire on the main drag, but, out of force of habit, snuck in through the back door on Canal Street, named romantically after an irrigation ditch with pastures and alfalfa fields on either side. Poking above the tree-tops and roofs of town with the campus of Picketwire College crowning its crest was Mount Witt, which despite the name was technically a hill. The land was donated, along with a large sum of money, to build and endow the college.

In his bequest, the unassuming man, who had occupied an equally unassuming house on the hill and who had not been as dirt poor as everyone assumed, stated that neither the college nor anything on the hilltop campus should be named after him. Since he didn't say anything about the hill, itself, the town named it after him, changing hill to mountain in recognition of the magnitude of his gift. The phonetic irony that the college's pillars of wisdom were built on "wit" has become an unofficial motto.

Howdy followed Canal Street into town until he reached the Last Ditch Bar where he'd had his last beer decades ago before leaving town. He turned right at the corner onto Las Animas Street. As he continued past the Tuttle mansion he wondered if Jemma Lu still lived there. A block later he rode by the Tumbleweed Theater where his still unfinished play would have its world premiere. To his left, on the other side of the street, he noted that the brick building with large plate glass windows that stretched along most of the block was no longer Fred's Ford Dealership but rather Fred's Furniture and Farm Implements.

He crossed the railroad tracks and passed Picketwire's historic train depot and entered downtown where he stopped for a red light. He remembered the joke that the light was there so people passing through town would have to stop for something. On the far corner a restaurant called Sue's Pretty Good Cafe now occupied the spot where Floyd's Four Star Barbershop had been, and next to it was Bunch of Books. The bookstore's owner, Harry Bunch, was the only person Howdy had stayed in touch with since he left town.

Next to Bunch of Books was the town's newspaper, the *Picketwire Press*. When he was a kid, Howdy delivered the paper on his bike as he followed his route through town. Howdy smiled at the thought of tossing smartphones onto front lawns so people could read the news online. He'd heard from Harry that out of the blue the paper's publishers, Jan and Steve Tiding, had decided to retire and had taken off in an RV, leaving their youngest son, Tom, in charge. Apparently their retirement and his appointment as the new publisher and editor-in-chief had surprised Tom as much as everyone else in town. Howdy added a shake of his head to his smile at the thought that someone who hadn't been born when he'd left town was now running the paper where he'd been a paperboy.

When the light turned green Howdy made a left turn. A couple of minutes later he lowered his kickstand in front of the Wobbly Building. The imposing, five-story brick building didn't get its name because it lacked solidity, but because it had been built by the International Workers of the World (IWW), known as the "Wobblies," whose Picketwire Branch still occupied half the first floor. Howdy was happy to see that the other half was occupied by the Mother Jones Bar, named in honor of arguably the most famous Wobbly who had been one of the leaders of the 1914 strike against Rockefeller's Colorado Fuel and Iron Company that included the infamous "Ludlow

Massacre" when 1200 strikers were attacked by troops from the Colorado National Guard and private security firms.

Howdy unfastened the worn leather valise that had been strapped behind him then walked through the entrance and took the elevator to the third floor lobby of the Wobble Inn, a bed and breakfast occupying the top three floors that had once been a hostel for IWW members.

***

"How long you staying Mister Hanks?" the desk clerk asked.

Howdy grinned, "That depends on how much trouble I can make before they run me out of town."

The clerk flashed a reciprocal grin, "We don't run people out of town we let them drive." He looked at the registration where Howdy had put down his motorcycle in the vehicle description box and added, "Or in your case ride."

Howdy signed the registration, took back his credit card and noticed that there was a stack of the most recent edition of the *Picketwire Press* on the front desk. The clerk told him they were free for guests so he took one, jammed it under his left arm and walked to the elevator. The top floor room was small and sparsely furnished with a wood desk and chair, single brass-framed bed, dresser, and sink (bathroom down the hall). Next to the desk was a box that had been delivered to his room and contained the clothes and books he'd shipped.

From his valise he took out a laptop computer and placed it on the desk, then walked over to the window and pulled back the drape. He had the best view in town except from the top of Mount Witt. Third place would be the tip of Picketwire Community Church's spire, although you would need to be a mountain climber to enjoy the view from its summit. The whole shebang would begin tomorrow in its sanctuary, which is where the Bard Wired Players had their rehearsals. The last time he'd been in a church was for a funeral. Hopefully, this wouldn't be his.

It had only been several months since Howdy had met Max Bergmann, the artistic director of Picketwire's local theater company, the Bard Wired Players. Although the play was only in Howdy's head at the time he'd contacted Max and asked him if he was interested in staging the world premiere in Picketwire, Max immediately drove the two hundred miles to Taos, New Mexico where Howdy lived in an Airstream trailer outside of town. By the time he got to the Mexican restaurant where he was to meet with Howdy, Max not only wanted the Bard Wired Players to perform the play, he wanted to direct it. It didn't matter that the only thing Howdy had shared with him was that it was set in Picketwire. It would be the world premiere of Howdy Hanks, the Sagebrush Shakespeare's new play. Howdy could see the "Great White Way" reflected in Max's eyes as he told Howdy that even though they were a regional theater the next stop could be Broadway. Howdy told him that he didn't care where it went afterwards as long as it opened in Picketwire.

After discussing logistics and reaching an agreement on how to proceed, they settled into dinner of enchiladas and tamales, tequila, and beer while trading stories until the restaurant closed, about people in the theater world they knew and those they wished they hadn't, the latter being the more entertaining. Somehow Max had been sober enough to write up the agreement after they'd parted that night, and he presented it to Howdy the next morning at the same restaurant over a breakfast of huevos, tortillas, frijoles, and lots of coffee. Howdy tried to read it, but since his brain was still a bit fogged in from the night before, he gave up and just signed the damn thing, sealing it with drops of salsa.

At that point, Howdy was committed. Not only to writing the play, but more importantly, to returning to Picketwire. As for writing the play, he'd finished a draft that he would need to refine during rehearsals based on what worked and what didn't. Except for the last scene. That would be written just before the play opened when there would be nothing to change because he would finally know how it had to end. At least he sure as hell hoped so, since knowing how it would end was the reason why he was writing the damn thing and returning to Picketwire.

Turning back from the window, Howdy's eyes caught a story on the front page of the *Picketwire Press* that he'd tossed on the desk. It was about Wylie Boone, and said that after the hit-and-run in Aspen that nearly killed him, he had returned to Picketwire and was staying at his ranch, the Double B. He knew about Wylie's hit-and-run, but his return to Picketwire at the same time as Howdy must be some sort of cowboy karma, although he wasn't sure if it was the good or bad kind.

CHAPTER TWO

When he walked on stage for the first meeting with the cast, Max was planning to recite the "band of brothers" speech from *Henry V* as he had always done before every first rehearsal. Since he had been both an actor and the director in every production of the Bard Wired Players, sometimes it had been more of a soliloquy to a one-man band than an address to a company. However, this time he was only going to direct, and there were almost a dozen people in the cast, so he could deliver it the way Shakespeare intended. As Max looked at the front row where everyone was seated, he was about to open his mouth when he was stopped by the new face. Not just new to the Bard Wired Players and new to Picketwire, but new to acting. Even her name was new, having told Max after she'd been given the part that she had decided on a stage name.

"I want to be called Zelda Zenn. Not Mary Ann Smithers. That's Zenn with two n's not one. I think a stage name will give me a bit of mystery."

Since Mary Ann or Zelda was already a complete unknown, Max was a bit mystified by her desire to be even more mysterious, although he could understand her wanting to have a name with more zip to it. He himself preferred to be called Max rather than Maximilian and unfortunately, the "silent" n added to his own last name transformed it from the name of the famous Swedish film director, Ingmar Bergman, into the German word for "mountain man."

Whatever her reason for wanting to be called Zelda Zenn, there was certainly no mystery as to why she was in the play since she was the only one who auditioned for the part. Fortunately, Zelda had talent in addition to her stage name. Still, she was only a seventeen-year-old high school student who had never acted in a play before so it was a risk, but Max liked to think of himself as a risk-taker. Besides, it couldn't hurt at the box office to have someone make her debut. Not that they should need any help since the play was the world premiere of a new work by the Sagebrush Shakespeare, Harold "Howdy" Hanks. Max had already been working on getting a front-page story in the *Picketwire Press* and a live interview on WTPW Radio as part of the publicity.

Max opened his mouth as he looked out at the cast and crew seated in the first row, which happened to be the front pew of the Picketwire Community Church. They were using the church for rehearsals although the play would be performed at the historic Tumbleweed Theater. Fortunately, the rehearsal space was free, courtesy of Reverend Dave Sanderson, who was also one of the members of the cast.

Sitting next to Dave was Zelda looking up at him and suddenly he couldn't remember a word of the speech and closed his mouth. Attempting to overcome Zelda's intense stare, he looked up at the large, oval, stain glass window that rose behind the balcony at the back of the sanctuary. A woman in a white robe with golden wings and surrounded by cherubs in a swirl of clouds looked down at him.

He opened his mouth again and "O, for a Muse of fire that would ascend the brightest heaven of invention! A kingdom for a stage, princes to act, and monarchs to behold the swelling scene!" came out. After a short pause he lowered his eyes. "I thought that these lines were more appropriate," he explained as much to himself as the others, "since we are not only beginning the fifth season, but we are doing so with a brand new play by our very own muse, the Sagebrush Shakespeare, Howdy Hanks."

"Well, I'm sure as hell not an angel or a Greek goddess, Max, but I try to amuse people," a gravelly voice bellowed from the back of the sanctuary. The only thing Max could see were the soles of two boots propped on the back of the next to the last pew and the top of a Stetson hat.

"Howdy! I didn't see you back there."

"I've always been a back of the church sort of guy," Howdy answered. "Not that I've spent much time in church at all."

Dave Sanderson turned and looked back toward Howdy. "Think of this as a theater, Howdy, rather than a church."

"You mean it's been re-consecrated to the theater gods?"

"It's always been a place for the Theater God."

"I guess that makes this a unitheatertarian church so I suppose I can come on up there without worrying about being damned by the Trinity."

Howdy stood up, took off his hat, revealing an unruly thatch of hair over a sun-creased face, and walked up the aisle to the front of the sanctuary. Max invited Howdy on stage to say a few words about his new play. Instead of stepping up onto the stage, Howdy sat down on its edge. His legs, clad in jeans that looked like they hadn't been washed in years, were long enough so that he could plant the heels of both of his scuffed cowboy boots into the carpet.

Max, being wider than he was long, knew that even if he managed to lower himself and sit next to Howdy, his short legs would be left dangling along with his dignity. Instead, he walked over to the pulpit on the stage behind Howdy. Judging that it was securely bolted to the floor he leaned against it with as much nonchalance as he could muster.

As Max introduced each member of the cast and crew, Howdy squinted at them, nodding without saying a word. When Max got to Zelda, he introduced her as Mary Ann Smithers and noted that this would be her debut performance.

Zelda stood up and reminded Max that she preferred to go by her stage name, Zelda Zenn. Then she turned to Howdy and said, "The only Howdy I've ever heard of was the puppet Howdy Doody, and he also wore a cowboy outfit."

"I hope you don't think I'm also a dummy," Howdy deadpanned.

"No, but a person who writes a play is sort of like a person who throws his voice."

"Howdy is not a ventriloquist," Max said firmly in an attempt to assert his directorial authority.

"Good, because I'm not a puppet," Zelda replied. "Now, what I don't understand is why we're only getting the first scene and it says draft on it?"

"Unlike the other plays we've done where the script for the play is completed, Howdy is still working on the play and will be refining it based on the rehearsals. In the theater we call it workshopping."

"That means I'm looking for your feedback as we rehearse," Howdy said.

"Constructive feedback," Max added, giving Zelda a look that he hoped reminded her that he was the director not her.

"That means there won't be a final script until we've finished the workshop-rehearsal process," Howdy said. After a dramatic pause, he added, "And we'll all know how it ends."

"In the words of Shakespeare, all's well that ends well," Max said.

CHAPTER THREE

Tom Tidings sat down at the counter of Sue's Pretty Good Cafe. He placed a steno pad and pen on the counter, opened the Denver Post with a snap so that it crackled the way only a newspaper can and was already reading as he poured the first of several cups of coffee into the slightly chipped mug with his name stenciled on it.

It was a big deal to have your name on a mug at the Pretty Good. It meant that you were now a regular, a regular being determined solely by Sue Cohen based on criteria that had never been shared with her customers, although it was generally agreed that just showing up was not enough. One morning you were drinking out of a plain old mug and next thing you know there was a brand new white mug emblazoned with your name in red block letters. However, you only got the first one free, so if you wanted a replacement you had to pay a buck fifty. Sue said it was a way to make sure regulars took their status seriously and treated the mugs bestowed upon them with the dignity they deserved, although most regulars were like Tom and just kept drinking no matter how many nicks and chips pitted its once glossy surface.

Tom read the news story about the hit-and-run in Aspen involving the billionaire Wylie Boone. According to the story, the police were still looking for a dark blue minivan that struck Boone's red Porsche. Boone was getting out of the car while talking on his cellphone. Unlike his bashed in Porsche and smashed cellphone, Wylie had miraculously escaped with only some cracked ribs and bad bruises. From eyewitness accounts it appeared that the minivan had intentionally sideswiped Boone's Porsche. Boone was the great-grandson of one of Picketwire's founding fathers and grew up there and still owned the family ranch outside of town, the Double B (some people said that the two b's stood for "Bottom line Boones"). Although it had been years since anyone had seen him around, he had returned to the ranch to recover from his injuries, Tom knew that it would be a real scoop if he could interview Boone.

"So, what's the column going to be on this week?" Reverend Dave Sanderson asked as he sat down on the stool next to Tom.

"Rev, I never give advance notice on my columns. Not because I want people to buy the paper and read it there first, which I do, but because I don't know for sure what I'm going to write until just before the deadline."

"Sounds like me on a Saturday working on my Sunday sermon," Dave replied, picking up the mug of coffee with his name on it that had miraculously appeared.

"At least you can ask for some divine intervention. You know, a little Holy Ghost writing on your sermon. I remember as a kid going to a revival where they were singing about God calling on his heavenly telephone. I guess now they're singing What a Facebook Friend I Have in Jesus."

Dave laughed then bent closer so he could whisper in Tom's ear. "I have a backup plan."

"A back up for God?"

"No, of course not," he chuckled. "I have Jane Takamoto."

Tom almost spat out the coffee in mouth. "Jane? Is she in town?"

"Not only in town but she's our new associate pastor and she's preaching this Sunday."

"How come I didn't know? I mean, this is news and I do run the newspaper."

"Now you know. Seriously, Jane didn't want any publicity until after she gave her first sermon, so we kept the whole thing under wraps. In fact, what I told you isn't for publication until after Sunday."

"Jane Takamoto," Tom rolled the name around a few times. "Coming back here? I thought she was gone for good. I mean she went to Yale."

"And then to Princeton Theological Seminary for her divinity degree."

"Some of us always thought she was divine," Tom said, then wondering how it sounded, added, "I mean a really nice person. So, she's come back to Picketwire. From the Ivy League to the minor league. Usually someone wants to be called up to the major league not the other way around."

"Are you calling my Church a farm team?" Dave said, pretending to be insulted.

"Of course not, Rev, although you've got some farmers in your congregation, including Jane's parents."

"Speaking of which, and this is definitely not for publication, it's not just a call from the church that Jane is answering, it's also one from her folks. Her mom and dad aren't doing all that well and you know she's not only their daughter, she's their only child. She gave up a good job in New York City." Dave paused then added, "You know that she's married."

Tom nodded. "We printed the announcement in our 'Getting Hitched' section."

"He came with her in case you were wondering."

"I'm looking forward to meeting him," Tom answered, feeling a twinge of guilt about lying not only to a member of the clergy but also a friend.

Dave finished his coffee and chuckled, "Now that could be a topic for your column."

"What?" Dave asked

"You can go home again."

***

You can go home again ran through Tom's mind after Dave left. Unlike Jane, it was Tom's parents who left home. He'd just graduated from high school and came home to an empty house and a note after a night out celebrating his graduation. He should have suspected something was up when his parents bought a twenty-eight-foot recreational vehicle at the beginning of his senior year. The RV was gone, and the note said that they had worked for almost forty years publishing the *Picketwire Press* without a break so they were going to make up for it by taking off and seeing the world, at least the parts you can get to in an RV. They hadn't decided exactly what places they were going to except that they were heading to Alaska first. They finished their note saying now that he was a high school graduate, he was old enough to take over the family business and they were appointing him the new publisher of the *Picketwire Press*.

It wasn't that Tom was an only child; he was just the only one still at home. He was ten years younger than his sister and twelve years younger than his brother. They'd both gone off to college and neither of them had any interest in returning to Picketwire or being in the newspaper business. Since the paper was held in a family trust established by his great-grandparents, Tobias and Hilda Tidings, who founded it, Tom knew he'd end up with it sooner or later. It turned out to be much sooner than later. He called his sister and brother with the news and learned that they'd both received a letter telling them the same thing. "They said that they wanted to retire while they were still young enough to enjoy it," his brother, Dick, said.

"It's more like they escaped than retired. It's a hell of a succession plan – running off and leaving behind the business to the kid who hasn't had a chance to leave home."

"All you have to do is get married and have at least one kid. That's not so hard," Dick laughed. "But seriously, this isn't really a bad succession plan since unlike me and Karen, you've always loved working at the paper and you know everything about it."

"Working at the paper isn't the same thing as running it and being responsible."

"It is now. The trust requires the family to continue as owner and a member of the family to be the publisher, and if the trust is violated...well, you know what happens then."

Yes, Tom knew all too well: It would be closed permanently and Picketwire would lose its only newspaper. A blessing and a curse had been passed down from one generation of Tidings to the other. So, there he was, the fourth publisher of the *Picketwire Press* at the age of 18. Since going away to college was now out of the question, Tom enrolled at Picketwire College. Unlike most of his classmates he knew what he was going to do when he graduated from college because it would be the same thing he was doing before he graduated. Fifteen years later that's exactly what he'd been doing.

And then Jane Takamoto comes home. The very person that he wished had never left came back, only now she was a reverend, with degrees from Yale and Princeton, and she was married. Jane had changed but he was the same old Tom. They would, of course, have to run a story in the next edition about her return to Picketwire. Just thinking about interviewing her made his hands tremble so much that he had to put his coffee mug down before it slipped out of his hands and shattered on the floor leaving his name in shards.

CHAPTER FOUR

Jemma Lu Tuttle descended the broad steps then walked down the brick paved path that cut through a manicured lawn of Kentucky Bluegrass until she reached the ornate, wrought-iron gate of the Tuttle Mansion on Las Animas Street. She paused and looked back at the house that had been built by her grandfather, Samuel. He believed that the family's success with Picketware, the business that his father and mother, Moses and Adouette Tuttle, had started, warranted constructing the largest and most palatial house in Picketwire. Jemma Lu thought it was dead wrong for descendants of a runaway slave and his Cherokee wife to live in what looked like an antebellum mansion, so she had moved out when she had inherited it along with the business.

For the past thirty years she had lived in the same modest adobe homestead that Moses and Adouette had built. It was the oldest house in Picketwire, on several acres where only original indigenous wild grass and plants were now allowed to grow. As Jemma Lu put it, she'd moved out of the big house on the plantation and back to the little house on the prairie. She'd donated the Tuttle mansion to the Picketwire Preservation Society when she moved and when she died they would also get the homestead and grounds.

Jemma Lu had just attended a breakfast meeting of the society's board of directors. She was not only a founding member but also a past chair, and her bequest of the Tuttle mansion along with an endowment for its upkeep made her by far the Preservation Society's biggest patron. Not that she threw her weight around. For one thing she barely weighed a hundred pounds so she wouldn't have made much of an impact, and for another, she believed that the nine heads of the board of directors were better than one big head. That being said, when she did make a point of sharing her opinion people tended to listen very carefully. It wasn't just because of her philanthropy, or that she owned Picketware, the town's biggest employer after the college and that Moses and Adouette Tuttle were two of the town's founders. It was because when Jemma Lu expressed an opinion it was only after she'd given it considerable thought. She'd never been one to run off half-cocked or spout something from the top of her head. Jemma Lu always had a plan before she acted.

Well, that wasn't quite correct, because she did have a child that she most definitely hadn't planned on, although she didn't know where he was or if he was even alive. So technically, she might not be the last of the Tuttle line, but she was the last one who would own Picketware, because Jemma Lu had a plan to keep the family business from ending after she was gone.

Her plan wasn't to sell it to someone else but to give it to the people who worked there, the Picketware family, in the form of an employee-owned cooperative. Of course, none of the employees knew that yet except for her lifelong friend Millie Pacheco, but now that she was past sixty there was more than a little concern as to what would happen to the business and their jobs when she was gone. Many of the employees had worked for Picketware for decades, and there were some who came from families that had worked there for two and even three generations. Other than Millie everyone would be surprised when she announced her plan, and Jemma Lu loved surprising others as much as she hated to be surprised.

But now she had to deal with not just one but three surprises. The first was that someone had tried to kill Wylie Boone, and the second was that Wylie had decided to come back to Picketwire. She hadn't seen Wylie in thirty years and she wasn't sure she wanted to see him now. They had not parted on good terms, to say the least, after she had refused to marry him. They had grown up together and, like Jemma Lu, he was a descendent of one of Picketwire's founders, and also, like her, he'd inherited the family business. What he had proposed was more like a merger than a marriage. He'd even written a detailed business plan.

"You have to understand, Jemma Lu," Wylie had explained, "Picketware can't survive the way it is now. Its business model isn't viable and hasn't been for a long time. You know your dad borrowed a lot of money to keep it afloat. Even worse for you, he personally guaranteed it so when, not if, it goes under you'll lose everything, including your home. When we get married, I can replace your personal family guarantee with one by Boone Enterprises. I've already checked with your creditors, and they've agreed that if Picketware becomes a subsidiary of my business then they don't have any problem with what is owed them. In fact, they offered to extend even more credit. Then Picketware will be streamlined and repositioned so it can pay off its debts and, even better, it will start racking up profits. Within five years we can make a public offering of stock and walk away with millions."

"Walk away?"

"It's a figure of speech. We can structure the deal so that Boone Enterprises retains control after going public."

"This seems like more like a business proposition than a marriage proposal."

"Don't you see, Jemma Lu, honey, if we get married and we don't do this then, as your husband, I'd be personally liable for Picketware's debt as well. That wouldn't be fair, would it?"

"No, Wylie, it wouldn't be fair, and we can't have a marriage that isn't fair to both of us, where one person has an advantage over the other. That seems to present us with an unsolvable problem, because just as it would be unfair to you not to give you control of Picketware if we married, it would be just as unfair to me if you had control. So, it seems that there is no way we can get married."

"You're calling off the marriage because you're not willing to give up control over something that you'll lose anyway, Jemima Louise Tuttle," Wylie said, drawing out her full name "Now that's crazy."

Maybe it was crazy to refuse Wylie, Jemma Lu thought after he left, but to be married to him would be worse than crazy. Of course, she didn't know then that she was pregnant. Although, even if she had, it wouldn't have been enough to change her mind. When she did find out a month later, she wasn't sure it was Wylie's, which kept her from feeling guilty about not telling him. When she could no longer hide her pregnancy she left town on what she told everyone was a grand tour of Europe several months before giving birth. Instead of Europe she went to Philadelphia and checked into a very private home for unwed mothers.

During those last three months of her pregnancy she did a lot of thinking and came up with a plan to save Picketware. She finished the plan just as she went into labor. After giving birth, her newborn son was immediately adopted by a nice couple. Later, she told herself that since the plan for Picketware's turnaround that she had birthed had been successful, the baby would grow up to be successful as well. After that she was equally successful at not thinking about her son until now with Wylie's return. The third surprise was that Howdy Hanks was coming back to town too. Unlike the first two surprises this one didn't fill her with dread.

This was all on Jemma Lu's mind when she rounded the corner onto Carson Street and almost ran into Sue Cohen. Like all of the main streets of Picketwire, Carson was wide enough for a wagon with a full team of oxen to turn around since getting an ox to back up is, well, oxymoronic. However, its sidewalks were narrow with the explanation being that people bumping into each other encouraged community and you didn't need to give a person the same amount of right of way as a thousand-pound ox. Jemma Lu stopped and exclaimed, "Why Sue Cohen! I almost walked right into you!"

"You're just in a hurry to get someplace, that's all."

"Hurry?" Jemma Lu replied. "But the place I was in a hurry to get to is yours. I could really use a cup of tea and some of your homemade cowboy fry bread and prickly pear jam."

"No scones with your tea?"

"This is low tea, not high, and it will go down even better if you join me, Sue." She threaded her right arm through Sue's left and said in a voice that must be obeyed, "And it's on me so don't even think about a freebie."

"How can I refuse an offer like that?"

"Why, you can't, of course," Jemma Lu said as she started walking, her right arm linked through Sue's left.

***

Ten minutes later Sue carried a tray with the tea and fry bread to the center booth next to the large plate glass window where Jemma Lu had seated herself. Jemma Lu might as well have her name on the booth in addition to the mug in her hand, Sue thought, since she always made a beeline to it as soon as she came through the door. If someone she knew already occupied it – and she knew just about everyone – they'd just scoot over to make room for her. Since it was after breakfast and before lunch the booth was vacant, and they pretty much had the cafe to themselves.

"Now Sue," Jemma Lu said, cradling the mug of tea, "has Rich Best tried to corral you into being a judge for this contest he's dreamed up?"

The contest was to be the centerpiece of FREDx, which stood for Farm and Ranch Entrepreneurship Dealmaking Expo. Rich Best had come up with the idea for FREDx and the fact that it just happened to have the same name as his business he insisted was a coincidence although its similarity to TEDx wasn't. Despite the doubts of many of its members, the Picketwire Chamber of Commerce had agreed to be the main sponsor. It didn't hurt that Rich was still the chamber's president when they made the decision. Now that the deed was done, Sue, as the newly elected president of the chamber, had to be supportive. "He didn't ask me to be a judge, but he did want me to ask you," she replied.

"He already asked me."

"He told me that you declined his invitation."

"So, he asked you to persuade me to change my mind?"

"Rich thinks you might reconsider and do it as a favor to me or for the chamber, but of course you shouldn't agree if you think it's a crazy idea."

"I do think it's a crazy idea, but that's not why I refused to be a judge. If it weren't for the crazy idea I came up with, Picketware would have gone out of business," Jemma Lu replied with a smile of amusement. "My concern is that all Rich has is the crazy idea. There needs to be a detailed plan on how to make Rich's crazy idea a success, and someone who isn't crazy to carry it out. Now," Jemma Lu paused and sipped her tea, "if you were in charge of running this contest it would be different."

"But it's not my idea and besides, I've got my own crazy idea."

"You do?" Jemma Lu asked eagerly as she picked up a piece of fry bread and spread some prickly pear jam on it.

"This is just between you and me, but I'm thinking of going into farming."

"You want to be a farmer?" Jemma Lu asked, arching her right eyebrow.

"If I want to serve the highest quality food then it's not enough to know how to cook it. I also need to know how to grow it."

"Now, Sue, you do know that there is a lot more to farming than growing things," Jemma Lu said, sounding somewhat like a schoolmarm as she took a bite of fry bread.

Sue chuckled, "You mean that farming is a great way to turn money into manure, which is how some of my customers describe it. It's like saying that the only way to make money owning a restaurant is to cook the books. Anyway, I haven't come up with a plan yet so it's only a crazy idea. I know the first thing, though, is that I have to find someone who really knows farming and is willing to teach me."

Jemma Lu wiped some crumbs off her lips with a napkin. "Well, you don't need to know much about farming to know that when it comes to farmers, like most people, being willing and being able don't necessarily go together."

"I also want to learn from someone who really knows about organic farming, which makes it even more difficult. It's like finding a needle in a haystack."

Jemma Lu's eyes lit up. "Sue, if I can find the needle in the haystack farmer who'd be willing and able to help you learn organic farming, can you find someone to help Rich turn his sow's ear of a contest into silk?"

"It won't be easy to find someone who knows what they're doing and is also willing to work with Rich, but I'll try. I think Desmond Goswami, the new owner of the Happy Trails RV and Trailer Park might be just the person."

"And I'll introduce you to an organic farmer. His name is George Takamoto, but everyone calls him Joji."

"The new assistant pastor at Picketwire Community Church is also named Takamoto. Are they related?"

"He's her uncle. Joji's brother is Jane's father, who is also a farmer. Their parents were among the first Japanese families to have established farms here."

"Well, then it's settled. Let's drink on it," Sue announced.

After they toasted and sipped some tea Jemma Lu said, "I do hope you're finding some time to get out."

"You mean other than going out with you and having tea?"

"I mean something more like a date."

"Well, I have been seeing someone."

"Can you tell me who or is that none of my business?" Jemma Lu asked with a grin.

"It's Max Bergmann."

"A girl from Los Angeles dating a guy from New York City," Jemma Lu said.

"And all both of us had to do was move halfway across the country."

"Those folks who say 'never the twain shall meet' should come to Picketwire, Colorado," Jemma Lu laughed.

"Maybe the chamber should use that in our promotional material. Picketwire, where the twain meet."

"Seriously, I'm happy that you two are seeing each other."

"I may be exaggerating when I say we're seeing each other since we barely have time between me running the cafe and the chamber and this crazy idea of Rich Best's, and Max rehearsing for the premiere of the new play by Howdy Hanks."

"Do you know what Howdy's play is about?"

"Max won't tell me a thing: Just that it's a new one and that Howdy wants it to be kept secret."

"Like your secret recipe for fry bread," Jemma Lu said, spreading jam on the piece of bread.

"A script as a recipe," Sue said. "I like the comparison. I'll have to share that with Max, although I have to see him first."

"Howdy kept his first play a secret as well, but it turned out to be a recipe for disaster. Of course, that was the play he wrote in high school."

"You saw it?"

"I was in it. We were classmates at Picketwire High. The play was the end of my stage career but, as it turned out, the beginning of his."

"Max said he's called the Sagebrush Shakespeare."

"That certainly wasn't one of the names he was called back then, and he was called quite a few." Jemma Lu said as her gaze floated out the window and into the street as if she was looking for something or someone from the past. She turned to Sue. "Although the Howdy I knew didn't give a hoot. I don't know what he's like now. With all his success writing plays he might have a head as big as a ten-gallon hat."

"You haven't seen him since high school?"

"We saw each other after we graduated, but then he left town thirty years ago and I haven't seen him since."

"Then you must be looking forward to seeing him again."

"Of course. But people change and...well..." Jemma Lu shrugged her slight shoulders. "Anyway, we've dawdled quite enough. Even though it's pretty darn difficult to stop eating this delicious fry bread and prickly pear jam of yours. In fact, I'll take the rest with me, if you don't mind?" Jemma Lu wrapped the leftover cowboy fry bread in a napkin and put it in her purse, then withdrew a ten-dollar bill that she slapped on the table, "I'm paying, and you keep the change."

CHAPTER FIVE

Everyone was long gone, but the curtain flapping in the window of the empty house was still waving goodbye. "Wonder what else they left behind?" Antonio "Tony" Medrano's voice filled the empty van before escaping through the open driver's side window. There was no point in keeping the words inside when there was so much silence outside to fill. He opened the van's door and stepped out into the settling dust blown up by his arrival. It was almost as dry as the baked ground beneath it and just as silent under the soles of his boots. He walked through the front yard, or what had been the front yard, although front and back and side or even the idea, the entire concept of yard didn't mean a whole hell of a lot to a house out here. He took a photo of it with his smartphone.

The door was open. In fact, the door was gone and so was most of the roof. You could have knocked down the house a long time ago with a couple of pushes from a bulldozer but what would have been the point? It's not as if there was some other use for the land it was on, and furthermore, it was adobe so it was basically dry mud and, unlike the houses now, it was biodegradable and would end up as unadulterated dust. After the housing boom a few years ago a whole bunch of new houses sprouted up on the prairie around Denver and Colorado Springs. They weren't little houses on the prairie, either, but big houses, and for a long time many of them were empty houses because their mortgages were far more than they were worth. They called that being underwater, an ironic description for houses built on the arid plains.

Looking around Tony couldn't help thinking that what was considered a piece of junk, worthless trivia, today could be an important archeological artifact years from now. Of course, he wasn't looking for artifacts but just scouting sites for a possible new tour that he had tentatively named "Ruins on the Range." This could be one of the ruins that was included on the tour, so Tony wanted to learn something about it from seeing what was left behind. It was like a tomb only the body was missing. Telling that story was a challenge. There wasn't much that these folks left, although they probably didn't have much to take with them. An overturned table with one of its legs snapped off, a tin bucket with a hole in it, and a lot of coyote scat.

That's when he noticed a Bible barely visible under a coating of dust on the earthen floor next to what was left of the overturned table. Tony brushed off the dust with a paintbrush he carried with him and took a photo. Carefully he opened the front cover. It was the King James Version, with a list of names, dates of birth, and, for many of them, their deaths. There were almost as many of the latter as the former. He was tempted to take it with him, but he was no tomb raider. He carefully returned the Bible to its shroud of dust then walked back to the van.

Tony sat in the front seat and drank the last of the coffee in the thermos that he'd filled that morning at Sue's Pretty Good Cafe. After writing a description of what he'd seen in his notebook he cranked the ignition and pulled away. When he got to the main road, which merely meant gravel instead of dirt, he stopped to let a couple of black Chevy Suburban SUV's barrel past on their way to the Double B Ranch. Tony wondered if they had anything to do with Wylie Boone moving back after the hit-and-run up in Aspen. Although he couldn't see through their tinted windows, he imagined they were probably surprised to see a purple van in the middle of nowhere.

Getting attention was, of course, one of the reasons for painting the van purple. The other was the name of his business, Purple Sage Tours. Although the business was new, Tony liked to think that he was picking up where his great-great-grandfather, Francisco Medrano, had left off. After all, "Don" Francisco, as he was still reverently called, had served as a scout and guide before helping to found Picketwire and starting its first (and last) stagecoach company. His son, Miguel, was responsible for bringing the railroad to Picketwire. After Tony's grandfather, Alejandro, sold the railroad to the Atchison, Topeka and

Santa Fe, the family business was primarily investing in businesses rather than running them. Tony's father, Roberto, had
been surprised when he told him that after getting an MBA at
the University of Colorado he wanted to start a business and not
just any business but a business that took visitors and sightseers
on tours of the area.

"What visitors? What sights?" His father asked, unable to
hide his disappointment not only at his son for not joining him
in Medrano Holdings, but also at what a bad investment he'd
made in paying for business school.

"That's the point, Dad," Tony had replied. "We won't get
tourists unless we identify and preserve the sights and have a way
to show them. Tourism is a big business, you know? What we
need to build is the infrastructure to support it."

"People come to Colorado because of the Rocky Mountains
and while we have plenty of rocks around here, we're not exactly
in the mountains."

"If you believe that then why are you still here?"

"I didn't say Picketwire wasn't a great place to live."

"Just not to visit, is that it? Well, how will people come to live
here if they don't visit? We need to invest to attract visitors or
they won't come."

"Okay, okay, maybe getting people to visit here would be
good," Roberto answered, grudgingly. "But why should the
Medranos be the ones to pay for it?"

If "Don" Francisco had thought that way we'd be in the fields
picking melons today instead of having this conversation, Tony

wanted to say but instead he answered. "I'm not asking you to pay. I'm asking for a small investment to get started." With that he handed over the business plan he'd written.

After looking at the plan his father was impressed. "But why do you want to call this business Purple Sage Tours?"

"It's named after *Riders of the Purple Sage* by Zane Grey."

"I prefer Louis L'Amour's books, but then I'm not a tourist; I just live here."

Medrano Investments indeed had provided some startup capital, and two years later, in addition to the van, Purple Sage Tours had a minibus, one full-time employee and several part-time tour guides. Although things hadn't gone exactly according to the business plan, Tony was confident that Purple Sage Tours was heading in the right direction and not riding into the sunset.

CHAPTER SIX

It would do. Oak bookcases covered most of the walls. Fortunately, they were already full since the room had been used as the church library and the books she brought with her would fill only a shelf. Jane did most of her reading on her iPad and Kindle but she found herself immediately drawn to the shelves filled with real books.

Instead of an office desk there was a wooden library table. Jane decided it should stay. She didn't need drawers, and a big office desk was just a barrier between her and those who came to see her. This way they would be sitting around the same table. And there was plenty of light from the large double window. True, with the bookcases there wasn't much space left to hang pictures on the walls, but she could always turn her chair and look out the window. It would be a good place to read and write and think, which is probably why the minister's office was called "the pastor's study."

But what about Bruce? He needed a place to work as well. They didn't even have a real home yet and were staying with her folks. There was no space to work there unless your work was farming, in which case there were acres. She laughed. Bruce? Bruce Levinson, born and bred in New York City as a farmer? Still, was that any more surprising than their marriage? A Japanese-American farm girl and a Jewish guy from Manhattan. Despite those differences they got married and had stayed married even when she went to seminary. But now she had uprooted them from their life in New York City to move back to her small hometown in the middle of nowhere. Bruce joked that if she was called to be a minister then he must have been called to be a wandering Jew.

In some ways, Jane felt like a stranger in Picketwire as well. Bruce, in fact, had an advantage because nobody there knew him and he wasn't expected to know anyone. If he were alone, people would introduce themselves to him but when they were together she was expected to introduce him to them, which was a problem since they all knew who she was, but she couldn't always remember who they were. She had to remind herself that not forgetting someone's name wasn't one of the Ten Commandments. What gave her the most anxiety was how she would handle running into someone whose name and face she couldn't forget as much as she'd tried. She only hoped that Bruce wouldn't be with her.

She opened her laptop and turned it on. The screen stared at her. It wasn't blank but cluttered with icons, but none of them said "sermon" and that's what she needed. This would be her first sermon at Picketwire Community Church. Her parents would be sitting in the front row as well as many people she knew. Reverend Sanderson – she had to remember to call him Dave – would be sitting right behind her as she stood at the pulpit and, of course, Bruce would be there next to her parents. He claimed that he would be there to give his moral, if not spiritual, support, but to be honest, his presence was what made her nervous.

In New York after seminary, she'd taken a job with an international social justice organization and "gave talks" rather than preached sermons. Bruce heard her "talks," but never one of the sermons she would give when she was a guest preacher at a church. Even then, her sermons weren't much different than the talks. In fact, she wasn't very comfortable preaching. She lifted her eyes from the computer screen and looked at the bookshelves. Her eyes drifted over the spines. She was too far away to read the titles. Why not just pick one of the books from here and use it as the basis for her sermon? Now, that would be something completely different for her, something that no one, not even Bruce, would imagine her doing.

The church secretary, Hazel Shanley, interrupted Jane's thoughts.

"Sorry to bother you, Reverend Takamoto," Hazel said standing in the open doorway.

"No bother, Hazel, and, please, you don't need to call me Reverend, Jane is fine. After all we've known each other for years." In fact, Hazel was the church secretary when Jane was baptized.

"I just want to say again, Jane, how proud we are of you and ever so happy that you've come back."

"So am I, Hazel. Can I help you with anything?"

"I just thought I'd clear some of the books off the shelves so you would have room for your own books. If you could just tell me what ones you want to keep then I'll put a little sticker on them so we don't move them by mistake."

"As a matter of fact, I was just going to take a closer look at them."

"Well, you'll find that all of the religious books, theology, Bibles and whatnot, are on these shelves," Hazel waved at the ones on the walls to the right and left. "But these," she put her hand on the bookshelf facing Jane, "Now these books I think it's safe to say we can get rid of. God only knows how they ended up here in the first place. We might be able to sell some to Bunch of Books."

"What kind of books are they?"

Hazel pulled a volume out, "I don't think you'll be needing the *Wizard of Oz*, for example."

Jane rose from her chair and walked over to where Hazel was standing. She took the book from her and looked at its cover. Staring back at her was Dorothy holding her dog, Toto, with the Tin Woodsman, Cowardly Lion and Scarecrow standing behind her. "I don't remember ever reading the book. I saw the movie with Judy Garland, of course, and musical, The Wiz, on Broadway, but I don't believe I ever read the book itself."

"I imagine you must feel a bit like Dorothy – having gone off to New York City and now coming back home. I've never been to New York, but I imagine it's sort of like the Emerald City."

Jane laughed, "Then, I should read it, Hazel. In fact, you can leave the other books here for now so that I can look through them as well."

Hazel hesitated at the door then said to Jane, "I hope you don't spend all your time in here reading books."

"I won't," Jane laughed. "As a matter of fact my husband, Bruce, and I are going on a long hike tomorrow in Canyonlands."

"You're going to see the dinosaur footprints?"

"Among other things," Jane said. The other things included trying to locate the ruins of a World War Two internment camp for Japanese-Americans that, according to her grandmother, was located somewhere near Canyonlands. She'd always wanted to try and find it but something had held her back. She hadn't told Bruce about it because she wasn't sure if she'd be able to find it or if she would even have the courage to look.

CHAPTER SEVEN

She was pretty sure that no one knew. At least they never said so if they did. Not a peep. Little kids sometimes gave her one of those scrunched face looks as if they wanted to say something but couldn't. Maybe it was the costumes she wore? Usually, it was the stripes of a convict, although sometimes it was the solid gray of a guard, and, when called on, the warden's three-piece black suit. She never wore the hangman's hood. A few goose bumps were okay but not screams of terror. Supposedly none of the people she portrayed were women, although she was pretty certain that a few had worked there disguised as men, just like they were known to have taken on other male roles in the West. When her role was a guard rather than a convict, she liked to think that she was reenacting a woman pretending to be a man.

Being thin, she had to pad herself before she played a warden or a guard but not when her role was a malnourished convict.

It was ironic that she only wore a traditional nun's habit when she had to fill in for Sister Cecilia in leading tours of the chapel. She and the other sisters didn't wear habits, but they lived in cells, the same cells where convicts, whose lives they re-enacted, had resided when it was the Purgatory State Penitentiary. Sister Mary Margaret, or Sister M's as she was known, put on the pillbox, striped cap and looked at herself in the mirror of her cell. A zebra stared back. She smiled, although it was hidden under the fake beard, which was just as well since an inmate wouldn't have much to smile about.

Sister M's walked to the Welcome Center at her usual fast gait then slowed to a shuffle that was more appropriate for the convict role she was playing. The Welcome Center was next to the main gate, which had hardly been a welcome sight for arriving prisoners. Looking through the gate she saw a large purple van parked in the visitors parking lot. "Purple Sage Tours" was painted on its side.

Sister Rachel was behind the counter when she entered. Unlike, Sister M's, she was dressed in a simple blue blouse and black pants with a small silver crucifix hanging from her neck on a slender chain. "They arrived a few minutes ago and they're in the museum waiting for you to start the tour," she said, nodding toward the door to the right. "You can count on Tony to be on time."

"He's sort of like a postman; neither snow nor rain nor heat nor gloom of night stays these couriers from the swift completion of their appointed rounds."

"It's easier when it hardly rains or snows and the night sky is lit by the moon and stars."

"Unlike what you had to deal with in Cleveland when you were delivering the mail."

"Yes," Sister Rachel answered with a smile. "I don't miss the weather or the skies being cloudy all day and night," she said, and then quickly added, "Although that certainly isn't why I joined the order, Sister M's."

"I think we both agree that we don't have any fair-weather nuns," Sister M's answered with a hearty laugh.

Sister Rachel joined in and then stopped and said, "My, aren't we just carrying on, laughing like little children."

"Can you think of a better place to fill with innocent laughter than a former prison? God knows it needs it."

***

"This may have been Purgatory Penitentiary but I'm pretty sure that the inmates thought it was hell." Everyone chuckled, the four adults because they knew that Purgatory was also the place that Catholics believed the souls of people who didn't go directly to heaven were condemned to do penance and the three kids because she'd said hell.

Sometimes people didn't laugh at all but Sister M's knew better than to try and explain. This wasn't a class in catechism but a tour of a former penitentiary. She did, however, explain that Purgatory, in this case, came from the location on the

Purgatoire River, from the French word for purgatory, and that prisons were named penitentiaries because they were supposed to be where people who had broken the law were sentenced to do penance through reflection on their bad deeds and learning how to be good and upstanding citizens. The adults all looked at the kids who responded by squirming in their seats.

Sister M's refrained from adding that they, in fact, were places where people were simply punished by being locked up. The "penitentiary" was the "pen" where society kept its human livestock.

"Do you still keep bad people here?" one freckle-faced, tow-headed boy of about eight asked.

"Why, do you want to stay?" an older girl, no doubt his sister, asked him. "Maybe they'd take you."

The adults laughed nervously, and the little boy looked at his sneakers as if he was hoping they would carry him away. One of the women said, "Now, Laurie, don't tease your brother."

"I prefer to say that we believe that it's now a place where anyone can come to reflect and learn to live a better life. We don't call people who stay here inmates and we don't have locked doors and guards."

"But aren't you an inmate?" the little boy asked.

"I'm dressed like a convict, but I'm really a sister." She pulled the beard down, exposing her face. "These are fake whiskers."

"I wish you were my sister not her," the little boy blurted out pointing at Laurie.

"Jack, stop that," the father snapped. "She's a nun."

"What's a nun?" Jack asked.

"None of your business," Laurie said, with a giggle.

"N-u-n," the older girl who had been trying to ignore the other two, spelled out. The two adults who smiled approvingly were obviously her proud parents. Then she asked, "But why aren't you wearing nun's clothes?"

"When we lead tours we dress up as either prison inmates or guards. It's called reenacting. When I'm not wearing this costume I just wear regular clothes. We don't wear habits in our order."

"You're just pretending," Jack said, nodding his head.

"She may be play-acting," Laurie said. "But little boys like you should remember not to make things up or you'll be sent to a real penitentiary."

The boy looked at his sneakers again.

"Laurie!" the mother snapped. "You shouldn't say things like that to your little brother."

"I was just joking."

"Telling your brother that he's going to prison isn't a joke."

"No, you're right," Laurie replied glaring at her little brother. "I wasn't joking."

CHAPTER EIGHT

Despite the bullet in his brain, Foster St. Vrain was feeling pretty damn good. There was a long neck bottle of beer in his right hand and his butt was in a La-Z-Boy and a Rockies baseball game on TV. Of course, his television didn't work anymore. He'd shot it and all he could see between the toes of the cowboy boots on the elevated footrest was a bullet hole in the middle of its screen. So now he was listening to the game on the radio. Well, hell, he liked to listen anyway. The way they called the game on radio was a lot more interesting than what he saw on television. When he turned the sound off the TV and listened to the play-by-play on radio it was like there were two different games: The boring as hell one he was watching on TV and the thriller he was listening to on the radio. He finally decided that he preferred the version that played out in his mind as he listened than what he saw and that's when he got his pistol and put the television out of its misery or maybe it was his misery. In any case, he felt better afterwards. Hell of a thing for a cop to do but he wasn't a cop anymore.

As he swigged his beer and listened to the game he looked out through the screen door of his bungalow. Was that Jemma Lu Tuttle standing on his front porch or was it someone else or maybe nobody? After all, his ability to make a positive identification of someone had been considered unreliable after he'd been shot in the head. He turned off the transistor radio.

"Foster."

Once he heard the voice he knew he had been right. "Sorry, Jemma Lu, I couldn't hear you over the radio," Foster replied as he pulled the handle on the recliner, got up and opened the door. "Come on in."

She accepted his offer to sit in the only other chair but declined the beer or a glass of tap water, which was the only alternative.

"So, Jemma Lu Tuttle," Foster asked after he settled back into the recliner. "What brings you to this part of town?"

"What's wrong with this part of town?"

"Other than me, nothing."

Now, what does that mean?"

"It means that if I knew I'd have me as a neighbor I'd have never moved here."

After Jemma Lu stopped laughing, she said. "You're too hard on yourself, Foster."

"You sound like the sister I never had."

"The big sister," she replied. Not that she had to remind him she was ten years older since that point had been made a long time ago.

"Since we haven't seen each other in a while there's been no one to put me in my place so I've had to do it myself. I hope you didn't come here to put me in some other place because I'm sort of attached to this one."

"This place?" Jemma Lu looked around the small living room of the one-story bungalow

"I believe this is the first time you've been here."

"Yes it is. Of course, I don't recall ever being invited to visit," she said. Then, without waiting for him to think of an answer that might sound halfway convincing, she let him off the hook by changing the subject. "What happened to your TV?" She asked, nodding toward the television.

"Shot it."

"Why on earth did you do that?"

"Got tired of its company." He took a sip of beer.

"Then I'll be sure and not overstay my welcome."

"Don't you worry, Jemma Lu, I only shoot television sets nowadays. Besides, I get the feeling you didn't come here just to keep me company."

Jemma Lu smiled. "I always enjoyed the times we spent together, Foster."

"All the times?" He asked, arching his right eyebrow.

"Okay, there might have been one or two that weren't so enjoyable. You're not the easiest friend to have."

Foster toasted her with his beer. "Easiest confession I ever got."

"Now that you've gotten it, I want to ask you something. Are you still doing private investigations?"

"It keeps me busy. Not that I've been really busy lately."

"So, you're free to take on a case?"

"Depends."

"On what?"

"Who asks me. I'm highly selective as to the cases I take."

"What are your criteria?"

"They have to be able to pay me," he snorted and took another swig of beer.

"Well, I'm asking and I can pay."

"Then the answer is yes."

"Before you know what it's about?"

"Well now that I've agreed, what is it about?" Foster asked then chugged some beer.

"It's about Wylie Boone."

Foster almost spit out the beer in surprise, "Did you say Wylie Boone?"

"Yes, you heard me right, Wylie Boone. I want to find out who's trying to kill him."

"I heard about the hit-and-run up in Aspen."

"What if it wasn't just a hit-and-run?"

"You think someone deliberately tried to kill him?"

"I don't know for sure and that's what I'd like you to find out and if it's true then find out who did it."

Based on what he'd heard Foster knew Wylie had a gift for making enemies. That and making money. "Could be that someone did run into him on purpose. Why do you want to find out? Wylie has been gone for years and someone told me that you and he didn't exactly get along when he left town."

"Who told you that?" Jemma Lu asked, sharply.

Foster chuckled "Now, Jemma Lu, you know I can't reveal my sources."

"Okay, Wylie and I had our differences, but..."

"But?"

Jemma Lu wished she'd taken Foster up on the beer. "But now that he's back..."

Foster put his beer down in surprise, "Back here...in Picketwire?"

"The ranch."

"Well by golly, Wylie is back at the ranch."

Jemma Lu smiled broadly and shook her head. "I would think a private detective would know things like that."

Foster picked up his beer and pointed the neck of the bottle at her. "I operate on a need to know basis and I didn't need to know until you just hired me." He took a swig, then said, "If someone is trying to kill him while he's at the ranch then that's the sheriff's jurisdiction."

"Jesse Riggleman?" Jemma Lu laughed. "You've got to be kidding."

"I'm just saying it's his responsibility."

"He's also the person who shot you, which doesn't sound very responsible."

"As you recall the prosecutor concluded it was an accident while assisting a fellow officer."

Jemma Lu shook her head in disbelief. "Riggleman is the one who called for your assistance and when you responded he tried to kill you."

"He claimed that he thought I was one of the bad guys," Foster said, wincing at the memory. "The only witness was me and they considered my account to be extremely unreliable on account of the bullet that was lodged in my head. Also, they couldn't come up with a motive for Riggleman shooting me. That was more than enough for Vince Lowery, the county prosecutor, to declare it an accident."

"Of course, he did. Lowery was probably in on the whole thing. Anyway, a lot of us here in Picketwire believe your account."

"There were enough folks outside Picketwire who believed his story. After all, he'd just been elected County Sheriff."

"His whole campaign was based on portraying Picketwire as the root of all evil and that if elected he'd stop it from spreading to the rest of the county."

"And he shot me because I was the police chief from hell," Foster said as he spun the empty beer bottle by its neck on the broad arm of the recliner.

"It's not something to joke about, Foster," Jemma Lu said wanting to grab the damn beer bottle out of his hand. "You wouldn't go along with him so he decided to get rid of you and then proposed that Picketwire get rid of its police department and let the sheriff, Riggleman, take over law enforcement. Fortunately, the City Council didn't go along with it."

Foster stopped the spinning beer bottle, picked it up and gently tapped the bottle's neck against the bullet scar on his forehead. "Believe me, Jemma Lu, it's no joke."

"Then, seriously, are you going to take the case or not?"

"I decided to take it as soon as you asked."

"Well, okay then. Just send me the bill. In fact, I should give you a retainer or advance," Jemma Lu said, pulling her checkbook from her purse. "How much should I make it out for?"

Foster waved his right hand, motioning her to stop. "I'm giving you the friends discount and since you can't put a price on friendship the discount is as much as the bill, so you can holster that checkbook of yours."

"You don't have to do that. You know I can afford to pay whatever you charge."

Foster smiled. "And I can afford to charge you whatever I want, which is nothing."

CHAPTER NINE

I t is a truth universally acknowledged that tourists in possession of a credit card must be in want of souvenirs. Jane Austen's opening line in *Pride and Prejudice* came to mind as Sister M's led the tour group into the Good Stuff Gift Shop next to the Welcome Center. She ended the tour by introducing them to Sister Rachel with the observation that, "Sister Rachel has a gift for helping people discern what they need rather than just selling them what they think they want."

Sister M's left the gift shop and walked over to Tony Medrano who was leaning against the Purple Sage Tours van. "You know, Sister," he said as she approached. "I'm trying to picture you giving a group of illegal immigrants a tour."

"They're undocumented immigrants not illegal and I won't be giving them the same tour I gave these folks or wearing this getup, that's for sure," she answered, tugging at the prisoner outfit she wore. Then she took off the striped prison cap, ran her fingers through her short hair, and asked, "Have you decided if you can help us?"

"Not yet," Tony replied with a nervous smile.

"We don't have much time."

"I know. I'll get you an answer by tomorrow at the latest," Tony replied. "It just seems strange to hide people in a prison so that they won't be arrested."

"It's not a prison anymore," Sister M's said, putting the cap back on.

"You have to admit it still looks more like a prison than a convent."

She stared at the red brick walls and towers with her hands on her hips. Maybe she couldn't shake Jane Austen, but with the turrets it actually looked sort of like a castle. Pemberley as a convent? Was that so farfetched? After all, *Pride and Prejudice* was as much about sisters as it was Mister Darcy, maybe more.

"There's also the name you gave your convent, Our Lady of Lost Souls. Lost souls are what some people call prisoners. And then the location here on the Purgatoire River. You know the original Spanish name is El Rio de las Animas Perdidas en Purgatorio."

Sister M's nodded her head, "which means in English the River of Lost Souls in Purgatory. But these people we're helping aren't lost souls and we didn't name our convent Our Lady of Lost Souls because we believe our community is Purgatory."

"I know, Sister," Tony held up both hands in surrender. "The lost souls in your convent's name means it's a place for folks who have lost their way in life and are searching for meaning and purpose. I did take your tour, you know."

"Then you should also remember I said that we welcome those who are outcast or given up for lost by society. However," Sister M's continued, "I agree that it's a convent that's camouflaged. Still, it's a convent, and that means it's a sanctuary, not a prison or purgatory."

"And you want to provide sanctuary for people who are here illegally?"

Sister M's nodded. "Like I said, they're undocumented not illegal and we won't ask them to sign the guest register."

"Isn't undocumented and illegal immigrant the same thing under the law?" Tony shook his head and looked down at his black cowboy boots. There was still dust on them from the abandoned house.

"Not necessarily. The law's a funny thing."

"I'd say a lawyer calling the law a funny thing is funny."

Not just a lawyer but a lawyer who'd once been a prosecutor. She'd put people in jail and now she was keeping them out. "That was the nun speaking, not the lawyer."

"Which one is breaking the law by hiding them – the nun or the lawyer?"

"We will be giving them sanctuary, which is not the same thing as hiding them," Sister M's corrected. "I will also be their legal counsel, and under the law everyone is innocent until proven guilty. That's the lawyer speaking. As a nun I also think it would be a sin not to offer sanctuary."

"So the good news for me is if I agree to transport these undocumented immigrants here to this convent-sanctuary then according to you, a nun, I won't be committing a sin?"

Sister M's nodded. "Yes, that's what I believe."

"And the bad news is that if I get caught, I'll be charged with committing a crime."

"I believe that's true, as well. However, I also believe that if the choice is between committing a sin by not helping and committing a crime by helping, then one should always choose not to knowingly sin."

"I shouldn't have asked, because now I know," he replied and looked at Sister M's in her black and white striped prisoner costume. It's easy for you nuns to choose to do something that would put you in jail, he thought, since you're already living in a cell. When Sister M's had asked if he was interested in helping after he'd told her about his anger as a Mexican-American at the way undocumented immigrants were being treated, he had hesitated. Going to jail wasn't exactly part of his business plan. "If I get arrested, will you be my lawyer as well?"

"Certainly," Sister M's said, and then added, "It will be pro bono, of course."

"As I said, I'll let you know tomorrow," Tony said. "Right now, I better round up my tour group. Next stop is looking at the dinosaur tracks and that's always a hit with the kids. Next to the prison tour, that is."

"I think it's ironic that this was once part of Mexico," Sister M's said as they walked toward the door to the gift shop.

"Everything south of the Arkansas River was until the U.S. declared war on Mexico in 1846 and took it all."

"Just think, if the U.S. hadn't taken it from Mexico, I could be the one who is arrested and deported for illegally immigrating."

Tony came to a dead stop and looked at her. "You know, Sister M's, the Medranos were living here back then, even before all that happened. One day my ancestors were living in Mexico and the next thing they knew they were in the United States. Instead of crossing the border, the border crossed them. Seems like what was legal or illegal was irrelevant."

CHAPTER TEN

"Enter into the rock and hide in the dust from the terror of the Lord, and from the splendor of his majesty." The words came suddenly to Jane as she looked at the dinosaur tracks imbedded in the banks of the Purgatoire River. The words were Isaiah's, not Fred Flintstone's, and they made her shiver even though she was standing in the hot afternoon sun of the Picketwire Canyonlands. Jane and Bruce had run into Tony and his tour group at the trailhead, and he'd invited them to ride along in one of the Purple Sage jeeps rather than hiking the three and half miles to the dinosaur tracks. Although Jane had suggested the hike as a way for them to explore on their own, Bruce quickly took Tony up on his offer to join the Purple Sage tour. The motorized tours were conducted by Forest Service rangers and only four-wheel drive, high clearance vehicles could be used. Jane returned her attention to Elise Plumb, a ranger who was explaining that there were more than

1,300 dinosaur footprints from the late Jurassic period in the hundred plus trackways. Forty percent of them were left by the four-legged, plant-eating apatosaurus and the remainder by the vicious, two-legged, flesh-eating allosaurus.

"The apatosaurus were up to 72 feet long and could weigh more than 24 tons. What were huge, plant-eaters doing here? Well, as hard as it is to imagine looking at this arid landscape with just the shallow, muddy Purgatoire River running through it, 150 million years ago this was the shoreline of an inland sea. There were lots of plants for the apatosaurus and other vegetarian dinosaurs to eat. There was even a forest here although that's not why the Forest Service has jurisdiction over the Canyonland. It's because it's part of the Comanche National Grasslands. That's why I'm a forest ranger not a grass ranger although we do enforce the law against growing marijuana on federal land." She waited for the anticipated chuckling to subside before continuing. "The allosaurus was only a third of the size of the apatosaurus but it had dozens of serrated teeth and it's estimated that it could run at speeds up to 34 miles per hour so it could take down prey that was much larger than it was. It's not hard to imagine that they were here to dine on other dinosaurs."

"Wow, this is like Jurassic Park," said the freckled-faced boy, who'd turned his Purple Sage Tours cap around so that the brim faced backward.

"Jurassic Park is just a movie, Jack," explained the girl standing next to him, letting him know that she was not only taller and older but much, much wiser. "All the dinosaurs are dead. They made those footprints a jillion years ago."

"Maybe all the dinosaurs didn't die?"

"Maybe you're right and we could leave you here and when we came back all we'd find would be little boy bones."

"Laurie, stop scaring your brother," the mom said and then turned to Jane and Bruce and explained. "First she was going to put her little brother in prison, and now she wants to feed him to the dinosaurs."

"Kids," Jane said, more as an expression of sympathy than an explanation.

"At least they aren't bored," the mom said. "Nothing is worse than when they are bored and they want to be doing something else." She looked around at the rugged landscape, "I mean, what else is there?"

"Are people ready to see some rock art?" Elise asked enthusiastically.

Laurie's hand shot up as she yelled, "I want to see the rock stars!"

"I hope you don't mind that these rock stars were artists who drew animals and other pictures on rock thousands of years ago."

"I can draw animals on rocks," Jack offered as Laurie withdrew her hand. "I've even got my own crayons in my backpack."

"I'm afraid we don't allow anyone to draw on the rocks," Elise said putting her right hand on Jack's shoulder. "However, if you have paper maybe you could draw something for us. We'd love to put them up in the Ranger Station."

"Will you put mine up too?" Laurie shouted as she jumped up and down.

"Of course," Elise answered.

"But I don't have anything to draw with?"

"Laurie," her dad said, "ask Jack if he'll share some of his paper and crayons with you."

"Why don't you just tell him to?"

"Because it's his decision."

Laurie walked over to Jack and, looking down on him, demanded, "Give me some paper and crayons."

"Laurie," her mom said, sternly, "there's a difference between asking and ordering someone."

"Please," Laurie said, forcing a smile.

"Okay, I can give you some paper, but I get to choose which crayons," Jack said to Laurie.

Laurie looked at her parents and when they declined to intervene, she turned back to Jack and nodded in agreement to the terms.

Jane said to Bruce, "Now that was a learning experience."

"You mean that whenever you go out with your kids be sure and bring extra paper and crayons?"

Jane jabbed Bruce's left arm with her elbow, "No, silly. It was better this way because they had to share."

"Well, if it was a lesson in free market economics and supply and demand, Jack should have demanded that Laurie pay him to supply her."

"You mean they should be taught that it's a dog-eat-dog world? Is that what you really think?"

"No," Bruce replied, calmly. "I don't know about dogs eating other dogs, but the ranger just told us that dinosaurs eat other dinosaurs, so it was a dinosaur-eat-dinosaur world 150 million years ago."

"Maybe if dinosaurs had learned to share they'd still be around."

"Dinosaurs are extinct because they didn't sit around the campfire singing kumbaya? Now, that sounds like what a preacher would say."

"What does that mean?" Jane asked not hiding her irritation.

"It was a joke, Honey," he said, with a weak laugh and slight shrug.

"Really?" She said staring at him and crossing her arms.

Bruce could hear the demand, but he wasn't sure he could supply the answer, and he was about to resort to his usual lame standby that he didn't mean it that way when Tony interrupted, "I hope you two are joining us on the rest of the tour?"

"Sure, we'd like to see the rock art," Bruce answered quickly, seizing the opportunity to avoid responding to Jane.

Instead of agreeing, Jane said to Tony that she had heard that there had been an internment camp in the area where Japanese-Americans were imprisoned during World War Two "It's not on any maps and even when I googled it there was nothing."

"I'm not surprised you didn't find anything," said Elise, who was now standing beside Tony. "In fact, you're among the very few people who have even heard that there was an internment camp here. Most people only know about Camp Amache that's located near Lamar. 7,500 Japanese-Americans were sent to Amache during World War Two. How did you hear about it?"

"I grew up in Picketwire and my grandmother said that there was another camp besides Amache. She didn't say where it was other than it was somewhere in this area near the Canyonlands."

"The Japanese-Americans who were sent to the camps were from the West Coast," Elise said. "The excuse was that they couldn't be trusted and might help the Japanese invade California."

"My family, the Takamotos, have lived here for more than a century," Jane said. "My great-grandparents came here from Japan in 1905."

"Then they were among the first Japanese immigrants who came to this part of Colorado."

"How do you know that?" Jane asked.

"I'm interested in more than dinosaurs," Elise laughed then reached out and put her right hand on Tony's left shoulder. "Actually, Tony here has been my personal tutor on the history of the area."

"Do you know where this other camp was located?"

"Sure," Elise spread a map of the area on the hood of the jeep. "It's here," she said, pointing to a spot. Jane noticed that her fingernails were trim but definitely manicured. "It's not very far from the ruins of the Dolores Mission."

"Look," Tony said, "We're stopping at the Mission on the way back after we look at the rock art, so we can drop you off and point you in the right direction."

"It should be an easy hike from there, although you should know that it's on the Double B Ranch property," Elise added. "I really wish we could include it as part of our research and education program, but every time we've approached the Double B they've refused to grant us access without giving us any reason."

"Does that mean we'd be trespassing?" Jane asked.

"Technically, I suppose," Tony answered. "But there's no fence in that section and it's not posted, so you can claim ignorance."

"I don't have a problem claiming ignorance," Bruce said.

CHAPTER ELEVEN

Money never sleeps and neither did Wylie Boone. For years he boasted about his ability to get along on only a few hours' sleep as a strategic advantage that gave him an edge. The point being that he had the ability to exert mind over matter in pursuit of money, although the truth was that it wasn't his desire to make money that kept him awake, it was his fear of the nightmares that came when he slept. The nightmares had started long before the recent hit-and-run, and avoiding them had played no small part in his accumulation of wealth. Instead of counting sheep to get to sleep he counted dollars and pounds and euros and pesos to stay awake. Not that he would have counted sheep since Boone grew up on a cattle ranch where even one sheep was too many.

This time staring at the numbers from different stock, bond, and currency markets throughout the world displayed on the three monitors in front of him didn't seem to be working and he felt himself slipping into sleep. He swiveled his black Herman Miller Aeron chair, got up, and walked out of one of the bedrooms of the ranch house that he'd converted into an office. What he needed was some fresh air and not the kind that comes from a stroll but through the open window of his Chevy going full throttle.

It was his first car and already classic when he bought it in 1973. The candy apple red paint job, the four shining mags on the wheels, the overhaul of the V8 engine and the installation of a four-speed stick shift on the floor with a black number eight cue ball as the knob, made it the perfect set of wheels for picking up girls and impressing the other guys. He had paid for it and the upgrades with his own money. Boone thought of it as his first investment and the only one that he hadn't sold. He'd told the reporters how upset he was that his 1960 Porsche Carrera had been totaled in the hit-and-run, but truth was that the only car he really cared about was the '57 Chevy. For years it had been kept safely in its own garage at the ranch, kept in tune and checked out regularly by a mechanic so that it would be ready when Boone decided to come back and take it for a spin. Now he was back, and he was ready.

Boone told the bodyguard on duty (whose name he couldn't remember) that he would be taking the car out for a spin.

"Are you sure, Mr. Boone?" The guard asked as he walked with him to the garage.

"Of course, I'm sure."

"But wouldn't it be better if I drove you in the Suburban? It's armor plated."

"That sort of ruins the whole idea. No, I want to drive myself and not in some two-ton tank."

After helping him take the protective cover off the car, the bodyguard opened the garage door. Wylie sat in the driver's seat. He didn't buckle the seatbelt, which wasn't original and had been added because it was required by law. His left foot pushed in the clutch, which was called a suicide clutch because you barely had to lift your foot for it to engage, then shift the stick through all four gears before settling back in first and taking off.

He quickly realized that he wouldn't be able to get beyond second gear without stirring up the gravel on the ranch road and pitting the candy apple finish so when he got to the front gate he ordered the guard to open it. A few minutes later he pulled onto the hardtop of the county road. He stopped and listened to the throb of the V8, inhaling the mix of leaded gasoline and sagebrush. There was a full-moon so he could see the road beyond the arc of his headlights as it ran straight across the flat, silver prairie. He knew that there wasn't a bend in it for at least five miles until it turned toward town just past the cut off to the old penitentiary.

He pumped the gas pedal a couple of times then pushed it down to the floor as he released the clutch and with a squeal the Chevy shot forward. When he reached a hundred, he shifted into neutral, turned off the engine and the headlights. Silently he coasted, surrounded by the silver, moonlit prairie and a rush of memories. When he finally rolled to a stop he pounded the wheel several times, leaned out of the window and yelled like a coyote. He turned the key, shifted into first and switched on the lights. Suddenly there was a bright light flashing above him. Looking up at the rearview mirror he was surprised to see a pair of headlights. They had come out of nowhere and were closing fast.

CHAPTER TWELVE

I t was a broad proscenium with an orchestra pit beyond the footlights followed by rows of plush, red upholstered seats. And above the main floor there was a balcony with more seats although less legroom. As far as Max was concerned, the Tumbleweed Theater was as good a venue as anything on the "Great White Way" except that it was a couple of thousand miles off Broadway. Although the house lights were on, Max had arranged with Fred Dimsdale to go to the lighting booth and turn them down and switch on a spotlight at his signal.

"It sure is different up here," Zelda said in a whisper.

She must be in awe, Max thought, which is exactly what he expected from someone who had never been on a stage before. Although each new member of the Bard Wired Players got a personal orientation from Max, he had particularly been looking forward to this one since Zelda had never acted. Ordinarily a new member had experience in a school play or musical or some amateur theater group and they had no idea how bad they were. Max would have to listen patiently as they recounted how they had honed their theatrical skills performing in *My Fair Lady* in a high school auditorium or *Our Town* at a Moose Lodge. That's why it was a relief that Zelda, who had never performed before, was a clean slate rather than a blackboard that needed erasing.

"It should be," Max answered. "You're up here instead of out there."

"I've only been in this place once and that was to see a stupid movie. Where's the screen?"

"Above you," Max pointed up. "It's lowered when there are films but otherwise it's stored up there. This was a theater for the performing arts long before movies were shown. They had performances of operas, concerts, musicals, some vaudeville and, of course, melodramas."

"Mellow dramas? You mean everyone was stoned?"

Max gave a mildly condescending smile and explained, "No, melodramas, not mellow dramas. A melodrama is a play in which everything is exaggerated and there's plenty of slapstick. They were very popular a hundred years ago. Usually it's some dastardly villain with a name like Snidely Whiplash who would kidnap a young girl with a name like Nell, and when she rejected his amorous advances, he'd tie her to the railroad tracks. Then the good guy, who's a real super straight Dudley Do-Right type, would rescue her."

"Why?"

"Because if she weren't rescued a train would run over her."

"I mean, why did she need to be rescued by some super straight jerk with a name like Dudley?"

"Because then Nell would fall madly in love with Dudley and live happily ever after."

"Sounds like something a guy would make up, especially the kinky, bondage stuff."

"Times were different then, Zelda."

""But not the male fantasies."

Changing the subject, Max pointed up. "The scenery is also hung up there so that it can be lowered and raised during a play. It's called the fly tower because the scenery flies up and down and the stagehands who pull it with ropes are called flymen." He pointed in front of the fly tower. "In front of that is the curtain and then going all the way around is the proscenium," Max continued pointing as his arm swung in a three-hundred-and-sixty-degree arc. As he did so, right on cue, Fred, hidden in the lighting booth at the back of the second balcony, dimmed the house lights and Max was suddenly lit up by a spotlight. "The proscenium is the frame the play is performed in." Max walked boldly to the front of the stage with the spotlight following him and stopped and put his right hand palm up as if it was pressing against clear glass. And this is the fourth wall."

"I don't see any wall," Zelda said.

"Of course not, Zelda," Max replied, disappointed that she didn't seem to notice the dramatic change in lighting. "It's an invisible wall that stands between the actors on stage and the audience on the other side."

"It's invisible because it doesn't really exist."

"Oh," Max shook his head and gave her his best, superior smile. He wanted to reach out and put his right hand gently on her left shoulder. That would have been a nice, dramatic touch. But Zelda being a teenage girl might get the wrong impression as to his intentions, so he just waved toward the empty theater and launched into the soliloquy that he gave to new members of the company. "It exists, even though it's invisible. The people out there, on the other side, the audience can look through it but what they see and hear exists only behind this wall. And what we do on this stage, on this side of the wall," he pointed to the floor of the stage, "is to create such a vivid world that while it exists, they don't." He pointed, forcefully toward the seats now shrouded in darkness. "They will be so absorbed that they are unaware of anything else, including themselves. This world that we create on the stage becomes their world, although they can only watch and listen in."

"Like all the world is a stage, right?"

"I bet you didn't know that you just quoted Shakespeare."

"You mean *As You Like It*, Act Two, Scene Seven?" Zelda replied as she walked quickly over to where he was standing. He was forced to move aside, and she took his place in the spotlight. Then thrusting her right hand out, fist first, she pushed past the edge of the stage into the darkness.

"For someone who's never acted before you sure know your Shakespeare," Max said, unable to hide his surprise at her response as well as her actions.

"I just haven't acted on a stage," Zelda answered. Then, without waiting for a reply from Max, she asked. "Are you going to show me the rest of this place or should I just stay here in the spotlight?"

Max was relieved at her request to be shown the rest of the theater. He could escape the improvisation and return to his orientation script. As he gave Zelda the grand tour of the rest of the beautifully restored, historic Tumbleweed, from the dressing rooms backstage to the lighting booth in the balcony where he introduced her to Fred, his confidence and command returned. He talked and she listened in silence. After they finished the tour in the ornate lobby, standing on the plush burgundy carpet, he asked if she had any questions.

"Only one. Why is this play supposed to be a big secret?"

"Howdy just made it a condition. Anyway, audiences like to be surprised."

"But I don't see why the actors need to be surprised as well. Why don't we get to see the last act now instead of waiting? You've seen it, right?"

"Of course. After all, I'm the director," Max replied with a straight face. After all, if you couldn't tell a convincing lie then how the hell could you call yourself a good actor? He couldn't tell her that he hadn't seen it either, because he was embarrassed that Howdy hadn't shared the entire play with him. He could have demanded it but Howdy had made it clear that he wasn't going to share it until they were ready to rehearse it. He told Max he should just think of it as a just-in-time production. After all, he'd joked, what's the point in having it until you need it? Max would have to direct the earlier scenes without knowing how it all ended. The fact was he had no choice since he could hardly afford to cancel the production and lose his chance to show everyone that this wasn't some podunk playhouse.

"So why can't you tell us how it ends?"

"Howdy doesn't want the cast to know until they've rehearsed the previous acts. Until you're ready."

"What if I hate it? I don't want to be in a play I hate."

"Listen, Zelda, trust me, you'll be happy with the ending."

"Not if it's a sappy ending."

"Of course not," Max replied, doing everything he could to hide his exasperation. "Howdy doesn't write sappy stuff. In any case, as soon as we finish rehearsing the first two acts we'll rehearse the final act, so you don't have long to wait. You know, Shakespeare himself would still be working on a play even as the actors at the Globe were rehearsing it. Apparently they would often get their lines just before they were ready to be spoken."

"You're saying that the reason Howdy is called the Sagebrush Shakespeare is because he doesn't finish his plays before rehearsals start?"

"No, I'm not saying that. It's just that, well," Max paused, for once at a loss for words, "let's just say that ours is not to reason why," he said firmly.

"That's not Shakespeare."

"No, I'm paraphrasing a line from Tennyson's poem 'The Charge of the Light Brigade.' You've never heard of it?"

"Just because I like Shakespeare doesn't mean I like everything that's written by old dead men."

"Tennyson is very famous, as is his poem."

"Okay, so how did the charge of this light brigade end?"

"They all died."

"Not exactly a happy ending."

"No, but..." Max stuttered as he searched for a comeback line.

"That's good, because I hate happy endings," Zelda declared.

CHAPTER THIRTEEN

Sister M's sat in her room. There were only two places to sit, either the one chair or the single bed. When it had been a prison cell there had also been a toilet one could sit on but that had been removed along with the bars. There was no need for a lock on either the inside or the outside of the cell since no one was going to break in and if someone wanted to break out they were more than free to escape. Anyone who wanted to lock themselves in their cell shouldn't be a nun. She was wearing a pair of Levi's and a black T-shirt with the words "Nun is our business" stenciled in white block letters. Hanging from a leather strap around her neck was a small crucifix made from piñon pine. Sister Darlene, who was a sculptor when she wasn't baking bread, carved them from wood that she found on her walks. They were the same ones that were sold in the gift shop. Sold was a misnomer since they were placed in a basket with the words "freely given" on a card next to it. There was also an unlabeled ceramic jar that Sister Bernadine made on her potter's wheel. The jar was empty when the shop opened but always seemed to be filled with coins and bills by closing time.

This was the time after supper and before compline. During dinner one of the sisters read aloud from a book while everyone else ate. It wasn't the Bible and, in truth, it wasn't always a good book. The reading time was limited to thirty minutes so that there was time for talking or just eating. Sister M's was scheduled as the next reader and she hadn't yet decided what to read. She wished that Sister Sylvia had picked something longer than Conrad's *Heart of Darkness*. It was certainly a story to contemplate and generated discussion, but it was only a novella and she'd be finished in a week.

Sister M's would have to get to the library quickly and check out a book she'd already read that she could read to people as they ate. It had to whet their appetite for discussion while not upsetting their stomachs. She'd given all of the books that she'd accumulated from her previous life to the library so the book she'd pick would more than likely be one that once belonged to her. The only book she kept was the Bible that she'd been given when she was an assistant district attorney.

It had been her first case that she had handled on her own: A rapist who had brutally beaten his victim. He refused to confess or accept a plea bargain, so it went to trial and she'd gotten the conviction and sent him to prison for thirty years. Seven years later she was in court facing him again. Only this time it was for his exoneration. DNA evidence had proven that another man had been the rapist and now the one she had prosecuted was being set free. 'The People,' who she as the prosecutor represented, had no objection and within minutes the courtroom was clearing out. The man who she had believed at the time was a vicious serial rapist and deserved no mercy was standing by himself. She walked over to him and said that 'the People' were sorry.

"The People are sorry?"

"The People is who we...I, represent."

"I'm people, a person, and you didn't represent me."

"That's not how the system works."

"That's how the system doesn't work, you mean."

She remembers wanting to walk away but something kept her there, looking up at him. "I guess not in this case."

"It wasn't a case to me, it was seven years, 2,555 days, 61,320 hours, in a cell in a maximum security penitentiary."

"Look, I know there's nothing I can say to give you back the time you lost but I do want you to know that the People apologize and..." And what? And what?

"No," he put up his right index finger. "I don't accept the apology."

"I understand."

"No, you don't understand, because what I don't accept is the People's apology because I don't see any people. I just see you." His brown eyes locked onto her blue eyes, seeing right through her. No, not through her but into her. A smile rippled across his lips and he said, "But I do forgive you."

"You do?" She exhaled the words. It was more than a sigh of relief. Much more. As if she'd been set free as well.

"Yes."

"Thank you," she heard herself say as he turned and walked away.

Just before he reached the door to the courtroom, where a group of people stood, probably his family and friends who'd waited for him for seven years, who'd believed that he was innocent, he stopped, and walked back to her. When he got to her, he reached into the pocket of the cheap, ill-fitting suit coat that the People had given him to wear in court and pulled out something. "Don't thank me, thank this," he said, handed it to her and walked out of the courtroom. The Bible he gave her was a cheap, pocket version with its black cover so worn that scotch tape had been applied liberally to keep it from disintegrating. Inside, every page from Genesis to the Book of Revelations had passages that he had underlined and every day she read one.

She read Exodus 3:11, "Who am I that I should go to Pharaoh and bring the children of Israel out of Egypt?" After nine years of reading the underlined passages Sister M's knew most of them by heart, including this one. Still, she always read the words. In the next passage Moses asks God who God is, and God turns Moses' words around and replies, "I am who I am." If she were still a prosecutor an answer like that would have drawn an objection from her that no judge would overrule, and God would have been held in contempt and if it was an immigration hearing swiftly deported. Although God wouldn't be one of the undocumented immigrants they would be providing sanctuary to and that she might have to defend, and if they were caught by Immigration and Custom Enforcement, there would, more than likely, be at least one with the name Jesus.

After closing the Bible and placing it on the single, wooden shelf fixed to the wall opposite the bed, Sister M's put on a faded blue hoodie sweatshirt. Whenever she had the time she liked to take a walk before compline. Since she ran for an hour every morning, she really didn't need the physical exercise, and this was more for thinking. There was a full moon, so she was planning to walk outside the walls. As she passed through the open gate she couldn't help thinking about how free the prisoners who'd served their time must have felt when they left through the gate and how free she had felt when she entered through the gate.

Suddenly, she was bathed in light. It wasn't the full moon but headlights and they were moving toward her at a high rate of speed. Whoever was driving was ignoring the speed limit they'd posted and she wondered if it was some teenagers on a joyride. She stepped to the side of the road and waved her arms. The car continued past her, then braked and came to a stop in front of the gate. She ran over to the idling car expecting to see some pimply-faced teenager. Instead, there was a man in his sixties with both hands gripping the wheel, looking intently in the rearview mirror. "Looks like I lost them," the man said somewhat triumphantly.

"Who?"

"Damned if I know. Whoever was chasing me. I couldn't sleep so I decided to go for a drive and they came up behind me fast, like they wanted to run me off the road. They must have something under the hood because I couldn't shake them. I took the turn off to here to try and lose them. I knew the road dead-ended here at the old penitentiary, so I didn't know what I was going to do if they were still on my tail. Maybe they decided they didn't want to go to prison," he laughed. "What are you doing here, anyway?"

"I live here," Sister M's replied, pulling the hood of the sweatshirt off her head.

"You live here? In the old Purgatory Penitentiary?"

"It's not a prison anymore."

"I know that. They shut it down when I was a kid. Are you some sort of caretaker?"

"I'm a nun."

"A nun? Why would a nun live in an old prison?"

"I don't live here by myself," she answered. "This is now a convent, a religious community."

"You're kidding me." He opened the car door and stepped out. He looked at the prison walls that even the moonlight couldn't soften and then at her. He was taller than Sister M's and a lot heavier and she could tell that he was used to throwing his weight around. "You're telling me this is now a convent?"

"It's also a retreat and educational center and we give tours of the old penitentiary."

"Well. I'll be da…" he stopped. "Sorry for the language, Sister. It's just a surprise." He looked at the sign next to the open gate that was lit up by his headlights. "It says Our Lady of Lost Souls Convent, Sisters of Saint Leonard. Who is Saint Leonard?"

"He's the patron saint of prisoners."

"Now it all makes sense," he said.

"It does?"

"I mean, that you live in a prison."

"But it's not a prison anymore."

He held up both of his hands in mock surrender. "Sorry, I meant former prison. Anyway, I'm happy to have a convent as a neighbor rather than a prison."

"You live on the Double B Ranch?"

He nodded his head, "I own it, but I haven't lived there for a few years."

"We've been here for almost ten years."

"I stand corrected, then. It's been more than a few years." He looked up at the walls of the former prison. "Guess if I'm going to be corrected then a former correctional facility is as good a place as any." He held out his right hand, "Anyway, I'm Wylie Boone."

"I know who you are. You may not have been around but your name has. I'm Sister Mary Margaret." They shook hands. He had a firm handshake like he enjoyed making people wince and seemed surprised when she didn't. "Do you have any idea why someone would want to chase you?"

He shook his head, "Like I said, I don't have any idea who they were."

"That doesn't mean you don't have an idea as to why."

"My but you are direct, Sister Mary Margaret. It almost feels like I'm being cross examined," he laughed. "Anyway, why covers a lot of territory. Lots of reasons why someone might want to chase me. Maybe they wanted to see if they could beat a '57 Chevy in a race.... They didn't."

"We should probably call the sheriff and report it."

He shook his head. "No, no need for that. Whoever it was is gone. No harm done. It was even kind of fun. I wonder if I can use your phone so I can call the ranch and tell them where I am and that I'm on my way back. I left my cellphone at home. Didn't think I'd need it."

"The cell service is pretty bad here, even if you brought it with you," she said, then looked over at the prison walls and added, "Even though we have lots of bars on our cells. I can let you use the landline in our Welcome Center."

He followed her through the gate to the Welcome Center where she turned on the lights and showed him the phone on the counter then asked, "You don't mind if I leave you here by yourself?"

"Should I lock up when I leave?"

"We don't have locks here," she answered. "Just shut the door when you leave. Now, I have to go, or I'll be late for compline."

"Compline?"

"Night prayers. It's what we do when we can't sleep. You're welcome to join us."

"Me? I think I'll pass. I mean, I haven't gone to church for years. I'm an agnostic now."

"We don't have any admission requirements. Everyone is welcome."

"I'll take a rain check."

"It hasn't rained in a month, but when it does you know where to find us." She pulled the sweatshirt hood over her head and started to walk out the door and then stopped and turned around. "I hope you don't mind, Mr. Boone, but I will include you in our prayers tonight."

"And if I said that I did mind?"

"That would be all the more reason to pray for you."

CHAPTER FOURTEEN

"You're asking me how to get an interview with Wylie Boone?" Gloria Herrera repeated Tom's question as she sat at her desk in the newsroom. The newsroom was not really a separate room but a couple of desks in the one-room office of the *Picketwire Press*. There was even an old Linotype machine in the corner that Tom referred to as a collector's item because all it did was collect dust. There was another room in the back with a loading dock where the printing press was. The new press was computerized and the shout to stop the presses had been replaced with the click on a computer screen. Digits instead of widgets.

Tom shifted uncomfortably in his chair. Not because of Gloria's response but because there was no way to get comfortable in the straight-backed oak office chair. It was the same one that his dad and grandfather had used. His father said it kept you on the ball, a hard ball. Better to have a numb butt than be a dumb ass was the way he'd put it. Besides, it went with the old rolltop desk that Tom loved even though he had to keep it rolled up to allow for the keyboard and two computer screens that had replaced the old Underwood typewriter. "I'm trying to get input from the members of the team, Gloria."

"The team? There's only me and you."

"What about Maggie and Rodney?" Tom pointed out.

"The business manager and advertising salesman? Really?"

"We've got our part-time reporters."

"Like Jim who covers high school sports and Virginia who writes the obituaries. Neither of them are trained journalists." Gloria never passed on an opportunity to remind him that she was not just a reporter but it was her full-time profession, backed by a degree in journalism from the University of New Mexico. Gloria had wanted to be a journalist ever since she was a little girl and she'd discovered Lois Lane and the *Daily Planet* in one of her older brother's Superman comic books. It had taken her years to work her way through college but by the time she'd graduated at twenty-four she felt she had the strength to bend words like steel.

"Okay, okay," Tom held up his hands in surrender. "It's a small team, Gloria. The point is that Boone is back in Picketwire and he's in the headlines because of the hit-and-run, so it would be a coup for us to get an exclusive interview."

She fidgeted in the black, ergonomic chair that Tom had bought for her that she liked to think of as her signing bonus, but that he had thought, mistakenly, might dampen her excessive energy. Finally she said, "Just call him."

Tom laughed and shook his head, "Just call him? Like you can just pick up the phone and get a billionaire like Boone on the line?"

Gloria didn't answer as she quickly paged through the dog-eared Picketwire phone book on her desk. "The Double B Ranch is listed," she announced holding up the page with the phone number. Without waiting for Tom to respond, Gloria was on the phone. She told whoever answered that she was Gloria Herrera, a journalist with the *Picketwire Press*. She smiled at whatever the response was and then told the person why she was calling. She wrote something down on a pad as she listened, then thanked the person and hung up. "We've got our interview. It's at the ranch tomorrow morning at nine."

"You got an interview with Wylie Boone just like that?"

"Uh-huh."

"How do you know the person you talked to has the authority to set up an interview with Boone?"

"Because it was Boone that I was talking to."

"Wylie Boone himself answered the phone?"

"Uh-huh. He told me he was surprised to hear the ring. He said it had been so long since he'd heard the ring of real landline telephone, he just answered it without even thinking."

"Okay," Tom waved his hands in surrender. "But what do you mean <u>we've</u> got our interview?"

"Me and you. It's called teamwork."

***

"I went to Picketwire High with your Mom and Dad. They were a couple back then and that must have been forty years ago," Wylie said. Although Wylie was addressing Tom, he was looking at Gloria who was perched at the edge of a chair facing him with a small digital recorder in her right hand like a race-horse waiting for the starting gate to open. Wylie was seated in a leather chair like a cattle baron on his cowhide throne. The sequoia sized beams high overhead, mammoth stone fireplace and custom-made southwestern furniture liberally draped with expensive, hand-woven Indian blankets added to the royal rus-ticity of the room.

"They're still a couple," Tom answered, passing on the op-portunity to ask Wylie about his three marriages, the last of which ended only a few months ago.

Turning his eyes from Gloria to Tom, Wylie asked "What are they up to since you took over the newspaper?"

"Traveling around in an RV."

"An RV? It's great to hear that after running a newspaper together for all those years they still want to run around together in an RV rather than retire to Florida or Arizona next to a golf course."

"They hate golf."

"Don't think much of it myself. It's not even a good walk since they make people ride around in a golf cart to speed things up."

"Don't you own some golf courses?"

"A few, and hell yes, I make people use carts. The more people I can get on the greens the more green gets into my pocket," Wylie laughed. He seemed awfully relaxed for someone who'd just escaped being killed in a hit-and-run, Tom thought.

"Can we ask you about the hit-and-run?" Gloria asked, sounding every bit the professional journalist.

"Sure, go ahead."

"Are you worried that they haven't found the guy who almost killed you?"

"Or gal. It could have been a woman, maybe one of my ex-wives," he said and then added, quickly with a grin. "That part about my exes was off the record, by the way. No, what really upsets me is that it totaled the car. You know it wasn't just any old Porsche, it was a 356 B Carrera GTL."

"But insurance should cover it," Tom said.

"Insurance? It was a classic – just like the Porsche that won at Le Mans in 1960. Didn't have a scratch on it. You can't replace a beautiful machine like that."

"Weren't you afraid you'd get a dent or something by driving it around?" Gloria asked.

"Afraid? What's the point in having it if I can't drive it? It's not a piece of furniture." Wylie leaned back in the chair and stretched out his long legs. Tom noticed that his cowboy boots were handmade.

"And you're sure it was an accident?" Gloria pressed, reaching out with her tape recorder.

Wylie leaned toward Gloria. "The running into me probably was, but the running away sure as hell wasn't. That's why they call it hit-and-run and the police are looking for the guy."

"Or gal," Gloria added. "But as someone who acquires companies, fires a lot of people, and then sells them for a big profit, you're probably not the most popular person."

"It's called restructuring, but I admit that I've made a lot of enemies. But any that would want to kill me with a minivan? That's not exactly the weapon a hit man, or hit gal, would use," he laughed and shook his head. "Still, the whole thing brought me up short. I mean, the idea that it could all be over just like that got me thinking about what's really important, and before you know it, I was thinking about this place. I've got plenty of houses. but this place," he looked around the room, "this place is my real home and, as they say, there's no place like home, especially this old home on the range. So, I decided that I'd been away too long."

"How long?" Tom asked.

Wylie looked up at the ceiling and then replied, "About thirty years."

"That sure is a long time. Although I've never left at all. It's hard to get out of Picketwire."

Wylie nodded. "It was easy for me, though. Nothing to keep me here after my dad passed away. My mom had already moved to California after she divorced the old cuss. I wanted to try my hand at something besides the ranch, and there weren't any business opportunities here in Picketwire."

"It turned out you were pretty handy at business since you've made a lot of money," Tom said.

"And enemies," Gloria added. "Those were your words, Mr. Boone."

"There doesn't seem to be a way to make one without the other, so, yes, I've made plenty of both." He slapped the leather right arm of the chair and declared, "Anyway, I'm happy to be back here."

"If that's the case, I imagine you're looking forward to seeing your old friends here?" Tom asked, trying to inject some cheer into the conversation.

"Old enemies are more like it. I seemed to have been able to make enemies even before I made money. There were lots of people who didn't mind me leaving."

"Did you know that one of your old Picketwire High class-mates, Howdy Hanks, just returned to town as well," Tom said.

Surprised, Wylie asked, "Howdy's back?"

"He's back for the premiere of his new play," Gloria said.

"Howdy wrote a new play?"

"He sure did, and it's going to be performed at the Tumble-weed Theater by our own Bard Wired Players," Gloria said, in a voice more animated than her usual professional journalist register. "Everyone's talking about it. You know, they call Howdy Hanks the Sagebrush Shakespeare."

"You seem quite enthused, Miss Herrera."

"Gloria also covers the arts for us," Tom explained.

"A premiere you say?" Wylie repeated, drawing out the word premiere. "The only premiere of one of Howdy's plays that I ever attended was the one he put on at Picketwire High when we were both seniors. It pissed off a lot of people." He looked at Gloria and added with a slight smile, "Excuse my language, it sort of rubs off from the ranch."

"My folks told me about that play," Tom said. "They said it upset a lot of people. But the fact that everyone is looking forward to the performance of his new play just shows that people in Picketwire tend to forgive and forget."

"I haven't forgotten. I walked out halfway through it."

"I was just using it as an example of people here letting bygones be bygones," Tom said.

"Easy to say about people when they're gone but when they come back it's another matter," Wylie said then looked around the room again then rose from the chair. "Enough of the strolling down bad memory lane, let me show you around the place."

Wylie took them on a tour of the ranch house. He explained that it had started with the one room that his great-grandfather C.W. Boone had built and then expanded along with the acreage of the ranch and the family wealth. The tour was a voyage of rediscovery for Wylie with each room evoking memories and stories that he would recount. They moved slowly into the past as they went through the newer rooms into the older ones until they reached the original one room ranch house. It was now completely enclosed by the later additions and, as Wylie explained, everything from the planks in the floor to rough-hewn beams in the ceiling to the sturdy wood furniture was original. "Except these windows that once opened to the outside," he said standing in front of one of them. "Now they have paintings inside the frames that show what the ranch looked like back then."

"It's like a museum," Tom observed as he gently pushed a rocking chair with his hand to see if it really did rock. It did.

Wylie looked around. "It does look like everything's been pretty well-preserved," he turned and winked at Gloria, "except the bodies. All the Boones are buried in the family cemetery on the hill outside."

Gloria, ignoring the wink, reached into her purse that was slung over her left shoulder. "Can I take a photo of you in this room?" Gloria asked pulling out a camera.

"Gloria's also our staff photographer," Tom said.

"Sure," Wylie said as he assumed a pose with both hands on his hips. "As long as you don't make me look like a ghost who came back to haunt this place."

"We don't generally interview dead people," Tom replied as the flash on Gloria's camera lit up the room.

Wylie laughed, "They may have killed my Porsche but they didn't get me. No, Wylie Boone is very much alive."

CHAPTER FIFTEEN

"I hope we're not lost," Bruce said.

"This is the trail that Tony and Elise said leads to the camp," Jane stopped and turned to Bruce who was several paces behind her. "Do you want to switch places?"

"No, honey. Without cell service and a GPS who knows where we'd end up if I were leading the way?"

"I have to admit that ever since we climbed out of the canyon everything looks pretty much the same," Jane replied, her hands on her hips.

"So how do we know that we're still going the right direction?"

"Dead reckoning."

"I don't like the dead part in that," Bruce replied. "Maybe we can reckon with the help of the map that Elise gave us?"

Jane pulled out the map she had tucked into her back pocket and opened it. "I'm pretty sure we're here." She pointed to a spot on a line that Elise had drawn in blue ink and then moved her finger along it until she stopped at a blue circle. "And this is where Elise said the camp is."

"You're sure?"

"Don't you know how to read a map?"

"I'm a New Yorker so I only know how to read a subway map. You, on the other hand, are a cowgirl so…"

"I grew up on a farm not a ranch so I'm not a cowgirl," Jane said, cutting him off.

"A farm has cows, doesn't it?"

"Yes, but they don't call girls on farms cowgirls."

"I married a farm girl when I thought I'd married a cowgirl."

"Cowgirls only marry cowboys. It's one of the unwritten laws of the West. You should have done your research before you proposed, Mister," she laughed. "Of course, if you feel cheated you can leave right now. Only," she waved the map, "I keep this and, this girl knows how to read a map."

"Leave you? I'll have you know I've always had a hankering for farm girls."

"Hankering?" Jane hooted.

"It was an inner hankering, but I believe it's becoming an outer hankering,"

Jane laughed, "Well, you'll just have to keep your hankering inside until we get back home."

"Right, the farm," Bruce said with a grin. "That's where you keep the hay you farm girls like to roll in. The kinky stuff."

"Kinky? More like itchy," she answered, trying to keep from cracking up.

"If you've got the hay then it must be only the cowgirls who like to roll out here in the cactus. It would be like making love to a porcupine."

"You've heard of cowpokes, haven't you?" Jane replied with as straight a face as she could muster. "And speaking of pokey, we need to get going. It shouldn't be far, but I want to have time to look around before we have to hike back to the trailhead."

As they walked, Jane called out the names of various plants and flowers: buffalo grass, cheatgrass, Bigelow sage, cane cactus, snakeweed, prairie clover, red paintbrush.

"I'm amazed that you know all their names."

"They aren't the proper names just what people call them around here. If you go somewhere else they often have different names for them. The only names that everyone accepts are the scientific ones they've been given and those are in Latin."

"Didn't you study Latin in seminary?"

"I only studied Biblical Greek and Hebrew. Remember, you tried some of the Hebrew you'd learned for your Bar Mitzvah on me and I told you I didn't understand a word you said because I'd learned to read it not speak it."

"And I told you that was okay because I didn't remember what any of the words meant. In any case, Honey, I prefer the common names of the plants we're looking at to the names in an old language that I don't understand."

"Speaking of old languages, I'm glad we had a chance to see the rock art. I think Elise did a great job of explaining how the pictographs are really a language, didn't you?"

"I thought it was interesting that people who know Native American sign language can read them."

"But that's only a theory," Jane said. "As you recall, Elise said that while sign language and pictographs may look similar there's no way to prove that the pictures mean the same thing because there's no Rosetta Stone like there was for hieroglyphics."

"Maybe there is but it just hasn't been discovered. There are plenty of stones out here and it could be under one of them." Bruce stopped, picked up a small rock and turned it over. "Not this one," he said and tossed it into a clump of what he now knew was buffalo grass.

"I'm afraid you'll have to leave the rest of the stones unturned because the camp is just ahead." Jane answered, pointing at a wooden watchtower fifty yards in front of them. The watchtower was lying on its side, tangled in the rusty barbed wire of the fence it had fallen on.

"It's a good thing you really can read a map," Bruce said and started walking toward the breach in the fence that had been created by the watchtower's collapse.

Yes, Jane thought, as they proceeded, but it's still dead reckoning.

CHAPTER SIXTEEN

Every year on the first Saturday in the first week of June Picketwire celebrated its founding with a big parade. Jemma Lu's earliest memory of the parade was watching it go by as she sat on a milk box in the shade of the Tumbleweed Theater's marquee. She was four years old then and decided that the parade didn't have a beginning or an end but kept on going clear around the world before showing up back in Picketwire a year later. When Milli, her best friend, pointed out that this couldn't be true because the world was flat, Jemma Lu responded in the authoritative voice that she had acquired almost as soon as she started talking that while Milli's world might be flat the real world was round and that she could prove it by showing her the globe in their house. Over the years as Jemma Lu's world grew, the parade route shrank. What she had once been sure had circumnavigated the earth was reduced to a dozen blocks. Likewise, as she got older what had seemed like an endless parade of horses, riders, wagons, floats, and marching bands was condensed into not much more than an hour.

Jemma Lu had read that some astrophysicists theorized that there were multiple universes where alternate versions of this universe existed. If that were true, then maybe the parade she remembered continued to exist in alternate universes where it marched around alternate worlds. But that would mean there was more than one Picketwire and more than one version of herself. If there were, what were her alternative Jemma Lu's up to? What happened to the Jemma Lu who married Wylie? What happened to the Jemma Lu who ran off with Howdy? What happened to the Jemma Lu who kept her son? What happened to the Jemma Lu who...

"Jemma Lu!"

"Yes." Jemma Lu looked at Milli who was standing next to her.

"Where on earth did you go this time?"

"Go?"

"I know when you're daydreaming."

"I wasn't daydreaming, I was just remembering when I saw my first Picketwire Day parade at this very spot."

"You remember the first one you saw?"

"Why, Milli, you were right here with me. We were both four years old. You don't remember?"

"That was almost 60 years ago, Jemma Lu."

"56 years, Milli."

"Only 56? Why I feel younger already. But, really, how can you expect me to remember one from the other? I mean you've seen one Picketwire Day parade and you've seen them all as far as I'm concerned."

Jemma Lu couldn't forget because that was when she found out who her great-grandparents were. After the parade her mother asked her which float she liked best and she answered without hesitation that it was the one with the Indian princess.

"Why, she's your great-grandmother," Jemma Lu remembered her mother answering with a smile that was even bigger than usual.

"Then I'm an Indian princess too," Jemma Lu asserted as she twirled around in delight at her unexpected coronation.

"And the man next to her, the black man dressed in buckskin with the long rifle," her mother added, "he's your great-grandfather."

Jemma Lu remembered that she stopped twirling at hearing this unexpected news. That was when her mother told her the story about the black mountain man who fell in love with an Indian maiden and that she was their great-granddaughter.

At the time Jemma Lu didn't fully comprehend what her mother was saying. The only black man she had met was Mr. Fraser who bore a striking resemblance to the man on the float. She didn't know any Indian princesses either, although that didn't stop her from believing in her royal lineage. A few years later she cried when she discovered that her great-grandmother hadn't been a princess after all and that her great-grandfather had been a slave before he escaped. "Just think," she said to Milli, "We've been friends all these years. Through thick and thin."

"I'm thick and you're thin," Milli laughed, patting her stomach.

"Let's celebrate with a milkshake. My treat." Jemma Lu hooked her right arm around Milli's left and tugged her toward the door of Tanneyhill's Drug Store.

"We should sit at the counter," Jemma Lu said, steering Milli toward the row of stools in front of the soda fountain. When Jemma Lu was a little girl she thought that the drugs sold at Tanneyhill's were dispensed from the soda fountain through the large faucets behind the Formica counter.

"I'm not sure I can still get up on one of these stools, Jemma Lu," Milli said. "Can we sit at our old booth, instead?"

They made a beeline for the middle booth and sat on its familiar red vinyl benches. The white top had been dulled by the years but the sunlight that played against it through the open blinds still managed to uncover the gold and silver flecks imbedded in the Formica. How many times had they and their friends sat at this very booth? Jemma Lu wondered if the wads of gum they stuck to the bottom were still there in some fossilized form. The teenage boy behind the counter who had watched them come in walked over, pad and pencil in his hand. The badge on his white apron said his name was Mike and Jemma Lu recognized him as a Tanneyhill. It was still a family business and even though Mike's father, Trent, now ran the place, his grandfather, Lyle, still came in several times a week to work in the pharmacy in the rear. She tried to fill her prescriptions with Lyle as much as possible since she knew after forty some years he could keep it private. That was no small feat in a small town.

"Can I help you," Mike asked.

"I'm..."

Mike interrupted, "Everyone knows who you are, Miss Tuttle."

In that case maybe you could tell me, Jemma Lu wanted to say, because she was beginning to have her doubts. But she didn't want to embarrass a teenage boy. She'd done enough of that when she was a teenage girl. "Just call me Jemma Lu, and this is Milli."

"Sure thing, and I'm Mike."

"We know."

"You do?"

"It's on the name badge pinned to your apron."

"Oh," Mike looked down at it. "Right."

"And we know you're Trent's son because you look just like your dad when he was your age," Milli added.

"Do you want to be a pharmacist like your father and grandfather?" Jemma Lu asked.

"I sort of like working at the soda fountain, but it's not exactly a career. I've thought about working for you – I mean Picketware. Everyone says it's a great place to work," Mike said with a sheepish grin.

"Picketware will be around if you still want to work for us when you've finished school."

"I'm going to graduate from Picketwire High next year."

"Aren't you going to college?"

"Sure, I guess so," Mike said without much enthusiasm. "Can I take your orders..." He paused and then added, tentatively. "Jemma Lu and Milli."

Happy that Mike had agreed to pursue higher education, Jemma Lu smiled and asked for a milkshake. Milli decided on a vanilla root beer float but with diet root beer as if that would cancel out the calories in the ice cream.

"We sure knew some soda jerks in our day, didn't we Jemma Lu?" Milli sighed after Mike retreated behind the counter.

"We also knew plenty of just plain jerks."

"I think I dated most of them," Milli giggled.

"At least you married someone who wasn't."

"Yes, I can't complain. Ricky's been a great husband and father."

"Four kids and six grandchildren."

"Going to be seven. I just found out that Martha's expecting another one."

"How wonderful, Milli. Another reason to celebrate!" Jemma Lu said.

"Do you ever wonder if your son has kids?" Milli was the only person who knew that Jemma Lu had a child.

"I just hope he didn't turn out to be a jerk." Jemma Lu replied. No, she hadn't thought that she might be a grandmother. She tried not to think about being a mother. It wasn't as if she'd done any mothering. She had settled on thinking of herself as being a surrogate mother for some lucky couple.

"Have you seen Wylie since he came back?" Milli asked "I was just wondering. It has been quite a while, hasn't it?"

"Thirty years."

"That long?"

"Not long enough," Jemma Lu, snapped.

"Jemma Lu, someone tried to kill him. At least that's what the news is saying and after all he's the..."

"He might not even be the father," Jemma Lu cut Milli off.

"But you and he were going together when you got pregnant."

"We were going together and, yes, the odds are he is the father, but there's still room for doubt."

"You mean after all these years you're telling me that there was someone else," Milli said.

"Briefly."

"How brief?"

"Once."

"Someone I know?"

"This is Picketwire, Milli, where everyone knows everybody."

"Are you going to make me start throwing names at you?" Milli asked.

"You sound like a wife who just found out her husband cheated and wants to know who it was with."

"Sorry, Jemma Lu. It's just that we're best friends so..."

"So, let's just change the subject."

"Okay, what about Howdy?"

"What about him?" Jemma Lu answered, sharply.

"You don't have to snap at me," Milli said. "I changed the subject like you asked. I just asked if you've run into Howdy Hanks since he came back to put on this new play of his?"

"Sorry, Milli. No, we haven't run into each other."

"Why Jemma Lu Tuttle and Milli Martinez. I see you two girls are sitting in your regular booth." Jemma Lu looked up at the sound of a drawl that she knew, even after thirty years, could only belong to Howdy Hanks. Despite the creases around his eyes and mouth, and wild strands of gray hair escaping from under his Stetson, she was surprised at how well he'd weathered.

"We're not girls anymore, Howdy," Jemma Lu answered, glad that her dark complexion was perfect for hiding a blush. "And it's Milli Pacheco now."

Howdy looked at Milli, who had moved over to let him sit down opposite Jemma Lu. "That's right, I heard you married Ricky Pacheco."

"You've actually heard something about us since you left Picketwire?" Jemma Lu said.

"Read it in the *Picketwire Press*, actually. I subscribe."

"We've sure read a lot about you, Howdy," Milli said, sounding more like a teenage member of his fan club than a grandmother. "You're famous."

"I thought no one was famous in their hometown," Howdy said.

"You're probably thinking of the Bible verse where Jesus said no prophet is accepted in their hometown," Milli offered.

"Good thing I'm a playwright and not a prophet."

"As I recall, before you left Picketwire you thought they were the same thing," Jemma Lu said.

"As I recall I was a bit full of myself back then, but at least I didn't think I was Jesus."

"That means we don't have to see your return to Picketwire as the second coming."

"Hi," Mike interrupted, handing Jemma Lu and Milli their orders.

Milli leaned toward Howdy and said, "This is Mike, he's a Tanneyhill."

Howdy looked up. "Howdy Mike."

"Howdy," Mike replied.

"Howdy is his name," Milli giggled. "Howdy Hanks."

"Are you the Howdy Hanks?" Mike asked. "My dad told me you were famous or something."

"Or something is a fair description," Howdy replied. "You can call me Howdy."

"Okay," Mike said, his pencil poised over the pad. "Can I get something for you, Howdy?"

"I don't think I can get what I really want, Mike, but a Coke sure would taste good."

"What do you really want, Howdy?" Jemma Lu demanded as Mike returned to the counter. "I mean, why did you come back after all these years?"

"Jemma Lu," Milli said. "You know perfectly well that Howdy's back for the world premiere of his new play."

"I heard that it wasn't finished," Jemma Lu said, as she churned her vanilla shake with a straw.

"I'm still working on the ending."

"You always did have trouble with endings as I recall."

"Here's your Coke, Howdy," Mike announced placing a glass on the table. "Say, Howdy," he asked, "is that your motorcycle parked outside?"

"Since you don't have a place to hitch a horse anymore I had to ride my bike instead."

"He's just joking again, Mike," Milli said before closing her lips around a spoonful of ice cream.

"Right." Mike looked through the plate glass window at the motorcycle. "Can I ask you what kind of bike it is? I know it's not a Harley."

"It's a 1950 Indian. They stopped making them in 1953. I don't count the ones that the snowmobile maker, Polaris, started making a few years ago. Stamping a name on something doesn't make it the real thing. It's like buying the brand without the beef. Of course, if it were a Harley it would be without the hog, which is another reason why nobody from cattle country should be riding one of them. Why don't you go out and have a closer look. Just don't kick the tires."

"I'll just go and have a quick look," Mike said, turning and walking out the door.

"And I need to go to the lady's room," Milli said.

After getting up and letting Milli out, Howdy sat back down and, ignoring the straw, took a drink of his Coke.

"Isn't that the same bike you rode out of town on?" Jemma Lu asked.

"The very one."

"Remember the time I rode with you in the Picketwire Day Parade?"

Howdy nodded his head and said, "I was in the back of the parade along with the jalopies, bikes, trikes, skateboards, and whatnot and you came up and said that you wanted a ride. Surprised the hell out of me that you wanted a ride."

"And you gave me one."

Howdy grinned. "I did, Jemma Lu, I sure did."

Jemma Lu hoped he wouldn't bring up the second time that he gave her a ride when he picked her up after she broke up with Wylie. She said quickly. "And now you're back after all these years, and on the very same bike,"

Howdy stared at the glass he held in his right hand. It was already half empty. He looked up at Jemma Lu and said, "How about another ride?"

CHAPTER SEVENTEEN

"All aboard," the short, stocky man wearing a turn of the century train conductor's uniform announced to the twelve passengers in the vintage Pullman railroad car that Tony Medrano had reserved for his new Rails, Trails, and Tales tour. Then, with a lurch that sent the man stumbling forward, the train pulled out of the La Junta train station at 10am. Regaining his footing, the man continued.

"I'm Clem the Conductor and this little lady here is Clementine," Clem nodded to the young woman standing next to him. She was dressed in a black skirt that brushed the ankles of her high-topped black shoes and a white, long-sleeve blouse with puffed shoulders, ruffles down the front, and a starched collar. "And she's a Harvey Girl. In case you don't know, Harvey Girls worked at the Harvey Houses where passengers on the Atchison, Topeka and Santa Fe Railroad could have a meal when the train stopped at a station. Mind you, not just any girl could be a Harvey Girl. They were very selective. You had to be single, between the ages of 18 and 30, and of good moral character. Most importantly, though, a Harvey Girl had to sign an agreement not to marry for at least a year."

"I was a Harvey Girl," Clementine said, curtseying as she smiled at the passengers. "But I'm not a Harvey Girl anymore."

"You mean you're married?" Clem asked in mock disbelief.

"Of course not. Not that I don't have plenty of proposals. I was working in a Harvey House but I wanted to ride the rails not just watch the trains go by. Now I work on this wonderful train whose next stop is Picketwire, Colorado, right Conductor Clem?"

"It certainly is my darling Clementine. This being the Picketwire Limited, there's no stops between here and there. Now a few words from our tour conductor."

Tony, who had been standing behind Clem and Clementine, stepped forward. "Thanks Conductor Clem," he said, flashing the biggest smile he could muster. "We will arrive in Picketwire at 11:45. After a brief tour of the Picketwire Train Station, which is over a hundred years old, we will walk across the street to the equally historic Picketwire House where a gourmet lunch will be served."

"It's not a Harvey House," Clementine said, batting false eyelashes the size of window awnings. "So, proposals are welcome."

"But no tips since they're already included in the tour package," Clem added.

Feeling like a straight man, Tony continued. "Then after lunch we'll board our luxury Purple Sage Tours bus and visit the historic, former Purgatory Penitentiary."

"However, the current occupants are not incarcerated desperados since it's now Our Lady of Lost Souls Convent," Conductor Clem chuckled.

"I used to visit one of my beaus there," Clementine said, batting her long eyelashes. "Before it was a convent, of course."

Tony waited for the laughter to stop then said, "Several members of the tour will be leaving us at that point. Not to be incarcerated, as Conductor Clem put it, but for a stay at the convent's retreat center." As he spoke Tony glanced at the two men and a woman who were sitting in the back row. For them this was a ride on another kind of railroad – one that was underground. They were the first group of undocumented immigrants that Tony had agreed to transport to the Our Lady of Lost Souls Convent disguised as members of his tour group. "After touring the historic Purgatory Penitentiary, we will return to the Picketwire House for cocktails, followed by dinner at the hotel's Home on the Range Restaurant. Tomorrow morning, after spending the night in the deluxe accommodations of the Picketwire House, we will tour the town of Picketwire with its many historic buildings, including the Tuttle Mansion, before concluding our Rails, Trails, and Tales Tour by boarding the train for our return trip to La Junta. Now sit back and enjoy the scenery."

***

"I never thought I'd say things that corny," Zelda Zenn, said as she lit a cigarette. "Or play someone like Clementine."

"It's supposed to be corny," Max Bergmann replied. "And you shouldn't be smoking."

"We're outside, aren't we?" Zelda waved the cigarette. They were standing on the open observation deck that stuck out from the back of the Pullman car.

"But women usually didn't smoke in public back then."

Zelda exhaled sending smoke wafting over the receding tracks in the otherwise trackless prairie. "Harvey Girls didn't, but Clementine would be smoking up a storm. That's probably why she was fired and had to do this 'I've been working on the railroad' gig."

"There's nothing in the script about her being fired. It says she quit to ride the rails."

"A character has to have a back story, doesn't she?" Zelda replied. "And Clementine's real back story includes being fired because she was a naughty girl. I bet Conductor Clem was a smoker so why not join me? I've got half a pack in my purse."

Max, who, truth be told secretly snuck a smoke now and then, was about to say that he might take one or two puffs just for the sake of his character when the door opened and Tony came out on the deck. "I think it's going pretty well," Tony observed. He'd wanted something different for the new tour and had asked Max if he would play the part of a conductor who could spin some tales while they were on the train. Max had proposed the Clementine character, telling Tony that he had just the person to play the role. Tony had been a little nervous after meeting Zelda who was a high school student that Max had cast in a lead role in the new play by Howdy Hanks. But he had to admit she was pretty good in the part and the original Harvey Girls weren't much older than her.

"You think it's going well now, just wait until I spin the tale about the Picketwire Railroad train robbery in 1905," Max said.

"I'm looking forward to it," Tony answered. "We've only got a few minutes before we reach the spot where it took place."

Max looked at the pocket watch that dangled from his vest on a gold chain, "Five minutes."

"That gives me time to finish my cigarette and touch up my lipstick," Zelda said, taking another drag.

"Remember," Max said, "when you hear me say that we're moving through a particularly scenic and pastoral area, you scream then open this door here and come in from the observation deck...."

"And shout 'There are train robbers chasing us, Clem, we need to escape!'" Zelda replied. "How could I forget a corn ball line like that."

"It may not be what you would say but it's Clementine who is saying it," Max replied. "Then I do my bit where I run back, chase off the robbers and come back in and tell everyone about the great train robbery."

"After which Zelda serves everyone lemonade and cookies," Tony said.

"Clementine does the serving," Max said. "That's what a Harvey Girl would do...."

"I'm not a Harvey Girl anymore, Clem."

"Well, you're still an actress and it's in the part you play." Max looked at his watch again. "Okay, I'm going in now."

"I'll be there in a second," Tony said to Max as he closed the door.

"If you ask me, I don't get it," Zelda said, her hand cupping the elbow of her right arm as she gestured with the cigarette in her right hand.

"Your lines?"

"No, the three members of your tour who want to spend the night in prison."

"They're going there for a spiritual retreat and, besides, it's a convent now not a prison"

"I thought they're the same thing," Zelda replied.

"I don't think the sisters would agree with you on that."

"I don't think they'd agree with me on anything."

"You should meet them," Tony replied. "You might be surprised."

Zelda took another long, seductive drag on her cigarette, then said, "Nothing surprises me. You may not believe it, but I've seen a lot and done a lot, too."

"Including pretending to smoke?"

"What?"

"You're blowing smoke out your mouth instead of your nose, so you're not inhaling."

Zelda looked at the cigarette as if it had betrayed her and then, as her face blushed the same shade as her rouged cheeks, she pleaded. "Please don't tell Max that I'm faking it."

"Sure," Tony said opening the door. "Just don't throw the cigarette overboard, we don't want to start a grass fire."

Tony closed the door and sat down in a vacant seat near the rear of the car. He looked at Max, who had resumed his position at the front of the car. Max announced, "Ladies and gentlemen if I can have your attention please. May I draw your attention to the scenic and pastoral area we are passing through that..."

An earth-shattering scream from the observation deck cut Max off. The door suddenly swung open and Zelda burst through, her face contorted in terror. She shouted, "They're chasing us. We need to get the hell out of here!"

"Don't panic," Clem the conductor responded in a calm voice, while Max the actor felt upstaged by Zelda's histrionic performance and use of a swear word. He would need to tell her of the importance of following the script.

Before Max could begin his story about the great train robbery, Zelda, slammed the door behind her and sprinted toward the front of the car, frantically waving her hands and yelling, "I don't know about you all but I'm getting off this damn train!"

Max stood speechless with his mouth open, as Zelda rushed past him followed by the three members of the tour who were going to stay at the Our Lady of Lost Souls Convent.

CHAPTER EIGHTEEN

A picture might be worth a thousand words but Tom couldn't find anything in Gloria's photos of Friday's high school football game between the Picketwire Prairie Dogs and the Bitter Creek Bisons that matched the account in Jim Harman's sports story. It was as if they had attended two different games. Jim's story was of young men in helmets battling each other on the gridiron while in Gloria's photos young women with pom-poms performed acrobatics on the sidelines. When he'd pointed the discrepancy out to Gloria, she reminded him that she'd never claimed to be a sports photographer as well as a journalist. That being said, she couldn't help pointing out that Picketwire's cheerleaders are gymnasts and had clearly outperformed those from Bitter Creek, which was more than could be said for the football team who had been trounced by the Bisons.

As Tom sat in a booth at the Sue's Pretty Good Cafe, he looked at the layout for the sports page. He could almost hear the kicking and screaming as he tried to drag one of Gloria's photos and drop it into a box next to Jim's story. It was the exact opposite of her photo of Wylie Boone that slid perfectly into place next to the front-page interview they'd run in yesterday's paper.

"Why if it isn't Tom Tidings."

Tom looked up at the man standing next to the booth holding a mug of hot coffee.

"Why if it isn't Foster St. Vrain," Tom replied.

"I didn't mean to interrupt you."

"You're not interrupting anything," Tom said closing his laptop.

"Seems like rush hour at the Pretty Good."

Tom looked around, "You're right. It was almost empty when I got here." He looked at his watch. "But that was a couple of hours ago and it's getting close to lunch time." Tom gestured to the vacant bench facing him. "I feel sort of guilty occupying a booth by myself. Care to join me?"

Foster took a seat facing Tom, set his mug on the table and rested both elbows on either side of it.

"You don't have a mug with your name on it?" Tom asked.

Foster laughed and tapped the mug, "I put so many chips in it that Sue finally confiscated it. Apparently, it would be bad for business if I cut my lip and bled to death. Now I get a new one each time. I sort of like it this way, to tell you the truth. It's like being undercover."

"Speaking of undercover, how is the private detective business?"

"I guess you could say it's more of a hobby than a business since I don't seem to make any money at it. Fortunately, I've got my pension. One of the benefits of being shot on the job was getting my pension early." He sipped his coffee, put down the cup and continued, "Of course, I hadn't planned on retiring early. Maybe that's why I fiddle around with private investigating. Makes me feel like I'm not some pensioner grazing the south forty. By the way, that was quite a story you ran on Wylie Boone yesterday."

"Thanks. Some wire services and internet news feeds have even picked it up. That doesn't happen often."

"Wylie Boone is pretty famous."

"Some people prefer infamous."

"Picketwire's favorite son...of a bitch."

"Is that what you think?"

"I don't think that Wylie just happened to be in the wrong place at the wrong time."

"Wylie claims it was an accident."

Foster smiled in response.

"You think he's lying?"

"Wylie tell a lie? And to the press? That would hardly be – what's the word they use now? – transparent, that's it."

"Okay," Tom threw his hands up in surrender. "Maybe he was lying to us. Maybe he does think someone tried to kill him but for some reason he wants to hide it. That's what Gloria thinks."

"Gloria Herrera, the reporter that shared the byline with you?"

"Yes, she and I did the interview and wrote the story together," Tom said. "No, wait, since we're talking about transparency, if it weren't for Gloria we wouldn't have gotten the interview and she also took the photo."

"Seems like this Gloria Herrera is a real go-getter."

"I just hope I can keep her from up and going somewhere else. She really wants to do investigative journalism."

"So?"

"So? If I want to keep her I've got to come up with some opportunities other than covering the high school football game."

"In any case this Boone story should provide a great opportunity."

Tom raised his mug and stared into it as if there were tea leaves at the bottom instead of coffee. He put it down and said, "The thing is, we've got to move fast and there are really only the two of us, and it's not like I know anything about how to do investigative journalism. I don't have a clue as to how I'm going to take advantage of this opportunity."

"It's just detective work."

"Easy for an ex-cop and a private eye to say," Tom replied. "I'm just afraid that we'll screw it up and not only hurt the paper's reputation but also Gloria's career."

"Sounds like you could use some help," Foster said.

Tom face brightened. "Say, you wouldn't consider helping us out, would you?"

"Me?"

"Who better to help us with our investigative reporting than a private investigator. It's pretty much impossible for us to cover all the bases on story like this. Us being mainly Gloria since I'm giving her the lead on this."

Foster sat back and drummed the fingers of his right hand on the Formica tabletop. Finally, he stopped, leaned forward, and answered. "I'll help, but I have three conditions."

"What are they?"

"First, that you don't pay me anything. I'm interested in who tried to kill Boone and was going to do some nosing around anyway."

"You don't want to be paid anything? That's an easy one to agree to. What's your second condition?"

"You have to agree to keep my name out of the paper."

"You don't want us to acknowledge your contribution?"

"Bad for business. Sort of undermines the private part of detective."

"Agreed. Now what's your last condition?"

"That Gloria agrees."

"I don't see why she would object to having some help from a professional investigator so that shouldn't be a problem."

"She needs to agree, not you, Tom."

"Right," Tom nodded. "She's in the office so if you have time why don't we go over and ask her?"

"I think it would be better if I met with her by myself."

"You think that she'd be afraid to speak her own mind if I was there?"

"You are her boss, aren't you?"

"Boss? I think of us more as a team."

"But you sign her paycheck," Foster pressed.

"I see your point," Tom replied. Unfortunately, he really was the guy who not only signed the pay checks, but had to have enough money in the bank to cover them. "But I have to tell you Gloria isn't afraid to speak her mind."

"Then she won't have any trouble speaking it to me. It's a non-negotiable, Tom. I need to know that she doesn't have a problem with me being involved. Being on the team, as you put it."

"Okay, but let me go to the office first and tell her our idea."

Foster grinned. "Your idea, Tom."

"My idea. Then I'll call you on your cell in about ten minutes. What's your number, by the way?"

After Foster gave him his number, Tom said. "I'll invite you over and introduce you and explain my idea about your helping us out. Then I'll find an excuse to leave. I'll say that I'm going to get us some lunch, which," he looked at his watch, "will be the truth."

***

"Let me get this straight, you were once Picketwire's chief of police?" Gloria asked Foster. Tom had introduced them then quickly excused himself and left to pick up the lunch for all three of them from the Pretty Good.

"I was."

"And you think you can help us with our investigative reporting on Wylie Boone's hit-and-run?"

"It depends."

"On what?"

"On whether you want me to, since Tom tells me that you're the investigative reporter for the *Picketwire Press*."

"He did?"

Foster arched his right eyebrow. "Did I misunderstand him?"

"No, of course not. Just like he said, I'm the paper's investigative reporter."

"Well, I'm a private investigator. Got into it after I retired early from the police department. Turned out being the police chief was bad for my health. Being a private investigator is a way to supplement my pension."

"I didn't know there were any private investigators in town."

"I've done a good job of keeping it private," Foster said, with a slight smile. "Seriously, it's hard to work undercover if people know that you're a PI."

She sighed, "I guess that's the bright side of no one knowing that I'm an investigative reporter."

"There you go." Foster wanted to give her a light tap on the shoulder but decided to pull his punch in midair and converted his fist into an okay sign.

"Tom said you don't want your role to be made public?"

"Correct."

"I guess I'll just refer to you as an anonymous source. Anonymous resource might be more accurate."

"I take that to mean you don't object to my being involved?"

Gloria shrugged, "I'm willing to give it a try. It's not like the *Picketwire Press* has a lot of resources to draw on when it comes to investigative journalism or any journalism for that matter."

"All right, Ms. Herrera..."

"You can call me Gloria. I think we can be on a first name basis since we're going to be working together."

"Okay, Gloria. It might be good if you can fill me in on what you've done so far."

She picked up a notebook from her desk, looked at it, and answered. "Well, there's the interview with Boone that was in the paper yesterday."

"Read it."

"Then I guess you know pretty much everything I do. I really didn't have any time since I had to work on the weekly police report that we publish on Friday."

"Read it as well."

She shook her head slowly. "Can you believe it's one of the most popular things we publish in the paper?"

"I can believe it. If you don't find your name in it, then you must be an honest person. Like reading the obituaries to see if you're still alive."

"Obituaries are popular as well. Fortunately Virginia Robertson writes them. She says she enjoys it." Gloria gave a mock shiver. "But to get back to the weekly police report. You might not believe how much work goes into it. People just think we print what the different police departments in the county send us but...well, let's just say there's more than a little editing that's required. The Picketwire police department gets their spelling and grammar correct, most of the time, and I can understand the other towns, because they only have one or two policemen, but what I can't understand is why the county sheriff's are so poorly written. It's a challenge to rewrite them so that they're intelligible for our readers. If we printed them the way they send them to us people would have serious doubts that they are professional law enforcement officers."

"Maybe they should have doubts."

Gloria looked at Foster to see if he was pulling her leg, but his face was stonier than Washington's on Mount Rushmore. "Then I had some other stories I had to write and to top it off I had to take photos of the high school football game because the photographer we usually use was grounded.”

“Grounded?”

“He’s a junior at Picketwire High and his parents grounded him for the weekend because of, get this, he was texting while driving…their tractor. So, I had to spend Friday evening doing about my least favorite thing, watching a football game.”

“I prefer baseball myself.’

“Me too!” Gloria exclaimed almost jumping out of her ergonomic office chair. “I was the short stop on my high school softball team. I was pretty good at double plays.”

“I bet you were,” Foster nodded.

“What positions did you play?”

“As I recall,” Foster replied. “I was a catcher and I also played third base and spent some time playing center field. I even did a little pitching. Not all at the same time, of course. I started with Picketwire’s pee wee league when I was seven.”

“You still play?”

“I was playing with the ‘Over the Hill Gang’ in the Picketwire recreation league until my illustrious career was cut short by an injury,” Foster replied then, quickly asked, “Now, that you’ve brought me up to speed what do you see as the next steps?”

“I was thinking that my next step would be to call the Aspen police and the Colorado State Police.”

“Patrol.”

“What?”

"They call themselves the Colorado State Patrol not the State Police like in New Mexico. It was originally called the Colorado State Highway Courtesy Patrol. I can understand why they dropped 'highway' from their name but not courtesy. It seems to me that if people were more courteous, they'd be less inclined to engage in criminal behavior."

Figuring it might be impolite to laugh if Foster was indeed serious, which was impossible for her to tell, Gloria looked at the notebook in her lap. "What about the Colorado Bureau of Investigation? Did I get that name right?"

"That's right. Courtesy was never part of the CBI name."

She underlined the name with her pen. "Should I call them?"

"Sure. They'd likely be involved in something as big as this. I'll get you the name of someone I know who will talk to you."

"Great. Then I was thinking I should interview Sheriff Riggleman since Boone's ranch is in his jurisdiction."

Foster nodded in agreement.

Gloria made a check mark with her pen. "This will be my first interview with the sheriff so I'm open to any suggestions you might have."

"I wouldn't tell him what you think about his police reports. He's a bit touchy."

"Was he the sheriff when you were police chief?"

"When I started he was a deputy sheriff."

"So, you knew Riggleman even before he was sheriff?"

"You could say we go back aways."

"In that case maybe he would be more open if I mention your name."

"I don't think that would be a good idea," Foster said.

"Why not?"

"You know that injury I was telling you about?"

"The one that ended your career as a ball player?" Gloria replied.

"You left out illustrious."

"Sorry," Gloria laughed. "Illustrious career. What did Riggleman have to do with your injury?"

"He caused it."

Gloria's smile vanished. "You mean he was playing against you?"

"That's one way to put it. He shot me."

"Shot you!" Gloria gasped, dropping the pen in her hand. "You mean with a bullet?"

"It wasn't with a baseball."

CHAPTER NINETEEN

J emma Lu didn't take up Howdy's offer for a ride on his motorcycle. It wasn't that she was afraid of motorcycles, but her taking a ride on his bike was how it all started the first time. Howdy might be the Sagebrush Shakespeare, but she'd already had enough drama in her life with the encore appearance of Wylie Boone. Besides, she had a lunch meeting to attend of the FREDx selection committee that Rich Best had persuaded her to serve on. Since she'd also agreed to chair the meeting on condition it would be held at her office, she couldn't very well miss it. She smiled as she recalled Rich's surprised reaction when she'd relented and agreed.

"Did you say yes?" Rich had asked.

"Yes."

"That's a yes to yes?"

"Really, Rich, can't you take yes for an answer?"

"I just wanted to make sure."

If Rich had asked one more time she would have said no, Jemma Lu thought as she watched him and Desmond Goswami, who Sue Cohen had persuaded to join the selection committee, enter the front door of the Picketware Building, a three-story brick structure occupying an entire block in downtown Picketwire. Her desk was on the mezzanine overlooking the main show room. She watched them as they walked toward the rear where the stairs and elevator were. Jemma Lu wondered if they would take the stairs or the elevator. She always took the stairs even when she had been on crutches from knee surgery a couple of years before. Unfortunately, she couldn't see the elevator doors or the stairs from her perch so she could only guess, which one they took. After waiting several minutes for them to appear she knew they had opted for the elevator. Taking the stairs was faster, even on crutches. When they arrived at Jemma Lu's workspace she waved them toward chairs on the other side of the desk.

"I sure get a kick out of taking that elevator of yours, Jemma Lu," Rich said. "What an antique. And Stan, that's the old gentleman who was operating it," Rich explained to Desmond, "he's such a card. You know, I ride the elevator every time I come here just so I can hear his jokes. Desmond says this is the first time he's ridden in it."

"This is the first time I've been above the main floor," Desmond admitted sheepishly. "If I might ask, why haven't you replaced the elevator with one that has automatic controls."

"Because while we can replace the elevator we could never replace Stanley," Jemma Lu answered.

"I see," Desmond replied, but Jemma Lu knew that he didn't, really. Not yet anyway. But there was no rush. A whooshing sound made her turn to a vacuum tube that ran up through the floor of the mezzanine next to her desk. It had been used for sending and receiving messages and documents at Picketware before the advent of computers. Still, not everything can be reduced to digits and attached to an email so they kept the tubes. Jemma Lu opened a lid on the tube and a glass container popped out. Inside was a bag with the words Sue's Pretty Good to Take Home printed on it. She placed the bag with their lunches on the table, put the container back in the tube, closed the lid and it immediately disappeared with another whoosh.

"Here's your Better Than Most Burger, Rich. Well-done as you requested," she said passing it to Rich, who sat across from her. "And this is your bowl of Some Like it Hotter Chili," she said to Desmond. After handing them all plates, napkins, forks, knives and spoons that she took from the top drawer of the mammoth oak desk they were all seated around, she placed the Rocky Ford cantaloupe half that would be her lunch on a paper plate in front of her.

"Thanks for lunch," Rich said before biting into his burger.

"Yes," Desmond added, looking around as he dipped his spoon into the bowl of chili. "I see you have adopted the open office plan."

"Adopted?" Jemma Lu said. "We've never had individual offices. There wasn't even an office desk for the first fifteen years and that was more than a hundred years ago. Then my great-grandparents had this made. The date and initials of the man who made it for them are carved right here." She ran the fingers of her right hand across the carved initials on the top of the desk. "It was big enough for both of them to use at the same time. In fact, anyone who needed a desk used it."

"It's called hot-desking," Desmond pointed out. "That's when different people use the same desk on a rotating basis. It's quite an innovation."

"I don't know that anyone thought of it as an innovation a hundred years ago. It was more like necessity. Not that we're against innovation at Picketware as long as it meets a real need."

"Necessity is the mother of invention," Rich offered, feeling he needed to put his two cents in even if it was a cliché.

"And desire can be the father of a lot of orphans," Jemma Lu replied. "Picketware isn't in the business of producing orphans, so we don't market our products to people based on desire, but to satisfy a need."

"Desmond, you said a rotating desk is a hot innovation? I wish I'd thought of that one." Rich said.

"I think what Desmond meant is that a hot desk is when different people use the same desk on a rotating basis not that the desk rotates," Jemma Lu said.

"Then the next innovation in office furniture after the hot desk could be a desk that rotates. It would be like a lazy Susan only I'd call it a lazy Fred. You know I think I'll submit it to FREDx."

"If you want to submit it for consideration you have to abstain from voting," Jemma Lu said.

"Why?"

"Because it would be a conflict of interest for you to vote on your own submission. In fact, you should leave the room so that you don't know who voted for or against it."

Rich looked around. "What room?"

"Well, you can wait downstairs or you can ride the elevator up and down listening to Stanley's jokes."

"Stan's my man," Rich said. "But if I leave then what happens if one of you votes for my idea and one against? There needs to be three people voting so there won't be any ties."

"Good point, Rich," Jemma Lu said with a smile "And since you can't vote because of the conflict of interest there's no other alternative than not to allow any member of the selection committee to submit an idea for consideration."

"I agree," Desmond said, then added sympathetically. "That doesn't mean it isn't a good idea, Rich, although I would be derelict in my duties if I didn't point out that it doesn't appear to be an innovation in either farming or ranching."

"Desmond is correct," Jemma Lu said. "On those grounds I'm afraid it's not eligible for consideration."

Rich sighed, "Yeah, I should have included furniture in FREDx."

Jemma Lu tapped a stack of paper on the desk in front of her and asked him and Desmond, "You met with everyone who submitted an application?"

Rich perked up and answered. "We sure did."

"So together with what was submitted in these application forms we should have all the information necessary to decide who should present at FREDx." After Rich and Desmond nodded, Jemma Lu continued, "Then let's discuss them in the order that they were submitted. She picked up the top sheet from the stack. The first submission is by Clint Crowley."

Rich looked at Desmond and then said to Jemma Lu. "We already sort of promised him that he would be included in FREDx."

"Sort of promised?"

"After Clint pitched us his idea for 'Rent-a-Rancher' it seemed like a no-brainer. We did tell him he'd need a little help with his presentation."

"Knowing Clint he'll need more than a little."

"Desmond agreed to coach him, right, Desmond?"

Desmond nodded.

"Then there's no point in reviewing Clint's submission. Did you sort of promise anyone else that you met?"

"Let's see," Rich looked at the list then pointed at a name. "We didn't promise Brady Barnes, although I have to say, I like this 'Hoofer' idea of his where ranches hitch their surplus horses to special hitching posts in towns and people can unhitch them by inserting their credit card and then ride them to where they want to go. Then they just hitch them to another post so someone else can use them. Desmond, though, has some doubts about it."

"I question whether there is really any market demand for it," Desmond said.

"If there's a demand for shared bikes and electric scooters in big cities then why not for horse-sharing here in horse country?" Rich answered.

"Aside from Desmond's point, which I think is quite a good one," Jemma Lu said. "It seems to me that this business Brady proposes could be really dangerous. Riding a horse isn't the same as riding a bike or electric scooter."

"Brady covered that. Everyone who rides has to sign a waiver that says they won't sue if they get hurt. A rider to ride, as he called it."

"What if the horse is injured?" Jemma Lu pressed. "Nobody shoots a bike when it has a flat tire. I can't vote for something that doesn't have proper safeguards to protect the horses. I don't see anything in his proposal about it. Did Brady tell you what the safeguards were when you met with him?"

"Well," Rich squirmed, "he didn't tell us."

"We didn't ask," Desmond said. "We should have."

"That's okay. You saved Brady the embarrassment of having to admit that he hadn't even thought about it."

"I can see now that Brady's idea isn't ready for FREDx," Rich said. "I'll let him know that it needs more work." He looked at

Jemma Lu who was staring at him with one eyebrow arched and added, "A lot more."

"You might want to tell him that successful entrepreneurs learn from their failures," Desmond added.

"You can tell him that, but the Brady Barnes I know is a very slow learner," Jemma Lu said, then with a forced smile said. "Anyway, that's settled. Is there anyone else on the list of applicants who you sort of promised?"

"Nope," Rich said.

"Then I guess there's nothing else for the selection committee to do."

"There is one more that we could consider who isn't on the list."

"I thought every idea that was submitted before the deadline was on this list," Jemma Lu said, tapping the paper. "Other than your idea for a rotating desk, which we decided isn't eligible."

"Technically, the idea was submitted before the deadline," Rich said. "But there was a condition that we would have to agree to. That's why it's not on the list."

"What's the condition?" Jemma Lu asked.

"That he presents the idea only to you and that you decide whether it should be included in FREDx."

"That means you and Desmond won't be able to hear it or vote on it."

"Yeah, but if we meet his one condition he'll cover all of our expenses plus another twenty five thousand dollars in prize money for the best ideas."

"I didn't know FREDx is going to give out prize money," Jemma Lu said.

"That's because we don't have any money but if we did, we could, and we could if we agree to his condition."

"Two coulds don't necessarily add up to a should," Jemma Lu said, shaking her head. "This offer sounds like a bribe, to me."

"It's not a bribe because he said he would give the money whether or not we, in this case you, accepted his idea. All he wants is a chance to submit it to you in person."

"I still don't like it. There has to be more to it than that one condition."

"Is that a no vote?" Rich asked.

"I think I should abstain. I'll go with whatever you two decide."

"In that case I vote yes," Rich said. "What about you Desmond? Are you willing to let Jemma Lu hear this fellow present his idea and decide whether it should be included in FREDx?"

"I think I'll abstain as well," Desmond said, dipping his spoon into the bowl of chili.

"That's one yes and no noes so the motion carries," Rich said slapping the table. Then taking a paper napkin he wiped off the greasy imprint that his burger stained hand had made.

Jemma Lu sat back in her chair and sighed, "Okay, but I just hope this fellow really has the financial resources to keep up his end of the bargain."

"You don't need to worry about that, Jemma Lu," Rich said, breaking out in a broad smile, "because the fellow we're talking about is Wylie Boone."

CHAPTER TWENTY

An old rancher once told Foster that ranching was ninety percent perspiration and ten percent trying to wipe it off. Square-jawed and broad-shouldered Clint Crowley sure looked the part of a trail boss itching to lead a cattle drive, but the truth was that ever since he busted his right leg when he was thrown from a horse and then stomped on by a steer, Clint lost his desire to head 'em up and move 'em out. Clint's output of perspiration declined along with his inspiration as did the reputation of his family's ranch, the Lazy C. But even if the Lazy C was no longer one of the best ranches around, it was next to Wylie Boone's Double B, which was hemmed in by the Comanche National Grasslands on every other side. One might say that the Lazy C occupied a position of geo-strategic importance as a check on any expansion of the Double B. In fact, Purgatory County's last range war had been between the Double B and the Lazy C in 1912. It ended in a show down in which the Crowley family somehow managed to fight the Boones and their gang of hired guns to a standoff. And that's where it still stood more than a century later. So while Gloria was off interviewing Sheriff Riggleman, Foster was at the Lazy C getting an exclusive of his own.

The entrance to the Lazy C was almost directly across from the massive gate of the Double B. At the end of its short drive was the Crowley's sprawling ranch house. It no longer burst at the seams with sons and daughters, all of whom could ride, shoot, brand, and pretty much do whatever needed to be done including taking on the Boones, as was done a hundred years before. Instead, it was mostly empty, occupied only by Clint and his wife, Rhonda, as well as two dogs and several cats. Merle, the second oldest of their three sons lived alone in a mobile home parked near the corrals. He did most of the perspiring on the ranch along with a hired hand named Diego who, ironically, had only one arm having lost the other in Iraq. Merle had been in the army as well and done two tours in Afghanistan. Unlike Diego, Merle had managed to come back with all his limbs still attached although based on the few interactions Foster had with him he was still working on getting his mind back together.

"Decided to re-invent yourself, huh?" Clint said after Foster told him that he was there as a reporter for the *Picketwire Press*. They were seated in Clint's office just off the entry hall of the house. Foster was seated in a well-worn easy chair with horsehair sprouting through the cracks in the leather upholstery while Clint sat in an old wooden office chair with wheels on its four legs. The only other furniture was a large oak desk with a desk top computer and a bookcase filled with what appeared to be ledgers.

"Seemed easier than being reborn. Dying was hard enough."

"You mean when you got shot in the head and almost died."

"I did die according to the docs but apparently they didn't want me up there or down there. Woke up with a hell of a headache."

"So now you're undead, like some kind of zombie."

"That's what I was beginning to feel like sitting there in my La-Z-Boy recliner watching the damn television."

"And you're a reporter now," Clint said, nodding his head slowly then pursing his lips like it was a lot to contemplate.

"I don't do the writing just the research. That's why I'm here."

Clint perked up. "The paper wants to do a story on my 'Rent-a-Rancher' idea? Rich Best says it's a big idea."

"I bet it is but that's not the story I'm researching. I'll let Tom know since he covers big ideas for the paper."

"Actually it might be better to keep it under wraps since Rich wants me to present it at this FREDx shindig he's putting on for people who want to invest in big ideas. He'd probably be mad as hell if it got out before then."

"No problem," Foster said and took the pen from his breast pocket and wrote in the small pad he was carrying that he shouldn't tell Tom that Clint Crowley had a big idea.

"So what is the story that you think I can help with?"

"It's about Wylie Boone. This attempt to kill him has made the headlines all over and now that he's come back to the ranch, the *Picketwire Press* wants to do a series on him."

"It's no secret that the Crowleys and the Boones don't exactly like each other, but I didn't try to kill him."

"No one's saying that, Clint."

"Yeah, well Riggleman has already been out here and asked me where I was the day Boone got run down. I told him it was none of his damned business, but if I had run him over it sure wouldn't have been with a minivan."

"Knowing Riggleman, I don't think he'll drop it. Especially after what you told him."

"I sure as hell hope you're right and he brings me in for questioning and asks me where I was, so I can tell him right there in front of his deputies," Clint stopped and held his right hand over his mouth to stifle a laugh.

"What's so funny?"

Clint wheeled his office chair closer to Foster, leaned forward and answered. "You see I was on jury duty at the Purgatory County Courthouse, which as you know, is right next to the Sheriff's Department. In fact, one of Riggleman's deputies testified in the case. He was the star witness for the prosecution, which didn't help them one bit since he was as big an idiot as his boss. You should have seen our equally incompetent DA, Vince Lowery, trying to get his star witness to make sense. It was like trying to turn on a light bulb when there's no electricity. Hell, after hearing his testimony we didn't even have to deliberate to find the defendant not guilty. The only thing we did in the jury room was shake our heads and laugh. Yeah, I sure hope Riggleman calls me in and asks me where I was."

"I wish I could be there to see his face if you do get the chance."

"Say, maybe you could be there as a reporter?"

"I don't think Riggleman's going to let any reporter witness his interrogation, especially not me. Besides I'm not a reporter. Like I said, I'm just doing research. But Gloria could cover it if you get called in. She could interview you and Riggleman afterwards. At least try to interview him because I don't think he'd be in any mood to meet with the press."

"I can see the headline: Sheriff Takes the Fifth."

After Clint finally stopped laughing Foster said, "I didn't actually come here because I thought you were under suspicion, Clint. I wanted to ask you if you've noticed anything suspicious since Wylie came back to his ranch. You know, any comings and goings that are out of the ordinary."

"You think I spy on him?"

"I'm not saying you spy on him. I just figure that given the past history between the Boones and the Crowleys you keep a sharp eye out for anything unusual."

"Sharp eye, more like an eagle eye. If I could afford it, I'd have a satellite up there with its camera focused on the Double B twenty-four seven."

"So have you noticed anything?"

"Well let's have a look in the log." Clint wheeled backwards and then spun his chair, so it faced the desk. He pulled a binder toward him and opened it.

"You keep a log?"

"Sure. Not just me. My father and granddaddy as well." He waved at the bookshelf filled with what Foster had thought were ledgers. "Now, let's see here. The only thing unusual happened the other night. My son, Merle, monitors our remote cameras and if he sees anything unusual he writes me a note and then I put it down in the logbook."

"You have remote cameras?"

"You bet. Got them set up at strategic locations along the border with the Boones. The border is what we call the property line. I guess you would say it's part of our early warning system. Lets us know if there's been any incursions from the other side. Merle's in charge of all that. Once in a while he and Diego even do some recon work. That's off the record of course."

"Of course. I won't even write it down."

"Anyway, the video monitors are in Merle's trailer, which he calls the CCC, Crowley Command Center. He even got us a drone with a camera for aerial surveillance. Anyway, he says, well, hell, you can read it yourself." He handed Foster the open book.

Foster read the entry that said that at 7:30 PM a '57 Chevy came out of the Double B front gate and turned south without coming to a full stop. Five seconds later a Jeep Wrangler appeared from the north at a high rate of speed and continued south and then at 8:05 a Chevy Suburban left the Double B headed south. Finally, there was a third entry that said at 8:20 the '57 Chevy followed by the Suburban returned to the Double B.

"Did Merle get any license plate numbers?" Foster asked handing Clint the ledger.

"If it's not in there then he didn't get them, either because he couldn't make it out from what he saw on the monitor or he didn't think it was important."

"So, it might be on the tape?"

"Maybe, if Merle decided to save something he looked at. If he did, he would have written that on the notes he gives me, so I can write it in the log. He's been talking about storing them in a cloud, whatever the hell that means. You're lucky, there's a note that says he saved it."

"Who do you think was in the Chevy and the Suburban?"

"Well, the Suburban is easy. That's the vehicle that Boone's security detail uses. I figure the person in the '57 Chevy was Wylie. He used to have a red '57 Chevy when he was younger. It was a real beaut, I have to say, and it was fast. He must still have it and keep it at the Ranch. I can't imagine Wylie letting anyone else drive it, so it must have been him."

"You have any idea who might have been driving the Jeep Wrangler?"

"Nope, and Merle would have mentioned it if he did. There's a lot of Jeep Wranglers around. Hell, Foster, you're even driving one." Clint pointed out the window at Foster's dented, dirt encrusted, black Jeep.

"Almost a hundred thousand on it. Thirty-five were there when I bought it."

Clint whistled, "And those are Jeep miles."

"Yeah, and I can feel every one of them. I'm sort of hoping it will jar loose the inoperable bullet in my head and pop it out through my ass."

"Good luck, I guess," Clint said. "To get back to the Jeep, you can look at the tape and see if it helps you figure out who the driver was."

CHAPTER TWENTY ONE

"I didn't expect it to be like this," Bruce said after they sat down on the front steps of a partially collapsed building in the center of the abandoned internment camp. He and Jane hadn't spoken more than a half dozen words since they passed through the break in the fence.

"What did you expect?" Jane asked him, although she could have directed the question to herself as much as Bruce.

"I thought we'd just find some crumbling foundations, piles of bricks and boards here and there, but I certainly didn't think there would be anything still standing. It's like a ghost town."

"It was an internment camp, not a town."

"So, it's a ghost camp," Bruce quipped.

"Funny you say that because I can't shake this feeling that we're not alone," Jane said as she looked around. There were at least half a dozen buildings surrounded by sage brush, bunch-grass, and tumbleweeds. They were weather-beaten and windowless with tin roofs that were caved in by years of wind, snow, and hail. "Not that I'm scared. It's not like I believe in ghosts."

"What about the Holy Ghost?"

"I mean ghost as in a dead person who's come back to scare people," she replied, jabbing him in the side with her left elbow.

"Gee, and I was hoping to practice my ghostbusting," Bruce replied, standing up and tucking his thumbs under the belt of his jeans. "Guess I'll have to try bronco busting instead. Of course, first I'll have to learn how to ride a horse."

Jane got up and stood beside him, "I can ask my dad to teach you. He taught me when I was a kid. I could teach you myself but I don't know if our marriage would survive."

"I'll ask your dad. After I learn you can call me Bruce the Kid."

"I think Bruce the kidder would be more appropriate," Jane laughed nervously and did a three hundred sixty degree turn. "But I wasn't kidding when I said I had this feeling that we're not alone."

"Maybe we should leave. It could be a security guard, and we are trespassers."

"If it's a security guard they aren't doing a very good job by not showing themselves. After all, it's not like we look as if we'd put up a fight if they told us to leave."

"Maybe it's a ghost guard."

Instead of laughing again, Jane gave Bruce her that's enough so cut it out look that she'd deployed on many an occasion in the years they'd been together.

"Sorry," he said quickly. "I don't mean to be disrespectful."

"It wasn't disrespect it was just a bad pun."

They lapsed into silence again. Jane remembered the words from Psalm 137 that recounted the Jewish exile and captivity in Babylon, "By the rivers of Babylon we sat down and wept when we remembered Zion." But then, instead of meditating on a story from the Bible, her mind shifted unexpectedly back to the *Wizard of Oz*. She pictured Dorothy, only she looked like Jane not Judy Garland and Oz wasn't emerald green but prairie brown and it wasn't Kansas that Dorothy wanted to return to it was Colorado and the Wicked Witch and the Wizard were...

"What are you thinking?" Bruce interrupted, bringing her runaway thoughts to a halt.

"Just feeling sad, but also curious," she answered, deciding that it was a whole lot easier to tell Bruce what she was feeling than what she had been imagining.

"Sadness I get, but why curious? I would be angry. That's what I felt when I saw Dachau, sad but angry."

"When did you visit Dachau?" Jane replied, wondering why he'd never told her before, although a German death camp wasn't something a person normally brought up.

"Before I met you. I was in Munich on business and it's near there. I had been in Munich several days working on a deal with colleagues in our German office and had a free afternoon before I flew back to New York the next morning. Dachau is right outside Munich so I decided to see it. I went there because I was curious about what a Nazi concentration camp, a death camp, was like. My family didn't talk about the Holocaust except to say that we were fortunate since none of our relatives were murdered by the Nazis. So, even though I'm Jewish, I didn't have a personal connection and it was all abstract to me.

"As soon as I entered the camp it wasn't abstract anymore and I wasn't curious, I was angry. When I got back to Munich I changed my return flight to New York from the next morning to that night. I wanted to get out of Germany as fast as possible. Of course, I got over the anger and I went back. I mean back to Germany, not Dachau. A long way of saying that I understand that you're feeling sad, but what are you curious about?"

"Curious as to why they were sent to this camp. Why is it such a secret even now, after all these years? I've visited the place where Camp Amache was and there's information about it and a memorial, but there's no mention of this camp. It's as if it never existed."

"You said your grandmother said there was another camp so some people knew about it."

"I asked her to tell me more but she didn't want to talk about it other than to say that they were lucky they hadn't been sent to the camps. When I asked my mom and dad they said that my grandparents and other older Japanese-Americans around here kept whatever they knew to themselves. It was as if was too painful to talk about."

"I wonder what people around here would have done if they'd rounded up their Japanese-American neighbors like your grandparents and thrown them in the camps."

"I imagine people were relieved that they didn't have to answer that question."

They walked over to one of the buildings that still looked in good shape. Unlike the other structures that were still standing, the door to this one was not only attached it was closed. Bruce twisted the rusted knob and gave it a shove. It swung open and he walked inside. "Now this is strange, truly strange."

"What do you mean?" Jane asked, stepping inside.

Bruce poked at several cans on the floor with the toe of one of his hiking boots. "This is a can of paint. It looks like it's been here for years."

Jane stooped down and picked up the can. "It's all dried out inside but it looks like it contained red paint at some point."

I wonder what they were painting. There's nothing in here. I'll look outside." He handed her the can and walked out the door.

Jane decided to put the can in her small backpack rather than leave it there.

"I know what they were painting," Bruce shouted through the open doorway.

"What?" Jane yelled back and then hurried out the door. Bruce was standing looking at the building from the other side.

"Someone painted graffiti on this wall. We couldn't see it because it faces the entrance to the camp. At least it's not a profanity that I recognize. More like the pictographs we saw earlier," Bruce said after Jane joined him in looking at what had been painted boldly in red across the wall.

"It's not a pictograph," she replied without hesitation.

"What is it, then?"

"It's Japanese."

"You're sure?"

"I think I would know what Japanese writing looks like."

"Okay, what does it say?"

Jane shook her head as she studied the red markings. They were more like angry slash marks than the delicate calligraphy she was used to seeing. "I don't know. I can speak some Japanese, but I never learned how to read it."

Bruce looked at her in astonishment. "You're telling me that you can read Greek and Hebrew but not Japanese, which is your ancestral tongue?"

"Says the Jew who can't read Hebrew."

"Good thing we both know English," Bruce said. "Hey, what about your parents? We can take pictures of it and show them."

"They can't read Japanese either, other than a few characters. The only person I know in our family who can read Japanese is my dad's older brother, Uncle Joji. You've never met him."

"Does he live around here?"

"He lives in my grandparent's old house. When my grandfather died, my grandmother moved in with us and their farm was divided between my dad, Uncle Joji and my two aunts. Since my Dad already had a farm and a house, and my aunts live out of state, the land Uncle Joji inherited included my grandparent's house. My dad bought his sister's land and added it to his own, but Uncle Joji lives in my grandparent's old house."

"Why haven't you mentioned this Uncle Joji before?" Bruce asked. "You met all of my uncles and aunts at our wedding."

"As well as all of your cousins and nieces and nephews."

"What can I say, my family loves a party."

"Anyway, I hardly know Uncle Joji. He went to Japan and lived there for a number of years. That's where he learned to speak and write Japanese. I only saw him as a kid when he came back to visit. He stayed with my grandparents when he was visiting here and didn't come back for good until my grandfather died and left him the house on the condition that my grandmother could continue living there. She decided to move in with us instead. My mom became the oldest daughter by default when my aunts moved away. Fortunately, my grandmother and my mom really got along. As I said, Uncle Joji moved into my grandparent's house and he's lived there ever since. The last time I saw him was at my grandmother's funeral and that was more than five years ago."

"If you don't really know your uncle, maybe your Dad could ask him what this means."

Jane shook her head, "My dad, along with my aunts, had some sort of falling out with Uncle Joji after my grandfather died. Since my grandmother's death they've pretty much kept their distance so it wouldn't be a good idea to ask my dad."

"That explains why he wasn't at our wedding," Bruce said. "If no one is going to ask your Uncle Joji, we'll have to see if there's someone else who can translate it. There might be someone at Picketwire College."

"That won't be necessary because I'm going to ask him," Jane said with a firmness that surprised Bruce. "I said it wasn't a good idea to ask my dad, but that doesn't mean I can't ask Uncle Joji."

"I thought you said you didn't really know him."

"Now's my chance."

CHAPTER TWENTY TWO

Instead of fingering a bead, Sister M's shot baskets while saying the Rosary. After each Hail Mary she'd launched the ball toward the basket, working her way clockwise in an arc from the right corner to the left as if following a hardwood Stations of the Cross. Basketball, unlike prayer, came easily to Sister M's. She had been playing the game since she was in grade school and had been a starting guard her senior year at Saint Joan of Arc Catholic High School. However, after college, where she played in an intramural league, she hadn't stepped onto a court until she'd arrived at Our Lady of Lost Souls Convent and discovered that there was a gym left over from when it was the Purgatory Penitentiary. The gym had been added in the 1930s as an alternative to the prison yard where walking in circles and brawling had been the only form of exercise. The theory was that good clean sports like basketball and volleyball would help in the convicts' rehabilitation by instilling in them the hygienic values of fair play and teamwork. The reality had been gladiatorial combat between teams composed of rival prison gangs. Still, it was better to have an elbow in the ribs than a shiv in the belly.

Now the space was used primarily for activities like yoga, tai chi, and even square dancing. The latter was called by Sister Rosalie with Sister Wendy on the fiddle. Although there was the occasional game of volleyball in the gym, Sister M's was the only one who used it to shoot baskets or, as she jokingly called it, engaging in "nun on none" instead of "one on one." Sister M's needed this bit of roundball meditation. Soon Tony would be delivering several undocumented immigrants, and she would have to be on her toes. She released a Hail Mary from her lips along with her shot from the top of the key. Watching it swoosh through the net, she heard her name being called.

"They're here," Sister Cecilia yelled from the open doorway.

"Who?"

"Our guests."

"They're early," Sister M's answered as she picked up the basketball and tucked it under her left arm. "The Purple Sage tour group isn't supposed to arrive for several more hours."

"It's not the whole tour group that is here, just those who are staying with us. You know, the ones we're providing sanctuary for."

"Where are the others?" The plan was for this to be seen as a regular stop on the Purple Sage tour so it wouldn't raise any suspicions.

"I guess they're still with Tony," Sister Cecilia replied. "Our guests came in the back of a pickup truck, not in the Purple Sage tour bus. A young lady was with them. Sister Rachel has taken them to the guest rooms that we have set aside for them. We thought it was best that they be out of sight in case they were being followed." Nothing was more out of sight than the area they had designated the Sanctuary Wing since it had once been the maximum-security cellblock.

"Is the young lady who was with them still at the Welcome Center?"

"No, I'm right here," Zelda blurted as she rushed past Sister Cecilia and stepped out onto the court. "And I'm wearing this costume because I'm an actor."

"I'm Sister Mary Margaret, although you can call me Sister M's," Sister M's replied, calmly as she looked at the young woman who was wearing a dress right out of the Victorian era and high-topped, buttoned shoes that were scuffed and coated with dust.

"My name is Zelda Zenn. Actually, that's my stage name although if I had my way it would be my real name."

"Which is what?"

"Mary Ann Smithers," Zelda said, then put two fingers in her mouth like she was going to vomit. Before Sister M's could think of a reply, Zelda dived right into recounting her story. "I was on the rear platform of the train car, which is sort of like being on a moving balcony. I was waiting to make my entrance as Clementine who's a character in the skit I was performing for the Purple Sage tour. She's the female lead..."

Sister M's held up her right hand to stop Zelda and then told Sister Cecilia who had been standing just inside the gym door on the waxed wood floor that it would be better if she wasn't present since this was likely to be something that fell under attorney-client privilege. Sister Cecilia nodded and left and Sister M's turned back to Zelda. "Could you get back to what happened when you were on the rear platform of the train?"

Without missing a beat, Zelda picked up where she left off, "As I was saying, in the skit I was supposed to run into the car screaming that there were train robbers on horses chasing us and Clem, that's the name of the character who's the conductor, was supposed to pull out a pistol, run back onto the rear platform and then there would be the sound of gunfire – blanks of course. Then Clem would come back in and say that he'd driven them off. That's when I was supposed to throw my arms around him and call him a hero. Of course, there wasn't supposed to be anyone actually chasing us."

When Zelda paused for dramatic effect, Sister M's asked, "Was someone actually chasing the train?"

Zelda nodded, "A whole gang of guys on horses appeared out of nowhere yelling for us to stop. Stop the train, they meant. I took off running right through the car past Clem and then the next car and then the train stopped and I jumped off and ran for the bushes by the tracks. That's when I realized that three people on the Purple Sage tour were right on my tail. We hid behind the bushes as a couple of the guys on horses trotted by heading toward the train engine. I could see that they were wearing badges and had patches on the arm of their shirt that said "Sheriff's Posse." That's when I turned to the three people who followed me and told them that we didn't need to hide because it was the sheriff, not train robbers. But then Gary..."

"Guillermo," Sister M's interjected. "Guillermo is one of the three guests we were expecting."

"He just told me his name was Gary. I like Guillermo better, actually. Anyway, he told me that they couldn't because they were the people the sheriff was after and if they were caught, they'd be thrown in jail and deported. Then the girl named Alice..."

"Alejandra," Sister M's said.

"She definitely said her name was Alice and she said it in English, which she spoke really well."

"Alejandra is her real name and Alice is a made up name, just like Zelda is for you. She has lived in the U.S. since she was one year old, so English is her first language and Spanish is her second."

"Her English makes some of the people I know who were born here sound like it's their third language," Zelda said. "But getting back to names, Zelda isn't a fake name, it's a real stage name."

"Sorry," Sister M's said, although she wasn't sure what the difference was between a stage name and the pseudonyms that Alejandra and the others were using.

"Anyway, like I was saying, Alice or whatever her name is, asked me to wait at least a few minutes to give them time to get a head start. You know, so that they had a decent chance of getting away. She wasn't just asking, she was begging and with tears, real tears, Sister. It was no act."

"Then the other guy, he called himself Art, although from what you just told me that's probably not his real name."

"It's Andres."

"Whatever," Zelda shrugged, the puffed up shoulders of her dress rising as if she were lifting barbells. "Art-Andres said that they could tie me up and gag me so I wouldn't be arrested for helping them. Well, I told him even if he was Snidely Whiplash and I was really Clementine I wouldn't let him tie me up and, besides, they didn't need to do that because I was going with them."

"And why did you decide to do that, if you don't mind me asking?"

"I don't know exactly. Everything happened so fast," Zelda said, leaving out that she'd always wanted to play someone on the run from the law. She used to imagine herself in the movie *Thelma and Louise*, only it would be Zelda and Louise.

Sister M's nodded and asked, "And they agreed?"

"Agreed? Of course they did. Who wouldn't? Gary did say that if they got caught they'd tell the sheriff that they had kidnapped me so I wouldn't be arrested as an accomplice. I thought that was really sweet of him. Then I asked them where they were going and he said they needed to get here because it was a safe house although a prison doesn't seem like a safe place from the sheriff."

"It's a convent now."

"Right. Anyway, when they told me that's when I understood that they were the three members of the tour that Tony Medrano told me about who were going to stay here at the prison, I mean convent, only it was supposed to be for a spiritual retreat not to hide out...."

Sister M's interrupted, "We're providing sanctuary."

"Isn't that the same thing as a hideout?"

"Not exactly," Sister M's answered although she would have been hard pressed to explain the difference.

"I think hiding out in a prison that's now a convent is a neat plot twist. It's sort of like that old movie *Sister Act* where Whoopi Goldberg has to disguise herself by dressing up as a nun and hiding in a convent to escape the hit men who are after her."

Suppressing a desire to break out laughing, Sister M's replied, "Dressing as a nun here wouldn't be much of a disguise because we don't wear habits except when we lead historical tours, but maybe you could continue with your story about escaping the 'Sheriff's Posse'?"

"Right. Well, we snuck off through the brush, but we didn't have to go far before we came to a dirt road. The others sort of looked at me like I was supposed to know where to go from there. Of course, I didn't have a clue where the road went. Believe you me, Sister, things were looking desperate," Zelda looked at Sister M's to make sure that she was impressed with how serious, not to mention melodramatic, the situation was. Clementine couldn't have told it better.

After Sister M's nodded Zelda continued, "But just then, out of the blue, a pickup truck came barreling down the road and stopped right in front of us. It turned out that the kid driving the pickup recognized me even in this get up. He also goes to Picketwire High. Anyway, Donny, whose real name is probably Donald but who would want to be called that, agreed to drive us here."

"Did you tell Donny what happened?"

"I just told him that we were on the train as part of the Purple Sage tour and I was giving a performance, which was why I was in this outfit, and that the train broke down and the three people with me were on the tour and needed to get here so I had volunteered to take them."

"And he believed you?" Sister M's asked.

"I am an actress," Zelda declared. "Besides, I told him that if he drove us here I'd go out on a date with him."

"Really?" Sister M's said, more out of marvel than as a question.

"Yes, really," Zelda answered. "I don't expect that you'd know much about dating, Sister, so you'll just have to take my word for it when I tell you it's a really big deal for a guy to get a chance to go out with me. Donny looked like he'd died and gone to heaven. Sorry, I guess I shouldn't be using the word heaven that way with a nun."

"You don't have to apologize. I'm just sorry that you were put in a position where you felt you had to lie to Donny."

"It wasn't lying, it was acting. I was just playing a part. Besides, I'm pretty sure that Donny wants to go out with Zelda Zenn, not Mary Ann Smithers."

"Well, Mary Ann, I mean Zelda, I just want to tell you how much we appreciate what you've done. You put yourself at risk to help people you didn't know."

"Do I have to hide out here as well?"

"As I said before, this is a sanctuary not a hideout, so no, you don't."

"But what if the sheriff finds out I helped them escape?"

"Sheriff Riggleman didn't find any undocumented immigrants, or 'illegals' as he calls them, on board the train. The obvious explanation as to why you and three members of the tour left is that you thought he and his gang were train robbers since he didn't identify himself as the sheriff. There's no way he can prove that you knew he was after the other three because he thought they were 'illegals,' so how could you have helped them escape? Anyway, this was just a publicity stunt by him. Riggleman formed this posse of his claiming that it will protect the county from what he calls an alien invasion. What he did by stopping the train is what's alien. It was not only outside the law he's supposed to be enforcing, but it also put people like you in danger."

Zelda knitted her mascaraed brows and asked, "Are you saying that he's going to just drop the whole thing and forget that it ever happened?"

"Let's just say that his publicly stunt turned out to put a big dent in his silver star. That doesn't mean he isn't going to give up this crazy crusade of his, and he'll probably try to find the three people that you brought here, but, as I said, you should be in the clear on this."

"What if the sheriff asks me if I know where they are?"

"Then you tell him you won't talk to him without your lawyer present."

"I don't have a lawyer."

"I'll represent you."

"Sorry, Sister, but I would need a lawyer not a nun."

Sister M's laughed, "I'm also a lawyer."

"That's good," Zelda sighed in relief. "Because as much as I consider myself an outlaw, I'm in a new play by the Bard Wired Players and being in jail would really mess up my big break."

"You're in the new play by Howdy Hanks?"

"You know about it?"

Sister M's nodded, "We already bought tickets even though we don't know what it's about."

"Well," Zelda hitched up her skirt, which had started to droop, "I'm not only in the play, but I'm the female lead. The director, Max Bergmann, got me the job playing Clementine and he plays Clem the train conductor, so I need to let him know that I'm okay."

"I'm sure Max will be relieved," Sister M's replied.

"Relieved that he didn't lose his star," Zelda said as she looked around. As if she suddenly realized where she was, she said, "Why this is a gym. I didn't know convents had them. Not that I know anything about convents."

"It was here when we took over the prison. Nuns need to exercise just like everyone else."

"I thought your body was supposed to be a temple not a gym. At least that's what they said in Sunday School, although to be honest I wasn't paying a lot of attention."

Sister M's couldn't help laughing. "That's from the New Testament, First Corinthians," deciding to leave out that St. Paul was referring to sexual immorality.

"I used to play basketball," Zelda said, pointing at the ball Sister M's had tucked under her left arm. "That was before we moved to Picketwire a year ago. I've given up playing in a gym for being on the stage. Sort of weird being in one dressed as the character I'm playing. I don't think Clementine played basketball."

"Well, here's her chance," Sister M's said passing the ball to Zelda. It was a slow, bounce pass to make it easier to catch. Zelda ran toward it, grabbed it and took off dribbling toward the basket, her long skirt trailing behind and her shoes clattering on the floor. Without stopping she launched a layup that bounced off the backboard through the net.

CHAPTER TWENTY THREE

As he cast the fly Dave Sanderson imagined he was on the banks of the lake near his cabin in the Sangre de Cristo Mountains instead of standing on the blue carpet between the pulpit and the lectern in the sanctuary of Picketwire Community Church. He waved the rod back and forth creating elegant loops with the line before flinging it out over the empty pews. Before the fly could land on one of the pews he whipped it back.

"Catch anything?" Jane asked from the back of the sanctuary.

Dave looked up, surprised to see Jane emerging from the shadows under the balcony. "Just practicing," he answered without taking his eye from the fly.

"Uh huh."

"Practicing for next Sunday's sermon."

"I've heard some people consider fly-fishing a religion but..."

"The sermon is on Matthew 4:19."

Jane laughed, "Fishers of men."

"I haven't done a sermon on this passage for a few years and I always use my fly rod as a prop, so I need to practice. Not the preaching but the casting. I'm going fishing on Saturday for the first time this year so I'll be able to practice then, but I figured it would be good to rehearse it once in the sanctuary as well." Dave began reeling the line in as Jane walked to the front.

"Have you ever hooked someone?"

"The first time I did it I caught a parishioner's hat. She always wore a hat in church that you couldn't miss and I didn't. That was years ago at my first church back in Pennsylvania."

"What did you do?"

"Ran down and unhooked the hat. It's called catch and release. Mrs. Matthews, that was her name, was a pretty good sport about it. She said she appreciated that I was demonstrating how Jesus fished for women as well as men. After that I've made sure there's no hook but just a weighted fly." He held up the end of the line to show Jane. "What brings you in on a Monday? You should be relaxing after preaching yesterday."

"I stopped by to pick up a book from my office and noticed that the doors to the sanctuary were open. But as long as we're both here..."

"When we should be on our day off."

"It will take some getting used to having Mondays as my day off now that as a pastor I'm working on Sunday."

"Good thing that Sunday is the first day of the week rather than the seventh or we'd be breaking the Fourth Commandment every time we preached."

"You said you were going fishing on Saturday so how does that comply with remembering the Sabbath day, to keep it holy?"

Dave smiled as he shook his head. "Jane, for me fly-fishing is a spiritual exercise, because every time I cast I say a little prayer."

"I have to admit that I haven't thought of incorporating fly fishing into a sermon."

"Well, I hadn't thought of the *Wizard of Oz* as part of one until I heard your sermon yesterday."

"How do you think it went over?"

"The way you opened by reading the first line from the book..."

"That Dorothy lived in the midst of the great Kansas prairies," Jane recited.

"Yes, right there you got everyone's attention since Picketwire, Colorado is where those great Kansas prairies end. You not only got their attention you held it. Why I even notice that Jim Arbogast stayed awake."

The only person she'd really noticed during the sermon, aside from Bruce and her parents sitting in the front row, was Tom Tidings. She knew they would see each other and had imagined some scenarios. None of them had her preaching her first sermon with Tom sitting in the back pew. He must have slipped out the side door during the recessional. Was it to avoid telling her that he didn't like her sermon or was it just to avoid her?

"What are you going to do on the rest of your day off?" Dave asked.

"Bruce and I are going for a drive in the countryside to see someone."

"Don't tell me that you're off to see the Wizard."

"No," Jane laughed. "We're off to see my Uncle Joji at his farm and the road to it isn't paved with yellow bricks."

"Uncle Joji?"

"Joji is how George is translated in Japanese. My grandparents named my uncle George, but when he came back from living in Japan he told everyone in the family that he wanted to be called Joji from then on. Most people wouldn't know that because he's a bit of a recluse."

"Now that you mention it, I've only met him twice that I recall, and both times were funerals. The first time was at your grandmother's funeral and the second time was at the funeral for Jacob Brewster who had a farm next to your uncle's. Brewster was a widower with no children and kept to himself, except for coming to church every Sunday. The only people at the funeral were members of the congregation, except for your uncle. I didn't have much to go on coming up with a eulogy other than Brewster's perfect church attendance, so I talked about his steadfastness. I used First Corinthians 15:58 where Paul talks about the importance of being steadfast and always doing the work of the Lord."

"Knowing that in the Lord, your labor is not in vain," Jane said, nodding her head.

"Yeah," Dave replied as he grabbed the fly at the end of the line. "Hopefully, Jacob was living a steadfast life and not just a creature of habit. Anyway, I'll never forget that your uncle came up to me after the service and gave me a really deep bow. Since he didn't say anything I assume that meant the funeral service met with his approval."

"You're right, he wouldn't have done that otherwise since bowing is a sign of respect. What did you do in response?"

"I bowed back. It wasn't quite as graceful as his. Probably the only opportunity I'll ever have to take a bow for leading a church service, much less a funeral." As they talked Dave untied the fly that was at the end of his line and started attaching another one.

"Why are you changing flies?"

"The one I'm taking off is a trout fly called a Parachute Adams and it's pretty effective since it resembles a number of different insects that are on the surface of the water. Its drawback is that as a dry fly it's for fish that come to the surface to feed. For those that don't, you need one that works underwater where it's darker and colder that looks like nymphs and leeches and other underwater critters. That's what a wet fly like this Wooly Bugger is good at," he pointed to a fly tucked into the band of the broad brimmed, cotton hat he wore. "I did some casting with that one before I switched to the Parachute Adams. There are different flies for different fish and conditions. So you have to decide first what kind of fish in general, like a trout or a salmon or a bass, you want to catch and then, this is where it gets even trickier, what particular ones are you after. Is it some young, small one who's impulsive and will go for just about anything flashy that you toss at them or one who's grown old and big by being wily and cunning? And then there are the conditions. Are you fishing in calm waters or fast-moving, shallow places, deep places, rocky places, marshes and so on. There are different flies for different conditions."

"Which one works best inside a church?" Jane asked, trying to sound serious.

Dave reached into one of the pockets of the fishing vest he wore and pulled out a fly. "I came up with this one on my own and have been using it for years when I give a sermon on this passage."

"What's it called?"

"The Jesus Fly, of course," he said with a wink as he deftly tied some brown feathers arranged in a cruciform to the end of the line. "As you can see there's just a weighted tail rather than a hook. Now let's see if I can get it all the way to the deep water where the souls are hiding in the back pew." He began flicking the rod back and forth, each time sending the line with the fly at the end farther out over the empty pews. "Almost there," he said as the fly flitted upward toward the vaulted ceiling. Then, as Dave's arm shot forward in one last cast, it and the rod came to a sudden stop. Instead of whizzing over them the fly had disappeared behind them. They both turned around and looked over their shoulders. Their eyes followed the line across the carpet, onto the communion table and up to the six foot high wooden cross attached to the back wall, where the fly had caught the left arm.

CHAPTER TWENTY FOUR

Why worry, Max told himself. This wasn't the first time he'd been questioned by the police. True, the other time was in the television series *Mean Streets of Manhattan*. He played the part of Sal Malpensa, a Mafia hit man, and was interrogated by Detective Liam O'Bannon, played by Troy Stone, the tall, broad-shouldered chiseled-face star of the show. No matter what O'Bannon threw at him Sal parried it without breaking a sweat. Finally, when O'Bannon offered Sal witness protection, Sal responded with a sardonic smile. "I'm the only protection I need," and walked out of the precinct station as cocky as ever. Sal was immediately cut down in a hail of hot lead and fell into the gutter where he sprawled in a pool of blood. Unfortunately for Max that was not only the end of his character but also the end of the steady paycheck he'd been getting. He'd had enough of waiting on tables and bartending while waiting for his big acting break so he drove off into the sunset across the Hudson River heading west, not to Hollywood but to Picketwire and a new job at the Bard Wired Players.

***

"So, where are they?" Sheriff Riggleman demanded after he'd climbed aboard the Pullman car and found Max inside, next to the door to the rear observation platform.

"They?" Max answered.

"The illegals you're transporting on this train."

"Illegals?"

"You know, the illegal immigrants?"

"I still don't know what you're talking about."

"You don't?" Riggleman sneered. "Then hand over the passenger list."

"Why would I have a passenger list?"

"You're the conductor and the conductor takes the tickets for all the passengers, right?"

"Right, except for the fact that I'm not the conductor."

"Then why are you dressed like one?"

"I'm acting as a conductor."

"I don't care if you're just an acting conductor, you're still responsible for knowing who the passengers are on this train just like a permanent conductor."

"No, I'm an actor playing the part of a conductor."

"You expect me to believe that you're pretending to be the conductor?"

"I'm not pretending, I'm playing a role in a melodrama. Actually, it's more like a mini melodrama."

"So, you're play acting, is that it?"

"I'm a professional actor in a play."

"By yourself?"

"No, there's another actor, Zelda Zenn. I guess you could call her the leading lady. She plays a Harvey Girl."

"Who's Harvey?"

"Harvey is the name of a chain of restaurants that used to be at train stations a long time ago. Like I said, she's just playing a part, she's not a real Harvey Girl just like I'm not a real conductor."

Riggleman points his right index finger in Max's face and asks, "Where's this Zenn woman now?"

"She took off when you and your gang..."

"It's not a gang, it's a posse."

"What's the difference?"

"A gang is, well, hell," Riggleman said dropping his right hand in exasperation. "Anyway, we didn't attack the train."

"What do you call it then?"

"Detaining it because of suspicious activity."

"What suspicious activity?"

"That this train is being used to smuggle illegal immigrants into Purgatory County."

"And you know that for a fact?"

"If we knew it for a fact it wouldn't be suspicious. When we catch the illegals and those helping them then it will be a fact."

"In any case, Zelda thought you were a gang that was attacking the train, so she took off."

"In other words, she fled the scene of a crime."

"She thought you were the ones committing a crime by robbing the train and she was just escaping, so we weren't committing a crime."

"Not you, them...the illegals. They're involved in a criminal enterprise."

"Well, my business is show business so I don't know anything about a criminal enterprise."

"Okay, you didn't know you were aiding a bunch of criminals," Riggleman said, scribbling in a small spiral notebook he held in his left hand. "Now, this Zelda, when she made her getaway where do you think she went?"

Max shrugged, "Maybe she jumped on one of your horses and rode off."

"You know they used to hang people for stealing a horse."

"I was just kidding."

"Kidding an officer of the law could be seen as obstruction of justice, which is a crime."

Max looked at the ceiling of the Pullman car and sighed, "Oh, jeez..."

"Now you're swearing."

"I'm not swearing."

"Using the Lord's name in vain is the same thing."

"Is that against the law, too?"

"It's one of the Ten Commandments in case you didn't know."

"Of course, I know what the Ten Commandments are, I'm Jewish and the Jews had them before anyone else."

"That also means you've had more time to break them."

"You know, Sheriff, I think what we've got here is a failure to communicate."

"So now you're playing Paul Newman in *Cool Hand Luke*?"

"Actually, the line in the movie was delivered by the character Strother Martin was playing, not Paul Newman who was playing Luke."

"Oh yeah, I remember, now. You know, my favorite scene is when Paul Newman ate all those hard-boiled eggs that made his stomach swell up like he was nine months pregnant. I'm more a John Wayne fan but that was some pretty good acting."

"I like Wayne in *The Searchers*. He did his best work when John Ford was directing him. You can't have good acting without a good director. Of course, I might be a bit biased since I'm a director."

"You're a director as well as a conductor."

"I told you I'm not the conductor. I'm doing this as a favor to Tony Medrano. My full-time job is artistic director for the Bard Wired Players and I direct most of their plays. In fact, I'm directing the new play by Howdy Hanks."

"I heard Howdy was back in town. What's this play of his about?"

"It draws on his experiences growing up in Picketwire."

"Does he mention me? He and I grew up here at the same time."

"I'm afraid I can't tell you anything more than that," Max replied. "Howdy wants the details of the play to remain secret until it's presented."

Riggleman waved the steno pad at Max and demanded, "If there's stuff in there about me I have a right to know what it is."

"Then I guess you'll have to see the play."

"What do you mean I have to wait to see the damn play?" Riggleman snarled.

Fortunately, Max was saved from answering by the train whistle.

Riggleman jerked his head. "Why did the train whistle blow?"

"It's signaling that the train is about to start moving," Tony Medrano answered from behind them.

Riggleman turned around to face Tony, "I didn't give my permission to move the damn scene of the crime, Medrano."

"I did," Tony answered. "We're already behind schedule."

Riggleman turned back to Max and said, "You can't just move the scene of a crime even if you are the conductor."

Exasperated, Max replied, "For the last time, I'm not the conductor."

"Is that right, Medrano?" Riggleman demanded.

"Like he said, Sheriff, he's not the conductor. Max is an actor pretending to be the conductor and he wouldn't know any of the people who left with Zelda, just like he said."

"And how do you know he doesn't know?"

"Because everyone in this car is a member of my Purple Sage tour and none of them are from this area so Max would never have met them before."

"Since it's your tour, Medrano, you tell me who's missing."

"Sheriff, the horses are missing!" a sheriff's deputy shouted from the open door to the platform.

"Horses? What the hell are you talking about?"

"All the horses are gone."

Riggleman quickly ran out onto the back platform with Tony and Max following him. Stopping at the railing he exclaimed, "What the hell happened?"

"I don't know, Sheriff. The train whistle spooked them, and they got loose and took off."

"Well, go find them and bring them back."

"They could be miles away by now."

"Then call dispatch and tell them to send out a couple of patrol cars to come and pick us up."

"There's no cell service here," the deputy answered.

"Well, damn to high hell!" Riggleman cursed then turned back to Max and Tony. "We'll just have to take this train into Picketwire."

"No problem, Sheriff," Max answered, repressing the urge to flash Sal's sardonic smile. "All you have to do is buy tickets."

CHAPTER TWENTY FIVE

This time she wasn't meeting Wylie on his home turf. The last time Jemma Lu saw him it was at the Double B. They had been dating for six months and she was expecting a proposal. What she got sounded like a business proposition for a merger rather than a marriage. The veil was lifted from her eyes, but it wasn't the bridal one. They argued and then she left, refusing Wylie's offer to drive her home. He had picked her up in the same candy apple red '57 Chevy he'd driven when they were in Picketwire High School. She realized that it was probably the only thing in his life that he would really cherish until death did they part.

Why had she ever started dating him much less think it would lead to marriage? She didn't want to spend another minute with him or his beloved Chevy and asked to use the phone to call someone to pick her up. Jemma Lu knew when she called Howdy that she wasn't burning the bridge between her and

Wylie, rather she was blowing it up. As she rode off on Howdy's motorcycle she could hear Wylie shouting at her but his words were lost in the roar of the engine and the rush of the wind.

Thirty years later Jemma Lu was prepared for Wylie. He wanted something from her and she was pretty certain it was more than wanting FREDx to include some "big idea" of his. Through the window of the first floor parlor of the Tuttle Mansion she saw the candy apple red '57 Chevy pull up. Behind it was a black Suburban with dark tinted windows. Jemma Lu had told him that she didn't want his bodyguards inside the Tuttle Mansion and the doors of the Suburban remained closed as Wylie got out of the Chevy and walked toward the front porch.

Jemma Lu turned away from the window. She didn't want him to see her watching. The front door opened and closed, there were footsteps in the hall. Jemma didn't get up from the Louis XVI chair that faced a French mahogany love seat. They were both antiques and upholstered in a soft pinkish-blue floral pattern that she knew would annoy Wylie. The chair she sat in was one of a pair but she had moved the other one out of the parlor for her meeting. She would have preferred the large couch instead of the love seat, but she would have been unable to move it without scratching the floors. As she surveyed the arrangement Jemma Lu was satisfied that it was the exact opposite of the intimidating masculinity of the Double B ranch house where she had last met Wylie.

Between the chair she sat in and the love seat was an antique French coffee table made of painted chinoiserie with an inlaid black lacquered top. Resting on the lacquer top was a silver tray with a porcelain china tea service and a plate of lemon tea cookies. She was pretty sure that she had turned the table, in this case one with tea and cookies, on Wylie. The footsteps stopped. Jemma Lu looked up at the parlor entrance, whose pocket doors she had slid back and left open. Wylie stood in the doorway. He was wearing jeans, a blue blazer and an open collared white western shirt with pearl buttons. The brown cowboy boots he was wearing added a couple of extra inches to his already six foot plus height. He was still handsome and he knew it. Her heart didn't flutter.

"I see that you're back on your feet after that run-in with a minivan in Aspen."

"You know what they say, it's hard to keep a good man down," Wylie replied in a voice that for Jemma Lu came across as a frayed attempt to sound off the cuff.

"That may be true for good men but what about you?"

"Same old Jemma Lu."

"Old but not the same, Wylie."

Wylie started to laugh but cut it off when she didn't join in. He looked around, noticed that she was sitting in the only chair and walked over to the love seat. She noticed that he had a slight limp as he walked and grasped the right arm of the love seat to steady himself as he sat down at one end. When he realized that Jemma Lu wasn't going to get up and join him on the love seat, he shifted toward the center and said, "You're as beautiful as I remember, Jemma Lu."

"That probably says more about your bad memory than my good looks, Wylie."

"I haven't forgotten, Jemma Lu."

Jemma Lu, deciding not to follow up on his compliment, bent forward and poured tea into both of the china cups. "It's Darjeeling. Help yourself. There's cream in the silver pitcher and sugar in the bowl," she said taking one of the saucers and cups and sitting back in her chair.

Wylie reached for the other cup with his right hand. Discovering that the handle was too small for his index finger he wrapped his hand around it and took a sip then with a reflexive grimace put it down, sloshing some of the tea in the saucer.

"Is it too strong for you?"

"No, I'm just not that thirsty."

"Then how about one of the cookies?" Jemma Lu asked. "They're homemade lemon tea cookies."

Wylie shook his head, "I'm not much for cookies."

"Really, it must have been someone else I was thinking of who liked cookies," Jemma Lu reached out and picked up a cookie, bit a piece off and, after slowly chewing and swallowing said, "Now, what exactly is this idea of yours?"

"You mean my big idea for FREDx or my idea of making it a condition that you had to meet me?"

"Both."

"Well, the first one is easy, but I can see already that the second one isn't going to be."

"Why, Wylie, I think I'm being ever so polite. This is my best tea set, which belonged to my grandmother, the cookies are from Dolly's Dough bakery, and you have that love seat all to yourself and are sitting in what is considered to be the nicest parlor in all of Picketwire and, possibly, the whole state of Colorado. So, please go ahead."

Wylie clenched and unclenched his fists, exhaled and then replied, "Okay, Jemma Lu, my big idea is to make Picketwire and Purgatory County the cannabis capital of Colorado."

"Cannabis capital," Jemma Lu relied, almost spitting out the tea she'd just sipped. She put her teacup down and said as calmly as possible, "The idea is big, but I guess that's befitting a Boone, and cannabis capital has an alliterative ring, but are you sure you haven't been smoking cannabis, that is marijuana, or, as we used to say, pot, because it sounds like more of a pipe dream than a big idea."

"Before you laugh it off, Jemma Lu, I'm not finished so hear me out." Wylie had moved to the edge of the love seat and was leaning toward her. "Picketwire and Purgatory County will be known for its marijuana just like Rocky Ford is for its melons."

"From what I know about farming, there's a big difference between growing melons and growing marijuana."

"The money you make from growing both is the same except you can make a hell of lot more of it growing marijuana."

"Wylie, what do you know about growing marijuana or anything except beef? The Boones have always been ranchers not farmers."

"The ranch," he spat out the word, "has been losing money ever since I left Picketwire. If it were one of my other businesses I would have sold it a long time ago."

"What's stopping you?"

Wylie shifted uncomfortably, "I suppose it's the sentimental value."

Jemma Lu shook her head, "Sentimental value?"

"Okay, it also has some value as a tax write-off."

"Tax write-off. Now that's the Wylie I remember."

"Really?" Wylie blurted and then stopped, looked down at his hands, which had moved from clenching to clutching his knees. He took a deep breath, looked up at Jemma Lu and said, "But to get back to my point, Jemma Lu..."

"Yes, your big idea. Please," Jemma Lu said then picked up her teacup, easily slipping her right index finger through the handle, and took a sip.

"When cannabis was legalized in Colorado I started thinking that I might be able to turn the ranch into more than a tax write-off. Something that would expand the Double B brand to include more than beef. I've been working on this for a while under the radar. I've invested millions. I hired a whole herd of experts and crossbred cannabis plants just like cattle to come up with the best breed. Those small growers who got the law passed to legalize cannabis aren't going to be able to compete with the big money and I've got plenty of that."

"And that's your big idea?"

"No, Jemma Lu, there's more. The second part is distribution – how to sell it. That's where Picketware comes in."

"Picketware?"

Wylie nodded. "Picketware is nationally known, even internationally, for selling only the highest quality, locally made products and that's exactly what this is."

"Picketware products aren't just made locally, the companies that make them are locally owned."

"Why Jemma Lu," Wylie said with a bit of hurt in his voice. "The Boones are among the founders of Picketwire. The Double B is the biggest ranch in Purgatory County. You can't get more locally owned than that."

Jemma Lu set her teacup down again, "The past thirty years you've been an absentee owner, Wylie. From what I've heard you have a lot of homes all over the world but the Double B isn't one of them. I don't call that local."

"That's not my fault, Jemma Lu, and you know it. I wouldn't have left Picketwire if you had agreed to marry me."

"You wanted Picketware more than me, Wylie."

"Now, that's not true."

"Okay, maybe just as much rather than more. Not that I was completely surprised."

"So why did you ever agree to go out with me? We dated for almost a year…"

"Half a year."

"Okay, but it seemed longer, and we also…I mean you haven't forgotten that we…"

"No, haven't forgotten, but it all happened a long time ago. We were younger."

"We weren't teenagers, Jemma Lu. We'd known each other our whole lives."

"Which is why I should have known better than to ever get involved with you. I had turned thirty and maybe I just wanted to start a family and you kept asking me out. You wore me down, Wylie," Jemma Lu looked into her empty teacup. There was a single leaf at the bottom. "But I came to my senses."

Wylie shook his head. "Now look at us. Neither of us is married. Neither of us has kids, has an heir."

"Are you sure about that, Wylie?"

"Sure? Just ask my ex-wives."

"You don't have to be married to have a child."

"Are you talking about that rumor about me and Pam Martindale back in high school when she and I dated?"

"You know I'm not one for rumors, Wylie. I'm just saying that you've been around and a man wouldn't necessarily know the result of his, his…"

"Screwing around."

"I was trying to find a more polite way of saying it, Wylie."

"Then I apologize for not being polite in the nicest parlor in Picketwire…and, possibly, the entire state of Colorado, but look, Jemma Lu, if you've got some sort of point you want to make just tell me straight."

"My point is that while I don't know about your heirs, mine are Picketware's employees."

Wylie sat back, stunned, then recovered and said, "Well, if you're thinking of giving them some stock in the company then it's all the more reason you should agree to go with my idea, Jemma Lu. The value of Picketware will soar and your employees stand to make a lot more money from any stock they have. And as for local ownership, I've moved back and I'm living at the Double B full time. In fact, I'd like nothing better than to have you come over. How about right now? I've got the old Chevy right outside."

"The last time I was at the Double B it didn't end very well."

"This time it can have a happy ending."

Jemma Lu rose from her chair and looked down at Wylie, "Well, Wylie, I've heard your idea."

Wylie slowly got up from the love seat and looked at her from across the coffee table. "And what's your decision? Yes or no?"

"The agreement was that I would meet with you alone, hear your idea and decide whether it should be included in FREDx. In return you will cover the expenses for FREDx and provide twenty five thousand dollars for prize money."

"That's the agreement. I'll certainly live up to my side of it." He pulled a check from the inside breast pocket of his blazer and showed it to her. "This is for fifty thousand – twenty five for the prize money and another twenty five toward the expenses. If the expenses are more than that I'll pay the balance. I lived up to my side, now, what's your decision?"

"And I lived up to it on my side, which doesn't include me telling you what I decided. You'll hear from Rich Best whether your idea will be part of FREDx. You can leave the check on the tray."

"I guess that means you're turning down my invitation," Wylie said, dropping the check on the tray. "You know that I don't take no for an answer."

"You did thirty years ago."

Wylie walked out of the parlor with Jemma Lu following him, several feet behind. He opened the front door and then said, "About taking no for an answer, you must not have heard what I shouted at you when you were riding off with Howdy Hanks' on his motorcycle."

"What did you say?"

Wylie didn't answer, he just turned and walked out.

CHAPTER TWENTY SIX

Hot off the press and right into a burning ring of fire. Just a couple of hours after the *Picketwire Press* published their exclusive interview with Wylie Boone it was picked up by the wire services, and shortly after that Tom got his first call from another newspaper. In a few hours he had fielded calls from media outlets from all over: not just all over the state of Colorado, and not just all over the country, but from all over the world. And not just print, but television, radio, and internet news sites. Not to mention the bloggers and tweeters.

"I'll get back to you," Tom said and hung up the phone on his desk.

"Who was that?" Gloria asked. She had just come back to the office and was standing by his desk. Other than her and Tom, no one else was in the office.

"He said he was a news curator," Tom answered looking up at Gloria. "I thought curators just worked in museums but he told me that a news curator takes news stories from news outlets and puts them into a thematic collection that can be published online. He wanted to collect our stories on Wylie Boone for a news feed, which is called, get this," Tom looked down at his handwritten notes, "Boone Buzz."

"I've heard of Boone Buzz. I came across it when I did an internet search on Boone as part my background research. "

"Did it have any good stuff?"

"Let's say it had stuff and leave it that," she shook her head. "Amazing the stuff that is posted online that no newspaper in its right mind would publish."

"You mean all the news that's unfit to print?"

Gloria grimaced, "Like having to eat a jumbo box of stale popcorn in order to find a kernel of truth."

"Speaking of which, were you able to get anything truthful from Riggleman?"

Gloria shook her head slowly, "That name sure suits him because he sure knows how to wriggle out of giving a straight answer to a question." She opened her notebook. "When I asked him if he was worried that the person who tried to kill Boone might try it again his answer was, quote, 'if they tangle with me, I'll have their hide.' What does that mean?"

"It's a line from John Wayne in the movie *Horse Soldiers*," Foster St. Vrain said. He'd entered the office while Gloria and Tom were talking.

Gloria rolled her eyes. "Thanks, Foster, I'll put in my story that Sheriff Riggleman's response is actually a quote from John Wayne."

"Is there anything from the interview that is news?" Tom asked.

"Nothing concerning Boone. What he really wanted to talk about was undocumented immigrants from Mexico that he calls illegals invading the county. He also said that these so-called 'illegals' include lots of violent criminals."

"Did he offer any evidence to back up his claim?" Tom asked. "Not that a lack of evidence ever stopped him from arresting people."

"He said he and his 'Posse'..."

"You mean the gang that can't ride straight?" Foster drawled. He had settled into a chair, crossed legs on the desk in front of him, his boots resting on the blotter, and hands clasped behind the back of his neck.

"Whatever," Gloria answered and then continued. "He said they had just intercepted a bunch of what he called 'illegals' who were entering the county on the Picketwire Railroad. They were, according to him, disguised as members of one of Tony Medrano's tours. He also said that Max Bergmann was there and that he was also in a disguise...as the conductor." Gloria looked up from her notes and added. "He refused to elaborate on what he meant by that."

Tom leaned back and laughed, "Max was working for Tony. He was playing the part of Clem the conductor on this new tour of Tony's called Rails, Trails, and Tales."

"How do you know that?" Gloria asked.

"Tony sent me a press release announcing his Trails and Tales tour and I included it in the Round Up section of the paper a few weeks ago."

"I guess I missed it. Sorry. I really do try to read every single word that's in each edition of the paper."

"Then you read more of it than I do," Tom replied. "Anyway, getting back to your interview, did the sheriff tell you what proof he had that these illegals, as he calls them, who he arrested on the train were actually violent criminals?"

"No, because he didn't arrest anybody. He says they got away before he could apprehend them."

"You mean he actually admitted that these desperados managed to escape him and his posse?" Foster asked.

"Riggleman said they jumped off the train and escaped before he could board it. He claims that they had accomplices who helped them get away, otherwise he would have caught them."

"Did he offer anything to back up this claim that there were accomplices?" Tom asked.

"He said he had no further comments on the accomplices at this time. He did say that their horses were spooked and ran off so they were unable to pursue the illegals."

Foster unclasped his hands. "Did he actually see these, again to use his words, illegals that he claims are violent criminals?"

"No but he's sure he'll, quote, 'have them rounded up and behind bars in no time so they won't be able to prey on the good, law abiding, citizens of Purgatory County.' I guess I should check to see if that's also from a John Wayne movie. I'm going to ask Tony for his version of what happened."

"You mean, the true version," Foster said pulling his legs from the desk and letting his boots hit the floor with a thump.

"I'll do it, you stick with the Boone story," Tom said, picking up the phone. The person who answered the phone at Purple Sage Tours said Tony was out of the office and they didn't know when he would return. Although the next person to call would be Max Bergmann, Tom hesitated for a moment. Even though he'd attended most of the plays performed by the Bard Wire Players he wasn't exactly a fan. Despite his best efforts he always dozed off during the performances although he was pretty sure no one noticed since he managed to keep his head upright and not snore. He also made a point of attending on opening night so he could sit next to Eleanor Perceval, the *Picketwire Press*'s theater critic. Eleanor, who was also a professor of fine arts at Picketwire College would not only nudge him awake as the final curtain came down but fill him in on what he missed so that he could reply intelligently when people asked him what he thought. She joked that this not only saved Tom from embarrassment but also from having to read her review, which, in fact, it did.

Instead of Max, his voicemail picked up. There was a lengthy message from Max in a dramatic voice informing the caller that

Mr. Bergmann was unavailable because he was at the rehearsal for the new play he was directing, by the world-renowned playwright, Howdy Hanks. Tom hung up as the message continued with details on the date of the world premiere and how to go about purchasing tickets. Tom knew that rehearsals were being held in the sanctuary of the Picketwire Community Church and decided to walk over since it was nearby.

Five minutes later Tom was at the church. The door to the sanctuary was closed with a note taped on it stating that there was no admittance during rehearsals. Hoping there might be a break when he would be able to talk to Max, Tom sat down on a bench in the narthex. As he waited he noticed the stack of church newsletters and picked one up. On the front was a story about Jane, which made him feel guilty that he had avoided her, including sneaking out at the end of the service when she preached her first sermon. Then he started worrying that she might walk in on him sitting there and he'd have to talk to her. He put the newsletter back in the stack, looked at his watch and decided to leave. As he got up the door to the sanctuary suddenly opened and Max appeared.

"What are you doing here, Tom?" Max demanded, "The rehearsal is closed to the press."

"Don't worry, I didn't go inside. I've been waiting out here."

"What for?"

"To talk to you."

Max relaxed his face, "Ah, you want a story. Sorry to disappoint the press but as much as I want to, I can't tell you anything about the play because Howdy wants to keep it a secret until it opens.”

"It's not about the play.”

"It's not?”

"I mean the play is really big news, don't get me wrong, but what I want to talk to you about is what happened when you were performing on the train yesterday as part of Tony Medrano's tour. Gloria Herrera, one of our reporters interviewed the sheriff about something else and he claimed that he had stopped the train searching for illegal immigrants and that you were playing the part of a conductor.”

"Clem the conductor. I also wrote the script and directed it. It was in the old melodrama style that was popular in the nineteenth century, especially in the Old West. I had to do quite a bit of research to make sure it was authentic.”

"Right,” Tom said, cutting Max off. "But what I'm interested in is that Riggleman told Gloria there were illegal immigrants on the train but that they had escaped. The sheriff refused to go into any detail but since you were there, I thought you might be able to tell me what took place.”

Max opened his mouth and then closed it, bit his lip and furrowed his brows and then answered, "As much as I would like to be quoted in the paper – not for me personally, of course, but for the positive publicity it gives to the Bard Wired Players – in this case I really don't want my name in the paper. I've been told that the sheriff can be vindictive.”

"I'm afraid you're right." Tom nodded. "But look, I don't need to name you; you can be an anonymous source."

Max smiled. "You mean, like deep throat in *All The President's Men*?"

"Sort of like that."

"And you're playing Woodward."

"I'm not exactly Robert Redford," Tom stammered.

"Neither was Woodward. That's what we call theatrical license. Of course, being a journalist, you want just the facts."

"Whatever you can recollect will be great."

"Then, what I recollect is that Sheriff Riggleman and his posse stopped the train just when we were reaching the dramatic climax of our performance. The actor who was playing the part of Clementine..."

"A man was playing a woman's part?"

"Whatever gave you that idea?"

"You said actor not actress."

Max sighed, "We don't call women actresses in the theater anymore. Everyone who acts, whether they are male, female or whatever combination they choose, is an actor."

"Isn't that confusing?"

"No more confusing than women journalists being called reporters rather than reportresses."

"Right. Sorry I interrupted."

"As I was saying, the actor playing Clementine came running from the back of the observation car, which is the last car in the train and has one of those platforms at the rear."

"I know, I wrote a story about riding on it for its inaugural run after it had been restored. Sorry for interrupting again."

"Yes, well, to continue," Max said, "she, the actor I mentioned, was yelling that there was a gang on horseback chasing us. Of course, she couldn't have known that it was the sheriff and his posse and not train robbers. She ran past me to the front of the car. Several other passengers leapt from their seats and followed her. She did give quite a convincing performance."

"But she wasn't performing if she thought the sheriff and his posse really were bank robbers."

"That doesn't mean she wasn't acting. All the world's a stage, so why not a train."

"Isn't all the world's a stage from Shakespeare?"

"*As You Like It*, Act Two, Scene Seven. You no doubt remember those words from the production that we staged last year."

"Of course," Tom said. "It was very moving."

"It's a comedy – you're supposed to laugh."

"I was moved to laughter is what I meant," Tom replied. "But getting back to what happened on the train, what did your actor and the three passengers do next?"

"It seems that they all jumped off the train."

"They jumped off a moving train?"

"No, the train had come to a stop. Someone had pulled the emergency cord and since it wasn't going very fast to begin with it stopped pretty quickly."

"Then what happened?"

"Sheriff Riggleman came aboard and walked down the aisle. Actually, he strutted like he wanted everyone to think he was John Wayne. He stopped when he got to me and demanded to know where the illegals were. It seems that he actually thought I was a real conductor instead of an actor. If he weren't such a dunce, I would be flattered that my performance was so convincing that he didn't realize I was an actor. Like your reporter told you, he had some crazy idea they were illegal immigrants. He seemed to think the Picketwire Railroad was the underground railroad."

"He didn't find the passengers who jumped off the train from what I understand."

"That's right, he and his posse couldn't find them near the train and they weren't able to continue their search because their horses had escaped as well. Apparently, the train whistle scared them off. Since there was no cell service where we were, he wasn't able to contact anyone to pick up him and his posse so they had to ride back to Picketwire with us. I don't know what happened to the passengers who ran off."

"What about the actor who played Clementine?"

"What about her?"

"What happened to her?"

"I don't know. She got here just in time for the start of rehearsal. All she said was that some guy she knows from high school was driving by and gave her a ride."

"Can I talk to her?"

"You can try but she said that she didn't want to discuss it with anyone. But you'll have to wait until after rehearsal is over, which won't be for another couple of hours. I just called for a short break because one of our actors hasn't shown up. I came out to see if he was sneaking a smoke or a drink before making his appearance."

"I didn't think smoking and drinking were allowed in a church."

"That wouldn't stop this guy. He's turned out to be completely unreliable." Max looked at his watch. "That's it, I've had it with him. I'll just have to cast someone else for the part. The show must go on." He stepped back and sized Tom up, "You look perfect for the part."

"You're kidding. Me? Act? In a play?" Tom stammered.

"Nothing to it. This isn't a lead or anything. You only have to deliver a few lines. You just need to look the part and you're about the right age for the character, who is a senior in high school."

"But I graduated from Picketwire High more than ten years ago."

"That's closer than thirty years, which is how long it's been for Larry, the guy I just fired. You can only do so much with make-up. Also, he couldn't remember his lines even when he did show up. You, on the other hand..."

"No way," Tom interrupted, holding up both of his hands in protest.

"Look, you said you wanted to talk to Zelda, right?"

"Who's Zelda?"

"Zelda Zenn is the actor who plays Clementine. That's her stage name, by the way."

"Yeah. But..."

"Well, this is your chance. We're about to rehearse a scene with her and the character you play. You can read your lines from the script."

"But that's acting not interviewing."

"Don't you see, you'll gain her trust and she'll agree to tell you everything. I think she has some very valuable information that will help you. It'll be a scoop. Come on, just try it out. No commitment although I'm a pretty damn good judge of talent and I think you've really got something, Tom."

"I do?"

"You may not believe this, but when we were doing our interview just now it felt like we were doing a scene together. It was like you really were Robert Redford playing Woodward." He poked Tom in the chest with his right index finger, "There's an actor inside you just waiting to get on stage."

Before Tom could reply, Max grabbed him by the arm and opened the door. To Tom's amazement he didn't resist and followed Max inside the sanctuary as if he was being called by some higher power.

CHAPTER TWENTY SEVEN

"Two riders were approaching and the wind began to howl," Sister M's listened to the last verse of Bob Dylan's "All Along the Watchtower" trail off into silence. She loved the song, and for many years she listened to the Jimi Hendrix version with his soaring guitar riffs. However that version had been replaced by the one Sister Rosalie and Sister Wendy performed under the name The Lost Souls Sisters. Sister Rosalie's voice transformed the lyrics into a soulful prayer and Sister Wendy's fiddle solo at the end was a veritable transubstantiation.

Sister M's turned off the ancient Sony Walkman, removed the headphones and placed them in the backpack that served as her briefcase. This was followed by the legal pad that she'd been scribbling on. Then she turned off the computer that she'd been using for the last several hours, engaged in one of her least favorite activities, legal research. At least with free online sites like Google Scholar she didn't have to wade through volumes of law books. She looked around at the room she was in. It had once been the prison library. When they took over it was filled with books and the largest section was devoted to law. In fact, when she had examined the books it was apparent that they had been some of the most popular volumes in the library. She couldn't help wondering how many jailhouse lawyers had sat where she was now, scouring the dusty pages of legal statutes, criminal code, and case law for something that would get them out. In comparison, the law books she had added from her own small library seemed pristine.

"Tony Medrano is here to see you," Sister Sylvia announced. She looked at Sister M's from her seat at the librarian's desk, cradling the receiver of the old black rotary phone that served as an intercom.

"Tell him I'm on my way," Sister M's answered, getting up from the library table.

After conveying the message and hanging up, Sister Sylvia asked, "Have you chosen the book you are going to read at supper?"

"I haven't decided yet."

"You don't have much time."

I would if you hadn't picked a novella to read, Sister M's was tempted to respond. "I suppose you wouldn't consider stretching out *Heart of Darkness* a bit, would you? I mean, it's such a great work that it's a shame not to allow every word to sink in."

"Well, I suppose I could go a bit slower to allow everyone to reflect more fully on what Conrad has written. I chose it because I thought we might benefit from something a bit deeper to digest as we ate our supper."

"I agree. Although I think that Sister Rachel did a very good job with her reading of *Bridget Jones's Diary*."

"It was entertaining, I'll grant you that," Sister Sylvia replied then turned her attention back to the papers on her desk, not even trying to hide the smile on her face.

***

When Sister M's entered the Welcome Center she found Tony Medrano standing next to a map on one of the walls. "Good afternoon, Sister M's. I was just looking at this old map of the area that you have on display. I guess I hadn't really noticed it before."

"That's because I just put it up this morning," Sister Louise chirped from behind the counter. "Sister Beatrice spent some time studying the original. As you know, being an archaeologist, she supervises all the restoration and preservation work here. Anyway, Sister Beatrice was very excited about the discovery, but she didn't want to display a copy until she was certain that the original was authentic. She said it was in excellent shape considering its age so not much preservation work was required. Of course, the original is safely stored in the archives."

"Where did you find it?"

"If you can believe it, we discovered it hidden under the floor in one of the cells that was undergoing restoration. When Sister Beatrice and Sister Melody, who is also a carpenter, pulled up the old floors, they found it. There's a little bit of space between the wood planks and the stone underneath. Fortunately, it had been wrapped in cowhide and with the dry air it somehow survived."

"How the heck did it end up there?"

"Considering who occupied the cells, we think it's highly likely that it was some inmate's ill-gotten gain, although who they stole it from and why they thought it was so valuable they would risk smuggling it into prison with them is anyone's guess," Sister Louise said, walking over to where Tony and Sister M's were standing. "Something must have prevented them from smuggling it out with them after they had served their time."

"Do you mind if I take a photo of it?"

"Go ahead, but you can buy your own copy." Sister Louise pointed to the price sticker for $4.99 affixed to the frame. "That price is without the frame, which would add ten dollars to the price."

"I'll skip the frame, Tony said then took out his wallet and handed Sister Louise a five dollar bill, adding that she could keep the change.

Sister Louise reached under the counter and took out a copy of the map, rolled it up, fastened a rubber band around it and handed it to Tony.

"Thanks. This could really be helpful with some research I'm doing," Tony said then turned to Sister M's. "Sorry for this unexpected visit, but I need to talk to you about something that's just come up."

"As a matter of fact, I need an excuse to get away from the legal research I'm doing."

"In that case, I think this will be a pretty good excuse: Sheriff Riggleman brought Donny Buford in for questioning."

"Who's Donny Buford?"

"Donny's the kid who gave Zelda and our visitors a ride in his pickup after they escaped from the train."

"Oh, that Donny. Zelda didn't mention his last name. Did he tell the sheriff that he dropped them off here? I mean, I wouldn't want him to lie."

"He refused to answer the sheriff's questions."

Surprised, Sister M's asked, "How do you know?"

"Zelda told me. She said that Donny called her when the sheriff pulled up in front of his house. Zelda told him not to say anything without his lawyer present."

"Who's his lawyer?"

"You are," Tony replied. "I mean Zelda told him that you were her lawyer so she didn't think you'd mind being his as well."

"Where's Donny now?"

"At the sheriff's department. That's where they took him for questioning. When he told them he wouldn't talk without his lawyer present they informed him that he could make one call. The problem is, Zelda didn't give him your name or phone number. Anyway, Donny called Zelda again and told her he needed his lawyer, so she called me and asked me if I could pick you up and take you to the sheriff's department and, well…"

"Well," Sister M's said, interrupting Tony in mid-stammer. "We should get going and save my new client from Riggleman's ham-fisted version of the arm of the law."

CHAPTER TWENTY EIGHT

Bruce looked at Jane from the corner of his eye as he steered their blue Subaru Forester that he had bought when they moved to Picketwire. He had discovered that driving could be relaxing rather than nerve-wracking when you didn't have to dodge and weave through New York City traffic with one foot on the gas and one on the brake. You could use cruise control out here because you were actually cruising. It also gave him a chance to think about something other than avoiding a fender bender. "This is exciting," he said.

Jane turned and looked at him with surprise. "You're excited about meeting my uncle?"

"What I mean is it's exciting to be involved in trying to solve a mystery, maybe even a crime, and your uncle could provide us with some important clues."

"We're not detectives, Bruce."

"Speak for yourself, Honey. Being a detective might be my true calling."

Jane laughed, "Your calling?"

"Don't laugh," Bruce said, stifling his own. "If you were called to be a minister why can't I be called to be a detective? We could be a team. I catch the sinners and you save them."

"We are already a team," Jane answered. "It's called being married."

Bruce stared at the road ahead and muttered. "I need to do something other than, you know..."

"What did you just mumble?"

"Fulfill my husbandly duties."

"You mean you're doing it out of a sense of duty?"

"No, I mean...," Bruce glanced at her and saw the teasing smile on her face. "Okay, so we can scratch off detective as my next career."

"I want you to do what makes you happy, fulfills you."

"Before I met you I didn't even think about it."

"So, you were happy until you met me, is that what you're saying?"

"Happy? No, what I mean is that I didn't know what happiness was until I met you so I didn't think about it." He slid his right hand off the steering wheel and onto her left thigh. "Did I ever thank you for saving a wretch like me?"

"I didn't save you, I married you," Jane said, giving Bruce a gentle punch on his right arm.

"You being a reverend, I thought it was the same thing. A twofer. Although, if I were a rabbi it would be like hitting the trifecta."

"Silly."

"You mean me being a rabbi?" he asked, sounding hurt.

"I mean I didn't decide to become a minister until after we got married."

"In other words, getting married to me drove you to God."

"Drove me to God!" Jane finally exploded in laughter. There, she thought, you won again. If bantering were an Olympic event, Bruce would have a string of gold medals dangling from his neck.

"Did I say God? What I meant was drove you to your Uncle Joji's." Bruce hunched over the steering wheel and peered out through the windshield as if they were driving in the dead of night rather than the middle of a sunny afternoon. It was an unsuccessful attempt to conceal the victory grin on his lips. "How much farther do we have to go?"

"We should be close."

"Does anything look familiar?"

"Not particularly," Jane replied as she gazed out the side window at the mix of pasture and prairie. "I remember visiting when my grandparents lived here before my grandfather died. I only saw Uncle Joji a few times when he visited my grandparents. I was just a kid. After my grandfather died and grandma moved in with us my dad would drive her here to see Uncle Joji but I was never invited to go along. The only time I saw him after he moved back from Japan and into the house was at my grandmother's funeral."

"You said there was some sort of falling out between your uncle and the rest of the family. You don't know what it was about?"

"My parents never wanted to discuss it."

"I guess it was a good thing you called first to see if he would agree to see you."

"I didn't think we should just show up at his doorstep."

"You said that he didn't seem to object to us wanting to see him."

It was like he expected her to want to come by for a visit even though they hadn't seen each other in years. "No, and when I asked him if he could translate something from Japanese into English he said of course."

"Does he know that I'm going to be with you?"

"Yes. He asked if I was coming by myself and I told him you would be with me."

"What was his response?"

"He said good."

"Do you think he meant it was good that it wasn't his brother, your father, or it was good that it was me, your husband?"

"I'm sure he meant it was good that you were coming with me because he wanted to meet you, not that he wanted to avoid seeing my dad," Jane replied.

"I just hope he isn't disappointed when he meets me."

"Why on earth would he be disappointed?" She didn't understand how Bruce, a man who could invest millions of dollars without a second thought, could be so nervous about meeting her uncle.

"He might not be happy when he asks what I do and I tell him I don't have a job. He might think that I'm just a moocher."

"Like you married me so you could get your hands on my measly minister's salary," Jane laughed. "You get more interest from your savings account than I'll ever make."

"Our savings account, not mine," Bruce replied, firmly. "Remember, I turned you down when you offered to sign a prenuptial agreement, remember? And it's not in a savings account, anyway. It's invested. Wisely, I might add. But no one knows about that except you and me."

"And I wish I didn't know."

"Because you feel guilty about it. You had nothing to do with it. I made it all before I met you." He paused. They weren't bantering now. "Think of it as an inheritance from my past life. It's like a nest egg."

"If that's what it's like then it was a really big bird that laid the egg,"

"How do you know? I thought you didn't look at our investment portfolio."

"I don't look at it. You told me your net worth when we were having coffee at Starbucks."

"When I took you out on our first date," he smiled at the memory.

"I didn't know it was a date and I insisted on paying for my coffee, which was actually a chai tea. The point is that you were trying to impress me by telling me how much you were worth."

"Right, I was," Bruce nodded. "And I could tell right away that I'd made a big mistake."

"I was going to get up and walk out but you wouldn't shut up and I didn't have a chance to tell you I was going to leave. Instead, I had to sit there and listen to you. Fortunately, you said you wanted to change the direction of your life and do something completely different that had nothing to do with making money."

"And that's why you agreed to go out with me," he replied, never tiring of the story.

"I also thought there was a pretty good chance that you were just feeding me a line."

"And all this time I thought you believed me," Bruce sighed.

"I did believe you." But it was a leap of faith, Jane thought.

"And here we are."

"Yes, here we are," Jane answered, smiling at Bruce. "together."

"I meant we're here at your Uncle Joji's farm," Bruce said, putting his foot on the brake.

"How do you know?"

"His address was on the mailbox we just passed." Bruce backed the car up and stopped next to the mailbox. Next to the stenciled address were some Japanese characters that had been applied with a black brush. "What does it say?"

"It says Takamoto. I did learn that much Japanese."

"I guess this must be the place, then," Bruce turned the wheel and they drove over a cattle guard and onto the gravel drive. "Is that the farmhouse in those trees?"

"Yes," Jane said. "Although when I was a kid it seemed a lot farther from the main road than it is now."

"Everything is farther away when you're a kid."

***

As they slowly approached the farm buildings Jane looked at the creek and the cottonwoods and then the red barn and the windmill. She looked at the corral near the barn and suddenly remembered riding a horse named Fiddlesticks when she was seven or eight. It was Uncle Joji who must have been visiting from Japan, who had boosted her onto the saddle then got on behind her. He let her hold the reins as they had trotted around the corral. That was the first time she had been on a horse. They had a couple of horses on their farm but her parents said she was too young to ride. She asked Uncle Joji not to tell them. That it was their secret. She never mentioned it to her father and when he taught her how to ride several years later she acted as if she had never been on a horse before.

As they pulled up in front of the farmhouse, Uncle Joji rose from a chair on the front porch and walked down the front steps with the dexterity of a man half his age. In fact, he seemed to have hardly aged since her grandmother's funeral only he was smiling now and wearing faded bib overalls and a white T-shirt.

Jane, hesitated, not sure if she should offer to shake his hand or give him a hug and, if she gave him a hug should she include a peck on the cheek? It reminded her of having to decide what to do when passing the peace at church. You tried to take your cue from the other person but what if they were waiting for you to act first. It was like playing the game rock-paper-scissors. More than once she'd put out her hand at the same time the other person embraced her in a hug. Uncle Joji cut off her thoughts by bowing. With relief Jane returned his bow and then introduced Bruce. When Bruce started to bow, Joji reached out with his right hand. It seemed to Jane that Uncle Joji's face morphed momentarily into a mischievous grin as they shook.

"Have you come for another secret riding lesson, Niece?" Joji asked.

"I know it was wrong of me to have asked you to lie to my dad," Jane answered, surprised that she was still embarrassed after all the years.

"But I didn't lie. I knew when you asked me to keep it a secret that he would never ask me. Now, why don't both of you come inside. It has been a long time since you have been in the house where your father grew up."

Uncle Joji gave them a tour of the house. It was smaller than what Jane remembered. Are walls also farther away when you're a kid she wondered. Upstairs, Uncle Joji opened a door and announced that the room was where her father and he had slept.

Inside, there was a bunk bed, a dresser, and a desk and chair under the one window.

"I remember the bunk beds," Jane said. "I always wanted to sleep in it, but when I stayed over when only my grandmother and grandfather were living here, I slept in one of the beds in Aunt Kate and Aunt Winnie's old room."

Uncle Joji rested his right hand on the upper bunk. "I slept on this one. I was older and so I got to choose first and I took the high ground. When your Dad had grown tall enough for his legs to reach the bottom of the upper bunk he would kick me at night. He claimed he did it because I snored and he wanted me to turn over, but I never heard myself snore so I told him he was just dreaming," He chuckled at the thought and then led them to a room next door that had been where Jane's aunts slept. Instead of a bunk bed there were two single beds separated by large dresser.

"I remember that when I stayed over Aunt Kate and Aunt Winnie's dolls were still here and I loved playing with them. The dolls are gone, but everything else looks the same," Jane said.

"There was no need to change anything except in your grandparent's room, which is where I now sleep." He pushed open a door that was half ajar revealing a room twice as large as the other two. The sun streamed in through several windows. It was empty except for a tatami mat on the hardwood floor. "As you can see, I removed the furniture. I sleep on a futon that I roll up and put in the closet during the day."

"No more upper bunk," Bruce joked.

"Yes, I have come down in the world," Uncle Joji answered with a grin. "Now, we should go downstairs to the kitchen and I can serve you tea."

After Jane and Bruce sat down at the large wooden kitchen table, Uncle Joji began boiling the water. He turned and asked them. "Would you like some botamochi that I made?"

"Oh, yes, please, Uncle!" Jane answered, clapping her hands like a little girl.

"Botamochi?" Bruce asked.

"It's a rice cake, a sweet pastry," Jane said, lowering her hands. "My grandmother made them. I wish I'd asked her to show me how she did it but...."

"Would you like me to give you a secret lesson?" Uncle Joji asked as the kettle began to whistle.

"Yes, that way if I ruin them no one will know," Jane laughed, "especially, this guy." She smiled and nudged Bruce with her left elbow.

"What I want to know is what's with these secret riding lessons?" Bruce asked.

"Uncle is just teasing me about something that happened when I was a little girl. Sorry, Mr. Detective, but it's no big mystery. I'll tell you about it later." Looking at Uncle Joji she asked, "So Grandma taught you how to cook them?"

"No," Uncle Joji said as he poured the hot water from the kettle into a teapot. "I learned when I was in Japan. When I came back and I moved in here I made them for her as a surprise the first time she came over to visit. She said that they were different than hers but she liked them just the same. I could tell she said that just to make me feel good so I asked her if she would show me her way. We made them together right here in this kitchen and I have made them her way ever since."

"Because Grandma's way was better."

"Of course," Uncle Joji answered. Then he placed a bamboo tray with the teapot and round teacups on the table along with, a plate of botamochi that had been warming in the oven. He sat down and poured the tea into the cups and passed them to Jane and Bruce. As he began to pass the plate of botamochi he said, "You said that you wanted me to translate some Japanese words that you found on the side of an old building?"

"Yes," Jane answered. "We almost forgot. Bruce, can you show Uncle Joji."

"We took a picture of the words on my cellphone." Bruce said, putting down the botamochi that Uncle Joji had just passed him and reaching for his iPhone from the breast pocket of his shirt.

"You don't need to show me, it says 'not forgotten.'"

"But, how do you know?" Jane sputtered.

"Because I wrote it."

"Why?"

"My father, your grandfather, told me about the camp when I was fifteen. We were driving on Highway 50 between Lamar and Granada when he told me about what had happened to the Japanese-Americans during the war and that there had been a camp up the road called Amache where Japanese-Americans were sent. It was called an internment camp, but was really a prison. He said he'd visited it when he was a young man. I already knew that he and Japanese-American men were barred from joining the military except for those who were able to volunteer for the 442nd that fought in Europe."

Uncle Joji stopped. Jane could see tears forming in his eyes and he looked away as if to hide them. "I am still ashamed of the memory of being embarrassed when my schoolmates bragged about their fathers serving in the war while my father stayed home and farmed. None of us knew then that my father would not have been allowed to serve in the military, so I lied and said he was 4-F. Now, I realize how fortunate my father and the other Japanese-Americans living here were that they were not put in the camps because they weren't considered to be as great a risk as those who lived on the coast."

Uncle Joji turned and looked at them, his eyes now dry. "My father went on to tell me that Japanese-Americans who lived here were allowed to visit Camp Amache. When he asked the people he met in the camp why there were so few young men he was told that many unmarried young men had been taken to another camp. They were told it was for security reasons. Although the camp was not far away its exact location was supposed to be a secret. However, they knew where it was on the Double B Ranch. They made him promise not to tell anyone because it would make trouble and they feared they might be sent to such a camp as well. My father also said that he still felt guilty that with so many of the young men missing he and his male friends were very popular with the girls in the camp."

"And this has been kept secret all these years?"

Uncle Joji had nodded his head in sadness "Yes, but there is another secret."

"There's more?" Bruce exclaimed. Jane had forgotten he was there.

"Some of the prisoners died and were buried in the Picketwire Cemetery."

"Where?" Jane asked him. "When I was a girl I used to ride out there on my bike and read the headstones and I never came across them."

"They are buried in the southwest corner where they don't even cut the grass. They are not visible unless you are looking for them. The markers look like small stones that have rolled off the prairie. There are no names on them, only dates. When I was young there were stories that there were bodies buried there in unmarked graves. People said that they were murderers who had been hung, crazy people, people who had died in an epidemic and couldn't be buried next to healthy dead people. All sorts of stories.

"One day a couple of my friends and I went to the cemetery to see if the stories were true. We found the markers at the far boundary of the cemetery. The only thing on them were dates in 1942 through 1945. Then I went to the county clerk's office and looked at the death records for those years. There were only a few deaths recorded during that period and those who died and were buried in the cemetery had headstones with their names on them, so the deaths of the people buried in those graves had never been kept secret. When I told my father he said there were rumors that people had died in the other camp and that no one knew what happened to their bodies, he said that the graves in Picketwire Cemetery might be where they were buried. I asked him where the other camp was located and he told me, but he said since it was on the Double B Ranch he'd never seen it. Then he said the best thing to do was to forget about the other camp and the bodies in the cemetery, because it would only stir things up with the Boones."

"You mean you never told anyone, including my dad?"

Uncle Joji shook his head, "I disobeyed my father and told him. Your father had overheard our parents talking about it and he kept asking me so I finally told him the secret. I felt relieved to tell someone. But your dad was still just a child and it disturbed him a great deal. He had nightmares and told our father. Our father was very mad at me for not keeping it a secret. He said it was wrong to burden anyone else with this knowledge. Then he made both me and your dad swear on our honor not to tell anyone." Uncle Joji looked off toward the mountains then said softly, "However, I decided that I needed to do something, so I went to the camp and painted the words not forgotten on the building. When I told your father he was very angry and said that we had given my word to our father not to tell anyone and that it was a great dishonor and I could not be trusted." He paused, and said, "I believe they should not be forgotten and I would do it again."

CHAPTER TWENTY NINE

"You can just let me off here," Sister M's told Tony as they pulled up in front of the Purgatory County Sheriff's Department in Kochia City. The red brick building, which also housed the jail, was attached like a carbuncle to the rear of the Purgatory County Courthouse.

"You have my cell number so just give me a call when you're finished and I'll swing by and pick you up."

"I don't think this will take long."

"You think Riggleman is going to back off and see reason?"

"I don't know about reason but I think he will let Donny go after he sees me," Sister M's replied with a wink and then got out of the pickup.

With time to kill, Tony decided to drive over to the Picketwire Canyonlands Park Headquarters and see if Elise Plumb was in. They were going out on their third date on Friday. For Tony, the third date was a decision point as to whether to be more than 'friends.' Since he and Elise had just been friends for a year before they'd decided to go out on a real 'date' he was feeling that there was even more riding on this third date. He thought that dropping in on her at work might take some of the pressure off.

When he walked in Elise was standing with a couple of tourists in front of a large wall map. Tony looked over the rack of brochures as he listened to her give them a brief history of Picketwire Canyonlands and some of the easier hiking trails. After they left, laden with maps and information pamphlets, Elise turned to Tony and asked, "This isn't Friday is it?"

"What?"

"You know date night, our third date? We're meeting in the Conquistador Lounge at the Picketwire House after work. Did you forget?"

"No, today isn't Friday and no I didn't forget. I just dropped Sister M's off at the county jail and I thought I'd stop by and see if you were in while I'm waiting to drive her back to the convent."

"What's she doing at the jail?"

"She's there to get somebody released."

"Some desperado, I imagine," Elise laughed.

"Not unless you consider Donny Buford a desperado."

"Desperate, maybe, but what teenager isn't. So why was he busted?"

"I guess you could say he was arrested for being in the right place at the right time."

"I didn't know that was against the law."

"It's not, but when did the law stop Riggleman."

"But Sister M's can stop Riggleman."

"You don't think she can?" Tony asked.

"It wasn't a question," Elise said. "I was stating a fact. There's not a shadow of a doubt that she can."

"Anyway, that's why I was in the neighborhood and stopped by so I'm glad you're in."

"I'd rather be out...there as you know," she waved at the map on the wall. "However, Jeanine called in sick and Bob is at an in-service training in Denver and then Ron decided to go on vacation. He went to New York City, of all places. Said he wanted a change of scenery and Dennis, well you know...." She rolled her eyes.

"Yeah, I know," Tony answered, "Dennis the Menace."

"What's that in your hand?" Elise pointed at the rolled up map in Tony's left hand.

"An old map of the area."

"You want to trade it in for a new one because we've got plenty of them."

"No, because this isn't just any old map, either. At least a copy of one, anyway." He peeled off the rubber band that bound it and spread it out on the glass counter.

Elise bent over and looked at it. "It does look old and there's the Rio de las Animas Perdidas en Purgatorio"

"The name is in Spanish, because the map was drawn when this was still part of Mexico."

"Where did you find it?"

"In a gift shop."

She stood up and looked at him as if Tony was pulling her leg. "No really," he insisted. "I saw it on the wall of the Our Lady of Purgatory Gift Shop just an hour ago. Of course, that was a copy, as well."

"Where's the original?" Elise asked.

"The sisters have it. They discovered it while they were renovating one of the prison cells. Sister Beatrice says that it's authentic. You know, she's an archaeologist."

"Of course, I know Sister Beatrice. She's on our archaeological advisory board and she helps out with our Digging for Dinosaurs program every summer. If she says it's authentic then it's quite a find. Is it something you're going to use in your tours?"

"Maybe, but this is more personal. It shows the land granted by Mexico to my family."

"You mean this is the boundary line for the Medrano Land Grant?" Elise said as she followed a line with her right index finger.

"Right," Tony said, pointing at the right corner of the map. "This right here is an official seal next to the signature of Manuel Armijo, who was the governor of New Mexico when it was still part of Mexico. It's dated April 7, 1840. Next to it you can see it says in Spanish that this map shows the land that is granted to Francisco Medrano and his family in perpetuity."

Elise shook her head. "Unfortunately, the 'in perpetuity' ended when the U.S. won the Mexican-American War in 1848."

"Yeah," Tony nodded. "Even though in the Treaty of Guadalupe the U.S. agreed to honor the existing Mexican land grants, the U.S. wasn't really all that committed to honoring the treaty. When the legality of the land grants was challenged, Don Francisco couldn't produce an official map showing the boundaries of the land grant."

"The story I heard was that he lost it."

"In fact, he said it had been stolen. He couldn't prove it and there were people who said that there was never a map and he was lying about it being stolen. Of course, without the map Don Francisco couldn't substantiate the claim. He also couldn't defend the Medrano family honor, which was probably worse than losing the land."

"I thought your family ended up with some of the land and that part of it was donated to establish the town of Picketwire."

"Don Francisco did get the government to recognize the land that our family had settled and was actively ranching but that was only a quarter of what was in the land grant and, as you said, some of it was donated by Don Francisco to establish Picketwire. Even though it's too late to do anything about the claim, at least this map shows that it was legitimate and that my great-great-grandfather wasn't a liar." Tony's cellphone jiggled in his breast pocket and he took it out. "It's a text from Sister M's saying she's finished," he said. He texted okay and put it back in his pocket.

"You know, what I don't get is how did it end up in a prison?" Elise asked as Tony rolled up the map. "I mean, if it were a map of the prison I could understand someone smuggling it in so they could use it to break out, but why this?"

"That's what I hope to find out," Tony answered securing the map with the rubber band.

CHAPTER THIRTY

"A funny thing happened at the Sheriff's Department," Gloria said to Foster after Tom left the office to interview Max Bergmann. "While I was waiting to see the Sheriff to interview him about the status of the Wylie Boone hit-and-run, a lawyer walked in and said that she was there to see her client."

Foster looked up from the current edition of the *Picketwire Press* he was reading. "What's so funny about a lawyer seeing their client?"

"She said her name was Sister Mary Margaret."

"You mean Sister M's," Foster said, sitting back in his chair and giving Gloria his full attention.

Gloria shook her head in amazement, "A nun called Sister M's who's also a lawyer? Now that's hard to believe."

"Then I guess you witnessed a miracle because Sister M's is a damn good lawyer as well as a darn good nun. She's one of the sisters that took over the old Purgatory State Penitentiary. They changed the name to Our Lady of Lost Souls." Foster smiled and added, "Talk about divine inspiration when they gave a former prison that name."

Gloria's eyes widened in surprise, "She's one of the sisters of Saint Leonard?"

"You know about the sisters?"

"It was in the news when they bought it and I've always wanted to visit the place. Maybe do a story on it."

"Bought might be a stretch since they were the only bidder when the state auctioned it as surplus property. It was more like a steal and you can use that quote in any story you write."

After groaning at his joke Gloria said, "You have to admit that it's pretty unusual for an order of nuns to take over an old prison."

"They're an unusual order. Not that I know much about religious orders or religion, for that matter. Who was she there to see?"

"Somebody named Donny Buford."

"Now that's strange, because Donny Buford isn't the sort of person that Sister M's would take on as a client."

"Why not?"

"She represents people who don't have any money and Donny Buford's father is the president of Picketwire Bank and Trust and his mom is a doctor."

"So why would Sister M's agree to be Donny's lawyer?"

"Must have something to do with why he was brought in, maybe something that Sister M's is involved with and Donny doesn't want his parents to know about."

"Like what?" Gloria asked, sensing a story.

Foster held up the section of the *Picketwire Press* that he had been reading, "You write these dispatch reports for the paper so why not call the sheriff's department and find out?"

Gloria quickly turned to the phone on her desk, dialed the number for the sheriff and spoke with the deputy who handled the dispatch reports. "What do you mean you're not allowed to disclose it?" She asked then twirled her right index finger in the air as she listened to the reply. "Why isn't the FBI handling it?" After listening to his reply she asked if she could speak with Sister Mary Margaret then after a pause said, "She's his attorney. I saw her when I was there." Shaking her head and this time rolling her eyes she registered a protest and hung up. Turning to Foster she said, "That was Deputy Doolittle..."

"You mean Deputy D O L I T T L E," Foster replied, spelling it out. "One of Riggleman's highly unqualified team."

"Anyway," Gloria continued, "he told me that he couldn't release any information on the arrest because it was a matter of national security. When I asked if that were so, why wasn't the FBI involved and he said that the sheriff didn't need any help from the feds. Does that make any sense?"

"Only if you put 'non' in front of it. My hunch is that Donny's arrest is connected to Riggleman and his sheriff's posse stopping the Picketwire Railroad in search of undocumented immigrants, or illegals as he calls them."

"But when Riggleman brought up the whole incident when I was at the sheriff's department he said there weren't any arrests. He did say that he was sure there were accomplices who helped with the escape."

"Didn't Deputy Do-Little tell you this was a matter of national security?"

Gloria nodded.

"Well, to Riggleman and his deputies that means lying is their patriotic duty, which confirms that patriotism is the last refuge of a scoundrel."

Gloria couldn't help laughing. "I guess that means Riggleman's also a refugee."

"And definitely an illegal one," Foster deadpanned. "Anyway, the best way to find out what's going on is to talk to Sister M's. What did he tell you when you asked to speak with her?"

"He said she'd left a half hour ago and gone back to her nunnery. Of course, he snickered when he said that."

"Then if we want to talk to her we should get to the nunnery as well," Foster said. He folded the newspaper, placed it on the desk and stood up.

***

As he walked with Gloria toward the gate of the old Purgatory Penitentiary after parking his Jeep, Foster suddenly recalled something that happened to him when he was ten years old. He was mowing the lawn of their home in Picketwire when their next door neighbor, Mister Malloy, appeared on the front porch of his house, a big two story place with peeling paint and a sagging roof, and called him over. This was the first time that Malloy, who hardly ever came out of his house, had spoken to him. Foster's parents had told him that Malloy's wife walked out on him shortly after he'd retired.

Foster remembered that he'd hesitated at first when Malloy called to him, but then let go of the handle for the push mower and walked over. Malloy had settled onto the top step of his front porch and looked at Foster, who would have declined to sit down even if he'd been asked. Malloy held a can of beer in his right hand and took a drink, wiped his lips with the back of his left hand and asked if he'd ever been in a prison?

"No sir," Foster had replied in a serious voice even though it didn't make any sense to ask a ten-year-old if they'd been in prison.

"Well, I have," Malloy spat out the words. "Thirty years in the Purgatory Penitentiary. I'd still be there if they hadn't closed it down."

"You were in Purgatory?"

"Yeah, but I wasn't an inmate, I worked there."

"As a guard?"

Malloy nodded, "Yeah, but my official title was corrections officer, because I was employed by the Department of Corrections. I should have been called a waste management officer because I guarded a garbage dump. That's what prisons are, they're just garbage dumps with walls. I was there to make sure the trash society threw away didn't escape and pollute the environment. Now they've closed the place and sent all the garbage to other dumps. And this...," he had waved his right hand with the can of beer at his house, "this is my dump." He laughed again until he started coughing. When he stopped coughing he looked down at Foster, his eyes squinting, and said, "If prisons are garbage dumps you know what cops are, right?"

"Policemen," Foster had replied, confidently.

"Nope," Malloy grinned and shook his head. "Cops are just garbage collectors with guns." He took a last sip from his can of beer, crumpled it in his hand and got up slowly then stood unsteadily at the top of the steps. "I just figured you should know that you're living next to a dump so when the cops show up you'll know they're just here to haul away the trash." As Foster stood there trying to figure out what he meant, Malloy turned and walked into the house letting the screen door slam shut behind him like a cell door.

"I wonder what the prisoners felt when they walked through these gates," Gloria said, bringing Foster back to the present.

Foster stopped and looked up at the massive gate and said to Gloria, "I suppose it depended on whether they were walking in or walking out. You know, someone I knew a long time ago called the prison a garbage dump."

"There's no way I could call someone a friend who thought people in prisons are garbage."

"I didn't say he was a friend. He was a neighbor of ours when I was growing up in Picketwire and had been a guard here until they closed it. He also called the police garbage collectors."

"How dehumanizing. Didn't that bother you?"

"Yeah, but it must have bothered him even more, because he killed himself the day after he told me. Guess he wanted to escape."

"Oh..."

"And I became a cop."

***

When they entered the Welcome Center Sister M's was talking to Sister Louise at the gift shop counter. "Why Foster St. Vrain, what a surprise," she said. Noticing Gloria next to him, she added, "And..."

Gloria quickly stepped up and held out her right hand, "I'm Gloria Herrera."

"Gloria's our ace reporter at the *Picketwire Press*. I'm doing some research for them. Right now, I'm helping Gloria on a story."

"I'm also the *Picketwire Press*'s investigative reporter," Gloria added as they shook hands.

"Is that why you were at the sheriff's department when I was there a couple of hours ago?"

Gloria nodded her head, "I was there to interview Sheriff Riggleman about the status of the search for the suspect in the Wylie Boone hit-and-run."

"Your interview with the sheriff should be interesting reading to say the least. Did he tell you if they are close to catching the person?"

"Not really. He didn't want to talk about it, in fact. What he really wanted to talk about was stopping the invasion of illegal immigrants. Those were his words."

"I'm sure they were," Sister M's said.

"Anyway, he said that he and his posse had just stopped the Picketwire Railroad trying to apprehend some illegals. The sheriff claimed they were disguised as members of Tony Medrano's Rails, Trails, and Tales tour. He said the 'illegals' got away and he was sure they had accomplices who helped them escape. That's why we're here. I overheard you say that you were there to see a client named Donny Buford and when I called the sheriff's department and asked if he had been arrested, they wouldn't comment. They said it was a matter of national security. It sounds crazy but was Donny Buford arrested as one of the accomplices the sheriff mentioned?"

"It does sound crazy, doesn't it?" Sister M's replied with a slight smile.

"Riggleman's no stranger to crazy," Foster stepped in. "But crazy or not why else would you be representing Donny Buford? Donny's not exactly poor."

Sister M's gave Foster a hard look, "I don't require my clients to take a vow of poverty just because I do. Anyway, other than I was there to represent him I can't tell you anything. Attorney-client privilege still holds even if the client's not underprivileged."

"In other words, you're giving us a no comment just like the sheriff?" Gloria asked, holding a pen poised over a notebook she had taken from her purse.

"At least I didn't insult your intelligence by saying it's a matter of national security."

"Can we quote you on that?" Foster said with a grin.

"But seriously, Sister Mary Margaret..." Gloria persisted.

"You can call me Sister M's."

"Okay, Sister M's, can't you at least tell me if Donny Buford was arrested?"

"Yes, I can deny that he was arrested. He was detained for questioning and walked out of the sheriff's department about fifteen minutes after I arrived."

"But if you hadn't arrived there was a good chance he would have been booked, right?" Foster pressed.

"No comment," Sister M's replied.

"If you don't give us something more, I'll have no alternative but to contact Donny Buford," Gloria pleaded, "and tell him I'm writing a story that will appear on the front page of the *Picketwire Press* about how he was hauled in by the sheriff in a matter concerning national security and that you, his lawyer, didn't deny it. I'll also have to contact his parents."

Foster added, "I have a hunch poor Donny's going to talk and he's going to say some things that you'd rather not have in the newspaper."

"Please don't contact him or his parents," Sister M's begged. "He was just being a good Samaritan."

Gloria wrote down what Sister M's said. "I'll be sure and include that quote in the story. It's a good quote. After all, as a nun you should be an expert on who's a good Samaritan."

"Can we go off the record?" Sister M's asked pointing at Gloria's notebook.

Gloria closed her notebook and put down her pen, "Okay, what can you tell us off the record?"

"It's not me that's going to tell you," Sister M's replied then asked if they would follow her.

As Sister M's led Gloria and Foster through a long, window-less corridor she explained that, although it was a tunnel, it led into the prison, not out of it. "This was the main entry point for new prisoners. For many of them it was one way. If you were serving life the only way to escape was to dig a tunnel or wait to have someone dig your grave."

"Did anybody dig a tunnel and escape?" Gloria asked.

"According to prison records there were tunnels that were dug but all of them were discovered by guards before they were completed. Most of them weren't very long, although there was one that was more than a hundred feet in length. Unfortu-nately for the prisoners who dug that one they were still several hundred feet short of the other side of the outer walls when they were discovered. Sister Beatrice, who's an archaeologist, suspects there are more."

The corridor ended with a pair of massive steel doors that, according to Sister M's hadn't been closed since they acquired the prison. "When I lead tours I joke that we threw away the key, but the keys are actually kept in a locked cabinet in the Captain of the Guards room even though we don't lock any of the cells."

Sister M's motioned for them to follow her through the doorway into the sunlight.

"I suppose you call this the light at the end of the tunnel," Foster said.

"No," Sister M's replied, "but I think I'll use that on my next tour if you don't mind."

They were now in a large courtyard. A wall was on their right topped by guard towers and in front and to the left were the former cellblocks. They rose two stories higher than the wall, which meant that the upper cells had a view over the wall. "This was what they called the yard, which is where the convicts were allowed to congregate for a couple of hours a day. They had to keep moving, so they just walked around in circles."

"Is that why those stones are arranged in a circle?" Gloria asked, pointing at paving stones that were laid out in a circular pattern in the middle of the courtyard.

"Oh, that," Sister M's laughed. "That's a labyrinth. You'll find them in the great cathedrals like Chartres in France. We use it for walking meditation. It's not lost on us that while we are free to walk in a labyrinth, meditating, the people who were imprisoned here were condemned to walk in circles."

"No doubt meditating on how to escape," Foster said.

They followed Sister M's through an open door and into a hallway. "This corridor leads to the cellblocks but we're not going that far." She stopped in front of another open door and motioned for them to enter.

They entered a long room with a high ceiling. Along the far wall were windows set high in the walls. Light streamed in from the courtyard. There was a black board on the wall opposite the windows that stretched almost the entire length of the room. "If you'll wait here I'll be right back," Sister M's said.

"Where are you going?" Gloria asked.

"To get the people who can answer your questions," Sister M's replied, then stopped as she was about to walk out the door and added, "off the record."

CHAPTER THIRTY ONE

Jemma Lu took a sip of the chamomile tea and placed the cup back on the tabletop of the booth in Sue's Pretty Good Cafe. She had ordered chamomile because it was supposed to have a calming effect, but she was beginning to think that she should have gone to the Last Ditch for a martini instead. When she saw Howdy at Tanneyhill's Drug Store Jemma Lu was relieved that he didn't say anything in front of Milli about her riding on the back of his motorcycle one other time, relieved because she'd never told Milli the whole story about her breakup with Wylie, in particular the part about riding off with Howdy.

The whole story was so surreal that Jemma Lu couldn't explain it to herself much less her best friend. Seeing no point in dwelling on it Jemma Lu had decided to push the entire episode out of her mind and she had succeeded... until both Wylie and Howdy returned to Picketwire. Running into Howdy a couple of days ago at Tanneyhill's and then meeting with Wylie at

Tuttle Mansion yesterday was like having a carpet pulled back. Jemma Lu couldn't avoid facing what she'd swept under the rug three decades before.

"Ready?"

Startled out of her rug reverie, Jemma Lu looked up at Howdy. He had slipped unnoticed into the seat across from her. She took a deep breath and replied, "For what?"

"Ready for our ride. Remember what you said when I saw you at Tanenyhill's the other day and asked you if you wanted to take a ride?"

"I remember that I said not now."

"Exactly. Well, this is not that now, it's the now that's now."

"What on earth do you mean Howdy Hanks?"

"What I mean Jemma Lu, is that my bike is right outside and I've got a helmet for you." He placed a motorcycle helmet on top of the table.

"I just asked if you'd meet me here."

"And I met you here," Howdy grinned. "Now we can go for that ride."

"But I asked if we could meet because we need to talk, Howdy," Jemma Lu sputtered in protest.

"I know, Jemma Lu, but we can ride and talk."

"We can't talk while riding on a motorcycle."

"We can talk; we just won't be able to hear each other," Howdy said and then looked around at the lunch hour crowd that was filling the cafe. He pushed the helmet toward her and stood up. "Actually, I've got just the place where we can talk and there won't be anyone around to listen in."

***

Outside the cafe Jemma Lu put the helmet on, climbed onto the saddle of the motorcycle, then wrapped her arms around Howdy's back as he kickstarted the old Indian. The engine coughed then caught and she felt her entire body vibrate. Then they took off. She was glad she was wearing the helmet. Not because it might save her life but because it might save her the embarrassment of people recognizing her as they sped down Carson Street. In a few minutes they were out of town heading south on County Road 12, whose blacktop was bleached gray by the sun. Five minutes later they turned left at the roadside marquee for the Star Dust Drive-In movie theater, then slowly followed the gravel drive past the closed box office toward the theater's large white screen before coming to a stop in front of the concrete concession stand.

"You brought me to the drive-in theater to talk?" Jemma Lu said after they dismounted and removed their helmets. Howdy opened one of the saddlebags on the motorcycle and pulled out a paper bag then pointed at a picnic table. "Just take a seat and I'll explain."

They sat down, side by side, facing the screen. Howdy opened the paper bag. Jemma Lu could smell the popcorn. "You brought popcorn."

"What's a movie without popcorn."

"What movie?"

"Why, the one we're going to watch, Jemma Lu." Howdy tilted the open bag toward her. "Go ahead and have some. I got it freshly popped from the Mother Jones Bar."

"I just see a blank screen up there, Howdy," Jemma Lu replied, her right hand reaching into the bag and pulling out a handful of popcorn.

"Perfect for projecting our thoughts," Howdy said, helping himself to some popcorn. "We'll both just look at the silver screen and tell each other what we see up there. Ladies first."

"Okay, Howdy," Jemma Lu looked hard at the screen. "Do you remember what happened between us thirty years ago?"

"After I picked you up at Wylie's? How could I ever forget."

"Yes, but also the week before that at the Picketwire Day Parade."

"When you hopped on my bike. How could I forget – it surprised the hell out of me."

"I was surprised myself. I was just standing there with Milli watching the floats go by and I started thinking about all the Picketwire Day parades I'd seen. I was thirty then and the first one I can remember was when I was four. I realized that there was nothing that surprised me anymore. It was all predictable. Then it seemed like I was watching my life pass by and it was all predictable as well. That's when I saw you at the end of the parade, riding on your motorcycle, the same one we just rode here on," Jemma Lu nodded at the bike. "And that was a surprise, so I just did something unpredictable. Something that no one would expect of Jemma Lu Tuttle. I surprised myself as well."

Howdy laughed, "So you ran out into the street and asked if you could get on the back of my bike."

"Then after the parade ended I told you not to stop and we kept going and ended up at that little place you were renting on Swink Street."

"I invited you in for a drink."

"We talked."

"You did most of the talking as I recall."

Jemma Lu nodded her head. "There was some crying as well."

"You did all of that."

"Then we...we..."

"If that memory weren't X-rated I'd project it up there on the screen," Howdy replied. Jemma Lu poked Howdy in the ribs with her elbow, then leaned against him. Howdy continued. "I didn't hear from you for almost a week until you called and asked if I could pick you up at Wylie's."

"You came over on your motorcycle."

"We rode off into the sunset."

"Happily."

"Until you told me to get lost."

"I did not," Jemma Lu said, pulling away from Howdy and looking at him.

"When we got to your house you gave me a peck on the cheek and said you'd be in touch. I waited a couple of weeks but you never called. I got the message and it was to get lost. So, I left town and I've been lost ever since."

"Something came up that made everything more complicated," Jemma Lu said, wiping tears from her eyes. "I needed some time to sort things out. That's why I wanted to meet, to tell you I owe you an apology, Howdy.

"I didn't come back after thirty years for an apology, Jemma Lu."

Jemma Lu turned from the blank screen and looked at Howdy, "Why did you come back?"

Howdy pointed at the screen and said, "I'm hoping for a sequel with a different ending."

CHAPTER THIRTY TWO

Other than the top of Mount Witt, there is no better view in Picketwire than from the hill at the western edge of town. Looking out over gently rolling prairie toward the Sangre de Cristo mountains it offers a truly sublime perspective. Of course, since it's also Picketwire's Cemetery, the view for its permanent residents is obstructed by six feet of earth. When Jane was a girl she would ride her bike on the paved walkways that meandered through the cemetery reading the epitaphs. The last time she'd been there was when her grandmother was buried next to her grandfather.

After parking her car, Jane walked through the cemetery to an area at the far southwest edge where she stopped. No more secrets, Jane repeated silently while she gazed at the grave markers barely visible in the grass. They looked like stone stumps of trees that had been cut down in their prime. The wind rustled the grass and blew strands of hair across her face. Clouds drifted across the sky. Some cattle grazed in the pasture just beyond. It wasn't just who they were but where they died, toiling as unpaid, captive workers for the Double B Ranch. At least Uncle Joji had done something when he painted 'not forgotten' on the side of the building in the secret camp. But who would see the words, and if they did and were able to translate them into English, how could they know what they referred to? Jane shivered and turned to begin walking back to her car.

"I see you found them," someone called out. Startled, Jane turned and saw an older man in coveralls standing behind a marble headstone. He was thin, slightly stooped and his face was weathered by years in the sun and wind. He held a pair of pruning shears in one of his gloved hands.

Regaining her composure, Jane asked, "You know about these graves over here?"

"Yep, in fact I was here when they were buried," he replied, removing his straw cowboy hat and wiping the sweat from his forehead with the sleeve of his left hand.

"You saw them buried?"

"I was only a kid, of course," he said, settling his hat back on his head. "My dad worked here as the caretaker. I took over as caretaker when he died and then my oldest son took over after me when I retired. I still help out a bit. My dad is right over there with my mom." He pointed at two headstones a few feet away with his pruning shears, then smiled and shook his head. "She used to complain that he spent more time with dead people than her. They both got what they wanted." He turned to Jane and said, "Anyway, I've worked here my whole life." He nodded at a headstone next to them, "That's mine. There's room next to it for my wife." He stopped and laughed. "She said she's still thinking about it. Anyway, as you can see my headstone has my birth date, but the day of my death as well as my epitaph will have to be carved by my son. I've trained him on how to do it and he's gotten so good he's taken up sculpture."

Jane walked over and read the name on the headstone. "Lazarus Lamont. Your first name is really Lazarus?"

"My parents had a sense of humor. My dad used to say that if Jesus came back and raised all the dead we'd be out of a job. I go by Laz. I tell people it's short for lazy." He placed the shears and weeds on top of the headstone, took off his gloves and they shook hands. Jane was surprised by the firm grip.

"I'm Jane Takamoto."

"You must be related to the Takamotos over there under the Elms. Nice folks. Never cause any trouble."

Jane couldn't help laughing.

"That's good," he said. "That you can laugh, I mean. Most people seem to think that because this is a cemetery you have to be deadly serious."

"To answer your question, yes, I'm related. I grew up here and moved away but just came back. This is the first time I've been out here since I returned but I used to come out here quite often. I'm sorry that I don't remember you."

"I try to be invisible. Sort of like an undertaker at a funeral. See but not be seen."

"You said you saw the people being buried over there when you were a kid?"

Laz's expression turned serious. He crossed his arms and looked at the small stone markers, "I can see it now even though it was in January of 1946, after the war ended. I was only five years old at the time. It was after sunset, twilight time. A truck drove up to the cemetery gate. The caretaker's house is right next to it. I heard it idling and looked out my window. My dad went out, talked to someone in the cab and then opened the gate. He started walking and the truck followed him. I snuck out of my room and followed the truck that was following my dad until he stopped over there. About half a dozen men got out of the back of the truck and dug the graves. It was winter so the ground was partly frozen, so it took them quite a while. Finally, they finished and took plain wooden coffins out of the back of the truck and buried them. After they covered them up with dirt they placed those little stone markers down and drove off."

"Did your dad ever say anything about it?"

"When I was twelve or thirteen, we were mowing the grass right about where we are now and I told him that I'd seen the burial. He said it wasn't a regular burial but a re-burial because the bodies had been buried somewhere else and then been dug up and reburied here. According to him the folks who buried them didn't want anything on the stones but the date the person died. The Cemetery Association changed the rules and now there has to be a person's name, but it was a little late for those fellows over there."

"I can understand why you never forgot what happened."

He nodded and said, "There was one more thing I'll never forget and that's what my dad did after the bodies were buried and the truck left. He just stood there for a few minutes and then bowed his head and said something. I couldn't hear what he said back then so I asked him and he told me that he felt something needed to be said but since he didn't know anything about the people who had just been buried he wasn't sure what was appropriate. He didn't have his Bible with him so he decided to repeat the only poem he knew by heart. He had to memorize it when he was in grade school."

"What poem?"

"'The Charge of the Light Brigade,'" Laz replied. "He thought that since it was about riding into the valley of death it seemed sort of appropriate. Anyway, it's not the words but the thought that counts, he figured and I agree."

"Did your father tell you who the men were that buried the bodies?"

"He said the only person he recognized was the guy he talked to who was in charge. The guy had stayed in the cab of the truck so I didn't see him."

"Did he tell you who the man was?"

"Charles Boone, Wylie's dad."

CHAPTER THIRTY THREE

"I must apologize," Sister Beatrice said to Tony, her gloved hands placing the map on the table. She had removed it from a former prison cell next to her workroom-laboratory where valuable artifacts were now stored. "I saw it as just a very old map of the area and not as a legal document recording the Medrano Land Grant. Otherwise, I would have come straight to you. After all, if it was stolen from your family then it should be returned to you. I don't know how I could have missed what seems obvious."

Tony liked Sister Beatrice. He had often shown her the items that he had found on his amateur expeditions around the area and she had treated his discoveries as if they were important artifacts worthy of careful examination. She had also been helping him develop his new Ruins on the Range tour. He hated to see how distraught she was. "I'm just happy that you discovered it," he replied. "I mean, we thought it had disappeared for good.

Many people said it never existed in the first place; that "Don" Francisco made it all up. Now, here it is in the flesh – I mean on paper," he said, bending over for a closer look at the map.

"It's actually drawn on parchment, which is made from calf-skin, so you were right the first time to say in the flesh," Sister Beatrice said. "I've carbon tested it and compared it to other maps of that time. It's the right age and the signature of General Armijo matches other documents he signed." She pointed at the seal next to the signature, being careful not to touch it even though she was wearing gloves. "Probably most important is that the imprint from his official seal is next to the signature, wax and all. The seal that he used is in the New Mexico History Museum in Santa Fe. I went down there and it's a perfect match for this imprint."

"Then this must be the genuine article," Tony said, his voice filled with excitement.

"Artifact," Sister Beatrice corrected Tony. "I also asked an authority on old maps and documents at the University of Colorado to look at it and he agreed that it seems to be authentic."

"Seems to be?"

"There is one issue."

"What's that?"

"Establishing provenance. It would help to be able to know the chain of ownership."

"The chain of ownership? There's only one link as far as ownership and that's my family. Whoever had it after that was either the thief or dealing with stolen property."

"Let's call it the chain of possession, then."

"Since you found it in a prison cell the guy who stole it was in possession. Talk about chains, the guy was locked up behind bars."

"The problem is that the map was reported stolen in 1850 and the Purgatory Penitentiary wasn't opened until 1875. Where was the map during those twenty five years?"

"The person who stole it could have concealed it somewhere for twenty five years and then he was convicted of a crime and snuck it in with him," Tony suggested. "Do you know who the inmates were who occupied the cell?"

"There is a master registry of all the convicts. The original is with the Colorado Department of Corrections, but we have a copy. It has things like their name, their date of birth, last known address, their criminal record, what they were sentenced for, the date they were incarcerated and the date they were released or died. Unfortunately, there's nothing in it that tells us who occupied a particular cell."

"Nothing," Tony repeated glumly.

"Not in the Registry, but, we do have the graffiti written on the walls of the cells. Those who knew how to write, that is. Sometimes they signed their name or initials."

"You mean like Kilroy was here?"

"Yes, only it would more likely be Killer Roy," Sister Beatrice chuckled.

"Did you find any signed graffiti in the cell where this was found?"

"As a matter of fact, we did. We found two sets of initials TW and BG. Unfortunately, a number of prisoners in the registry had the same initials, but at least it narrows it down. There was also a prisoner who wrote Ruf Ryder on the wall."

"There was actually a convict with the name Rough Rider? That's what you call someone who rides wild horses."

"It's spelled R U F not R O U G H and R Y D E R not R I D E R There's a Rufus Ryder in the registry, so it must be the same person."

"Probably preferred being known as a rough rider instead of a Rufus. Anyway, with a name like that I sort of hope he did it."

"He was only twenty-five when he was incarcerated here so he couldn't have been the person who stole the map."

"Maybe the thief gave it to him or, more likely, he stole it from them. After all, he was a crook."

"It could also be any of the convicts with the same initials on the wall or it could be someone who didn't feel like leaving his mark for history. However, he would seem to be our prime suspect, so to speak."

"What does your database have on him?" Tony asked.

"I can pull it up on our computer." She walked over to a desktop computer. It was already on so with a few keystrokes she pulled up the file labeled Rufus Ryder. Tony looked over her right shoulder as she scrolled slowly through the information.

"Wait," Tony said. "It says he was convicted of committing grand larceny here in Purgatory County."

"Right, he's the only one on the list who was serving time for a local crime."

"Local boy makes bad."

"Not just local but right next door," Sister Beatrice replied. "The Double B Ranch was the place he robbed."

***

Francisco Way was more like a country lane than a street. It wasn't straight and it wasn't wide and it wasn't smooth, but it did get you to where you were going, at least if that place was the Hacienda Medrano because the street had originally been the road from the Rancho Medrano gate to the Hacienda. When "Don" Francisco Medrano contributed part of the Medrano land to establish Picketwire one of his conditions was that "the paseo," as he called it, would not be altered in any way. Another stipulation was that the Hacienda could never be sold and if no Medrano chose to live there it was to be donated to the town of Picketwire.

Tony's parents were the current Medranos in residence and they might be the last since no one else in the family, including Tony, had expressed any interest in living there. After Francisco died the town council decided that the street should be named in his honor. Paseo Medrano was the favorite candidate until his oldest son, Alejandro, objected and argued that it be called Francisco Way because their father was so stubborn. That was a trait Alejandro shared and so he got his way.

Tony's father, Roberto, had his office in the Medrano Building, a modest two story brick building at the beginning of Francisco's Way not far from where the old gate once stood. Roberto's office looked out at the canopy of sycamore trees that lined Francisco Way. His name was stenciled in bold, black letters on the frosted glass of the door. It was only slightly bigger and bolder than the names stenciled on the doors of the other five offices on the second floor. The frosted glass allowed the names to be scraped off without leaving a trace, but that rarely happened. There wasn't much staff turnover at Medrano Holdings, which reflected its investment strategy. As Roberto liked to point out, it was called Medrano Holdings not Medrano Droppings.

Roberto's door was open, so Tony walked in without knocking. His father was sitting behind his desk staring at a computer screen. He was wearing his usual white shirt, suspenders, and tie. Tony knew that his suit coat was on a hanger in the closet. Every employee at Medrano Holdings dressed for work. Each had a clothing allowance that they could use at The Fashion Farm, whose motto was "clothes for the cultivated." Roberto believed that dressing for work was like an actor putting on a costume so that they could play their role. In the same way, when they left work they took it off and could leave the role behind. He also believed that companies that encouraged their employees to wear the same casual clothes that they wore when they weren't working, blurred the line and resulted in the person never being able to leave their job behind.

Roberto looked up from the computer screen when Tony said, "Hi, Pop."

"Hello stranger," his father replied swiveling around in his chair to face Tony.

"Stranger? I was just over for dinner the other night."

"The other night was a week ago. You must have someone else cooking for you."

Tony smiled broadly. He enjoyed going back and forth with his father. The two of them might not always have rapport but they sure had repartee. "Come on, Pop, nobody can compete with Mom."

"If that's the reason you aren't married, maybe I should cook when you come over instead of your mother."

"Pop, I'm not looking for someone who can cook for me. Mom taught me the basics and she said I'm not that bad. Hey, why don't I cook something next time I come over?"

Roberto grimaced and said, "If that's what it takes to have you visit I guess I can stomach it."

"Actually, I've been dating someone and maybe I'll bring her with me."

Roberto's face brightened, "Will she help you cook?"

"No, we just started dating. Isn't it enough that I bring her to dinner? I mean, this will be the first time I've brought a woman I'm dating to dinner with you and Mom."

"Of course, it's more than enough, son. I promise that if you bring this woman I will eat whatever you cook and I will also say that it is not bad. Now," Roberto said, cutting off any rejoinder by Tony, nodding at the rolled up document Tony had placed on the desk, "what do you have there?"

"That's the reason I came by," Tony answered, unrolling the map and turning it so his father could see it.

"What's this?" Roberto asked leaning forward to examine the document.

"This is a copy of an official map that shows that our land grant is for real. The one that was stolen. Don Francisco was telling the truth."

"Of course, he was telling the truth, son."

"Of course, but this proves it."

"I hope you didn't need proof to believe Don Francisco."

"Of course not. Still, we can now show the world."

"You say this is a copy? Where is the actual map?"

"It's in prison," Tony answered as he sat down in one of the two chairs facing his father's desk.

"Prison?"

"Actually, it's in Our Lady of Lost Souls but Sister Beatrice found it in one of the former prison cells. It had to have been stashed there by a convict. He probably thought it was a pretty safe place. I mean, who would look for stolen property in a prison?"

"Yes, who indeed. No wonder they could never find it," Roberto sighed. "Does Sister Beatrice know who hid it there?"

"Not exactly. Sister Beatrice has a copy of the records for all of the convicts but there's nothing in them that says which convicts occupied which cell. Still, there were six whose names match the initials that were scratched on the cell's wall and one convict who occupied the cell wrote Ruf Ryder, spelled R U F R Y D E R, on the cell's wall."

"You mean he stole the map and hid it in his cell?"

Tony shook his head, "The map was stolen in 1850 and the prison wasn't built until 1875 and Ruf Ryder was incarcerated in 1883."

"Maybe he held onto it for thirty-three years."

"He was only twenty-three when he was sentenced to prison. What's interesting is he was convicted for stealing from the Double B."

"Of course, it all makes sense," Roberto nodded. "This Ruf Ryder guy stole the map from the Boones."

"How did the Boones get it?"

Roberto got up from his chair and went to the door and closed it. He walked back to the desk, sat down, and finally said, "What I am going to tell you is a secret."

"A secret?"

"Not any old secret, but a family secret, so you must promise to keep it confidential."

"Sure, Pop."

"Your grandfather Don Francisco was certain that C.W. Boone stole the map."

"How did he know that?"

"He didn't trust C.W. Boone. Besides, C.W. gained the most when the land grant was denied, because the U.S. government would own the land and with C.W.'s political connections he could buy it for next to nothing."

"I never knew that."

"There was no need for you to know. What would be the point since there is nothing that can be done about it?"

"But now we have this," Tony said, reaching over and picking up the map. "It's proof that the land was granted to our family."

"And what can we do with this proof? The federal government ruled against us in 1854. The matter is settled."

"How do you know? Maybe there's some legal action we can take.

"Legal action? The statute of limitations has long since expired."

Roberto walked over to the window. He stared at the sycamore tree. Finally, he went back and sat down in his chair. He looked at Tony and said, "Besides, there is more to our family secret. You see, Don Francisco accused C.W. of stealing the map."

"And?"

"C.W. didn't deny it, but he told Don Francisco that if he tried to pursue this accusation he would not only pull his support for establishing the town of Picketwire he would also make sure it never happened. In that case that part of the land for the town that Boone had agreed to donate would revert back to him. He also said that if we tried to establish it on the land that we and the Tuttles had agreed to donate then he would stop that as well."

"How could C.W. stop our family and the Tuttles from going forward in establishing Picketwire?"

"As I said, C.W. had political connections including people in high places in Denver and not just a mile high, but political friends whose support was necessary for Colorado to approve a town charter for Picketwire. Don Francisco knew that C.W. could carry out his threat so he told him that even though they both knew it was the truth he promised not to pursue the matter and that he would keep his word as would all the Medranos after him because we were an honorable family." He paused and looked at Tony. "The Medranos still keep their word. You understand what I am saying?"

Tony nodded, although he felt more disappointed than honorable.

"But," Roberto waved his right index finger for emphasis, "the Boones are not an honorable family and Don Francisco believed that C.W. would break his word and secretly use his political connections to stop Picketwire from getting its charter. To prevent this he drew up an agreement that if Picketwire did not get its Town Charter then the promise he made was null and void."

Tony shook his head and whistled. "Don Francisco sure knew how to negotiate."

"That was because everyone knew he was a man who kept his word and everyone knew that C.W. was not such a man...including C.W..."

"Do you still have that agreement?"

"No, Don Francisco, being honorable, burned it after Picketwire got its charter."

CHAPTER THIRTY FOUR

It was four in the afternoon and the Conquistador Lounge was empty except for the bartender. Elise had left work early and was still wearing her low couture ranger outfit, although she'd left her Smokey Bear hat in her jeep. She would have preferred to change, but Tony had called and asked if they could meet at the lounge at four and then pick a place for dinner. Elise hoped meeting for drinks didn't mean he wasn't taking the third date seriously and saw their relationship as drinking buddies. She'd never been in the bar before, which was tucked away like an afterthought behind a door off the ornate lobby of the Picketwire House hotel, and noticed immediately that it was quiet with subdued lighting. Instead of the usual big screen televisions found in most bars there was a mural that filled the entire wall opposite the banquettes. It was lit with lights recessed in the ceiling and depicted an armor clad conquistador on his horse pointing at one of the mythical Seven Cities of Gold that seemed to float on top of a distant mesa.

Elise ordered a margarita from Raul the bartender, whose name was embroidered on the red vest he was wearing. She told Raul that she was there to meet someone. He nodded as if a lone woman in the bar in the middle of the afternoon dressed as a forest ranger needed no explanation. Elise walked over to the middle of three banquettes that faced the mural and sat down at one end of the curved, black leather bench. A minute later Raul placed the margarita as well as a small bowl of chili-coated peanuts in front of her.

Elise took a sip of her margarita and looked at the mural more closely. She couldn't help noticing that the conquistador resembled Tony and wondered if he picked this place to meet so she would have to look at his dead ringer on horseback. Elise smiled and in a low voice started singing the chorus of the Carly Simon song "You're So Vain." It was a song that described the guy she had dated prior to Tony. So far she hadn't noticed that trait in him. Suddenly her singing was interrupted by Tony's voice. "What are you singing?" Elise looked up at Tony who was standing next to the banquette.

Elise hoped it was dark enough to hide her blush. "I didn't realize I was singing out loud. Just keeping myself company, that's all." She slid over on the bench to make room for him.

"Sorry I'm late," Tony said after he sat down next to her.

Elise nodded at the mural, "It's given me time to admire your conquistador doppelganger."

Tony smiled broadly. "That's my great-grandfather, Miguel, so I guess there is a family resemblance."

"How did your great-grandfather end up on a mural in a bar?"

"Owning the hotel had something to do with it," Tony answered just as Raul set a bottle of Dos Equis beer on the table in front of him.

After Raul walked back to the bar, Elise asked, "Your great-grandfather owned the Picketwire House?"

"Miguel built it to serve the passengers on the Picketwire Railroad that he also owned. When his son, my grandfather Alejandro, sold the railroad to the Atchison, Topeka and Santa Fe, he kept the hotel. Our family still owns it."

"Is that why you wanted to meet here, because you can get free drinks?" Elise said, jiggling her margarita.

Tony smiled and shook his head slowly, "The drinks are not free."

"That means we're going Dutch?"

"We're going Tony Medrano, which means I pay. Besides, the family business doesn't allow for family freebies. If we want something from the business then we have to work for it. In this case, I'd probably have to wash dishes or something like that."

"Why didn't you go into the family business?" Elise asked.

"That's better told over a long dinner than a couple of drinks. We can eat here if you want. The food's pretty good."

"And then you'll disappear into the kitchen to wash dishes," Elise laughed. "Why not come over to my place for dinner instead? I'll cook."

"I think I'll like washing dishes at your place," Tony smiled then tapped the neck of his bottle of Dos Equis to her glass in a toast.

After sipping her drink, Elise asked, "Why did your great grandfather want to be painted as a conquistador?"

"There's a story behind it, obviously. It seems that Miguel caught polio when he was in his twenties and although he was lucky to survive he didn't see it that way. He'd have to use crutches to walk for the rest of his life and that meant he could never be a real man. As a good Catholic...maybe good is an overstatement...but he was a Catholic and believed that if he committed suicide he'd go to hell. So, as my dad puts it, he started riding horses as if he was hell-bent for leather. I mean, he didn't have to worry about being crippled if he was thrown and he wouldn't be damned to hell if he was killed. Anyway, what he discovered was you not only don't use crutches when you're riding a horse, you can be as good a rider as anyone with two good legs. It turned out that he was not only as good, he was better than most. He became one of the best horseback riders in the county, which is saying a lot. In fact, he competed in the Mexican charro competitions that are part of the Picketwire Rodeo and won most of them. He even had a portrait painted of him on his horse, Esperanza, dressed in his charro outfit with the big sombrero and vest."

"Why isn't that on the wall instead of this mural of him dressed as a conquistador?"

"That was the original idea, but the story is that when he saw a sketch for this mural that had been commissioned for the hotel he changed his mind. Instead, he asked the muralist, Manuel Vargas from Mexico City, to make some changes including putting his face on the conquistador." Tony waved at the mural. "I forgot to mention that this wasn't a lounge bar then. It was part of the lobby so everyone who came in the front door immediately saw the mural. It was only later, in the 1960s, that they decided they needed a bar and they walled this off from the lobby to create this space. Naturally, they named it the Conquistador Lounge because of the mural. By that time all the people who would have recognized the conquistador as my great-grandfather were long dead. The charro portrait ended up in our family home, Hacienda Medrano."

"I can imagine the impression this mural must have made when it was in the lobby. If he didn't want to be seen as a crippled person this certainly succeeds at that."

"Yes, and that's the story that was passed down, but now...."

"But now what?"

"But now I think there's more to the story and that's why I wanted to meet here," Tony got up and walked over to the mural and stood there like a teacher in front of a blackboard. "I didn't notice this until yesterday when I came here for a beer after meeting with my dad." He extended his right hand toward the conquistador's outstretched arm. "You think the conquistador is pointing at one of the Seven Cities of Gold, right?"

"Yes."

"But as we know the Seven Cities of Gold didn't really exist." Tony moved his arm and pointed his hand at the cities floating hazily in the background behind the one on the mesa, "They were a mirage."

"A mirage of mud would be a better way of putting it since the only thing the conquistadors found were pueblos made of adobe, not gold."

"Exactly. No cities of gold exist," Tony said, then lowered his hand to the mesa on which the city in the foreground rested. "But this mesa sure does."

"It's Mesa del Oro on the Double B Ranch. I recognized it immediately. Oro means gold in Spanish so it makes sense that the painter used that mesa like a pedestal for one of the mythical seven cities of gold."

Tony sat back down beside Elise, "That does make sense and that's why everyone thinks that's the reason. But what if it's been positioned on top of the mesa for another reason and that's because it's the mesa, not the mythical city, that the conquistador, my great-grandfather, is really pointing at?"

Elise looked at the mural, then sipped her margarita and turned to Tony, "Okay, I give up, why is he pointing at the mesa?"

"The Mesa del Oro is on the Double B Ranch, right?"

"Right," Elise replied.

"And that means it's also part of the land that was originally part of the Medrano Land Grant not the Double B, according to the map that my great-great-grandfather, Don Francisco claimed was stolen."

"So, what you're saying is that Miguel isn't just physically pointing he's also pointing this out?"

"You've got it," Tony said as if she'd found the prize in a box of Cracker Jack. "You know, I've probably looked at this mural more than a hundred times but didn't see what Miguel was really doing, but now it's obvious. My great-grandfather wanted to point this out in a mural that was prominently displayed in the lobby of this hotel because he wanted certain people to see it."

"Who?" Elise asked.

"The people who stole the map and, as a result, the Medrano land."

"And you know who they are or were?" Elise pressed Tony.

Tony looked at Elise and explained, "I learned from Sister Beatrice that the cell where they found the map had been occupied by a convict named Rufus Ryder, but he called himself Ruf Ryder, that's spelled R U F R Y D E R, I kid you not. Anyway, it turns out that Ryder was convicted of stealing from the Double B Ranch."

"You think he stole the map from the Double B?"

"Don Francisco said the map was stolen in 1850 and this Ruf Ryder character wasn't even born until 1860 so he would have had to have stolen it from the Double B. Not that it would have been listed among the items stolen. The last thing the Boones would want to claim is that this map was part of the property that was stolen from them, because they would be admitting that they stole it first. Of course, all of that is just circumstantial because there's no direct evidence that Ryder stole the map or that it was Ryder who even hid the map and not some other convict who occupied that cell."

"If this mural is Miguel's way of accusing C.W. Boone of stealing the map and, as a result their land, did he know that the map had been stolen from the Double B by this Ryder character and was hidden in a cell at Purgatory Penitentiary?"

"No, I don't see how he could have known that," Tony let out a sigh. "But he did have some other evidence that his father, Don Francisco, passed on to him. Only he couldn't make it public. I only found out about it yesterday from my Dad when I showed him the map."

"What is it?" Elise asked.

"I can't tell you. In fact, no Medrano can tell anyone."

"Why not?"

"It's got to do with our family honor," Tony said, "about keeping our word. I'm sorry, but I can't tell you anything more than that. My dad made it clear that as far as we Medranos are concerned the case is closed. Miguel could only accuse them indirectly using a mural because our Medrano family honor wouldn't allow him to tell anyone what happened between Don Francisco and C.W. Boone. Anyone looking at the mural today wouldn't even know that's my great-grandfather Miguel

Medrano in the conquistador outfit, much less what he's really pointing at and why. It's just some background decoration, like wallpaper."

"It's hardly wallpaper," Elise protested. "The mural is a message. It reminds me of the pictographs drawn on the rock walls near Dinosaur Tracks. They were also intended to communicate a message. The prehistoric people that the message was intended for understood it but for the people who visit the park today, they're just some decoration."

"Unless they hear you talk about them. I know the people on my tours tell me that they see the pictographs differently after hearing you."

"They also want me to translate what the pictographs are saying," Elise explained. "Of course, we don't know for sure because there's no Rosetta Stone that we can use to decipher them."

"I really like the way you turn the tables and ask them what they think the pictographs are saying. Especially, when you tell them it's their opportunity to solve a mystery."

"Some of the things that visitors suggest are quite plausible based on what we know from research, so who knows? It's sort of like crowdsourcing. Although in the case of your tour groups it would be toursourcing."

"Toursourcing," Tony repeated and clinked his beer against Elise's margarita glass. "I like it."

Elise said laughed. "I can see you up there instead of your great-grandfather only you're leading one of your tours. It would be called the Mystery of Mesa del Oro or something."

"That's it, Elise!" Tony slammed the glass down, sending a geyser of Dos Equis onto the tabletop.

"What is it?"

"I'll tell you over that dinner at your place."

"Before you wash the dishes."

CHAPTER THIRTY FIVE

Jane walked quietly through the sleepy wood-paneled reading room of the Picketwire Public Library, past the long oak tables, illuminated by green-shaded lamps to the elevator. Exiting the elevator on the third floor, which was as far as it went, she walked down the center aisle between the steel book stacks that branched off left and right like slot canyons where someone could easily get lost and be swept away by a flash flood of printed matter. Finally, she reached a gray metal door with PICKETPEDIA stenciled on it in black letters. Opening the door Jane climbed a set of stairs up to the library's attic. Massive roof trusses crisscrossed the ceiling and crowding the space below were filing cabinets and metal shelves laden with boxes. Jane felt like she'd just climbed a mountain to meet a guru only this guru was in an attic instead of a cave and wasn't squatting on the ground in a lotus position. Jane made her way to the far end where Drexel Herbert, the editor-in-chief of Picketpedia, sat behind a large desk in front of a crescent window.

Jane stepped on a loose floorboard that let out a groan. It echoed in the cavernous space and Drexel looked up, his face peering at her through the thick lenses of round wire rim glasses. He smiled, then pressed his hands against the desktop, pushed down, and unwound his eighty-five-year-old body until he was fully erect. Unlike a guru in a white robe, he was attired in a black suit, starched white shirt, and black bow tie. He stepped around to the front of the desk to greet Jane.

"Jane Takamoto, what a surprise," he said, shaking her hand.

"Mr. Herbert," she replied, pleasantly surprised that he remembered her.

"You can call me Drexel. I'm not your high school history teacher anymore."

"I'm sorry if I'm disturbing you...Drexel." It felt strange using his first name, especially since it was a strange name to begin with.

"Not at all. I needed to get up and stretch. This way I know I'm still alive and it's not rigor mortis that's made me stiff. I usually do some Tai Chi rather than a stroll around my desk to get the blood pumping." He took a clean, crisply folded, white handkerchief from the inside pocket of his coat, bent slightly demonstrating that he was, indeed, limber for a man of his age, and wiped the dust off the chair facing the desk. Folding the handkerchief, he tucked it back into his coat pocket and waited as Jane sat down before returning to his side of the desk. "I heard that you had returned and are now a minister at Picketwire Community Church. You know, I have to admit when you went out east to college I never expected you to come back, much less as a minister."

"Neither did I. I guess that's why it's referred to as a calling not a career choice."

"A calling," Drexel replied. "That's what happened to me when I took this position five years ago. I was called to it. Only in my case I wasn't called by God but by Paul Strand. He telephoned and told me he was finally stepping down as editor-in-chief after thirty years. He said Picketpedia needed some young blood and wanted me to be his successor." He laughed heartily, "Only someone who is in his nineties would think of an eighty-year-old as young. Anyway, that was that. You can say no to God, but there was no exercising free will as far as Paul was concerned." He sighed, "It seems I was predestined for Picketpedia."

"So how is the work going?" Jane asked.

Drexel swept his hands in the air over the sheets of paper on the desktop. "The work is never-ending. An encyclopedia is like a garden of knowledge that requires constant tending or it will be overcome by the weeds of ignorance. Somehow we've managed to keep Picketpedia blooming for over a hundred years."

"And you're the chief gardener, I mean editor-in-chief."

"Yes, but we depend on our many volunteers, our Picketpedes, who, if you will indulge me in continuing with the garden metaphor, plant, water, and fertilize. Of course, I have to prune with my editorial shears here and there. In some cases, such as this one," Drexel tapped the sheets of paper on his desk, "more like winnowing the kernels of fact from the chaff of circumlocution." He pushed the paper aside and looked at Jane. "Now, Jane, did you come here just to ask how my work is going?"

"No, it isn't the only reason. I'm trying to find out more about a particular place and I thought if anyone knew about it, you would."

"What place?"

"It was an internment camp for Japanese-Americans."

"You mean Camp Amache."

"Not Camp Amache, but another camp.

"The only entry we have in Picketpedia is for Camp Amache."

"I know, I looked, and I can't find anything about it in the library or online, but there must be something on it somewhere. I know it existed because Bruce, that's my husband, and I saw it. Well, what's left of it. It's on the Double B Ranch, close to Dinosaur Tracks. Also, my Uncle Joji and Lazarus Lamont, Picketwire Cemetery's retired caretaker, confirmed its existence." Jane proceeded to tell Drexel what both of them had told her about the camp and the burial of the bodies.

When Jane finished, Drexel rubbed his hands together and declared with gusto, "I love a good mystery, Jane. Any historian worth his salt does. Just let me contemplate this for a minute." He placed his elbows on top of the ink blotter, pressed the fingertips of both of his hands together and closed his eyes. It seemed to Jane like he was praying. Suddenly, he opened his eyes, slapped his hands on the blotter and announced. "It is possible that we have something on this mysterious place."

"You might?"

"Picketpedia receives many submissions that don't meet our rigorous standards. You would be amazed at what we get," Drexel laughed. "Based on the reports of paranormal activities and UFO sightings that are submitted to us every year, Picketwire is overrun with ghosts and little green men. But there are other submissions that would be accepted except that they just miss the bar because they lack sufficient supporting evidence. Those we retain in case such evidence is discovered."

"You're saying that you think that something about the camp was submitted but you couldn't publish it?"

"It's just a theory but one we can test by looking in purgatory. That's what we call the files where we keep submissions that are awaiting final judgement. If we get the supporting evidence then they are freed from purgatory and published in Picketpedia. If we get evidence that shows they are false they are cast into the flames of hell, which is the incinerator. They used to be, anyway, but now they're shredded and recycled. Instead of burning in hell they are reincarnated as a roll of toilet paper." Drexel opened the top drawer of his desk and pulled out a flashlight and held it up. "Our purgatory isn't in the most enlightened place so we'll need this for illumination. Now, let's go see what we can find."

Jane got up from her chair and followed Drexel. After winding their way through rows of files and shelves, Drexel stopped at the beginning of a row of olive-colored metal filing cabinets. He used the flashlight to read the small cards attached to the front of each of the filing cabinet's four drawers. "Ah, here we are. Now if you hold the flashlight I'll see if we can find what we are looking for inside." Drexel slid open the cabinet drawer and rummaged through the files before pulling out one, "Eureka."

"You found something?"

"The file is labeled Internment Camp with a question mark." Drexel pulled out a sheet of paper and an envelope. He opened the sheet of paper and said, "This is a note from my predecessor, Paul, that says the enclosed envelope contains an anonymous submission received by Picketpedia on March 12, 1986 and cannot be reviewed for publication unless supportive evidence is found that a camp existed on the Double B Ranch where persons of Japanese descent were interned during World War Two." He turned to Jane and said, gleefully, "From what you told me we now have evidence. Let's go back to my desk so we can see what's in the mystery envelope."

After returning to his desk, Drexel sat down, took a letter opener from the top drawer and deftly sliced the envelope open. He extracted several sheets of paper yellowed by age, gently unfolded them and began reading. After reading each typewritten page he placed them face down on the desktop. When he was finished he took off his glasses, wiped them, and put them back on.

Finally, he spoke. "Paul told me that being Picketpedia's editor-in-chief is like playing god because you have to make the final judgement. I always assumed that it was an observation on our power to accept or reject what is to be included. However, in this case the judgement goes beyond the pages of Picketpedia. I imagine he was relieved he didn't have to make the final decision in this case," Drexel sighed and handed Jane the sheets of paper. "You can read it for yourself since the indictment is now unsealed."

CHAPTER THIRTY SIX

Sister M's released the tumbleweed in her hands as she sat on her meditation mat. She was just outside the walls near the edge of the bluff overlooking the Purgatoire River. Sister Flora, who taught Sister M's the spiritual exercise she was practicing, was a master gardener and explained that the tumbleweed was once rooted in the prairie but it was only after it freed itself from the soil and tumbled in the wind that it could release its seeds. She added that keeping your eyes and mind focused on the tumbleweed was the opposite of keeping your eye on the ball. "I like to think of it as the Tao of tumbleweeds." Her instructions were that you didn't throw the tumbleweed, you simply held it out and let the wind take it.

Sister M's kept her eyes on the tumbleweed as it cartwheeled in the breeze until it vanished over the edge of the bluff twenty feet away. She closed her eyes and felt the wind tug at her. Hearing something stir, Sister M's opened her eyes. Facing her was a prairie dog who had popped its head out of a hole about six feet away that she hadn't noticed. Neither of them moved as they stared at each other. Finally, she blinked and the prairie dog ducked back into the hole.

Sister M's had been struggling with what her next step should be since Sheriff Riggleman had stationed one of his deputies outside the convent's gate a few hours before. This could only mean that Riggleman suspected that the three 'illegals,' as he called them, were inside. Sister M's had no doubt that the sheriff would soon show up with a search warrant. She had to find another place to hide them but first she had to find a way to get them out of the convent and past the deputy. Now, the tumbleweed and prairie dog had given her an idea. She rose from her lotus position, rolled up her mat, and walked around to the front and through the gate.

Sister Beatrice looked up from the table she was hunched over as Sister M's entered her workroom. "What are you working on?" Sister M's asked.

"I wish I knew. I've been looking at these fragments for an hour trying to figure out how they come together."

Sister M's looked at the pieces laid out on the tabletop, "What is it or was it?"

"I won't know until I can figure out how it all fits together. It's like doing a jigsaw puzzle without the picture on the box that shows you what it's supposed to look like when you're done." Sister Beatrice stood up from the bench and stretched her arms to the ceiling, "I need a break, especially my back."

"You know the tunnels that prisoners dug to escape from here?"

Sister Beatrice nodded as she continued to stretch.

"You've said that you are certain there are some that were never discovered by the guards."

"I'm not certain, I'm positive," Sister Beatrice replied.

"Does that mean you've discovered some?"

"Only one so far, but there may be more."

"Do you think it's possible for someone to get out through this tunnel that you discovered?"

"Maybe, but leaving through the gate is much easier."

"Not if you want to avoid being arrested by the sheriff's deputy parked in front of it."

Sister Beatrice dropped her arms, looked at Sister M's and asked with some alarm, "You think the sheriff is going to arrest you?"

"No, but he's after the people we're giving sanctuary to and that's why he's parked a patrol car outside our gate. I'm pretty certain that he's going to be here soon with a search warrant. That means we need to move them to a place where he can't find them."

"There are plenty of places we can hide them," Sister Beatrice said. "I know, because I've found them."

"But, we would have to lie when the sheriff asks if they're here," Sister M's replied.

"We could plead the Fifth," Sister Beatrice offered. "I've always wanted to do that."

"Refusing to answer would be like admitting they were here," Sister M's replied. "No, the right thing is to tell him that we aren't hiding them, which would only be true if they aren't here anymore. So, you see, the best thing to do is to move them to a safer place and the only way I can think of doing that is through a tunnel to the outside. I imagine he won't believe us and will conduct a search anyway, but he won't find them because they'll be gone."

Sister Beatrice clapped her hands, "A prison breakout! There couldn't be a better way to test my theory."

"Theory? I thought you said you'd found at least one tunnel that you think had been completed," Sister M's said, unable to hide her disappointment.

"Think I found, as in high probability, but not proven. Let me show you a schematic that shows where this tunnel is."

Sister Beatrice walked over to a filing cabinet, rummaged around, pulled out a file, and placed it on her desk. She then extracted a large sheet of paper that she unfolded revealing a schematic drawing. "This is a drawing I made showing the tunnel. I discovered it in the boiler room of the old power plant here," she said tapping a spot on the sheet of paper. "Like I said, I think it was completed but when I entered the tunnel I never got all the way to the end, but only twenty feet. If I weren't so tall I might have made it farther, but my sciatica started acting up. Unlike just now I couldn't touch my knees much less my toes. I guess you could say I wasn't able to stoop to conquer. However, I was able to measure the tunnel's length using my laser distance measure device and it was almost two hundred feet long. That would put it well beyond the prison walls." She pointed to a dotted line from the power plant that ended past the walls. "Let's go find out if I'm right," she said, gleefully. "I assume that since you practice yoga you won't have any trouble stooping."

***

Ten minutes later they were inside the old power plant, a squat, brick building with a smokestack that rose more than five stories. Sister Beatrice opened a steel door and they descended a stairway into a subterranean room with several large rusting boilers. She flipped a switch turning on the naked lightbulbs hanging from the ceiling high overhead. "I had a heck of time getting up there to replace the bulbs in those fixtures, but at least they work," Sister Beatrice said. "It's still pretty gloomy down here. Of course, the boilers, when they were going, would have provided some light. It was probably unbearably hot as well. I imagine that for the convicts who were assigned here it was like being condemned to hell rather than Purgatory." She led Sister M's over to a large wooden three sided enclosure. "This was the coal bin. The coal came down a chute from up there. It's gone now. And this," she pointed at a rectangular opening in the wood side, "is the tunnel entrance." Sister M's stooped down and looked into the opening, following the beam from the flashlight Sister Beatrice had handed her. "The opening, as you can see, is quite large for a tunnel: four feet high by three feet wide so a person could stoop instead of having to crawl on their hands and knees. It's also level. Because this is the basement they didn't have to dig any deeper."

"Why wasn't it discovered?"

"Since this was the old coal bin for the boilers the convicts who dug the tunnel would have worked here. That meant they had access to shovels. No one would have questioned the dust and noise that was coming from down here. As for the guards, they would have left them alone figuring there was no way they could escape from this hellhole. However, you can see the bin has wooden sides so all they had to do was clear away enough coal to get access and then remove some of the boards. You can see the section of boards next to the opening. They would place them back over the tunnel entrance when they weren't using it and then pile coal in front."

"Wouldn't the guards have been suspicious when some of the convicts working in the boiler room were missing and realize they'd escaped?"

"You're assuming that some convicts escaped, but as you know there's no record of anyone escaping from Purgatory."

"So if no one escaped that would mean the tunnel was never completed," Sister M's said in consternation as she stood up.

Sister Beatrice shook her head. "Not if my theory is correct. I believe this tunnel wasn't a way for prisoners to get out but a way to smuggle things in."

"What makes you think that?"

"I found a small notebook hidden in a niche in the tunnel wall near the entrance. It turned out to be a ledger. Not only did it record items being sold, it included a mark-up for each item that was labelled 'T Tolls.' I thought 'T' meant transport, but the volume was much greater than one would expect from the usual method for smuggling in contraband that takes place in a prison. I couldn't figure it out. Then I realized 'T' meant tunnel and that the convicts who dug this tunnel charged a toll for every item that was smuggled in. Of course, it's only a theory, but if I'm right there's light at the end of this tunnel."

"There's only one way to find out," Sister M's said, then crossed herself, bent down and entered the tunnel. As she walked slowly, hunched over, aware that if the beams that shored up the walls and ceiling gave way she would be trapped or, even, crushed to death. She whispered a Hail Mary as the dust swirled in the beam from the flashlight Sister Beatrice had given her. She counted her steps as she walked, estimating that each step was approximately two feet. After fifty steps she stopped and called back to Sister Beatrice that she thought she was halfway.

"Turn off your flashlight and see if you can see any light." Sister Beatrice's voice sounded as if she was shouting into a well. "Now with the flashlight off your eyes should adapt to the darkness," Sister Beatrice shouted.

"They are but I can't say that the rest of me has. Anyway, it's still coal black, so to speak." She turned the flashlight back on and resumed walking. After another twenty five steps she turned her flashlight off again. She thought it was a shade lighter than before. "It might be my imagination but I think it's a little bit lighter," she called back to Sister Beatrice. Sister M's turned the flashlight on again and continued walking.

It was not her imagination since she could soon see light falling like gold dust from the tunnel's ceiling. When she got closer she could see that the tunnel widened and the ceiling was higher. It was a small roomlike space. It was also the end of the tunnel. A wooden ladder leaned against the side of the tunnel and stopped just below several boards nailed together to form a square. The light she had seen had sifted through the cracks between the boards.

Sister M's shouted back to Sister Beatrice that she had found the end of the tunnel and that it was a space with a ladder leading to what appeared to be a hatch. "The rungs on the ladder are intact and it looks sturdy so I'm going to try it." Sister M's put her right foot on the first rung of the ladder and it held her weight, so she climbed carefully up until she reached the hatch. After pushing back and forth on it she was able to slide it away and sunlight flooded in blinding her momentarily. I wonder if this is what God experienced after saying let there be light, she thought.

After stepping on the next rung and pushing her head out of the tunnel she was surprised to see that she was only five or six feet from her meditation spot. Looking at the top of the hatch that she had pushed aside she also saw that it was nearly indistinguishable from the surrounding prairie. She swatted away a tumbleweed that blew in front of her and climbed out into the sunlight. The top of the hatch was covered with several inches of soil so that when it was pulled over the tunnel entry it would have been undetectable. Looking around she thought that while it may not match the description in Genesis, she was pretty sure this would have been the Garden of Eden to the convicts who dug the tunnel.

Less than fifteen minutes later Sister M's was back at the entrance in the boiler room. "Well?" Sister Beatrice asked.

"It comes out behind the east wall, about fifteen feet from the edge of the bluff overlooking the river."

Sister Beatrice hugged Sister M's. "Thank you for proving my theory, M's."

"Thank you for coming up with the theory, Bea."

"When do we stage the breakout?" Sister Beatrice could hardly contain her excitement.

"First, I have to arrange for someone to help me get them to the safe house once they're through the tunnel..."

"Where's the safe house?" Sister Beatrice asked. "No, don't tell me. That way I won't have to plead the Fifth if the sheriff asks me."

Sister M's laughed, "I can't tell you, anyway, because it's still in the works."

"Yes, but I'm sure you've worked it out in your head."

"In my head, but it's all theoretical until I work it out on the ground."

CHAPTER THIRTY SEVEN

Jane was both astonished and saddened at what she read in the pages from the file Drexel had retrieved from Picketpedia's 'purgatory.' "You have to publish this in Picketpedia after what my Uncle Joji and Lazarus Lamont told me," she said, handing the pages back to Drexel.

Drexel held the sheets of paper in his hand, as if weighing them, "What you told me is certainly evidence that supports what's written in this account. However, there is still the fact that there is nothing in this document that identifies who wrote it. The only thing we know about it is that Picketpedia received it on March 12, 1986. What the person who authored this has written will create quite a stir, to say the least, and without knowing who that person is, we can't judge its veracity. Were they an eyewitness or are they relating something they were told and, if so, how did that person come by their information? Without that knowledge we will need corroboration from other sources that can back this up. Until then, I'm afraid this must be cast back into purgatory."

"But Mr. Herbert..."

"Drexel."

"Drexel, there must be some way to make this public," Jane pleaded. "It's just wrong to return it to the Picketpedia purgatory. People need to know what's written on those pages."

"Yes, I see. There is the call of history to consider," Drexel placed the sheets of paper on his desk and tapped them as he knitted his eyebrows in thought. Finally, he said, "There is one possibility...."

"What?" Jane almost leapt from her chair.

"I'm not a religious person unless there's one I don't know about that combines Confucianism, Stoicism, and Christianity. However, it's my understanding that what someone tells a member of the clergy is confidential. Like what a priest hears in the confessional. Is that correct?"

"Yes, but what does this have to do with what we are talking about?"

"Just wait here a minute. I'll be right back." Drexel took the file and walked behind a partition next to his office space. There was the hum of a copier and a couple of minutes later he returned and placed a manila envelope on the desk and pushed it toward her. Then he clasped his hands together and looking directly at Jane said in a solemn voice, "I confess that I am giving you, a bona fide member of the clergy..."

"Ordained," Jane interjected.

Drexel opened his eyes in response, then cleared his throat, closed his eyes again and continued, "...an ordained member of the clergy a copy of this file and suggesting that you might want to show it to Tom Tidings and see if the *Picketwire Press* will do a story on it. And by doing this I also confess that I have sinned against Picketpedia by violating my responsibility as its editor-in-chief." He opened his eyes, and pushed the envelope toward Jane and said with a wink, "I hope I haven't committed some mortal sin and won't end up in a file drawer in purgatory."

***

Back in her office at Picketwire Community Church, Jane slipped the copy of the account out of the manila envelope that Drexel Herbert had given her. She decided to follow the ancient mystical practice of Lectio Divina in which you read the text several times slowly, after which you meditate, then pray, and finish with a few minutes of contemplation. As she contemplated, the internment camp appeared in her mind's eye, but it was now populated by people who looked like her. Then the scene shifted to the unmarked graves in the Picketwire Cemetery. They were open and empty. The bodies in the "ghost camp" had been resurrected. Jane was convinced that the account was a true one. As Drexel had suggested in his "confession," she needed to show it to Tom and ask him to publish it in the *Picketwire Press*.

Jane collected the sheets and held them suspended in the air above the desk as if she was weighing them the same way Drexel had. She and Tom hadn't talked to each other since her return to Picketwire. When she spotted him sitting in the last pew as she gave her first sermon, she had expected they would meet. As she stood at the back of the sanctuary greeting people after the service, Jane had wondered what he would say, what she would say, whether they would even say anything, or just shake hands like two strangers. As she exchanged words with each person she glanced over their shoulders at the line behind them, hiding her anxiety beneath a pastoral smile. After the last person filed past, she stood there wondering if Tom was waiting until everyone was gone to suddenly appear so that they could talk in private. When he didn't appear, it was clear to her that Tom had skipped out so that he could avoid her. Jane slipped the sheets of paper back into the manila envelope, stuffed the envelope in her purse, slung her purse over her shoulder, and walked out of her office.

***

Tom was in the middle of writing his weekly column and having the usual hard time when Jane burst into the *Picketwire Press* office. Fortunately, the high rolltop desk hid his stunned expression. Recovering, he rose from his chair, which like the desk had also been passed down from his grandfather.

"Oh, there you are," Jane said, then walked toward him, her right hand clutching the manila envelope. "I hoped I'd find you here."

"You did?" Tom stammered as he stepped from behind the desk. "I mean, well, here I am. I was meaning to come by the church and say hello."

"I beat you to it," Jane replied with a smile, deciding it was better not to mention that she had seen him in church.

"Please, have a seat," Tom said, pulling the chair from Gloria's desk over for Jane. "This is one of those ergonomic chairs with all the knobs and levers so you can adjust it. It does everything except eject people. I bought it for a reporter I just hired but she's out right now." After Jane sat down he retreated to the straight back, oak chair from behind his desk.

"I see you're still sitting in your grandfather's chair."

"Yeah," Tom said running his hands along the arms of the oak chair that had been polished by years of elbows. "The same chair, the same desk, the same job. Unlike you. I mean you left and went off to the East Coast..."

"And now I'm back."

Tom nodded, "And you're a minister... and you're... married." There, Tom thought with relief, he'd said it. "I was surprised when I heard."

"That I'm married or that I'm a minister?"

"You always said you wanted to get married and have kids," Tom answered, leaving out that he had expected at one time he would be the husband and father. "But I don't remember you mentioning that you wanted to be a minister. That surprised me."

"It surprised me as well. I guess that's why it's a calling rather than a wanting. What about you?"

"Nothing surprising has happened to me," Tom sighed, looking around the office. "This must be my calling because it sure isn't something I wanted. But, as the Rolling Stones song goes, you can't always get what you want."

"But you might get what you need," Jane said, paraphrasing the song's next line. Then with all the earnestness she could muster she said, "And not just what you need, because you're doing something here that is really important for the community when you report on things that they need to know."

"Like what?"

"Like this," Jane replied, swiftly pulling the sheets from the manila folder and handing them to Tom.

"What's this?" Tom asked, looking at the papers that were suddenly in his hands.

"Just read it...please," Jane pleaded.

Tom read the papers, placing each sheet he'd finished face down on the desk after he'd read it. When he finished he turned the pile face up and looked at Jane. "Where did you get this?"

"Picketpedia. It was in their files where they keep submissions they received but have never published."

"Why didn't they publish it?"

"Because it requires independent corroboration, especially since it was submitted anonymously."

"How did you get a copy? Was it Drexel Herbert?"

Jane looked down at her clasped hands and said, "I'm afraid I can't tell you how I got this because it's covered by pastoral confidentiality."

Tom rolled his eyes and said, "In other words, it wasn't Mister Herbert but Mister Anonymous."

"Whatever you want to call it, you need to print it."

"You said that Picketpedia didn't publish it because they didn't have evidence to back it up. The *Picketwire Press* would also need evidence if we were to do a story."

"I can verify that the camp existed because Bruce, that's my husband..."

"I know your husband's name," Tom cut her off. "We published a wedding announcement. Bruce Levinson. Native New Yorker. BA from Columbia. Harvard MBA. Works for one of those big consulting firms in New York..."

"Bruce quit when we moved here," Jane said, stopping Tom's recitation. "To get back to what I was saying, Bruce and I found the abandoned camp when we were on a hike. When I asked my Uncle Joji if he knew anything about a camp, he said that he'd heard about it from my grandfather. He also told me that he'd found the unmarked graves that are mentioned in what you just read. I went to Picketwire Cemetery and saw the blank stones marking the graves. While I was there I spoke with the retired caretaker, Lazarus Lamont, who told me that in 1946 when he was five years old he had seen the burials. When he was a teenager he asked his Dad about the incident and his dad told him that the bodies had been disinterred from the camp and were being reinterred in a corner of the cemetery."

"That supports what's written in here about burying bodies just outside of the camp and then moving them later to the cemetery," Tom said, fingering the pages as he rocked back and forth on the rear legs of the chair. Suddenly there was a crack and he was on the floor looking up at Jane. Tom scrambled to his feet and looked at the chair, his hands on his hips. One of the back legs had snapped. "What the..."

"Hell," Jane laughed.

"The hell," Tom repeated then turned to Jane with a grin on his face. "I think granddad just sent me a message that I shouldn't sit on this story. But if Wylie Boone sues there's no way we can survive the legal cost we would incur."

"So what do you do?"

"Show Wylie the story we're planning on printing and hope he won't say he'll sue."

"And if he says he will?"

Tony picked up the severed leg of the chair, "I'll do what my granddad's chair just told me to do. Then, I guess I'll have a chance to do something else with my life than publish a newspaper."

CHAPTER THIRTY EIGHT

When Tony called Sister Beatrice to ask if they could meet about the new tour he was planning she quickly agreed. In fact, she added, she and Sister M's had something they wanted to discuss with him as well. While he drove to Our Lady of Lost Souls Convent, Tony went over what he was going to say. His thoughts were disrupted when he saw a sheriff's department patrol car on the side of the road. Instead of a radar gun pointing at him through the window Tony saw a deputy sheriff with a sandwich in his hand. It was certainly a better spot for a lunch break than a speed trap, Tony thought. Still, to be safe, Tony kept his speed down as he drove on.

Sister Rachel, who was sitting behind the reception desk in the Welcome Center, informed Tony that Sister Beatrice and Sister M's were in the museum next door. Inside the museum entrance he found them standing next to an exhibit mounted on the wall that showed the layout of the old Purgatory Penitentiary superimposed on a map of the area.

After greeting both of them Tony asked what they wanted to discuss. "No, you go first, Tony," Sister Beatrice insisted. "Tell us about this new tour you're working on?"

"I'm putting together a mystery tour and I'd like your help."

"My work is all about solving mysteries," Sister Beatrice said, her eyes sparkling with delight. "Do you have any particular one in mind?"

"Sure," Tony responded with enthusiasm. "The mystery is how a map that was stolen from my great-great-grandfather, Don Francisco Medrano, that was proof of the Medrano Land Grant, ended up hidden in a cell here that was once occupied by a convict named Ruf Ryder who was serving time for robbing the Double B Ranch." Tony paused as he considered what to say next since Don Francisco had given his word of honor to C.W. Boone that the Medrano family would never publicly accuse the Boones of stealing the map. "But I want to make it clear that our family isn't accusing the Boones of stealing the map before this convict stole it."

"Good, because there aren't enough facts to prove it in my opinion," Sister M's said. "The evidence we have – that the map was found in a former prison cell, that someone wrote Ruf Ryder on the wall, and that there was a man named Rufus Ryder in prison for stealing from the Double B – is circumstantial. There's no proof that C.W. Boone stole the map from your family, or that Rufus Ryder stole it from the Double B."

"If there were proof it wouldn't be a mystery, which is what my tour is all about," Tony replied. "All I'm asking is that you let me bring the tour group here and show them the cell and the map of the stolen land grant and that you'll tell them how you discovered it and show them the name Ruf Ryder on the wall and that a Rufus Ryder was incarcerated for stealing from the Double B. That's all."

"That's all?" Sister M's asked. "That's enough for people to conclude that the solution to your mystery is that Ryder stole the map from the Boones. You don't have to be the one who accuses the Boones of stealing it from your great, great grandfather, Don Francisco, the members of your tour will do it for you. It's trial by tour."

"Does that mean you won't agree to be part of the tour?"

"Of course, we'll be part of it," Sister Beatrice said firmly. "After all, you're only asking us to show your tour group the evidence that's been uncovered. Besides we love a good mystery, don't we Sister M's?"

"In fact, we have a mystery tour of our own we'd like you to help us with," Sister M's answered. "Actually, it's more of a mystery escape than a mystery tour since it involves several people mysteriously escaping from here."

"But no one ever escaped from the Purgatory Penitentiary," Tony said.

"You're correct that no one has ever escaped. This escape hasn't happened yet."

"Why would someone want to escape from a convent?"

"You no doubt noticed that one of Riggleman's deputies is parked in front of the entrance?" Sister M's said.

Tony nodded, "He was eating lunch, why?"

"He isn't parked there on a lunch break. Riggleman is keeping us under surveillance while he waits for approval for a search warrant. As soon as he gets the warrant he can come in and look for the three undocumented immigrants we're hiding."

"That's why we need to bust them out," Sister Beatrice added.

"Your plan is to sneak them past the deputy?" Tony said, shaking his head in disbelief.

"No, they're going to escape through a tunnel that Sister Beatrice discovered," Sister M's said.

"It starts here in the old power plant," Sister Beatrice said turning to the diagram on the wall and tapping the power plant on the prison layout. Then she drew an invisible line with her finger to a point halfway between the east wall and the edge of the bluff overlooking the Purgatory River. "And it comes out here."

"I don't get it. What was the point of digging a tunnel if no one used it to escape?"

"No one escaped through the tunnel," Sister Beatrice explained, "because it was used to smuggle in contraband, not for prisoners to escape."

Tony looked closely at the diagram, then turning to face Sister M's and Sister Beatrice he said, "In other words, what you're planning is a breakout right under the sheriff's nose."

"That's what I meant by calling it a mysterious escape," Sister M's said, "because it needs to remain a mystery as far as Sheriff Riggleman is concerned."

"Why do you need me?"

"We need your help because once they escape through the tunnel and get to the other side of the wall they still need to get to a safe house without the sheriff catching them."

Tony shook his head slowly. "The problem is there's only one road in and out of here and that's the one the sheriff is watching. If they try to slip by the deputies on foot it will be a long walk and the only cover to hide behind is sagebrush."

"You have a tour that you do on horseback, right?" Sister M's asked.

"It's our signature tour called Riders of the Purple Sage."

"We'd like you to lead a special Riders of the Purple Sage tour that includes this stretch of the Purgatoire River below the bluff," Sister M's traced a route on the diagram. "There's a path from the top of the bluff down to the river. I'll lead them down the path to where you'll be waiting with the horses on the other side of the river. It's shallow enough this time of year at that spot that they can wade across."

Tony scratched his chin and looked at the diagram, "When does this have to happen?"

"As soon as possible. Tomorrow at the latest. I know through my sources at the county courthouse that Riggleman will likely get his search warrant by tomorrow afternoon."

"Well, at least I'll only need four horses. One for me and three for them. That makes it easier on such short notice. After they wade across the river we can ride to a spot I know of near the river about a mile from here where I'll have parked my van. From there I can drive them to the safe house you mentioned. Where is it, anyway?"

"We don't know,' Sister M's said.

Tony's jaw dropped, "You don't know where the safe house is?"

"That's because we don't have one yet. It isn't easy to find a safe place, especially on such short notice. Ideally it should be a place that no one would suspect and would be outside Riggleman's jurisdiction."

"You mean somewhere outside the county?

"Inside. We don't have time to arrange something like that. Someplace in Picketwire would be best since it's the only town in the county that has its own police force, so Riggleman doesn't have free rein.

Tony put his hands on his hips and looked at the ceiling as he thought. Finally, he said, "I know a perfect place in Picketwire."

***

Tony's father, Roberto, sipped from a glass of brandy while his mom, Delores, knitted as they listened to Tony. When Tony stopped talking, his father hunched forward, rolling the half empty glass between his palms and said, "If I understand what you just said, you are asking us to hide three undocumented immigrants from Sheriff Riggleman here at Hacienda Medrano: To be what you call a safe house."

Tony nodded, "If he catches them, he'll hand them over to ICE and they'll deport them without even a hearing. ICE stands for Immigration and Customs Enforcement."

Delores looked up from her knitting, "Your father and I know what ICE stands for, but what we don't understand is why you haven't told us until now that you're involved in helping undocumented immigrants."

"I didn't want you to worry about me getting arrested."

"But you're not worried about us, your parents, being arrested?" Roberto asked, reaching for the bottle of Presidente brandy and pouring some more into his glass until it reached the brim.

"Of course, I am," Tony said. He was standing with his hands on his hips in front of the large fireplace framed by tiles in the rustic living room of Hacienda Medrano, the piñon scented fire basting his backside. "But this is one place where Riggleman wouldn't suspect that they'd be hiding. Even if he did, he doesn't have jurisdiction in Picketwire, so he can't just start searching houses. He'll need the cooperation of the Picketwire Police and he can't get that if he doesn't have a warrant to search the Hacienda Medrano. Besides, they'll only be here a couple of days until we can arrange their safe passage out of the area."

"And if we refuse to take the risk?"

"It's your house..."

"No," Roberto cut him off. "This is our family's hacienda and it's our duty to avoid doing anything here that brings dishonor."

"And you believe this would bring dishonor, is that it?" Tony said, unable to hide his disappointment.

"No," Roberto smiled. "It would bring dishonor if we refused."

"You're saying they can hide here," Tony said, returning the smile.

"We are saying that they are welcome to stay here as our guests," Delores answered, putting her knitting down and rising from her chair. "Now, since we don't have much time before they arrive, I need to prepare three bedrooms."

After Delores left the room, his father filled an empty glass with brandy and handed it to Tony. As they clicked glasses, Roberto said, "To doing what is honorable."

After taking a drink, Tony said, "Speaking of honor, I should probably tell you about a tour that I'm putting together..."

CHAPTER THIRTY NINE

As soon as she saw the sheriff's patrol car blocking the gate of Our Lady Of Lost Souls Convent, Gloria knew that this would be a scoop. She pulled off and parked. Looking at the two purses on the seat next to her, she picked the smaller one. The last thing she wanted was to be delayed as the deputy made her empty everything in the larger one. Making sure a small notebook and her cellphone were in the purse, she put the lanyard with her *Picketwire Press* ID around her neck, got out of her car and walked up to the deputy sheriff who was leaning against the patrol car with his arms crossed over his ample belly. He stood up straight, rested his right hand on the butt of his holstered gun and looked at Gloria as she approached, at least she assumed he was looking since his eyes were hidden behind aviator sunglasses.

The bigger they are the harder they fall Gloria said to herself before she stopped several feet from him and asked, "What's going on, officer?"

He pulled down his sunglasses, looked at her press ID and growled, "No comment."

Gloria took out a pen and the small pad from her purse, and said out loud as she wrote slowly, "Deputy Sheriff..." Gloria looked at his nametag, "Tucker refuses to state why he is blocking the entrance to Our Lady of Purgatory. It appears that he is part of a raid being conducted by the sheriff's department on a convent."

"I didn't say that. What I said was no comment."

Gloria held her pen poised over the pad, "You deny that this is a raid on a convent, a community of nuns?"

Officer Tucker put his hands on his hips and looked up at the sky.

"You really think you're going to get help answering my question from up there, because I'd say the nuns have a better chance than you do," Gloria said.

He looked at her, shifted his weight back and forth, "It's not a raid. Okay? It's a search. We started..." He looked at his wristwatch, "at 0700."

It was already 9:30 AM, so Gloria knew she needed to move quickly. "What are you searching for?"

"You'll have to ask Sheriff Riggleman."

"And where is the sheriff?" This time it was more of a demand than a question.

Deputy Tucker looked down at the pointed toes of his cowboy boots that peeked out from behind his pot belly, and mumbled, "He's inside...searching."

"Thanks," Gloria said, stuffed the pad in her purse and quickly walked around him.

Deputy Tucker called after her, "Wait, where do you think you're going?"

Without stopping, Gloria shouted back over her right shoulder, "No comment."

Inside the Welcome Center, Gloria told Sister Rachel and Sister Louise that she'd heard about the search and asked where the sheriff was. "He and his deputies – there are several of them – are inside searching for some undocumented immigrants that they claim we're hiding," Sister Rachel answered.

Sister Louise added, "Sisters Mary Margaret and Beatrice are with them."

"I wonder if I can talk with the sheriff and Sister M's and ask them some questions?"

"Sure," Sister Louise, answered. "I believe they are in cellblock B. I can take you there."

Fifteen minutes later they entered cellblock B where they found Sister Beatrice and a deputy sheriff. Gloria flashed her press ID at the deputy with Miller on his nametag. "Where's Sheriff Riggleman, Deputy Miller?"

"I don't know. He said we should split up and me and Bernie...Deputy Peters, who's up there," he looked up at the top tier of cells where a deputy was leaning over the railing looking down at them, "we should search this cellblock while he'd go ahead with JT, that's Deputy Thomas, and the other nun...."

"You mean Sister Mary Margaret?"

"Yeah, the nun who's a sister and also a lawyer," he spat out the word lawyer as if it was a plug of chewing tobacco.

Gloria pulled out her cellphone, "Give me the Sheriff's number so I can call him and find out where he is."

"Don't waste your time," Deputy Miller replied. "There's no service here."

Sister Louise explained, "We have bars on our cells but none on our phones."

"Then I'll just have to go and find him," Gloria said, putting her cellphone back in her purse.

"I better go with you or we'll be searching for you as well," Sister Louise said.

When they entered cellblock C another deputy was jogging toward them. "We're looking for the sheriff?" Gloria asked.

The deputy stopped and said, "He's trapped in a cell."

"What?"

"He's locked inside one of the solitary confinement cells at the other end of the cellblock."

"How did he do that?" Sister Louise asked, incredulous.

"We split up and I was searching the cells at this end and he went down to the other end. A few minutes later I heard this heavy metal door slam shut and the sister who was with us started shouting something so I hightailed it over to where they were. I figured the sheriff had found the illegals but when

I got there the sister was standing in front of one of the solitary confinement cells. Its steel door was shut and she told me the sheriff was locked inside."

"But the cell doors can only be locked from the outside with a key so it's impossible for someone to lock themselves inside," Sister Louis said.

"Well, the Sheriff sure as hell found a way," Deputy Thomas said. "Sorry for the language, Sister."

"Don't be, we use the word all the time, although not the way you just did."

"Anyway," Deputy Thomas continued, "the sister said that all the keys are kept in the Captain of the Guards office, which is all the way at the other end of the prison, or convent, or whatever you call this place. It seems that our cellphones don't work in here so I'm on my way back to get the key. I'm sure the sheriff is mad as... well you know. He's probably cursing a blue streak although you can't hear him. There's only a small slot in the door and it seems to be rusted shut. Well, I got to get going."

"I'm going with you," Sister Louise said. "Otherwise, you'll never find the Captain of the Guards office much less the right key. You can run if you want, but it won't get you there any faster because I'm walking."

After they left, Gloria walked to the end of the cellblock where she found Sister M's standing beside a closed steel cell door.

Surprised, Sister M's asked Gloria, "What are you doing here?"

"Covering what started out as a breaking news story, but's now seems more like a breaking out story," Gloria replied. "How did the sheriff lock himself in there? Sister Louise said it was impossible since it can only be locked from the outside with a key."

"You'll have to ask him yourself after we get him out. The slot that allows the guards to check on the inmate inside is rusted shut so our only communication has been pounding on the door. Unfortunately, he doesn't know Morse code."

"You know Morse code?'

"I still remember a bit from when I was a Girl Scout. They gave me a merit badge for it, but probably would have preferred that I'd earned it for selling cookies."

"What happens now?"

"We wait."

"You think he's okay?"

Sister M's looked at Gloria and said, "The sheriff is locked inside a fifty square foot cell behind a solid steel door in total darkness. On the bright side, he could see this as an opportunity to pray." She paused and added, "That was off the record, by the way."

***

They waited almost an hour before Deputy Thomas and Sister Louise returned, accompanied by Sister Beatrice and the other deputies. "Sorry it took us so long but first we had to find the key to open the cabinet where all the keys are kept," Sister Louise explained, as Deputy Thomas held up a ring with half a dozen keys attached. "Fortunately, even though we don't lock people in the cells, we didn't throw away the keys. Inside the cabinet we found this ring with six keys on it hanging on a hook labelled solitary confinement. There are six solitary confinement cells so one of these keys should fit the lock on this door."

Deputy Thomas tried the keys in the lock one after the other until he reached the last key on the ring. "If this one doesn't work we'll have to get an acetylene torch and cut through the steel," he said, inserting it into the keyhole and turning it. The lock clicked and he pulled open the heavy door. When Riggleman didn't emerge Deputy Thomas went inside the cell. A minute later they came out with the sheriff's right hand on Deputy Thomas' shoulder to steady himself. He held up his left hand to shield his eyes from the sunshine that flooded into the cellblock from the windows high overhead. Deputy Thomas plucked a pair of aviator sunglasses from his breast pocket and gave them to the sheriff. After putting them on, Sheriff Riggleman withdrew his hand from Deputy Thomas' shoulder and stood there silently, his eyes now hidden behind the dark lenses.

Finally, Deputy Miller broke the silence. "How are you Sheriff?" The sheriff looked at him but didn't say anything so Miller said, "Tucker can drive you back to the sheriff's department and me, Bernie, and JT will continue the search."

"Sheriff," Gloria called out. "Before you leave can you answer some questions about your search of the convent?"

The sheriff shook his head and said with a slight quiver in his voice, "I'm calling off the search. Now, I'd appreciate it if everyone left except Sister Mary Margaret. I want to talk to her about what just happened."

Deputy Thomas, who was standing next to the sheriff, leaned over and said softly in his right ear, "Okay, Sheriff, but you should know that if you think the sister locked you inside that cell I don't see how she could have. It takes a key to lock it and the only key is on this ring I'm holding and I had to go all the way to the other end of the prison to get it."

"I don't want to talk to the sister because I think that she locked me inside the cell, I need to talk to her because of what happened while I was in there."

CHAPTER FORTY

Jemma Lu finished her dinner of Mexican braised short ribs with squash and, since it was impossible for her to cook anything worth eating for just one person, she placed the leftovers into several containers that she would take to work and share with Picketware's employees. As she sat down with a fresh pot of tea there was a knock on her door. Not many people visited Jemma Lu at home so she peeked out the window near the door and saw the lanky frame of Foster St. Vrain.

When Jemma Lu opened the door, Foster apologized, "I know it's late, Jemma Lu but I have some information on the person who tried to kill Wylie."

Jemma Lu invited him in and Foster took off his cowboy hat and followed her into the living room where she directed him to sit in one of the antique armchairs with a lace antimacassar draped over its back. "I just made a fresh pot of tea if you'd care to join me."

"Sure," Foster replied.

After getting another teacup and saucer from the sideboard in the dining room, Jemma Lu placed it on the coffee table next to the teapot. She sat in a chair facing Foster and poured the steaming tea into both of their cups. "It's a Native American herbal tea made from a blend of sagebrush and prickly pear cactus. We sell it as part of our PickeTea brand." She explained, pushing a small jar with a spoon in it toward him. "It's a bit strong so you should add some honey."

Foster stirred in a generous dollop of honey and then tried to fit his thick right index finger through the small handle of the dainty cup. Finally, he gave up and clasped it in his hand then took a sip. "This is pretty good, Jemma Lu."

"It's good for you as well. Calms a person down."

"I guess if I drank this instead of beer I wouldn't have shot my television set."

Jemma Lu laughed then took a sip of tea. Foster noticed that her index finger fit the cup handle with room to spare. She placed the cup back in the saucer on the coffee table and asked, "Now, what's this new information you have?" Foster shifted uncomfortably in the straight back chair. "I know it's not as comfortable as your recliner," Jemma Lu said. "These antique chairs have horsehair padding."

"I guess it's like being back in the saddle," Foster answered, then leaned forward and gingerly set the teacup into the saucer resting on the coffee table. He pulled a small notepad from the breast pocket of his shirt. "Like I said, I think I might have found who tried to kill Wylie. They really dislike Wylie," he said, opening the notebook.

"There are a lot of people who dislike Wylie."

"Yes, but these people want to stop him from stealing water."

"Stealing water?"

"They claim that Wylie is illegally diverting water from the Purgatoire and using it to grow cannabis. I know it's hard to believe."

"You're right that it's hard to believe," Jemma Lu said. "And I wouldn't if Wylie hadn't told me that he was doing it."

"Wylie told you?"

"It was part of a business proposition about growing cannabis that he pitched to me the other day. He left out the part about stealing water. Still, stealing water doesn't seem like enough of a reason for someone to want to kill Wylie."

"They lynched people for stealing water when this was still the wild west, Jemma Lu."

"This isn't the wild west, anymore, Foster."

"That's why they'd use a minivan instead of a noose. I guess you could call it progress although it seems that the intent wasn't to kill Wylie," Foster said then took a sip of tea and added, "at least not according to the guy who did it."

Jemma Lu almost dropped her cup of tea, "He confessed to you?"

"It wasn't an actual confession. I need to refer to my notes so I can tell you exactly what happened." Foster put down his cup of tea and took a small notebook out of his breast pocket shuffled through it until he found the page he was looking for and then continued, "It all started when I was over speaking with Clint Crowley who has the place across from the Double B. I asked him if he'd seen any suspicious activity and he showed me a tape from the security camera at his gate which is across from the Double B's. On the recording was a Jeep Wrangler following Wylie from his ranch. Later I saw the same Jeep parked in front of the Pretty Good and I observed the driver meeting with two other people. I tailed them from the Pretty Good and it turns out they were going to my house of all places. I was able to go in the back door and meet them at the front one. I even picked up a bottle of beer I hadn't finished – I have a few of them sitting around - and held it in my hand when I opened the door. They said they wanted to talk to me so I let them and they told me about Wylie stealing water and his illegal cannabis operation."

"Why on earth would they tell you that?"

"Because they wanted to hire me to gather evidence for a lawsuit they can file to stop Wylie," Foster said with a grin then stuffed the notebook back in his pocket, picked up the cup of tea and took a sip.

Jemma Lu shook her head in amazement, "What did you tell them?"

"I told them I'd work with them but not for them. I didn't want to have a conflict of interest."

"You didn't tell them you were working for me, did you?"

"Nope, that's client confidentiality. I told them I was doing some investigative work on Wylie for the *Picketwire Press*."

Jemma Lu shook her head in amazement, "You're also working for the *Picketwire Press*?"

"It's more like volunteering. Tom needed someone with my investigative skills to help him with his coverage of Wylie and I told him that I had a personal interest in finding out who was trying to kill him. I didn't tell him that you were the person who had the interest."

"If these people know that Wylie is diverting water illegally to grow cannabis why don't they just tell the authorities?"

"The authority in this case is the sheriff, since it's in his jurisdiction. That means they'd have to report what Wylie is doing to Riggleman, which means it would go nowhere," Foster explained then added, "It wouldn't surprise me if Riggleman knows all about it."

"Me neither. I must have been crazy to suggest that." Jemma Lu poured some more tea for herself as she mulled what he'd said. After sipping from her cup, she said, "I still don't understand why you think one of them tried to kill Wylie."

"That's because I haven't told you that I'm pretty sure the guy who was driving the Jeep is hiding a blue minivan."

Surprised again, Jemma Lu asked, "Why do you think that?"

"After they left my house I followed them back to the Pretty Good where this guy, Will, who was driving the Jeep, dropped them off. I put his age at around thirty and he works for the Picketwire Institute, which I gather is some sort of think tank affiliated with Picketwire College."

"I know about the Institute," Jemma Lu nodded her head, "but I've never met this fellow you described. Who were the other two people?"

Once again taking his notebook from his pocket, Foster looked at it then said, "The woman introduced herself as Gretl Johan and said she was the Director of this Institute." Foster looked up. "Since you know about the Picketwire Institute I'm guessing that you know her?"

Jemma Lu nodded. "I've met her."

"The other guy said he was a professor of philosophy at the College. His name is Ari Naxos. I suppose you know him as well?"

"I haven't met him, but Sid Tenken, who's the chair of the philosophy department, told me Professor Naxos is a new member of the faculty. Sid speaks highly of him."

Foster scratched his chin and said, "I don't think this has anything to do with philosophy."

"Philosophy has something to do with everything, Foster, that's why it's called philosophy, which means love of wisdom."

"He may teach philosophy, but the way he looked at Gretl Johan he's in love with more than wisdom."

"I didn't know you were also an expert at detecting love. Who knows, Doctor Naxos might be drawn to Doctor Johan because they share a love of wisdom," Jemma Lu said. "Anyway, tell me what happened next."

"This Will guy dropped off the two wisdom lovers," Foster continued, clearly loving the bantering between them. "I proceeded to tail him to a house on Bisonview. He parked in the driveway and after he went inside I checked out the Jeep Wrangler. It was unlocked so I looked in the glove compartment and found the registration. It's registered to Gretl Johan. I figured that if he was using her Jeep there must be something wrong with his own vehicle. At the end of the driveway was a single car garage. I tried the door and it was locked, which made me suspicious because most people in Picketwire don't lock their houses much less their garages. I looked through the window and could see a vehicle with a tarp covering it. Seemed to me that it was covering something larger than a subcompact and smaller than a semi, which would be about right for a minivan. With the police looking for a blue minivan with a bashed in front end he obviously couldn't take it to a body shop to get it repaired so he'd have to stash it somewhere and my hunch is that place is the garage. That's also why he's using this Johan's Jeep Wrangler. Now that it's dark, I'm planning to go over there after I leave here and see if my hunch is right."

"You mean you're going to break into the garage?"

"Pick the lock and walk in was more my idea."

"If your hunch is right, what happens then?"

Foster shrugged, "That's for you to decide, Jemma Lu. I'm working for you. If I find a blue minivan with a Porsche size dent in its front end under that tarp, then this Will Raines guy is who you're looking for."

"Raines?" Jemma Lu asked with surprise.

Foster chuckled. "Yeah, heck of a name for someone who studies water. Anyway, I'll let you know if my hunch is right." Foster got up and started to leave.

"No, you won't," Jemma Lu declared, stopping Foster in his tracks, "because I'm going with you."

"Why?"

"Because I have a hunch as well," Jemma Lu said, "only I hope it's wrong."

***

Foster parked a short distance down the street from the house on Bisonview. Fortunately, it was a moonless night and there were no streetlamps. Even better, the Jeep Wrangler was no longer in the driveway.

"We're in luck," Foster said. "He isn't here."

"Maybe he's here but he parked the Jeep somewhere else."

"If he did there would be a light on in the house."

"Maybe he's asleep."

"It's Friday night and he didn't strike me as an early to bed guy. Anyway, we'll find out after I pick the lock." Foster reached under his seat, grabbed a flashlight and stuffed it into his back pocket. As Jemma Lu started to open the passenger door, he asked, "You sure you want to do this?"

"If I'm going to make the decision that could send this young man to jail, I need to see for myself what's in that garage."

"Okay, but put this on," Foster reached back, picked up a gray sweatshirt with a hood and gave it to Jemma Lu.

"What's this?"

"One of my hoodies."

Jemma Lu held it up. "It's huge, Foster. I'll look like I'm inside a tent. We're not going camping, we're breaking and entering."

"The more of you it covers the less of you can be described in case someone sees us."

"What about you?"

"My excuse is that I'm a private detective involved in an investigation, but it would be hard to explain why Jemma Lu Tuttle is breaking into a garage."

Jemma Lu couldn't argue with that, so she pulled on the hoodie and got out. They walked to the house. Foster peeked into one of the windows and gave Jemma Lu an all-clear thumbs up then they continued up the driveway to the garage's side door. "Should I hold the flashlight so you can see?" Jemma Lu whispered.

"If we turn on the flashlight someone might see us as well. Besides picking a lock is all touch. Sort of like unhooking a ..." Foster cut himself off.

"A bra," Jemma Lu whispered, her own grin hidden by the shadows.

"Shhh," Foster replied then inserted something resembling a paperclip into the keyhole and turned the doorknob. He pushed the door open and they both entered, then he closed it behind them, pulled the flashlight from his pocket, and turned it on. Just as he had said, a brown tarp covered something large enough to be a minivan. He went over and yanked the tarp off and proclaimed, "Sure looks like a blue minivan to me."

They walked to the front of the minivan. The beam from Foster's flashlight played across the badly dented front end that was streaked with red paint. "I'm pretty sure that's a Porsche's red paint and not lipstick."

"Maybe the minivan belongs to someone else and this Will Raines agreed to let the person use the garage," Jemma Lu said, as if she was trying to convince herself that was what happened.

"I agree that a minivan isn't exactly the vehicle of choice for a guy his age. Anyway, there's one way to find out. We'll just check the registration." Foster asked Jemma Lu to hold the flashlight while he opened the passenger side door and then the glove compartment. After fishing around he pulled out the vehicle registration and looked at it, "His name isn't on the registration."

Jemma Lu exhaled in relief, "Then, it doesn't belong to him."

"Nope, the registration says Linda and David Raines and the address is in Fort Collins. Must be related to him."

"Let me see," Jemma Lu said, snatching the registration out of Foster's hands and looked at it intently with the flashlight.

"We should put the registration back and get out of here before Will returns," Foster grabbed the registration out of Jemma Lu's hands then stuffed it into the glove compartment and quietly closed the minivan's door.

Foster had just shut the garage's side door behind them when they were lit up by the headlights of a Jeep that was turning into the driveway. "Pull the hood over your head, look down and let me do the talking," Foster ordered Jemma Lu.

The Jeep stopped, the driver's door opened and Will Raines stepped out. "I'm Foster St. Vrain," Foster said before Will opened his mouth, "the detective you met with today."

"Sure, I recognize you, but what are you doing here?"

"I came by because I wanted to ask you some questions. We've been waiting here for you to return."

"How did you know where I live?"

Foster laughed, "If I couldn't find out where you live I'd be a piss-poor detective."

Will nodded, "Okay, I'll buy that." He pointed at Jemma Lu, "Who's the guy in the oversized hoodie?"

"Oh, this is Jim. I just hired him and I brought him along as part of his training."

Jemma Lu peered up at Will from under the hood then turned on the flashlight that was still in her hand and pointed its beam directly at Will's face.

"What the hell," Will said, startled. "Why are you shining that light on me?"

"Practice," Foster said.

"What do you mean practice?"

"You're supposed to shine a light in a suspect's face when you're interrogating them."

"But I'm not a suspect."

"Jim's a little over eager," Foster said, patting Jemma Lu on the top of the hood that covered her face, "Turn off the flashlight, Jim, this isn't an interrogation." Then turning back to Will he said, "We'll get going now. Sorry, to disturb you." With that he tugged on Jemma Lu's sweatshirt as a signal to leave.

"What about the questions you were going to ask?

"While we were waiting for you I got a call about a lead I need to follow up on in person. I'll give you a call about the questions. I've got your number."

"Of course you do," Will laughed. "You'd be a piss-poor detective if you didn't."

CHAPTER FORTY ONE

A core principle in Sheriff Riggleman's political creed was never to confess to making a mistake. People might forgive you but they wouldn't vote for you, because it was a sign of weakness. But that's what he was about to do. Not only confess, but to a nun, not a priest, and he wasn't even a Catholic. He had seen the light. It had appeared after the door of the windowless, solitary confinement cell had slammed shut. In the pitch black he felt a panic attack, remembering his dad locking him inside the root cellar of his family's sorry excuse for a farm when he was a small boy. Most of the time he didn't even know why his dad was punishing him and probably his dad didn't know either.

When he pulled the flashlight from his belt that also held a holstered gun and handcuffs, his shaking hands lost their grip. The sound of the flashlight hitting the floor was like a stone hitting the bottom of a dry well. Riggleman got down on his knees and frantically tried to find the flashlight, cursing the darkness and wiping away tears. Suddenly a blinding light appeared. It was just like the light from the bright desk lamp he used during interrogations at the sheriff's department, only this time it wasn't his voice demanding a confession from the squirming suspect.

"What did the voice say?" Sister M's asked.

"He said...," he paused and looked up at Sister M's. "It was a man's voice, but I'm not saying God is male."

"That's okay, I know she isn't."

"Anyway, he said he already knew all the execrable things I'd done in my life. I didn't know what the word meant but I figured it was pretty bad..."

"Detestable is one meaning, but the one you're familiar with begins with the letter 's'," Sister M's said.

"That bad, huh?" Riggleman nodded his head. "Well, who am I to argue with God, especially when I'm locked in a cell."

"And you think God told you that you didn't need to confess to him?"

"Not think, I know. Believe me, when God speaks you know. I mean, you're a nun so you know that. But he told me I had to confess to someone and they would tell me what I needed to do to atone."

Yes, I should know, shouldn't I, Sister M's thought. "And who is this someone who is supposed to tell you what to do to atone?"

"Why you, of course. That's why I told you about the vision."

"Me?"

"God said that after I told you, then you would tell me what I should do."

"I'm not doubting that you had some sort of vision, Sheriff..."

"Call me Jesse."

"Jesse," Sister M's repeated, more than willing to call him anything but Sheriff.

"It was a real vision from God. It was like in the Bible when Paul is blinded when he was on the road to somewhere."

"The road to Damascus."

"Right, that road. I know I wasn't on a road but locked in a cell and I wasn't blinded like him, but being in a pitch black cell was almost the same thing. I was blinded by the sunlight, though, when I came out of the cell. Until I put on these sunglasses." Riggleman touched the pair of Ray-Bans that Deputy Thomas had given him. "But while God told Paul to stop prosecuting the Christians, he told me that I especially had to atone for prosecuting the illegals, only he called them undocumented immigrants like you do. Then he said that you could help me with that."

"It was persecuting not prosecuting and it was Jesus who appeared in the vision and he asked Paul why he was persecuting him," Sister M's couldn't help pointing out.

"Okay, so maybe it was Jesus who was in my vision as well. I only saw the light and heard the voice. He didn't give me his name."

"In any case the voice you heard said that I would help you atone for persecuting the undocumented immigrants, is that what I'm hearing?"

Riggleman nodded and said, "Do you think that ordering my deputies to drop the search for the illegal, I mean undocumented immigrants, counts as atonement?"

"Atonement is not just refraining from doing bad deeds in the future, it's also making amends for your past actions."

"That's why God, or Jesus, I'll just call him the Voice, said you'd help. I only know about sending people to jail."

"There's a fine line between punishment and penance." Sister M's explained. "In fact, America's first penitentiary, as opposed to a jail, was built by Quakers in Philadelphia. It was supposed to encourage penance rather than inflicting punishment, reform rather than retribution."

"I get it, they wanted criminals to have the same kind of vision I just had when I was locked up in that solitary confinement cell," Riggleman said, nodding his head.

"Not quite. Quakers believe that God appears as an inner light and speaks in a still, small voice."

"Then I sure didn't have any Quaker vision. The voice I heard wasn't still and small and although it was inside the cell, it wasn't from inside me."

But, certainly a quaking experience, Sister M's thought, noting that Riggleman's hands were still shaking from his spiritual sound and light show. No, the Quaker experience was more like hers when she sat in her cell, in silence, inner eyes wide open, scanning the dark night of the soul for a faint glimmer from God. Truth be told, she was more of a Quaker Catholic than a Roman one.

"You are going to help me aren't you? The Voice said that you had first-hand experience in atoning."

How could Riggleman know that atoning for sending an innocent man to prison when she was a prosecutor was the reason she joined the Sisters of Saint Leonard and why she was providing free legal counsel to those in need. He couldn't know. Sister M's never told anyone except a priest when she had gone to confession at a church near the courthouse right after the incident. She didn't even think the priest listened to her because he just told her to say an Our Father and three Hail Marys twice a day for a week, which was hardly penance for what she'd done. It was more like putting a bandage on a child's knee for a minor scrape to make the kid feel better.

The point wasn't for her to feel better, it was to make things better for others. And that's what a still, small voice told her after her confession. Riggleman wouldn't know any of this. Was this proof that God or Jesus had actually spoken to Riggleman, only in a loud voice? The answer was that it didn't matter. Sister M's knew what her answer should be. She said, softly, "Yes, I'll help."

***

"Sheriff Riggleman wants to atone for persecuting the undocumented immigrants?" Sister Beatrice repeated Sister M's words as if she couldn't possibly have heard them correctly.

"He claims he had a vision from God or possibly Jesus when he was locked up in the cell."

"And you believe him?" Sister Beatrice asked, skeptical that someone like Riggleman could have a vision of the divine while she had never had so much as a glimpse despite her hours of devoted prayer and meditation.

"Whether I believe him or not, the important thing is that he believes he had the vision," Sister M's replied. "Riggleman and I agree that his vision should be kept a secret. Not only would people think he was crazy, but it would eliminate the element of surprise, which is necessary for the atonement plan to work."

"You've already got a plan?"

"It just came to me all at once and Riggleman agreed to it."

"Sounds like you had a vision of your own."

CHAPTER FORTY TWO

Dave Sanderson sat in his pastor's study at the Picketwire Community Church, Bible open, reading Psalm 23. Even though he knew it by heart he didn't want to bypass any of his exegetical duties when it came to preparing a sermon. When he got to "leadeth me beside the still waters" he envisioned the still waters of the mountain lake where he would soon be spending a week fly-fishing. When he continued, "Thy rod and thy staff they comfort me" prompted another vision, but this time it was of him casting with his fly rod. Suddenly the door opened and Jane appeared. "I hope I'm not disturbing you, Dave."

"I was just thinking about a sermon on Psalm 23. I'm trying to come up with something new that will hook people," Dave sighed. "What's on your mind?"

"I need to give you a heads-up."

"Okay," he nodded toward the chair in front of his desk. "Have a seat."

"I have to give you some background first," Jane replied after she sat down.

"I've got time," Dave answered settling back in his chair.

Jane told Dave about finding the World War Two internment camp for Japanese-Americans on the Double B Ranch, discovering the unmarked graves of prisoners of the camp in the Picketwire Cemetery, and the anonymous report found in Picketpedia's purgatory. "I just came from meeting with Tom at the *Picketwire Press*. I told him the same thing I just told you and said that he needed to run a story on it. He agreed. And now I realize that I should have spoken with you first, because when people read it they might think the church is involved."

After taking a minute to consider what Jane had said, Dave responded, "No need to apologize about the church, but are you ready to have your name in the paper? It's likely to create quite a stir."

"Yes, but I told Tom that there needs to be a disclaimer that makes it clear I am doing this as a private citizen and it has nothing to do with the church."

Dave leaned over the desk and looked Jane straight in the eyes, "You'll do no such thing, Jane. Speaking truth to power is what this church and our ministry are all about. Should be, anyway." Dave sat back and patted the open Bible. "Like it says in Psalm 23, though I walk through the valley of the shadow of death,

I will fear no evil, nor Wylie Boone who's going to be pretty ticked off when he reads it, to say the least."

"He won't have to wait until he reads it. Tom is going over to the Double B this afternoon to tell Wylie Boone that the *Picketwire Press* intends to run the story and ask for his response."

"My guess is that his response is going to be unprintable. I'd sure like to be a fly on the wall, though," Dave said, imagining the flies in his tackle box and picking the Wooly Bugger.

"I'm going to be there as well," Jane said, then noticed that her hands, which she had placed on top of the desk, were now clasped together as if she were praying. She moved them to her lap.

Dave's face erupted in surprise. "Did I hear you right, that you're going to be with Tom when he confronts Wylie?"

"It's only fair since I'm the one responsible for the story."

"I understand," Dave sighed. "But keep in mind that Wylie Boone's version of the Golden Rule doesn't include as you would have them do unto you so he's likely to do unto you just about anything to get off the hook."

***

With several feet and the center console of Tom's SUV separating them, Jane was reminded of the intimacy they once shared in the old Volkswagen Beetle he drove in high school. My god they talked and talked, she almost exclaimed out loud. Not that they didn't do some other things as well. Especially the last time when they parked at Rendezvous Ridge just before she left for college. Amazing how you can contort your body in a confined space when you're a teenager. She looked out the side window to hide the smile the memory had aroused.

"You're awfully silent," Tom said.

Turning to him, smile suppressed, Jane replied, "I was just thinking about how much bigger this SUV is than that VW Beetle you had in high school."

"Yeah," Tom laughed. "It was like driving a cardboard box on roller skates. Still, it was my first car and I miss it. For me, that car was freedom as much as transportation. As much about getting away as going somewhere." Not that he'd succeeded in getting away, unlike Jane.

"Now, instead of getting away in a car people just use their cellphones," Jane said. "I've turned mine off, by the way."

"Me too," Tom answered. "Guess we have nobody to talk to but each other. Not that I don't want to talk to you. In fact, it reminds me of the times we spent together. I mean..."

"Are you dating anyone?" Jane said, cutting off Tom's stammering.

Relieved, Tom answered, "If I were dating anyone, you and everyone else in Picketwire would probably know. People have a hard time keeping their love life secret around here: Two dates and you're halfway to the altar."

"I'm sorry, it's none of my business."

"I don't know, as a minister you're sort of in the marriage business."

"Believe it or not, I haven't married anyone."

"What?" Tom gave Jane a quick look. "You haven't married anyone?"

"I married Bruce, of course. What I mean is I haven't officiated at a marriage. Even though I graduated from seminary several years ago I wasn't ordained until I was called to be associate pastor at Picketwire Community Church."

"Then I've got you beat," Tom said with a grin.

"What do you mean?"

"A year ago a friend of mine asked me if I'd officiate at his wedding. I went on the internet, paid twenty five bucks and was ordained a minister in the Church of Living Happily Ever After. I even did some premarital counseling over drinks at the Last Ditch."

Jane laughed, "I can't believe there is actually a church that exists just to ordain people so they can perform marriages like this Church of Living Happily."

"You left out Ever After."

"Whatever," Jane rolled her eyes. "Calling that a real church is like calling something that only publishes wedding announcements a newspaper."

"I get your point, although wedding announcements are some of the most popular items in the *Picketwire Press*…along with the obituaries. Anyway, I didn't renew my ordination so if anyone asks me to marry them I'll send them to you."

"I'd much rather be doing that than meeting with Wylie Boone."

"Yeah," Tom said. "But remember you're the one who insisted on coming with me."

"I know. It's just something I have to do."

***

"Where's the lady reporter who was with you the last time?" Wylie asked after Tom and Jane had been ushered into the living room of the Double B Ranch house by a butler dressed in blue jeans and cowboy boots.

"You mean Gloria Herrera?" Tom answered. "As I said on the phone this isn't about the hit-and-run story, which is what Gloria is covering."

Wylie looked at Jane, somehow managing to convey both intimacy and intimidation. "What story are you reporting on?"

"I'm not a reporter," Jane answered.

"This is Reverend Jane Takamoto," Tom jumped in. "The new associate pastor of Picketwire Community Church."

"A reverend!" Wylie seemed genuinely surprised, which Jane sensed, was a rare and uncomfortable feeling for him. Good, she thought.

"But I'm not here in that role," Jane said.

"It would be a waste of time for both of us if you were," Wylie replied. "I stopped believing in God a long time ago. It was only fair since from what I could tell he'd stopped believing in me. Now, why don't you both take a seat and tell me about this story that you want me to respond to."

After settling into leather easy chairs Tom launched into a description of what they had uncovered, including the role Jane played. When he'd finished, he asked, "If there's anything you want to challenge as inaccurate this is your chance."

"Nice to know that you want it to be fair and balanced," Wylie said with more than a little sarcasm. "Can I see this submission that was discovered in a file at Picketpedia?"

Tom pulled out some papers from his briefcase and handed them to Wylie. Wylie put on a pair of glasses that had been sitting on the side table next to him and read the papers. When he was done reading, he took off the glasses. "Since the person who wrote this chose to remain anonymous how can you verify any of it?"

"Even though we don't know who wrote it, parts of it are consistent with what we do know from other sources. For example, the part that describes how people in the camp worked on your ranch and that those who died were buried in unmarked graves in the Picketwire Cemetery is corroborated by an eyewitness."

"That same eyewitness says that it was your father who supervised the burial," Jane added.

"You're really going to include that bit about my father in this story you print?"

"We haven't written it yet," Tom answered. "We want to give you a chance to respond so if you have anything to tell us this is your chance."

"And you believe it's your chance to keep me from suing you," Wylie said.

Tom shifted uncomfortably in his chair and started to respond, but Wylie held up his right hand to stop him.

"Thanks for the opportunity of letting me read this," he said. "Before I say anything in response I'd like to talk to Reverend Takamoto. Alone. I suddenly feel the need for some spiritual guidance."

"Jane said she wasn't here in an official capacity," Tom said, protectively.

"That's okay," Jane said.

Wylie stood up and, looked down at Tom, "You can wait here while we go somewhere else where Reverend Takamoto and I can have our spiritual discussion."

Jane followed Wylie from the living room, down a hallway, then through a door and onto a broad stone patio. Stretching out beyond the patio was a corral and half a dozen ranch buildings. Wylie stopped and without prompting pointed at one of them. "That's the old bunkhouse. A hundred years ago more than thirty ranch hands and cowboys – quite a few were Mexican vaqueros – slept there. Tried to sleep, anyway what with all the night noises that a bunch of men can make, especially after eating beans for dinner. That building next to it was the cookhouse and dining hall. There was an entire community here. Even had a church. Sort of, anyway. It's called a morada..."

"A morada is what the Hermanos Penitentes call their meeting house."

Wylie nodded, "A lot of the Mexican vaqueros who worked here were Penitentes and they asked my great-granddad, C.W., if they could build a morada where they could worship. C.W. said that he'd rather have them whipping themselves for their sins in a morada than getting drunk and shooting each other in a saloon. Anyway, he let them build it and that's it over there." Wylie pointed at a long adobe building set back from the others. "Dad closed it after my granddad, C.W. Junior, died since none of the people who worked here were living on the ranch at that point. Dad was going to use it for something else but...," Wylie paused and looked down at the ground for a second, "he never got around to it. It's pretty much the way they left it."

"There's a morada near my family's farm," Jane said. "From what I understand it's still being used for meetings."

"You ever see the inside?"

"Since it's a secret religious society for men I'm not allowed inside."

"Well, now's your opportunity."

They walked to the building. Wylie pushed open one of the double cedar doors and Jane followed him into a long narrow room with a high ceiling supported by thick wooden beams. The only light came through some windows set high in the walls. "There aren't many windows so it's pretty dark in here. They lit it with candles and lanterns."

Jane went over to look at a series of pictures that had been painted on the white plaster walls. "These are the stations of the cross." She walked to the far end of the room where there was a large painting on the wall, "And this one is the Virgin Mary."

"Our Lady of Sorrows is what the Penitentes called her according to my dad."

Jane moved to the left several feet and stopped, "The altar and crucifix must have been here."

"My dad gave the crucifix to some Penitentes when he closed the place but he said that it was life-size and painted."

"Where does this lead?" Jane asked walking over to a closed wooden door to the left of where the altar would have been.

"To a sort of a storeroom. It's not locked if you want to look inside, but it's pretty dark in there. I'd rather stay out here, if you don't mind."

"I can use the flashlight on my cellphone," Jane said, taking it out of her purse. She swung the door open and stepped inside. Other than the sunlight that traced the vents in the wooden shutter on the window set high in the far wall of the room, darkness filled the space. She switched on her iPhone's flashlight and shined it around the room. "There's a big wooden cross in here," Jane called back to Wylie. "It's not a crucifix. The Penitentes could have used it when they re-enacted Christ carrying the cross to Golgotha." She bent down. "There are also yucca leaves on the floor. They might be from the whips they used to scourge themselves."

"Dad said they called those yucca leaf whips disciplinas."

Jane emerged from the room and said to Wylie, who stood with his hands tucked into the front pockets of his jeans, rocking slowly on the high heels of his cowboy boots, "It felt like I was in a tomb."

"You're the first person who's been in there since my dad died," Wylie replied, slowly as if each word was being hauled up from a deep well. "I found him slumped over that cross in there. His shirt was off and he'd been whipping himself. Caused a heart attack. I carried his body to his bedroom. Then I washed off the blood where he'd whipped himself and dressed him in his pajamas. I told everyone that he died in his sleep. Our doctor and the undertaker knew better than to contradict me."

Jane reached out and put her hand on Wylie's left arm. He looked at her and said, "I've never told anyone this before."

"Why do you think he was in there whipping himself like he was a Penitente?"

"It didn't make sense to me, until now when you showed me that anonymous submission to Picketpedia."

"What do you mean?"

"Dad wrote it."

"How do you know?"

"For one thing the date on it is a couple of days before he died and for another I recognized the type as the same as an old typewriter we had. It was one of those old Underwood manuals and the letters for a and d were worn the same way as the ones in the report. I know because I used it to write my papers for high school. It's probably still in a closet. I think that he was in that room trying to punish himself for what he'd done by setting up that camp and using the Japanese...."

"Americans," Jane said. "They were Americans."

"Right," Wylie nodded his head. "All of his drinking must have been his way of dealing with what he'd done. Then the doctors told him that if he didn't stop he'd be dead of a heart attack or cirrhosis of the liver in less than a year. I was still living here at the ranch and I told him that he had to do what the doctor ordered. He promised me he'd stop. When I found his body there was an empty bottle of tequila next to it. I thought the empty bottle explained why he'd gone in here and did what he did. It was because he was drunk. Not totally convincing because by then he could drink a bottle and seem to be cold sober, but it was the only explanation I could come up with at the time. But now..." Wylie shook his head and looked away, toward the painting of Our Lady of Sorrows.

"He was trying to atone for what he'd done."

Wyllie shook his head and sighed, "Seems like he got religion and I lost it."

"By telling me this you're confirming that what was in the submission is true."

Wylie looked at Jane, "I asked you to meet with me privately for spiritual advice and because you're a minister that means whatever I just told you is confidential. You can't tell anyone without my consent, right?"

"Yes, but..."

"I'm not going to say that my dad wrote it. That he, the Boones, did the things that it says."

"But..."

Wylie held up his right hand to stop Jane, "But I'm also not going to try and stop Tom from printing his story or sue him afterwards. I'm not going to say anything. I won't confirm or deny what's in it. Call it a Mexican standoff."

CHAPTER FORTY THREE

Tony stood at the door to the Conquistador Lounge in the Picketwire House at the conclusion of his new Mystery Tour. Next to him was Olathe Sweetgrass, who'd been driving the Purple Sage's minibus. The tour had started at the hotel six hours earlier at 10:00 AM when Tony had greeted the group, some of whom had stayed the night at the hotel. The tour had sold out even though Tony had advertised the tour through the Purple Sage website and the Picketwire Visitors Center only two days before. The fact that lunch and cocktails at the end of the tour as well as a fifty percent discount on dinner were included in a ticket price of only twenty five dollars no doubt had something to do with it.

It wasn't just this tour that Tony was celebrating, there was also the private one for three people. Their tour began with Purple Sage's new Rails, Trails, and Tales Tour from which they exited before it concluded to be transported by pickup truck to the former Purgatory State Penitentiary, now Our Lady of Lost Souls Convent, where they were provided an exclusive stay as special guests of the Sisters of Saint Leonard. Their stay ended with a tour of a hidden tunnel that had been dug by inmates and they rejoined Tony as the only members of his Riders of the Purple Sage horseback tour along the Purgatoire River. The tour concluded with an all-inclusive stay in the historic Hacienda Medrano. Unlike the Mystery Tour that one would not be publicized.

The Mystery Tour, on the other hand would get maximum publicity, including a front page story in the *Picketwire Press*. In addition to the twelve people signed up for the tour, a thirteenth person was added as an "ex officio" member when Tony asked Tom Tidings if he would assign Gloria Herrera to cover the tour. Tom had hesitated at first, but agreed after Tony suggested who would be better suited for covering a mystery than the *Picketwire Press'* investigative reporter.

During the tour the group was presented with clues that spanned two centuries, involved multiple thefts, an imprisonment, and the discovery of a map documenting the Medrano Land Grant. The stops included the former Purgatory State Penitentiary where they viewed the cell while Sister Beatrice told them about the discovery of the map and pointed out the name Ruf Ryder scrawled on the wall. Sister M's then presented the evidence that pointed to Rufus Ryder as the inmate who had stolen it from the Double B and hidden it in the cell. Another stop on the tour was the gate of the Double B Ranch where

Tony pointed out that the Mesa del Oro in the background had been part of the original Medrano Land Grant. Returning to the Picketwire House, they inspected the mural in the Conquistador Lounge. The tour concluded where the participants discussed the clues that had been presented while imbibing cocktails. After arriving at a unanimous, if not entirely sober, solution for the mystery, they headed to the dining room for dinner.

"That reminded me of *Clue*," Olathe said to Tony as they stood in the empty lounge, "Except that this is a cocktail lounge not a library and this isn't one of those manor houses and none of the people looked like Miss Marple or Hercules Poirot, although that tall, skinny guy was a dead ringer for Sherlock Holmes except for the Colorado Rockies baseball cap he had on instead of a deerstalker hat with ear flaps. Anyway, I'm sure glad they didn't decide that the chauffeur did it since I'm the one who drove them around today."

Tony laughed, "Were you surprised at their solution to our 'whodunnit' mystery?"

Olathe scratched her chin and drawled, "Let's see, based on the clues they decided that this Ruf Ryder character was a convict named Rufus Ryder and that he stole a map of a Mexican land grant from the Double B that Wylie Boone's ancestors had stolen from your ancestors, the Medranos, which meant that the Medranos couldn't prove what land had been given to them under the grant. Based on that they concluded that the Boones stole the land from the Medranos and made it part of the

Double B Ranch. No big surprise that they decided that C.W. Boone did it."

"And what did you decide?"

Olathe looked at Tony and gave a weary shake of her head, "That everyone 'did it'… to us Native Americans since all of our land was stolen."

"Got a minute to answer a few questions?" Gloria interrupted, saving Tony from figuring out how to respond to Olathe.

"Don't mind me," Olathe said. "I'm heading into the dining room for my complimentary dinner. Solving the mystery has worked up my appetite."

After Olathe left, Gloria held up a small digital tape recorder and asked Tony, "One thing I don't understand is why you used this tour to accuse the Boones of stealing land from your family."

"Wait a second," Tony said holding up his right hand, "I didn't accuse the Boones of anything! The members of the tour group decided that based on the evidence that C.W. Boone was the most likely culprit," Tony laughed. "That laugh is off the record, by the way."

"Too late, I've already got it on tape."

"Let me then add for the recording, that I'm just a tour operator who conducted a mystery tour in which certain evidence in an unsolved crime was presented."

Fighting an urge to break out laughing, Gloria said, "Right, and it's just a coincidence that when it was over the people on the tour voted that C.W. Boone stole your family's land?"

Tony nodded and said solemnly, "Just like it's a coincidence that a jury has twelve people, which is the same number who were on the tour, excluding you of course."

Gloria rolled her eyes and then switched off her tape recorder and stuffed it in her purse. "I assume it's okay if I interview the members of the jury, I mean, tour group?"

"Of course, and please fill out the tour evaluation form."

Gloria grinned and said, "You can read my evaluation on the front page of the *Picketwire Press*."

"You should interview Olathe as well."

"Okay, but I hope she's going to actually tell me on the record who she believes the guilty party is unlike her boss," she replied over her shoulder as she left the lounge and headed for the hotel dining room.

"In her case it's guilty parties," Tony said to himself, remembering Olathe's comment as he looked at the mural of his great-grandfather attired as a conquistador, astride his horse, pointing at the stolen land.

CHAPTER FORTY FOUR

"I need a drink," Jemma Lu announced once she was in the passenger seat of Foster's Jeep after they left Will standing in his driveway.

"I do too," Foster replied. "But it's not tea."

"Let's go over to the Last Ditch."

"People might see me with you and wonder what we're up to."

Foster reached over and pulled the hood of the sweatshirt Jemma Lu was wearing over her head, "Just keep this hoodie on and they won't know who you are."

Five minutes later Foster parked next to the bar. Jemma Lu was still wearing the hoodie that blocked her peripheral vision as they walked through the bar to a table in the far corner. She was pretty sure no one could see her face hidden under the hood.

"I'll go up to the bar and order drinks," Foster said.

A couple of minutes later Foster returned with a long neck bottle of beer and the vodka and tonic that Jemma Lu ordered.

They both sipped their drinks and then Jemma Lu asked, "You won't tell anyone what happened back there?"

"You mean you don't want to have the guy who was trying to kill Wylie arrested?"

"No I don't, but that's not the only reason," Jemma Lu paused and took a drink. "I'm his mother."

Stunned by what Jemma Lu said, Foster swigged some beer and finally replied, "I didn't know you even had a son."

"Nobody does. I got pregnant by mistake thirty years ago and had the baby at a place out east. I put him up for adoption. It was all kept secret."

"How do you know this Will fellow is your son?"

"I suspected when you mentioned the name Raines and then when I saw the registration I knew he must be my son, because the names on the registration are the same as the people who adopted him and they also lived in Colorado Springs."

Foster took another swig of beer and said, "Can I ask who the father is?"

Jemma Lu sipped her drink and replied, "It could be Wylie Boone."

"Wylie," Foster exclaimed, spitting out some of the beer.

"I can see that you're surprised."

"Damn right," Foster declared.

"Wylie and I were engaged thirty years ago."

"I never knew you were going to marry Wylie."

"Not many people did. I called it off before we made it public."

"You called it off even though you were pregnant."

"I didn't know I was pregnant until a few days after I told him, but it wouldn't have made any difference. I wouldn't have married him anyway. Besides, I didn't know for certain that he was the father...and I still don't."

"You mean there was another guy?"

Jemma Lu nodded her head, the hood bobbing up and down, "Howdy Hanks."

"Howdeee Hanks," Foster repeated, drawing out the last syllable of the first name. "Now that isn't a surprise. I could see you two together unlike with Wylie."

"They each have a fifty-fifty chance of being the father."

"In other words, the kid's father is either the Sagebrush Shakespeare or Wylie Coyote."

"Neither of them knows I was even pregnant," Jemma Lu said and sipped some more of her drink.

"If you want to know which one is Will's father you can do a paternity test."

"I would need them to agree to a paternity test and that means I'd have to tell both of them they might be a father."

"Not necessarily. We just need some DNA from one of them. If it doesn't match then that person isn't Will's father and the other one is. Of course, we'll need a sample of Will's DNA as well. It just so happens that when he and his friends paid me a visit at my place I asked them if they wanted something to drink and he said he'd like some water. I haven't washed the glass he drank from, so I can get a sample from it. As for you all I have to do is pocket that glass you're drinking from.

"I don't know if I'll be able to tell Will any of this. It will be enough of a shock to learn that I'm his mother, but how on earth will he be able to handle Wylie, the man he tried to run over, as his father."

"Look, the lab results will come back from the DNA lab in a sealed envelope sent directly to you. You can do what you want with it. You can open it or not. It's your call. We'll still need a sample of either Howdy or Wylie's DNA. I don't think Wylie is going to accept any invitation from me to get together for a drink, so that I can get his DNA from the glass, but Howdy will probably agree to a beer."

"No," Jemma Lu said, emphatically. "If I want to go ahead with this I'll get it from Howdy somehow."

"Okay, you're the boss or client..."

"How about friend," Jemma Lu suggested, "because I could sure use one."

"That too. Now, why don't I drive you home? It's been quite a night."

"Okay," Jemma Lu said. "I can't wait to take off this hoodie. Wearing it makes me feel like one of the seven dwarfs."

"You'll be Snow White once again."

"I don't know about that, but at least I won't be Dopey anymore," Jemma Lu replied and looked around. "Hold on," she said to Foster. "Howdy is sitting at a table over there and it's a chance for me to get his DNA. But I can't go over to him in this get up." She tugged at the hoodie.

"Just go in the rest room and take it off then go over and do what you have to do with Howdy to get his DNA. I'll go in after you and retrieve the hoodie."

"Won't somebody notice that you've gone into the women's room."

"This is the Last Ditch, Jemma Lu. People use whatever restroom is available."

CHAPTER FORTY FIVE

"I see you're hard at work on the sermon you'll be giving this Sunday."

Jane looked up at Dave Sanderson, who was standing in her office doorway.

Dave stepped into the room and looked at the blank screen. "I know it was bad timing that the story on the internment camp is coming out on the day you're scheduled to preach," Dave said. "Look, I can preach instead. I can preach one of my golden oldies."

"And what do we tell people since it's already on our website, not to mention the directory on the front lawn outside that I'm giving the sermon. Oh my God, there's even a title for it."

"Rolling Back the Stone," Dave said. "I have to confess that when I saw it my first thought was the Rolling Stones, but, of course, it's on Mark 16:1-8 when the three women find the empty tomb."

"That was the title for the sermon that I was going to preach and not the one that I now have to preach. It was already written." Jane smiled, forgetting her troubles for a minute, "Mary Magdalene, Mary mother of James, and Salome find that the stone in front of the tomb where Jesus was buried has been rolled back." Jane pressed her left palm on the sheaf of papers. "The whole tone of the sermon I was going to give is upbeat and joyful. The tomb is empty and Jesus has risen. I don't see how I can use any of it now. Of course, I am stuck with the title."

Dave reached down and typed 'Rolling Back The Stone" on the keyboard. "At least the screen isn't completely blank anymore and you can start rolling."

The space Dave vacated when he left the room was immediately filled by Hazel Shanley, the church secretary who announced that someone named Elise Plumb would like to see her. What's another distraction, Jane thought after she told Hazel to show Elise in. They had only met the one time when Bruce and Jane had joined Tony Medrano's tour to see the Dinosaur Tracks and Elise had given them directions to the internment camp, which was now the subject of her as yet unwritten sermon."

A minute later Elise appeared. She was dressed in her ranger outfit and placed her Smokey Bear hat on the desk. After exchanging greetings Elise sat down in the chair opposite Jane and said, "I hope I'm not disturbing you"

"Not at all," Jane replied. "I wanted to get in touch with you anyway and thank you. After all, if you hadn't given Bruce and me directions to the internment camp it might still be a secret. Tom said you didn't want to be mentioned in the story that will run on Sunday?"

"If my boss knew I was involved, well let's say he definitely does not like surprises."

Unlike my boss who seems to love surprises, Jane thought. "In that case, you're welcome."

"But I didn't come here just to talk about the upcoming story in the paper," Elise said and then went on to explain about Wylie Boone calling Tony after the front page story by Gloria Hernandez on Purple Sage Mystery Tour ran in the *Picketwire Press*. "Wylie asked Tony what exactly he hoped to gain from stirring things up and then hung up."

"Tony discussed it with his family and they decided that they didn't want the land back, but that it was a stain on their honor that the internment camp is located on the original Medrano Land Grant. Tony then suggested that a way to remove the stain would be to ask Wylie to donate the land to the Comanche National Grasslands, which happens to be who I work for, as you know. It could then be open to the public like Camp Amache is."

"That's a terrific idea," Jane said. "That would bring the camp and what happened out from the shadows where it has been hidden for more than half a century. Is there any way I can help?"

Elise pursed her lips and then moved to the front of her chair, "In fact, there is something very important you can do to help. Not just important, but crucial."

"What would that be?"

"We are pretty sure that if the Medranos propose this to Wylie Boone, he'll turn it down. It's no secret that C.W. pledged that no Boones will ever part with any of the Double B."

"What do you think would persuade Wylie to break a family pledge?"

"To get rid of the negative publicity is all we can think of," Elise said.

"Although I've only met Wylie once I got the impression he didn't care what people thought of him?"

"You're right," Elise paused and looked down at her hands that she was wringing nervously. "But because of the story that will be in Sunday's paper, everyone will know that Japanese-Americans were imprisoned and forced to work on the Double B like they were prisoners in a chain gang and then hiding the internment camp and the secret burials. That's not behavior that Wylie can just shrug off as doing business. It's not something that is going to be forgotten. He and his family will be branded by it forever...and there's not a damned thing, excuse the language, he'll be able to do about it."

"But if he donates the land he can avoid the branding," Jane said.

"Like John D. Rockefeller escaped from being branded forever as a robber baron who engaged in despicable acts like the

Ludlow Massacre by becoming a philanthropist. It's not that the Boones' role in what happened would be covered up, but it would be a form of restitution that will lessen the sentence, so to speak."

Jane clasped her hands on the desk as if in prayer while she listened. When Elise was finished she said, "What's the crucial role you think I can play?"

"I know it's a long shot, but if you come with me to ask Wylie if he would donate the land, there is at least a chance he will agree even if he breaks C.W.'s pledge that the Boones will never part with any of the Double B. You were the one who brought it to everyone's attention, both the hidden camp and the secret burials, and because you're a Japanese-American he might be more receptive if you were the one to offer him a way out."

"When I met with Wylie Boone I was with Tom Tidings and we saw Wylie in order to give him a chance to respond to the story before it was published. While we were there Wylie asked to speak with me privately. It was an off-the-record meeting, so it wasn't mentioned in the paper."

"Does off the record also mean you can't tell me what you talked about."

Jane shook her head, "Not just because it was off the record journalistically, but it was also off the record pastorally."

"You mean like a confession?"

"I'm not a Catholic priest, obviously, so it wasn't like a Catholic confession. In our church we call it pastoral counseling not confessing, but it's as confidential as something said in a confessional booth."

"I suppose it's too late to tell him that donating the land would be penance? You know, instead of saying a bunch of Hail Marys."

Resisting the temptation to laugh, Jane replied, "Unlike a Catholic confession, pastoral counseling doesn't end with me giving the person a list of things they must do as penance for their sins. I believe that is ultimately between the person and God."

Elise gave Jane a quizzical look and asked, "Did Wylie tell you if he even believed in God?"

"I can't tell you."

"Pastoral confidentiality, got it," Elise said. "But can you at least tell me if this previous meeting between you and Wylie will be an obstacle in asking him for the donation?"

"Not for me."

"What about Wylie?"

"I guess we'll find out."

CHAPTER FORTY SIX

There Zelda was, sitting between a famous playwright and a director. Okay, maybe the director wasn't famous yet, but he would be after the play opened on Broadway, which Zelda was certain would be its next stop after the world premiere in Picketwire. Of course Max wouldn't be as famous as her after she reprised her leading role on the "Great White Way." She imagined all three of them sitting in one of those swanky restaurants in New York City reading the rave reviews instead of the swankless Last Ditch Bar. She looked at Howdy who was drinking a beer from a long neck bottle and Max with a glass of red wine in his hand and shamefully sipped her glamorless Coke through a straw.

Zelda had only been in the Last Ditch once before and on that previous occasion the bartender, Shep somebody, refused her request for a Margarita because she was underage, dismissing with a loud laugh her assertion that she was over twenty one and could prove it, except that she hadn't bothered to bring her ID because she'd never been carded before since it was so obvious. She was relieved that where they were sitting a waiter took their order, so Shep wasn't able to recount the humiliating event in front of Howdy and Max. Just as fortunate was the absence of Mike Arnold, the guy playing Clay to her Jolene in the play, After the rehearsal Howdy and Max had asked if they wanted to join them for a drink. To Zelda's delight, Clay declined, announcing that he had a date. Obviously not a date with destiny like Zelda.

"I think the rehearsal tonight went well," Max announced. He turned to Zelda and said, "You've improved dramatically since our first rehearsal, Zelda."

Well, it is a drama, after all Zelda was tempted to reply as she played with her straw. Instead, she turned to Howdy. "Mister Hanks...I mean Howdy, I know you don't want us to know the ending yet, but it would help if my Jolene, stands up to Clay because I would never let someone treat me that way."

"That's why it's called acting, Zelda," Max said without waiting for Howdy's reply. "In a play a world is created that is different than your own, or mine."

"The thing about this play..." Howdy began to say.

"Exactly," Max cut him off. "The play's the thing."

"Yes, I know the play is a thing," Zelda said. "But..."

"The plays the thing/Wherein I'll catch the conscience of the king," Max's voice soared and some of the bar's patrons turned their heads to see what the commotion was. Max lowered his voice and continued, "That's from Hamlet's soliloquy in Act Two Scene Two in which Hamlet says that he is going to write a play that shows a king being murdered just like his uncle Claudius killed his father so that he could become the King of Denmark and marry Hamlet's widowed mother. Then the play is performed in front of Claudius and his mother. So, you see, Zelda, the play is the thing Hamlet uses to get his revenge on the man who killed his father."

"Okay, I get what Hamlet is doing even though I would have just kicked Claudius' ass," Zelda replied.

"What I was going to say before," Howdy said, "is that the thing about this play is that it is based on real life experiences."

"You mean Jolene is based on a real person?" Zelda said, hardly hiding her surprise.

"That's not her real name but there is a person that I based Jolene on."

"What about Clay?"

"Let's just say that I didn't make Clay out of nothing, like God made Adam."

Zelda's eyes widened. "And the crappy way that Clay treats Jolene, did that really happen?"

Howdy nodded.

"Where did all this stuff happen?"

"Here in Picketwire," Howdy answered then took a sip from the long neck bottle of beer, placed it on the table and added. "It was a long time ago,"

"Are any of the people still alive?" Zelda pressed.

"Most of them, including me. Unlike in Hamlet where all the main characters end up dead, including Hamlet."

"You're in the play?" Max asked in astonishment. "I mean, there's a character in the play based on you?"

"Which one?" Zelda quickly followed up.

Howdy shifted uncomfortably in his seat feeling like a trout trying to shake the hook lodged in its lip. Then, to the rescue, a voice cut through the silence. "I hope I'm not interrupting anything?"

"Jemma Lu," Howdy answered with relief.

Jemma Lu was standing next to the table holding a half finished vodka and tonic. "I was just having a drink with a friend over in the corner when I saw you come in."

"We're unwinding after rehearsal," Max said.

"Zelda's the lead in my play," Howdy added.

"Mind if I join you," Jemma Lu asked. "My friend is just leaving," she turned to where Foster had been sitting and saw him walk out of the women's room with the hoodie tucked under his arm. "In fact, he just left."

Howdy pulled out the chair next to him and invited Jemma Lu to sit down.

"I play Jolene," Zelda declared to Jemma Lu as soon as she was seated. "Howdy was just telling us that she's based on someone he knew a long time ago only that's not her real name."

"Anyone I know?" Jemma Lu asked, arching her right eyebrow and looking directly at Howdy. She couldn't help noticing that Jolene and Jemma Lu sounded similar, but if Zelda was playing her she was woefully miscast.

"You might remember her, but she moved away right after we graduated from high school," Howdy answered, trying to sound as if the whole thing was no big deal.

"What happens to Jolene?" Jemma Lu said, relieved that he didn't base the character on her.

"That's what I'd like to know," Zelda said glaring at Howdy.

"If you'll excuse us," Max said. "Zelda and I have to leave."

"We do?" Zelda said.

"Remember, I promised your Mom I'd get you home by nine."

Zelda reluctantly rose from her chair and walked away with Max, her empty glass of Coke with its straw in her hand. She marched over to the bar and placed it directly in front of Shep and said, loudly, "Thanks for the rum and Coke," then joined Max, who stood speechless at the door.

"How was your meeting?" Howdy said as Max hustled Zelda out the door of the Last Ditch.

"What meeting?"

"With your friend."

"Oh, you know, just catching up on things."

Howdy leaned toward her and whispered, "I know that we have a lot to catch up on."

"You mean like what happens after people from the past suddenly show up," Jemma Lu replied and took a sip of her drink.

"I didn't mean to…"

"I wasn't just talking about you Howdy. You I can handle."

"Handle, what does that mean?"

"I mean," Jemma Lu replied, placing her right hand on his left forearm, "I'm glad you're back."

"You're talking about Wylie," Howdy nodded and placed his right hand over her left one. "You don't know how to handle that he's back."

Jemma Lu nodded, "Wylie is a handful. I met with him the other day and it didn't go well, to say the least."

"You should have called me and I'd have come to your rescue. Just like I did thirty years ago."

Jemma Lu clinked her glass against Howdy's bottle of beer, "To memorable rescues."

"Past and future," Howdy added with a broad smile then finished his beer.

"I need to get going," Jemma Lu said. "I'm walking home. The person I was meeting with drove us here."

"I'll run you home, and don't worry, I only had this one beer. Let me just settle my tab and I'll meet you at the door." As Howdy walked to the bar Jemma Lu wrapped his empty beer bottle in a napkin and stuffed it in her purse.

CHAPTER FORTY SEVEN

S ister M's looked up at the tiers of cells in cellblock C that had been preserved just as it was before the Purgatory Penitentiary became Our Lady of Lost Souls Convent. Guards could see everything through the bars of the cells. It wasn't just the cells, no matter where they were in the prison inmates were watched. The only place where the guards couldn't directly observe a prisoner was if they were in one of the solitary confinement cells directly behind her. Ironically, the prisoners who were confined in the small, bare, soundproof cells without any light as punishment were the only ones free from the oppressive surveillance.

She and Riggleman were seated next to each other at a folding table in front of the solitary confinement cells with members of the press facing them. Riggleman turned to Sister M's and whispered, "Are you sure this is necessary? Can't I just put out a press release instead?"

"Paul didn't issue a press release after his vision on the road to Damascus."

"Yeah, well, I'm no saint. I'm a sheriff."

"Anyway, remember that we agreed to have this press conference and it's too late to back out without looking like you have something to hide. The same goes for refusing to answer questions. You can't dodge them with no comment."

"And you remember that we agreed that I don't have to tell them what I saw and heard in there," he pointed his right hand thumb to the solitary confinement cell less than six feet behind them.

"Unless you're specifically asked."

"Yeah, well..."

"That was the agreement."

"Okay, okay. At least we also agreed that this would only last fifteen minutes."

Sister M's rose from her seat and welcomed the members of the press. "I believe this is the first press conference we've had here. After we're finished if any of you would like a tour please see Sister Louise." Sister Louise who was standing in the back, raised her right hand. Sheriff Riggleman will make a statement then he has agreed to take questions..."

"Only for fifteen minutes," Riggleman whispered.

"...for fifteen minutes." Sister M's looked down at Riggleman who seemed glued to his chair. "Sheriff, the floor is yours."

Riggleman unglued himself and slowly stood up, then cleared his throat and read from a piece of paper in his hands, "I want to inform the public that the Purgatory County Sheriff's Department after a careful review and due consideration has changed our policy and will no longer arrest people for being undocumented immigrants sometimes referred to as illegal aliens or immigrants or...whatever. That's it." As soon as he finished everyone jumped out of their chairs and started lobbing questions.

"Please," Sister M's said sternly, like a school teacher addressing an unruly class. "If everyone will sit down then raise your hand, the sheriff will give each of you a chance to ask your questions."

"Remember you only have fifteen minutes, because I've got to get back to my job protecting the citizens of Purgatory County," Riggleman said then looked for someone who would pitch him a softball. He pointed at a young woman sitting in the first row next to hard ball reporter Gloria Herrera. "Fire away...I mean ask your question."

Instead of the young woman, Gloria stood up. "Gloria Herrera of the *Picketwire Press*..."

"I was pointing at the young woman."

"I'm young and a woman."

"Of course, Ms. Herrera," Riggleman sighed. "What's your question?"

"Sheriff, does this change in policy have anything to do with you searching this place, which is a convent..."

"I know what it is."

"Then you know it's a religious institution, like a church."

"We had a warrant and information that there were illegal…I mean undocumented immigrants hiding here."

"Did you find any?"

"No," Riggleman replied and before she could ask a follow up, he quickly pointed at the woman who looked to be in her late teens sitting next to Gloria and said, "You had your hand up before I took the question from Ms. Herrera, what would you like to ask?"

"I'm Fiona Gilroy of the *Prairie Dog Pantograph*," the woman said as she stood up.

"Isn't that the name of the Picketwire High School paper?"

"Yes, I'm the editor-in-chief."

"I didn't think a school paper would be covering something like this," Riggleman said, cracking a nervous smile. "By the way, I always wondered why the Picketwire High School paper is named for a panting prairie dog instead of a barking or growling one.

"For your information, Sheriff, our paper isn't named for a panting prairie dog, a pantograph is a device that copies what a person is writing by moving a pen that is connected to a second one. Also, our paper was named the Pantograph when it was established more than a hundred years ago and only added Prairie Dog when Picketwire High adopted it as its mascot."

"Thanks for clearing that up," Riggleman said looked around, "Next question."

"You didn't answer my question," Fiona said.

"Oh, right, okay what is it?"

Fiona looked at the screen of her smartphone and read, "My question is that since you just said that searching this place and finding no undocumented immigrants wasn't the reason for changing your policy, then what was your reason?"

"We, uh, reviewed our policy. It was a very careful review...as I said..."

"Yes, we already know that you said that, Sheriff," Fiona interrupted Riggleman's stammer. "My question is was there any particular thing that came to light during your review that led you to change your policy?"

"Yes there was." Before Fiona could ask a follow up question, Riggleman spotted a woman in her sixties sitting in the front row holding a pad of paper and a pen rather than a smartphone or digital recorder. He pointed at her and said, "How about you, Ma'am? You must have a question?"

"A question?"

"Yes, I want to give every member of the press a chance so I'm spreading it around."

"Thank you Sheriff, I'm Sister Gabrielle with the *Prairie Psalms*."

"*Prairie Psalms*?"

"It's the Our Lady of Lost Souls Convent weekly newsletter. Anyway, now that you've asked me if I have a question I do have one." She held up her pad and read, "Did anything happen to you while you were locked in the solitary confinement cell?"

"What do you mean by happen?" Riggleman said, shifting uncomfortably.

"I mean, for example, did you see anything?"

"How could I? It was pitch black and I dropped my flashlight and couldn't find it in the dark."

"How about hearing anything?"

"How could I hear anything? The cell is soundproof and the little slot in the door was rusted shut.

"You're saying there was nothing you saw or heard while in the cell?"

Riggleman looked at Sister M's for help. She smiled back at him. He looked at the ceiling, then said, "Let me put it this way, I didn't see or hear any...body. Now if you don't mind, Sister, let's give someone else a chance to ask a question," Riggleman said. Immediately everyone's hand shot up and he called out, "How about someone in the second row."

A young black man in a gray hoodie stood up quickly, "Lemoyne Parry of the *Picketwire College Pundit*."

"What's your question?"

"Same as the Sister's. Did anything happen to you when you were incarcerated in that cell behind you?"

"I wasn't incarcerated."

"Incarceration is defined as being in prison or confinement and you were confined in a prison, weren't you?"

"A former prison, now it's a convent."

"Okay, you were confined in a cell in a former prison that's now a convent."

"I wasn't confined."

"You couldn't get out and you wanted to get out and that's being confined."

Riggleman held up his hands in surrender, "Okay, okay, I was confined, but not incarcerated." Now that I've answered your question as to whether I was incarcerated or confined, let's move on and give another member of the press a chance to ask a question."

"But that wasn't my question," Lemoyne said. "My question is similar to the one the sister asked that you didn't really answer."

"I answered that I didn't see or hear any body when I was...confined in the cell."

"And my question is whether anything at all happened in the cell?"

Riggleman looked at Sister M's who whispered back, "Remember our agreement."

Riggleman said through clenched teeth, "You could say that I saw the light."

"You mean you understood your policy of arresting undocumented immigrants wasn't right?"

"Just what I said, I saw the light," Riggleman replied with exasperation then looked at his watch. "Okay, time's up."

"There are two minutes left, so there is time for one more," Sister M's whispered.

"Okay, I'll take one last question," Riggleman sighed and pointed at a white cowboy hat in the second row whose wearer's face was hidden behind Fiona Gilroy's head. "Does the man in the white hat in the second row have a question?"

The man stood up and took off his battered, white Stetson. Riggleman said, "Hey, aren't you the bartender at the Last Ditch."

"Shep Woolsey," the man nodded.

"This is a press conference," Riggleman laughed, "but I'll sure need a drink when it's over."

"I also publish the *Picketwire Dialectic*."

"Never heard of it."

"It's a new alternative paper."

"Alternative to what?"

"To pretty much everything."

"Where does someone get a copy of this dia…" Riggleman stammered as he tried to get his tongue around the word.

"You can get a free copy at the Last Ditch. The drinks you have to pay for. I named it the dialectic after the method Socrates, the great philosopher, used to expose falsehoods and get to the truth."

"I suppose that since you publish an alternative paper you must have an alternative question?" Riggleman said with a weak grin.

"I just hope you give an alternative answer, since so far you've been ducking and dodging the ones pitched at you by my fellow members of the press," Shep said, bowing to the others present.

"Now, wait a second," Riggleman shouted. "I gave everyone a chance to ask a question and I answered them. So, what's yours?"

"When you ran for Sheriff, an election that you narrowly won I might add..."

"I carried all of the county but the city of Picketwire," Riggleman blurted.

"Which you lost by four to one," Shep said, unperturbed. "But if I could continue, you stated in an interview with the *Picketwire Press* that the county is supreme and not the state or federal government, and that within the county the sheriff is authorized to enforce all local, state, and federal laws, and also refuse to enforce any that the sheriff believes contrary to the U.S. Constitution, which happens to be the philosophy of the constitutional sheriff's movement." Shep held up his hand stopping Riggleman with his mouth open. "Those are your own words I'm quoting, so it's not my question."

"Okay, maybe I said something like that, but I was running for sheriff not county philosopher."

"Not maybe, you did say it."

"Okay, okay, so what's your point?"

"Hold your horses, Sheriff," Shep replied. "You've renounced a policy that you not only have the right, but it was your duty as a constitutional sheriff to protect Purgatory County from the 'illegals' who were invading the county, state, and the nation." Shep held up his hand again as Riggleman opened his mouth. "That's also a statement of fact and not a question."

"Yeah, that's what I said in the old policy, but now I'm saying something different, so get to your question."

"Since you agree with the facts that I've stated, it means logically you no longer believe in a core belief of the constitutional sheriff philosophy. Now here's my question, Sheriff. What law enforcement philosophy do you believe in?"

"Well…I…I mean…this isn't something that I can just spout off the top of my tongue."

"You mean you can't tell us what you believe the role of county sheriff is?"

"Give me a second to think about it."

"We at the *Picketwire Dialectic* encourage thinking, Sheriff," Shep said, nodding his head.

Riggleman looked at his watch and announced with relief, "Time's up."

"But you didn't answer the question," Shep objected. He was joined by a chorus of protest from the other members of the press.

"I tell you what. I'll meet with you later today and answer your question."

"What about us?" Gloria yelled. "You're supposed to answer the questions in front of all of the press at a press conference."

"That's easy to fix," Shep drawled. "The sheriff and I will meet at the Last Ditch and you're all welcome to join us."

Before Riggleman could say anything in reply, Sister M's stood up and announced, "Then we will adjourn this press conference and reconvene at the Last Ditch later today," she looked at Shep and asked. "What time?"

"Four o'clock," Shep replied. "That's when happy hour begins."

CHAPTER FORTY EIGHT

Tom sat at his rolltop desk, looking at a mock-up of the front page for Sunday's paper. Talk about hot off the press, Sunday's edition would be right from the frying pan with his story on the World War Two internment camp on the Double B Ranch and the secret burial of some of the Japanese-Americans interned there. Jane had asked him to wait until Sunday so she could inform her congregation before they saw it. The day before they had run the story by Gloria on Tony Medrano's Mystery Tour that accused C.W. Boone of stealing land that had been granted to the Medrano family.

"Where are you going to run the story on the internment camp?" Gloria asked, her head barely clearing the high top of the rolltop desk.

"Front page, of course," Tom replied, leaning back in the chair that was the temporary replacement for the one he'd broken while engaging in a similar maneuver. "Both the print and the online edition. I have no doubt that other media outlets are going to pick it up. Just like they picked up your front page story on the Mystery Tour. You're going to be getting a lot of job offers, by the way."

"The only one I'm interested in is right here."

Tom suddenly sat up straight, the front legs of the chair slamming onto the floor. "You'd really consider staying on here in Picketwire?"

"Why wouldn't I?" Although the desktop hid everything but her head, he knew she had both hands on her hips. "And what makes you think I didn't have other offers before I decided to come here in the first place? You think I took this job out of desperation. I did my research like any good investigative reporter before I took this job."

Tom sat back in his chair. "I'm not badmouthing my own paper but we're a small town newspaper. A lot of people consider us in the same category as the dinosaurs who left their tracks in the Picketwire Canyonland."

"That's what's nice about being a small town paper. You don't have to consider what a lot of people think. As for being a dinosaur, who knows, maybe people will be looking at the tracks I leave on the pages of the *Picketwire Press* a million years from now."

Tom nodded his head, "You do have a way with words."

"I better have," Gloria laughed.

"I can give you a raise and a promotion to assistant editor," he said as he wrote on a pad of paper Gloria's name, the date, a salary amount, and the new title."

"Look," Gloria said, "I could sure use the extra money and the title is nice but what I'd really like is an assurance from you that I can have the freedom and time to do investigative reporting."

"Freedom and time," Tom repeated as he scribbled the words on the pad. "Anything else?"

"Since you asked, it would be great not having to take photos at high school football and basketball games."

Tom made a crude drawing of a camera with a slash mark through it then gave a mock grimace, "You sure do drive a hard bargain." He looked at the sheet then signed his name with a date, tore it out of the pad and handed it to Gloria. She looked at it and walked over to her desk.

"Wait," Tom said. "You didn't tell me if it's enough to keep you here."

Gloria wrote something on another sheet of paper than folded it lengthwise, placed it on her desk and turned it toward him, then leaned back in her ergonomic chair and placed her feet on the top of the desk. Tom grinned as he read what she'd written on the paper name tent, "Gloria Hernandez – *Picketwire Press* Assistant Editor and Investigative Reporter."

CHAPTER FORTY NINE

Before Jane and Elise could ask Wylie Boone if he would be willing to donate the land occupied by the internment camp, they had to come up with a way to meet with him in person. As Elise put it, "We can't just call up the Double B and ask to talk to him or, worse leave a message. He'll either refuse to speak with us or he'll want to do it by phone, which won't work because in order to have a chance at persuading him we need to meet in person so he can feel our presence – well your presence, anyway."

"Then I guess we'll have to surprise him," Jane said.

"But how can we set up a surprise meeting with Wylie Boone?" Elise asked.

"I don't suppose we could just show up at his front door and ring the doorbell?"

"Now that would be a surprise," Elise laughed, "because it would mean we somehow got through the Double B gate and snuck past his security systems and bodyguards."

"How would we ever manage that?"

Elise slapped the desk with her right hand, "Can you ride a horse?"

"Of course," Jane replied. "I grew up on a farm. Why?"

"We may not be able to walk through Wylie's front door, but we can ride through his back one."

***

Jane and Elise had been riding for an hour after leaving the Picketwire Canyonland trailhead where they'd unloaded the two horses from the trailer that Tony had towed there with his pickup.

"Remind me what century we're in," Jane said as they stopped to drink from their canteens.

"Yeah, riding a horse out here on the prairie is like being in a time machine with a saddle," Elise said. "Hopefully it's taking us to a time when miracles happen, because we may need one."

"Speaking of miracles is that a herd of buffalo?" Jane said pointing to a cloud of dust on the horizon. She lifted her aching hips off the saddle and stood up in the stirrups. She'd forgotten how hard a saddle was compared to the padded seat of her trail bike.

"Not unless they've decided to switch from four-hoof drive to four-wheel drive."

Several minutes later two men in what looked like a dune buggy came bouncing over the prairie and stopped in front of them. After the dust settled they could see it was a Land Rover with a roll bar instead of a roof. Wylie Boone in the passenger seat looked up at Elise and Jane who were still astride their horses. "If you're looking for the Double B welcome mat you won't find it out here...or anywhere."

"How did you spot us?" Elise asked.

"You tripped one of the sensors we have along the property line and we sent a drone over to check it out," He pointed at a dark speck in the sky that Elise thought was a circling buzzard. "Got a good look at you and when I saw you were wearing your Smokey Bear hat I knew it wasn't rustlers or some folks out for a trail ride who got lost and strayed onto the ranch by mistake."

"It's not a mistake," Jane said, easing herself back in the saddle."

"Why its Reverend Takamoto. Don't tell me you decided to go for a ride here because of the pastoral setting," Wylie waved at the prairie with buttes and mesas in the distance.

"We want to talk with you and we didn't think you'd be willing to meet."

"And you'd be right. What with someone trying to kill me and then the story in the paper about the Boone's stealing land not to mention the one that's going to appear Sunday on...well you know all about that one. Let's just say it sort of dampens my interest in that regard." He took off his black Stetson and wiped his forehead with the back of his hand, then put it back on. "But now that you're here, what do you want to talk about?"

"We have a proposal..." Elise said.

"A business proposal?"

"I wouldn't call it business."

"Other than marriage what other kind of proposal is there? Actually, marriage is a business since in my experience it's been more about money than love," Wylie laughed then said, "However, I'm willing to hear your proposal."

"Here?" Jane said.

"Well, it is private...property, that is, but there's a real pretty canyon only a half mile from here that I think would be more suitable and more comfortable from what I can tell by the way you're sitting in the saddle. It's the part of Picketwire Canyonlands that belongs to the Double B..."

"I know," Elise nodded.

"I know you do and I bet you'd love to get your government hands on it," Wylie grinned.

Without waiting for a reply, Wylie whispered something to the driver and the Land Rover took off leaving Elise and Jane in a cloud of dust. They spurred their horses and followed the trail of dust until it settled when the jeep stopped. Elise and Jane dismounted and led their horses over to where Wylie was standing. As they got closer the prairie suddenly parted and a chasm appeared. If it had been a moonless night they could have easily walked right over the edge and fallen into the canyon, Jane thought. They tied the horses to the Land Rover and leaving its driver behind they followed Wylie down a path. Fortunately, it wasn't too steep since cowboy boots don't provide much traction and they would have slid down on their backsides, which in Jane's case, was sore enough already. When they reached the bottom still upright, they continued to follow Wylie, who despite the limp from the hit-and-run was remarkably agile. They caught up with him at an alcove in the canyon wall. Water from a spring seeped from the rocks creating a pool that was surrounded by cheatgrass and a small grove of cottonwood trees.

"Well, here we are," Wylie announced, his hands on his hips and his face beaming. "Have a seat. The grass is a lot softer than the saddles you've been on."

"What a beautiful spot," Jane exclaimed as she and Elise sat cross-legged next to each other on the grass, "and so tranquil."

Wylie sat down on a boulder near where the spring bubbled out. Behind him the rock face of the canyon wall rose fifteen feet and then curved out in an overhang that created the alcove.

"This is why my great grandfather, C.W., named it Eden Canyon, because it's our own little garden of Eden. When I was a kid I'd ride here and go skinny-dipping. In case you're wondering there wasn't any Eve to share it with." He took off his Stetson and put it on his knee and looked around. "You know when my dad brought me here for the first time I was twelve. He told me that when C.W. brought his son, my grandfather, here for the first time he was also twelve. He said that C.W. told my grandfather that he'd sworn an oath that he wouldn't allow anyone to kick us Boones out of our garden of Eden and that my grandfather had to swear to the same thing or he was banished. He also had to swear that his oldest son would take the same oath and so on for every generation. So, my grandfather brought my father here when he was twelve and made him take the same oath. Well as you no doubt guessed, my dad brought me here when I was twelve and I swore the same oath, one of the few times that my swearing wasn't a profanity. If I'd had a son or, hell, even a daughter, I'd have brought them here as well and ask them to take the same oath."

After what she'd just heard Jane didn't see how she would be able to convince Wylie to change his mind on donating the land where the internment camp was. She closed her eyes for a moment in silent prayer and heard Elise whisper to her, "Just ask him. If he says no we'll go to Plan B." Jane opened her eyes and said, "I'm asking you to donate the land that the internment camp is on."

"Give some of the ranch away! Did you hear a word of what I just said?"

Jane replied softly, as if this was a pastoral counseling session. "You said that your great-grandfather, C.W., told his son that the Boones wouldn't allow anyone to kick them out of their garden of Eden and that all of his descendants including you have sworn to do the same, right?"

Wylie nodded his head.

"Well, for you and your family the Double B might be the garden of Eden, paradise," Jane continued. "But for the Americans who happened to be of Japanese ancestry who were imprisoned in the camp, who were forced to work on the Double B, who were buried in the middle of the night in unmarked graves, your ranch wasn't the garden of Eden, it was hell."

"My dad only agreed to let the government locate the camp on the ranch because he could use the Japanese-American prisoners as a labor force. Without the free labor the Double B wouldn't have been able to provide beef to the army during World War Two."

"You're telling us that your father believed that allowing the camp on the Double B was an act of patriotism?" Elise asked, shaking her head in disbelief, resisting adding Samuel Johnson's observation that patriotism was the last refuge for a scoundrel.

"Let's say that he and the government considered it to be in the national interest to help the war effort. However, I don't deny that it was in the Boones' interest. Without the money from selling the beef my father couldn't pay off the family's debts that were incurred during the Great Depression. Boones always pay their debts, but the only asset we had was ranch land and, as I told you, he believed that selling off any of the ranch had been expressly forbidden by C.W. and he was bound to it. I guess you could say my dad was between this rock and a hard place. He decided that the only way out was to make enough money selling the beef to the army to pay off the debt...which he did."

"The Japanese-Americans who were forced to work for him paid off the Boones debt," Jane said. "Aren't they owed anything?"

"You're a reverend, so you must believe they'll get their reward in heaven? But you see if I were to give away any of this," Wylie waved his arm, "I'd feel like hell for the rest of my life and even if there is heaven I'm pretty sure I won't be going to it, so there's no reason for me to go to hell before I have to." Wylie put his Stetson back on and stood up. "So, I have no choice but to decline your request. Now that you've got your answer I believe your horses are waiting for you."

After they got up Jane whispered to Elise, "What's our Plan B?"

Elise immediately said to Wylie, "Before we leave can I take a closer look at the pictograph and petroglyphs on the rock of the canyon wall behind you?"

"Those things?" Wylie, said looking at the painted and carved figures behind him on the face of the rock. "I'm so used to them I don't notice them anymore. The canyon walls and the overhang up there provide some protection from the wind and rain so that's why they haven't been washed or worn away."

"There are a lot of these rock shelters, which is what we call them, in Picketwire Canyonlands," Elise said as she walked toward the rock wall. "Some of the petroglyphs and pictographs in them go back thousands of years." Without waiting for Wylie to reply, Elise climbed up on the boulder next to him and pointed at one. "This pictograph here is of a teepee and you can see very faintly that it has red stripes. That means it was done by Cheyenne."

Jane and Wylie looked at where Elise was pointing.

"How do you know that Cheyenne painted them?" Wylie asked.

"Because what's depicted is a Cheyenne medicine teepee. That's where powerful medicine men had visions of supernatural beings."

"I thought they were done by Apaches," Wylie replied, suddenly interested in what Elise was saying.

Elise pointed at some of the petroglyphs, "Now these figures with headdresses over here that are carved into the rock, we call them petroglyphs, they were done by Apaches and would predate the Cheyenne pictographs. The Apaches wouldn't have shared this spot with any other tribe unless they'd abandoned it or been driven away."

"You mean those squiggly lines are supposed to be a person with a headdress on?" Wylie asked.

"Not a human being but a spirit. The Apaches believe that spirits reside inside rocks like this one. That would make this a sacred spot."

"C.W. wasn't exactly spiritually inclined, none of us Boones are. However, according to my dad what was painted and carved on the rocks up there made a powerful impression on C.W. He seemed to know what they meant and said that they were supposed to provide protection. Although he wasn't a churchgoer it's possible that he believed this was some sort of sacred place. In fact, my dad said that C.W. had the Double B painted up there as a way to protect the ranch. See," Wylie pointed at a large BB and a stick figure with a cowboy hat on hanging from a tree that was painted on the rock face next to the petroglyphs. "The Double B brand is larger than all the others so people wouldn't miss it and he drew that stick guy hanging from a tree next to it to make sure that people got the message to stay away."

Elise said, "In that sense the brand and the older pictographs and petroglyphs are similar because they also served as a warning to outsiders to stay away. They were boundary markers because they were at the boundary of the land they wanted others to stay out of. Obviously, they didn't keep others away forever. The Apache and Cheyenne pictographs and petroglyphs that I pointed out are an example of how one tribe replaced another."

"And the last one is the Double B brand and I'm the last of the Boone tribe," Wylie sighed, with a wry smile and a shake of his head. "And as long as I'm alive none of the land inside the boundary of our land marked by our brand up there is going to be given or taken away. After I'm gone, well..." Wylie shrugged his shoulders.

"Because the pictographs and petroglyphs up there were intended to be boundary markers for this place, Eden Canyon, and since C.W. knew that's what they were for, then he would have also known that the brand he painted up there would only apply to the same area and not the entire Double B."

Wylie sat back down on the boulder, took off his Stetson and gave the rock face a hard look.

"That means your dad didn't have to agree to the internment camp and using the prisoners as free labor to pay off his debts to avoid selling any of the Double B property. Instead, he could have just sold off any of the land that was outside of Eden Canyon."

Wylie sat there, stunned, then finally said, "My dad sure would have benefited from a bite of the apple of the tree of knowledge because he sure as hell didn't know that what C.W. painted on the rock up there marked a boundary only for Eden Canyon. Neither did I until now."

"You said earlier that the Boones always pay their debts," Jane said, picking up where Elise had left off.

"Nothing worse than being indebted to someone, because it gives them power over you."

"But you're indebted to the Japanese-Americans who were imprisoned in the camp and forced to provide free labor for the Boone family," Jane pressed.

Wylie picked up his Stetson hat from his knee and slapped it against his thigh sending dust into the still air. "I know, I know." He looked at both Jane and Elise, "You're telling me that I can pay it off by donating the land that the camp is on?"

"To be honest, I have to tell you that donating won't erase the role that your dad played from the historical account," Elise said.

"Can you at least promise that this historical account, as you put it, will include that my dad thought he had no choice but to do what he did."

"I can promise you it will."

"And there is one condition on the donation,"

"What's that?" Jane said, hoping it wasn't a deal breaker.

"That you two don't tell anyone about Eden Canyon," Wylie said, putting his black Stetson back on.

***

"That was nothing short of a miracle," Elise said as they hiked out of Eden Canyon leaving Wylie standing beside the pool. "I mean, after he told us about swearing to not give away any of the Double B..."

Jane cut her off, "It was your Plan B that did it. The way you used those figures painted and carved on the rock to convince Wylie that C.W. meant that his descendants could never give up Eden Canyon rather than other parts of the ranch."

"There was no Plan B," Elise replied. "I just wanted to bolster your confidence. When Plan A didn't work, the only thing to do was improvise. The fact that it wasn't planned made it a miracle."

"God really does work in mysterious ways," Jane said, as much to herself as Elise.

CHAPTER FIFTY

As much as Sister M's had hoped that the press conference would conclude in cellblock B in front of the solitary confinement cells, she had to admit that a bar named the Last Ditch was an appropriate setting given Sheriff Riggleman's desperate situation. Still, she had no idea what his answer would be to Shep's question. What philosophy would the sheriff run on in his next election since he had renounced a key tenet of the constitutional sheriff philosophy that he espoused three years before? Riggleman had told her in confidence what had happened in the solitary confinement cell and his answer to Sister Gabrielle that he'd seen the light was true. However, he had cleverly dodged that it had been more than a light that shook him to his core. Of course, if he had elaborated it was likely that he'd be accused of hallucinating, which would not help his chance for re-election.

Sister M's said a quick prayer as she entered the Last Ditch a few minutes before the appointed hour of four. She was surprised to see that in addition to those sitting at two tables with 'Reserved for the Press' cards propped up by bottles of ketchup, mustard, and hot sauce, the place was filled with people. She walked over to the bar where Shep and another bartender were making drinks.

"I didn't realize your happy hour was this popular," she said to Shep.

"You're not exactly a regular, Sister," Shep replied with a sly smile. "But I confess this is a lot more customers than the usual number we get." He winked and added, "Seems the word spread that the Last Ditch was hosting the last question."

Sister M's choked off a laugh, "The last question?"

"Last question at the Last Ditch," Shep chuckled. "Kind of catchy isn't it? Anyway, it seems to have caught on with the social media." He tilted his head at the other bartender. "I called Dick, here, to help with the bartending, so I can take my seat with the other members of the press corps."

"It's almost as if you had this planned out as a way to boost your business."

"I'm not following a plan, just striking while the iron is hot, the iron in this case being the sheriff's tin star."

"Where is Sheriff Riggleman by the way?" Sister M's asked.

"He came in a few minutes ago, saw the crowd, winced, and asked if there was some place private where he could hang out until four. I told him there was the storeroom, but he said he'd prefer not to be in a confined space, so I said he should go out back where there's a courtyard for the smokers." Shep grinned, "I told him if he was thinking of escaping he'd have to climb a fence."

"I'll go back there and see if he's ready," Sister M's said.

"You want a drink to take with you?"

"I don't suppose you have tea, do you?"

"I could make you a Long Island Iced Tea."

"I'll have a black coffee instead, unless you don't have that either."

"Coffee we always have. It'll be here when you come back with the sheriff."

Sheriff Riggleman was pacing back and forth in the courtyard smoking a cigarette. As soon as he saw Sister M's he dropped the cigarette and squashed it with the toe of his boot. "You know, they used to have trials in bars before the Purgatory Courthouse was built," he said. "When I saw all the people inside I figured they were here for my trial by press conference. This being Picketwire where most of the citizens voted against me, they can't wait for me to be found guilty."

"It depends on how you answer the last question, doesn't it, Sheriff?"

"You're an attorney and know that anything a person says can be used against them, and this being the press 'it will be' instead of 'it can be'."

"You're not testifying in court," Sister M's pointed out.

"It's the court of public opinion," Riggleman snorted.

"Anyway, you can't plead the Fifth."

"Maybe I should drink a fifth," he said. "This being a bar I can choose my poison. If I were under the influence, I couldn't be held responsible for what I say. I might even pass out if I'm lucky. What do you think?"

"I think we need to get in there and get this over with, Sheriff," Sister M's replied then raising her arm so that he could see the dial of her wristwatch. "It's four."

"Really?" he said grimly. "It feels like high noon."

"Then it's high noon and now is your Gary Cooper moment."

Silence descended over the crowded room like a hangman's shroud when Sister M's entered followed by Sheriff Riggleman. They halted in front of two empty stools. Dick pushed a coffee mug toward Sister M's, who whispered, "On second thought, could you add some Irish whiskey to it, without anyone noticing?"

"Let me get you a fresh cup, Sister," Dick answered in a loud voice and took the mug. He turned his back to the room, and a minute later placed the same mug, this time with a shot of Jameson's in it, back on the bar. "Now this should perk you up." Sister M's took a couple of swallows and winked at Dick. She then turned and addressed the assembly, recounting what had taken place at the press conference that morning and that the answer to the final question, which was asked by Shep Woolsey, was deferred until now at the sheriff's request for more time."

She looked at Shep who was now seated in the front row at the press table and asked him to repeat his question."

Shep stood up front at the press table and turned to face the crowded room, "For those of you who know me only as a bartender here at the Last Ditch, I'm also the publisher, editor and so far sole reporter for the *Last Ditch Dialectic*, copies of which are at the end of the bar. The question I put to Sheriff Riggleman was, 'What law enforcement philosophy will you run on in the upcoming elections for sheriff of Purgatory County?'" He turned and addressed Riggleman, "Sheriff, you said you needed more time to come up with your answer. It's four o'clock and your time is up."

All eyes turned to Sheriff Riggleman. "Most of you know about what happened at the old Purgatory Penitentiary," he began, then glancing at Sister M's, added, "that's now a convent run by the nuns..."

"We prefer sisterhood to nuns," Sister M's interjected, then took another sip from the mug.

"Right, the sisterhood," Riggleman answered then stopped and pulled out a handkerchief from a back pocket. He slowly wiped the sweat that had formed on his forehead then raised it to his nose and blew.

"Stop stalling and answer the question, Sheriff," someone at a back table yelled. This was followed by the sound of bottles of beer being drummed on the tables.

Sister M's raised her hands, "Please, give the sheriff a chance to respond." When the room quieted, she turned to Riggleman, and asked him to answer the question.

Riggleman jammed the handkerchief back in his pocket with his left hand and with his right he unpinned the sheriff's badge on his chest. He tossed it on the bar. Then, looking directly at Shep, he said, "That's my answer and it should be enough to pay for a drink."

"Hell," Shep yelled in reply as the Last Ditch erupted in pandemonium. "From now on all of your drinks are on the house."

Riggleman turned to Dick and said like a man who had escaped the gallows, "I'll have whatever the Sister is drinking, but you can skip the coffee."

CHAPTER FIFTY ONE

The office of the Bard Wired Players was in the basement of the historic Tumbleweed Theater. Its walls were covered with theatrical posters and there were several filing cabinets, boxes of playbills, a half dozen folding chairs, a large wooden desk, and a sagging couch. The couch wasn't for casting, but for thinking and that's exactly what Max was doing as he lay there looking at the bare piece of wall trying to envision what the poster for their new play would look like. The problem was he didn't know how the play would end.

His contemplation was disrupted by the ringing of the black phone on the desk. It used to be an outside line, but since the advent of cellphones it now served as the Tumbleweed Theater's intercom. Putting the pad and pen on the floor, Max reached out to the desktop and picked up the receiver. It was Bert, the house manager, telling him that there was someone to see him.

"I'm in a conference at the moment," Max replied with irritation.

"With who?"

"Myself."

"Okay, I'll tell Mister Boone you're busy and can't see him."

Max jumped off the couch, "You mean Wylie Boone?"

"Is there another Boone?"

"No, but you say he's...here...to see...me?"

"That's what he claims," Bert replied. "There's also a couple of men dressed in black with him that I assume are his bodyguards."

"Tell him I'll meet him. Not down here, but in the theater. On the stage. Give me five minutes to get up there then turn on the house lights and show him in." Without waiting for a reply, Max slammed the receiver down shoved his feet into his loafers and rushed out the door, down the hallway, and up the back stairs that led to theater's stage, which he managed to walk onto just as Bert was ushering Wylie Boone into the theater.

"Ah, Mister Boone," Max said from center stage. "Sorry to keep you waiting, but I've been working on some technical aspects for our new play. You know, the one by Howdy Hanks that will have its world premiere right on this very stage."

"That's why I'm here," Wylie replied as he limped down the center aisle.

"You want to buy a ticket?"

"I want to make a donation."

"A donation?"

"A substantial donation," Wylie said, as he seated himself in a front row seat while his two bodyguards sat down several rows behind him. "There's only one condition."

Max walked to the front of the stage and looked down at Wylie. "Don't worry Mister Boone, you'll get full recognition..."

"I don't want to be recognized, I want the play cancelled."

"What did you say?" Max's broad smile froze then melted.

"I said the one condition for my very generous donation is the cancellation of this new play by Howdy Hanks."

"But, as we say in the theater, the show must go on."

"Yeah, well I'm saying the play must be shut off, because it's crap."

"How do you know that it's bad if you haven't seen it? In fact, no one has seen the completed play, including myself."

"Why not?"

"Because I haven't finished it," a voice bellowed from above.

"What the hell..." Wylie wheeled around in his seat and looked back and up at Howdy Hanks who was leaning over the balcony railing.

"As they say, long time no see, Wylie."

"Not long enough, Howdy," Wylie growled. "And I'm not about to sit here looking up at you."

"As much as I enjoy looking down on you, Wylie, I'll meet you on the stage in a jiffy. I was just up here running a scene through my head. Helps me to imagine it being played out on the stage."

After joining Max on the stage, Wylie looked around the theater, "I guess it's as good a place as any for a showdown."

"A showdown," Max said, with alarm and began side stepping toward stage left.

"Not a shootout, if that's what you're worried about."

"So, you think it's terrible even though you haven't seen it," said Howdy as he ambled down the right aisle to the steps that led to the stage.

"I don't need to. I saw the play you wrote for our senior year at Picketwire High and it was crap."

"As I recall you walked out before it was over."

"I wasn't the only one."

"Still, Mister Boone," Max pleaded, "people can disagree on what's a good play. Even Shakespeare had his detractors."

"Yeah, well Shakespeare didn't use me as one of his characters," Wylie spat out the words then turned and glared at Howdy who was now on the stage.

"Then you've never seen a performance of Richard the Third," Howdy replied with a grin.

"A horse, a horse, my kingdom for a horse," Max spouted dramatically, and added for Wylie's benefit. "Richard the Third, Act Five Scene Four."

"Not that part, Max," Howdy said. "I was thinking of the line at the beginning of the play in Act One, Scene One where Richard says, 'since I cannot prove a lover, I am determined to prove a villain.'"

"You left out a few words," Max said.

"I think Wylie knows what it means without me filling in the blanks," Howdy replied, looking at Wylie, "don't you?"

"What I know is that you made me a laughingstock in front of the whole town. The character named Dick was the son of the biggest rancher in town, so everyone knew that he was supposed to be me."

Max stepped between the two men, "That was all years ago when you were both in high school. Why, we all do things when we're that age that we later regret."

"I regret a lot of things I did back then," Howdy said, "but that isn't one of them."

"And the only thing I regret is that you got away with it," Wylie said, clenching his fists. "But not this time."

"What is it that you're afraid I'm going to get away with?"

"Making me look like a fool again."

"Then you have nothing to worry about, Wylie. Although the play isn't finished I can promise you that there won't be any characters in it who are fools."

"There you are, Mister Boone," Max said with relief. "You've heard it straight from the playwright's mouth and if that isn't enough you have my own assurance."

Wylie put his hands on his hips and looked around the empty theater. Finally, he muttered, "Okay."

"Is there any chance you'll still make that sizeable donation?" Max asked with uncharacteristic meekness.

Wylie shook his head in disbelief, "Nope, but I will buy a ticket, because like I said, it's going to be terrible and I want to see the audience walking out on it."

As they watched Wylie limp up the aisle away from the stage followed by his bodyguards, Max turned to Howdy and whispered, "I'm sure glad you were able to convince Boone that there wouldn't be anything in the play that he had to worry about."

Howdy grinned, put his hand in front of his mouth and whispered back, "I said there wouldn't be any characters in it who were fools. I didn't say he had nothing to worry about."

CHAPTER FIFTY TWO

Jemma Lu sat in her favorite booth by the window at Tanneyhill's letting the tea she'd ordered – instead of her usual vanilla shake – grow tepid, a temperature that perfectly matched Jemma Lu's feelings as she stared at the sealed envelope with the results of the DNA test. The silver and gold flecked Formica table top it rested on didn't lighten her mood.

When she had arrived the place had been empty and Mike, the owner's teenage son, greeted her, "You're lucky, because this place will be packed in a few minutes. A lot of kids come here right after high school is out. I have to pedal my bike like a bat out of hell, I mean heck, to get here before them."

By now all the booths and counter stools were filled with high school students. She felt guilty hogging the entire booth but she was waiting for someone and they would need the space. Jemma Lu picked up the mug of tea, tasted it and quickly put it down.

"Do you mind if I park here for a sec?"

Jemma Lu looked up and there was Zelda Zenn, who she remembered meeting briefly at the Last Ditch, looking down at her. She was wearing a black leather newsboy cap, an acid washed denim jacket with a heart shaped out of rhinestones on the left pocket, lavender parachute pants and high top sneakers. Before she could respond, Zelda slid onto the bench opposite her, "I'm trying to avoid meeting somebody."

"I'm not sure you'll go unnoticed with the clothes you're wearing."

"Oh, this is my costume."

"Costume?"

"From the play. Since it takes place a long time ago, in the 1980s I threw together this outfit as a way to get into the character. It's amazing what you can find in thrift stores. I added the rhinestone heart – sewed it on myself. Hopefully they'll let me wear this in the real play. Do I look the part?"

"You look rad. It's short for radical and was what we teenage girls back in the eighties called someone who looked super cool."

"Rad, that's dope, which also means super cool. I should ask Mister Hanks if he can put rad in the script to describe my character. But, anyway, the reason I'm in my rad costume is because rehearsal starts in a couple of hours and I want to wear it. Like I said, it helps me get into my character. The problem is I told someone I'd meet them here for a date. I won't have time to change before rehearsal, so I did it before I left school. Then, when I just walked in here I saw a guy sitting at the counter who I definitely do not want to meet. He plays my boyfriend in the play and wants to play the same role offstage as well. Anyway, I didn't know what to do, so here I am sitting with you."

"I can definitely relate to not knowing what to do when it comes to guys," Jemma Lu muttered under her breath then glanced down at the envelope and flipped it over to hide the sender's name, Genomic Labs, before saying, "Zelda Zenn is certainly a memorable name for an actress."

"Actually, it's my stage name, but I've decided to make it my real one. I mean, do I look like a Mary Ann Smithers?"

"I'm not sure what a Mary Ann Smithers should look like."

"Well, she wouldn't look like me," Zelda declared, emphatically. "My mom changed her name back to her maiden name after she divorced my dad. She gets to be Shirley McIntyre. It's not fair that she could leave Smithers behind in LA when she left him and we moved here, while I'm still stuck with it until I turn eighteen. That's when I'm old enough to legally change it without my dad's permission."

"How do you like living in Picketwire?" Jemma Lu asked, hoping to change the subject.

"I hated it at first. It seemed like nothing ever happens here, but then a whole lot of stuff happened. My gosh, I'm the lead in a brand new play by Howdy Hanks, who even though I'd never heard of him before, I now know he's a famous playwright. Then I ended up helping some undocumented immigrants who were chased by the sheriff and his posse escape to an old prison where some nuns live and I played basketball with one of them, who's now my lawyer. There's also all the stuff going on around

here like this Wylie Boone guy's family stealing land that belonged to Tony Medrano's family. I met Tony when I worked as
an actor on his railroad tour, which is how the sheriff ended up
chasing me. And it turns out that the father of this same Wylie
Boone had a secret camp on their ranch where Japanese-Americans were kept as prisoners and had to work for him for free
and…"

Zelda suddenly stopped when Jemma Lu held up her hand
and said, "Yes, a lot has happened and you seem to have been in
the thick of it."

"Been, I still am, and it's so dope or rad or whatever," she said
with a big smile.

"Yes, there's definitely a lot happening right now," Jemma Lu
said, although unlike Zelda, she wasn't feeling dope or rad about
it.

"I can't believe I'm telling someone who is old enough… well,
you know…."

"To be your grandmother," Jemma Lu said.

"Yeah, I sure wouldn't be telling either of my grandmothers
any of this, but here I am telling you and I don't even know
your name. Nobody told me your name when we met at the
Last Ditch."

"It's Jemma Lu Tuttle."

"Are you the Tuttle that lives in that big old mansion?"

"I haven't lived there for a very long time."

"I don't blame you. It sure looks like its haunted. Did you
ever see ghosts when you lived there?"

"No," Jemma Lu replied, just a ghost from my past that I saw recently, she thought to herself.

"Here's your vanilla shake," Mike announced, placing a tall, fluted glass garnished with a straw on the table.

"But I didn't order it," Jemma Lu objected.

"I did," Zelda said. "Mike knows what I like...to drink."

"Zelda's a regular," Mike smiled broadly and then his face turning serious, he asked Jemma Lu if she wanted more tea.

Jemma Lu looked at the mug and then the shake and said, "You know, Mike, I think I'll skip more tea and switch to my usual."

Mike's smile returned as he said, "Another vanilla shake coming up."

"You like vanilla shakes too," Zelda said.

"Since I started coming here when I was your age."

"Do you want a taste to tide you over? It's pretty busy here, so Mike could take a while." Zelda stopped sucking on the straw and turned it toward Jemma Lu. "Don't worry, I don't have cooties."

"I'm not worried about cooties," Jemma Lu laughed and thought, worrying about old coots is another matter. She took a sip from the straw and handed the shake back to Zelda.

"What's in the envelope?" Zelda asked.

"Nothing. I mean, it is something, but I don't know what, exactly."

Zelda sighed, "And you can't decide if you want to know, right? I know how that feels."

"It's that, but even more its whether it's my right to open it."

"Who's it addressed to?"

"Me."

"You think it was sent to you by mistake?"

"No, I requested the information that's inside, but it involves some guys and depending on what that information is their life could change for the better or worse. To add to my dilemma, the guys whose lives will be affected don't know anything about this – not a clue."

"Most guys don't seem to have a clue about anything," Zelda said, then looked toward the door. "Oh, I've got to go, my date just arrived and we have to get out of here before the other guy I told you about sees us."

"Why that's Donny Buford. His parents are friends of mine."

"Yeah," Zelda replied as she slapped a five dollar bill on the table. "I promised to go out with him after he helped me escape from the sheriff. Actually, this is our second date.... I never thought I'd be interested in a nice guy. Anyway, good luck with your clueless guys." Before Jemma Lu could reply, Zelda had scooted from the booth and in less than a minute she was at the door with Donny, where she turned and gave a quick goodbye wave.

Jemma Lu fingered the envelope. She had asked Howdy to meet her at Tanneyhill's where she would tell him that she had a son and he was either his or Wylie's. She would then open the envelope. But now she realized that she didn't really know what would come next. If Howdy was the father then, together, they should decide whether to tell Will. But if it wasn't Howdy, Jemma Lu couldn't imagine telling Wylie they had a son together. But if she didn't tell Wylie, did she still have an obligation to tell Will that the man he hated and almost killed was his father? She sipped on the straw, wondering if the sugar rush from the milk shake would bring some clarity.

"I see you picked our favorite booth," Howdy drawled as he stood next to the booth.

"Your seat should be nice and warm," Jemma Lu replied, quickly slipping the envelope off the table and into her open purse on the bench beside her, where it would be out of sight until she decided what to do.

"Warm is better than being on the hot seat," Howdy said, patting the bench opposite Jemma Lu before sitting down.

"It shouldn't be hot considering that Zelda

Zenn, the teenage girl who I met the other night at the Last Ditch was just sitting there, is pretty cool."

"She's my leading lady," Howdy said, smiling as he shook his head.

"Based on our conversation, I think she'd be insulted to be described as a lady. Zelda wouldn't tell me anything about the play, in case you're worried about your secret."

"I'm sorry it's a secret."

"That's fine as long as keeping it a secret doesn't hurt someone. At least someone you like."

"There's nothing in the play that is going to hurt you, I promise. And, in case you're worried, Zelda's character isn't based on you."

Jemma Lu sighed, "That's a relief, because when I was in high school I never wore the kind of clothes she had on. She says they help her with her character. She's going to wear them to the rehearsal tonight, by the way, and hopes she'll be allowed to wear them as her costume."

"Based on what she usually wears, I'm sure it's quite a getup. Nothing like that preppy style you wore."

"It wasn't preppy, it was just understated," Jemma Lu replied in mock indignation.

"Then please accept my apology for misstating."

"Apology accepted," Jemma Lu smiled. "Do you want some of my vanilla milkshake?" Jemma Lu pointed the straw in his direction.

Howdy grinned broadly and said, "Sharing the same milkshake means we're going steady."

"I don't think 'steady' would be an accurate description of our relationship," Jemma Lu said. If anything, her life had become very unsteady since Howdy rode back to Picketwire.

"Then how about we're ready rather than steady?" Howdy asked, the straw poised at his lips.

"Ready for what?"

"For whatever comes next."

Jemma Lu reached down with her right hand and touched the envelope inside her open purse, then she snapped the purse closed and said, "I'm ready."

THE END

ACKNOWLEDGEMENTS

I would like to thank the following:

My wife Kathleen Sutcliffe and my oldest sister Wendy Wintermute for their feedback on multiple drafts and encouragement.

Elizabeth Baer for her excellent copy editing.

Kiley Grantges for her artful cover.

Marianne Monson for her engaging book description and back cover blurb.

The town of Las Animas, Colorado.

ABOUT THE AUTHOR

Tim Wintermute it is a novelist and short story writer as well as the publisher of the Prismatist e-magazine (www.prismatist.com). Until age twelve he lived in southeast Colorado where the fictional town of Picketwire is located and has visited the area numerous times since then.

ALSO BY TIM WINTERMUTE

SAHALEE INN

CURIOSI CASEBOOK